## More Praise for *Boneshaker*

"Cherie Priest wove a story so convincing, so evocative, so terrifying that I read this book with the doors locked and a gun on my lap. *Boneshaker* is a steampunk menagerie of thrills and horror."

—**Mario Acevedo, bestselling author of** *Jailbait Zombie*

"Everything you'd want in such a volume and much more. . . . It's full of buckle and has swash to spare, and the characters are likable and the prose is fun. This is a hoot from start to finish, pure mad adventure."

—**Cory Doctorow, bestselling author of** *Little Brother*

"A gorgeously grim world of deadly gases, mysterious machines, zeppelin pirates, and a relentless plague of zombies. With *Boneshaker*, Priest is geared up to begin her reign as the Queen of Steampunk."

—**Mark Henry, author of** *Road Trip of the Living Dead*

"A rip-snorting adventure in the best tradition of a penny dreadful. Priest has crafted a novel of exquisite prose and thrilling twists, populated by folk heroes and dastardly villains, zombies and air pirates, incredible machines, and a heroine who'll have you cheering. *Boneshaker* is the definitive steampunk story, absolutely unique and one hell of a fun read."

—**Caitlin Kittredge, author of the Nocturne City novels**

"If *Wild, Wild West* had been written by Mark Twain with the assistance of Jules Verne and Bram Stoker, it still couldn't be as fabulous and fantastical as *Boneshaker*. Cherie Priest has penned a rousing adventure tale that breathes a roaring soul and thundering heart into the glittering skin of steampunk. Stylish, taut, and wonderful, it's a literary ride you must not miss!"

—**Kat Richardson, bestselling author of** *Greywalker*

"It's awesome. I loved everything about it, and I can't wait for it to come out so the rest of the world can read it and understand why I loved it as much as I did."

—Wil W

**Tor Books by Cherie Priest**

THE EDEN MOORE BOOKS

*Four and Twenty Blackbirds*
*Wings to the Kingdom*
*Not Flesh Nor Feathers*

*Fathom*
*Boneshaker*

# Boneshaker

*Cherie Priest*

**TOR**®

A Tom Doherty Associates Book *New York*

This is a work of fiction. All of the characters, organizations, and events portrayed in this novel are either products of the author's imagination or are used fictitiously.

BONESHAKER

*Map by Jennifer Hanover*

A Tor Book
Published by Tom Doherty Associates, LLC
175 Fifth Avenue
New York, NY 10010

www.tor-forge.com

Tor® is a registered trademark of Tom Doherty Associates, LLC.

Library of Congress Cataloging-in-Publication Data

Priest, Cherie.
    Boneshaker / Cherie Priest.—1st ed.
        p.    cm.
    "A Tom Doherty Associates book."
    ISBN 978-0-7653-1841-1
    1. Mothers and sons—Fiction.    2. Zombies—Fiction.    3. Northwest, Pacific—Fiction.    I. Title.

PS3616.R537 B66    2009
813'.6—dc22

                                                                2009018700


Printed in the United States of America

0   9   8   7   6   5   4

*This one's for Team Seattle—*
*Mark Henry, Caitlin Kittredge,*
*Richelle Mead, and Kat Richardson—*
*for they are the heart and soul of this place.*

## *Acknowledgments*

This one requires many rounds of thanks, so please allow me to make a list.

Thanks to my editor, Liz Gorinsky, for her superlative skills, astonishing patience, and unparalleled determination; thanks to the publicity team at Tor, specifically Dot Lin and Patty Garcia, both of whom rock quite thoroughly; thanks to my ever-encouraging and unrelenting agent, Jennifer Jackson.

And thanks to the home team, too—in particular, my husband, Aric Annear, who is subjected to most of these stories in excruciating detail and for dissection before they're ever finished; to my sister Becky Priest, for helping to scan all my proofs and passes; to Jerry and Donna Priest, for being my number-one cheerleaders; and to my mother, Sharon Priest, for keeping me humble.

Thanks go out to the aforementioned Team Seattle, and to our friends Duane Wilkins at the University of Washington bookstore and the incomparable Synde Korman at the downtown Barnes & Noble. Speaking of Barnes & Noble, I also send love and thanks to Paul Goat Allen. He knows why.

Yet further thanks must be showered upon my favorite lycanthrope, Amanda Gannon, for letting me use her LiveJournal handle as the name of a dirigible (she's the original *Naamah Darling*); to the guides of the Seattle Underground tour, who keep offering me a job because I've taken the tour so many times; and to my old friend Andrea Jones and her Usual Suspects, because she's always got my historical back—and she provides me with the *best* lead-in quotes. Thanks also to Talia Kaye, the amazingly helpful speculative-fiction-loving librarian at the Seattle Public Library's Seattle Room; to Greg Wild-Smith, my intrepid webmaster; to Warren Ellis and everyone in the clubhouse; and to Ellen Milne, for all the cookies.

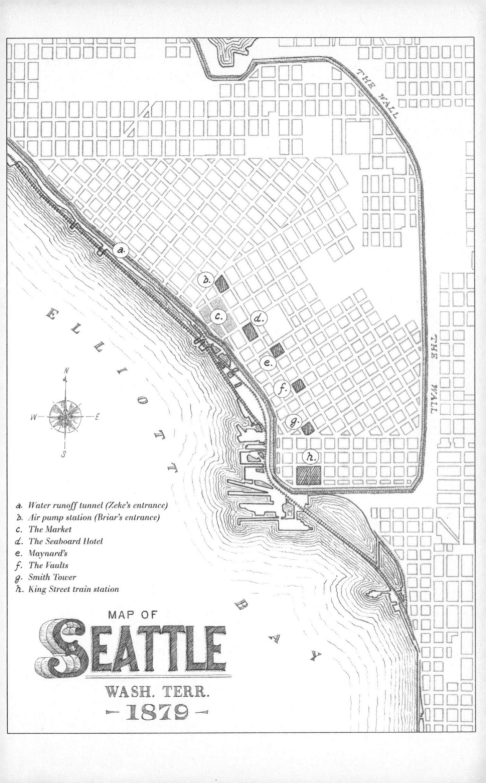

a. Water runoff tunnel (Zeke's entrance)
b. Air pump station (Briar's entrance)
c. The Market
d. The Seaboard Hotel
e. Maynard's
f. The Vaults
g. Smith Tower
h. King Street train station

MAP OF

# SEATTLE

WASH. TERR.

~ 1879 ~

In this age of invention the science of arms has made great progress. In fact, the most remarkable inventions have been made since the prolonged wars of Europe in the early part of the century, and the short Italian campaign of France in 1859 served to illustrate how great a power the engines of destruction can exert.

—THOMAS P. KETTELL, *History of the Great Rebellion. From its commencement to its close, giving an account of its origin, The Secession of the Southern States, and the Formation of the Confederate Government, the concentration of the Military and Financial resources of the federal government, the development of its vast power, the raising, organizing, and equipping of the contending armies and navies; lucid, vivid, and accurate descriptions of battles and bombardments, sieges and surrender of forts, captured batteries, etc., etc.; the immense financial resources and comprehensive measures of the government, the enthusiasm and patriotic contributions of the people, together with sketches of the lives of all the eminent statesmen and military and naval commanders, with a full and complete index. From Official Sources* (1862)

# Boneshaker

From *Unlikely Episodes
in Western History*
CHAPTER 7: *Seattle's
Walled and Peculiar State*

*Work in progress, by
Hale Quarter (1880)*

Unpaved, uneven trails pretended to be roads; they tied the nation's coasts together like laces holding a boot, binding it with crossed strings and crossed fingers. And over the great river, across the plains, between the mountain passes, the settlers pushed from east to west. They trickled over the Rockies in dribs and drabs, in wagons and coaches.

Or this is how it began.

In California there were nuggets the size of walnuts lying on the ground—or so it was said, and truth travels slowly when rumors have wings of gold. The trickle of humanity became a magnificent flow. The glittering western shores swarmed with prospectors, pushing their luck and pushing their pans into the gravelly streams, praying for fortunes.

In time, the earth grew crowded, and claims became more tenuous. Gold came out of the ground in dust so fine that the men who mined it could've inhaled it.

In 1850 another rumor, winged and sparkling, came swiftly from the north.

The Klondike, it said. Come and cut your way through the ice you find there. A fortune in gold awaits a determined enough man.

The tide shifted, and looked to the northern latitudes. This meant very, very good things for the last frontier stop before the Canadian border—a backwater mill town on Puget Sound called Seattle after the native chief of the local tribes. The muddy village became a tiny empire nearly overnight as explorers and prospectors paused to trade and stock up on supplies.

While American legislators argued over whether or not to buy the Alaska territory, Russia hedged its bets and considered its asking price. If the land really was pocked with gold deposits, the game would absolutely change; but even if a steady supply of gold could be located, could it be retrieved? A potential vein, spotted intermittently but mostly buried beneath a hundred feet of permanent ice, would make for an ideal testing ground.

In 1860, the Russians announced a contest, offering a 100,000 ruble prize to the inventor who could produce or propose a machine that could mine through ice in search of gold. And in this way, a scientific arms race began despite a budding civil war.

Across the Pacific Northwest, big machines and small machines were tinkered into existence. They were tricky affairs designed to withstand bitter cold and tear through turf that was frozen diamond-hard. They were powered by steam and coal, and lubricated with special solutions that protected their mechanisms from the elements. These machines were made for men to drive like stagecoaches, or designed to dig on their own, controlled by clockwork and ingenious guiding devices.

But none of them were rugged enough to tackle the buried vein, and the Russians were on the verge of selling the land to America for a relative pittance . . . when a Seattle inventor approached them with plans for an amazing machine. It would be the greatest mining vehicle ever constructed: fifty feet long and fully mechanized, powered by compressed steam. It would boast three primary drilling and cutting heads, positioned at the front of the craft; and a system of spiral shoveling devices mounted along the back and sides would scoop the bored-through ice, rocks, or earth back out of the drilling path. Carefully weighted and meticulously reinforced, this machine could drill in an almost perfect vertical or horizontal path, depending on the whims of the man in the driver's seat. Its precision would be unprecedented, and its power would set the standard for all such devices to come.

But it had not yet been built.

The inventor, a man named Leviticus Blue, convinced the Russians to advance him a sum great enough to gather the parts and fund the labor on Dr. Blue's Incredible Bone-Shaking Drill Engine. He asked for six months, and promised a public test display.

Leviticus Blue took his funding, returned to his home in Seattle, and began to build the remarkable machine in his basement. Piece by piece he assembled his contraption out of sight of his fellow townsmen; and night by night the sounds of mysterious tools and instruments startled the neighbors. But eventually, and well before the six-month deadline, the inventor declared his masterpiece "complete."

What happened next remains a subject of much debate.

It might have been only an accident, after all—a terrible malfunction of equipment running amuck. It may have been nothing more than confusion, or bad timing, or improper calculations. Or then again, it might have been a calculated move after all, plotted to bring down a city's core with unprecedented violence and mercenary greed.

What motivated Dr. Blue may never be known.

He was an avaricious man in his way, but no more so than most; and it's possible that he wished only to take the money and run—with a bit of extra cash in his pocket to fund a larger escape. The inventor had recently married (as tongues did wag, his bride was some twenty-five years his junior), and there was much speculation that perhaps she had a hand in his decisions. Perhaps she urged his haste or she wished herself married to a richer husband. Or perhaps, as she long maintained, she knew nothing of anything.

What is certain is this: On the afternoon of January 2, 1863, something appalling burst out from the basement and tore a trail of havoc from the house on Denny Hill to the central business district, and then back home again.

Few witnesses agree, and fewer still were granted a glimpse of the Incredible Bone-Shaking Drill Engine. Its course took it under the earth and down the hills, gouging up the land beneath the luxurious homes of wealthy mariners and shipping magnates, under the muddy flats where sat the sprawling sawmill, and down along the corridors, cellars, and storage rooms of general stores, ladies' notions shops, apothecaries, and yes . . . the banks.

Four of the major ones, where they were lined up in a row—all four of those banks were ravaged as their foundations were ground into mulch. Their walls rattled, buckled, and fell. Their floors collapsed downward in a V-shaped implosion as their bottom buttresses dropped away, and then the space was partially filled with the toppling roofs. And these four banks held three million dollars or better between them, accumulated from the California miners cashing in their nuggets and heading north in search of more.

Scores of innocent bystanders were killed indoors as they stood in line for deposits or withdrawals. Many more died outside on the street, crushed by the leaning, trembling walls as they gave up their mortar and crashed heavily down.

Citizens clamored for safety, but where could it be found? The earth itself opened up and swallowed them, here and there where the Drill Engine's tunnel was too shallow to maintain even the thinnest crust of land. The quaking, rolling street flung itself like a rug being flapped before beaten clean. It moved hard from side to side, and in waves. And wherever the machine had gone, there came the sounds of crumbling and boring from the underground passages left by its passing.

To call the scene a disaster does it a terrific disservice. The final death toll was never fully calculated, for heaven only knew how many bodies might lie wedged in the rubble. And alas, there was no time for excavation.

For after Dr. Blue lodged his machine back beneath his own home, and after the wails of the injured were tended, and the first of the angry questions were being shouted from the remaining rooftops, a second wave of horror would come to afflict the city. It was difficult for Seattle's residents to conclude that this second wave was unrelated to the first wave, but the details of their suspicions have never been explained to anyone's collective satisfaction.

Only the observable facts can be recorded now, and perhaps in time a future analyst may provide a better answer than can presently be guessed at.

This much is known: In the aftermath of the Drill Engine's astonishing trail of destruction, a peculiar illness afflicted the reconstruction workers nearest the wreckage of the bank blocks. By all reports this illness was eventually traced to the Drill Engine tunnels, and to a gas which came from them. At first, this gas appeared odorless and colorless, but over time it built up to such an extent that it could be discerned by the human eye, if spied through a bit of polarized glass.

Through trial and error, a few particulars of the gas were determined. It was a thick, slow-moving substance that killed by contamination, and it could be generally halted or stilled by simple barriers. Temporary stopgap measures cropped up across the city as an evacuation was organized. Tents were disassembled and treated with pitch in order to form makeshift walls.

As these barriers failed one ring at a time, and as thousands more of the city's inhabitants fell fatally ill, sterner measures were called for. Hasty plans were drawn up and enacted, and within one year from the incident with Dr. Blue's Incredible Bone-Shaking Drill Engine, the entire downtown area was surrounded by an immense brick, mortar, and stone wall.

The wall stands approximately two hundred feet high—depending on the city's diverse geographic constraints—and it averages a width of fifteen to twenty feet. It wholly encircles the damaged blocks, containing an area of nearly two square miles. Truly, it is a marvel of engineering.

However, within this wall the city spoils, utterly dead except for the rats and crows that are rumored to be there. The gas which still seeps from the ground ruins everything it touches. What once was a bustling metropolis is now a ghost town, surrounded by the surviving and resettled population. These people are fugitives from their hometown, and although many of them relocated north to Vancouver, or south to Tacoma or Portland, a significant number have stayed close to the wall.

They live on the mudflats and up against the hills, in a sprawling nontown most often called the Outskirts; and there, they have begun their lives anew.

# One

She saw him, and she stopped a few feet from the stairs.

"I'm sorry," he said quickly. "I didn't mean to startle you."

The woman in the dull black overcoat didn't blink and didn't move. "What do you want?"

He'd prepared a speech, but he couldn't remember it. "To talk. To you. I want to talk to you."

Briar Wilkes closed her eyes hard. When she opened them again, she asked, "Is it about Zeke? What's he done now?"

"No, no, it's not about him," he insisted. "Ma'am, I was hoping we could talk about your father."

Her shoulders lost their stiff, defensive right angles, and she shook her head. "That figures. I swear to God, all the men in my life, they . . ." She stopped herself. And then she said, "My father was a tyrant, and everyone he loved was afraid of him. Is that what you want to hear?"

He held his position while she climbed the eleven crooked stairs that led the way to her home, and to him. When she reached the narrow porch he asked, "Is it true?"

"More true than not."

She stood before him with her fingers wrapped around a ring of keys. The top of her head was level with his chin. Her keys were aimed at his waist, he thought, until he realized he was standing in front of the door. He shuffled out of her way.

"How long have you been waiting for me?" she asked.

He strongly considered lying, but she pinned him to the wall with her stare. "Several hours. I wanted to be here when you got home."

The door clacked, clicked, and scooted inward. "I took an extra shift at the 'works. You could've come back later."

"Please, ma'am. May I come inside?"

She shrugged, but she didn't say no, and she didn't close him out in the cold, so he followed behind her, shutting the door and standing beside it while Briar found a lamp and lit it.

She carried the lamp to the fireplace, where the logs had burned down cold. Beside the mantle there was a poker and a set of bellows, and a flat iron basket with a cache of split logs. She jabbed the poker against the charred lumps and found a few live coals lingering at the bottom.

With gentle encouragement, a handful of kindling, and two more lengths of wood, a slow flame caught and held.

One arm at a time, Briar pried herself out of the overcoat and left it hanging on a peg. Without the coat, her body had a lean look to it—as if she worked too long, and ate too little or too poorly. Her gloves and tall brown boots were caked with the filth of the plant, and she was wearing pants like a man. Her long, dark hair was piled up and back, but two shifts of labor had picked it apart and heavy strands had scattered, escaping the combs she'd used to hold it all aloft.

She was thirty-five, and she did not look a minute younger.

In front of the growing, glowing fire there was a large and ancient leather chair. Briar dropped herself into it. "Tell me, Mr. . . . I'm sorry. You didn't say your name."

"Hale. Hale Quarter. And I must say, it's an honor to meet you."

For a moment he thought she was going to laugh, but she didn't.

She reached over to a small table beside the chair and retrieved a pouch. "All right, Hale Quarter. Tell me. Why did you wait outside so long in this bitter weather?" From within the pouch she picked a small piece of paper and a large pinch of tobacco. She worked the two together until she had a cigarette, and she used the lamp's flame to coax the cigarette alight.

He'd gotten this far by telling the truth, so he risked another confession. "I came when I knew you wouldn't be home. Someone told me that if I knocked, you'd shoot through the peephole."

She nodded, and pressed the back of her head against the leather. "I've heard that story, too. It doesn't keep nearly as many folks away as you might expect."

He couldn't tell if she was serious, or if her response was a denial. "Then I thank you double, for not shooting me and for letting me come inside."

"You're welcome."

"May I . . . may I take a seat? Would that be all right?"

"Suit yourself, but you won't be here long," she predicted.

"You don't want to talk?"

"I don't want to talk about Maynard, no. I don't have any answers about anything that happened to him. Nobody does. But you can ask whatever you want. And you can take your leave when I get tired of you, or when you get bored with all the ways I can say 'I don't know'—whichever comes first."

Encouraged, he reached for a tall-backed wooden chair and dragged it forward, putting his body directly into her line of sight. His notebook folded open to reveal an unlined sheet with a few small words scribbled at the top.

While he was getting situated, she asked him, "Why do you want to know about Maynard? Why now? He's been dead for fifteen years. Nearly sixteen."

"Why not now?" Hale scanned his previous page of notes, and settled down with his pencil hovering over the next blank section. "But to answer you more directly, I'm writing a book."

"Another book?" she said, and it sounded sharp and fast.

"Not a sensational piece," he was careful to clarify. "I want to write a proper biography of Maynard Wilkes, because I believe he's been done a great disservice. Don't you agree?"

"No, I don't agree. He got exactly what he should have expected. He spent thirty years working hard, for nothing, and he was treated disgracefully by the city he served." She fiddled with the half-smoked wand of tobacco. "He allowed it. And I hated him for it."

"But your father believed in the law."

She almost snapped at him. "So does every criminal."

Hale perked. "Then you *do* think he was a criminal?"

One more hard draw on the cigarette came and went, and then she said, "Don't twist my words. But you're right. He believed in the law. There were times I wasn't sure he believed in anything else, but yes. He believed in that."

Spits and sparks from the fireplace filled the short silence that fell between them. Finally, Hale said, "I'm trying to get it right, ma'am. That's all. I think there was more to it than a jailbreak—"

"Why?" she interrupted. "Why do you think he did it? Which theory do you want to write your book about, Mr. Quarter?"

He hesitated, because he didn't know what to think, not yet. He gambled on the theory that he hoped Briar would find least offensive. "I think he was doing what he thought was right. But I really want to know what *you* think. Maynard raised you alone, didn't he? You must've known him better than anyone."

Her face stayed a little too carefully blank. "You'd be surprised. We weren't that close."

"But your mother died—"

"When I was born, that's right. He was the only parent I ever had, and he wasn't much of one. He didn't know what to do with a daughter any more than I know what to do with a map of Spain."

Hale sensed a brick wall, so he backed up and tried another way around, and into her good graces. His eyes scanned the smallish room with its solid and unadorned furniture, and its clean but battered floors. He noted the corridor that led to the back side of the house. And from his seat, he could see that all four doors at the end of it were closed.

"You grew up here, didn't you? In this house?" he pretended to guess.

She didn't soften. "Everybody knows that."

"They brought him back here, though. One of the boys from the prison break, and his brother—they brought him here and tried to save him. A doctor was sent for, but . . ."

Briar retrieved the dangled thread of conversation and pulled it. "But he'd inhaled too much of the Blight. He was dead before the doctor ever got the message, and I swear"—she flicked a fingertip's worth of ash into the fire—"it's just as well. Can you imagine what would've happened to him, if he'd lived? Tried for treason, or gross insubordination at least. Jailed, at the minimum. Shot, at the worst. My father and I had our disagreements, but I wouldn't have wished that upon him. It's just as well," she said again, and she stared into the fire.

Hale spent a few seconds trying to assemble a response. At last he said, "Did you get to see him, before he died? I know you were one of the last to leave Seattle—and I know you came here. Did you see him, one last time?"

"I saw him." She nodded. "He was lying alone in that back room, on his bed, under a sheet that was soaked with the vomit that finally choked him to death. The doctor wasn't here, and as far as I know, he never did come. I don't know if you could even find one, in those days, in the middle of the evacuation."

"So, he was alone? Dead, in this house?"

"He was alone," she confirmed. "The front door was broken, but closed. Someone had left him on the bed, laid out with respect, I do remember that. Someone had covered him with a sheet, and left his rifle on the bed beside him with his badge. But he was dead, and he stayed dead. The Blight didn't start him walking again, so thank God for small things, I suppose."

Hale jotted it all down, mumbling encouraging sounds as his pencil skipped across the paper. "Do you think the prisoners did that?"

"*You* do," she said. It wasn't quite an accusation.

"I suspect as much," he replied, but he was giddily certain of it. The prison-boy's brother had told him they'd left Maynard's place clean, and they didn't take a thing. He'd said they'd laid him out on the bed, his face covered up. These were details that no one else had ever mentioned, not in all the speculation or investigation into the Great Blight Jailbreak. And there had been plenty of it over the years.

"And then . . . ," he tried to prompt her.

"I dragged him out back and buried him under the tree, beside his old dog. A couple days later, two city officers came out and dug him back up again."

"To make sure?"

She grunted. "To make sure he hadn't skipped town and gone back east; to make sure the Blight hadn't started him moving again; to make sure I'd put him where I said I did. Take your pick."

He finished chasing her words with his pencil and raised his eyes. "What you just said, about the Blight. Did they know, so soon, about what it could do?"

"They knew. They figured it out real quick. Not all the Blight-dead started moving, but the ones who *did* climbed up and went prowling pretty fast, within a few days. But mostly, people wanted to make sure Maynard hadn't gotten away with anything. And when they were satisfied that he was out of their reach, they dumped him back here. They didn't even bury him again. They just left him out there by the tree. I had to put him in the ground twice."

Hale's pencil and his chin hung over the paper. "I'm sorry, did you say—do you mean . . . ?"

"Don't look so shocked." She shifted in the chair and the leather tugged squeakily at her skin. "At least they didn't fill in the hole, the first time. The second time was a lot faster. Let me ask *you* a question, Mr. Quarter."

"Hale, please."

"Hale, as you like. Tell me, how old were you when the Blight came calling?"

His pencil was shuddering, so he placed it flat against the notebook and answered her. "I was almost six."

"That's about what I figured. So you were a little thing, then. You don't even remember it, do you—what it was like before the wall?"

He turned his head back and forth; no, he didn't. Not really. "But I remember the wall, when it first went up. I remember watching it rise, foot by foot, around the contaminated blocks. All two hundred feet of it, all the way around the evacuated neighborhoods."

"I remember it, too. I watched it from here. You could see it from that back window, by the kitchen." She waved her hand toward the stove, and a small rectangular portal behind it. "All day and all night for seven months, two weeks, and three days they worked to build that wall."

"That's very precise. Do you always keep count of such things?"

"No," she said. "But it's easy to remember. They finished construction on the day my son was born. I used to wonder if he didn't miss it, all the noise from the workers. It was all he ever heard, while I was carrying him—the swinging of the hammers, the pounding of the masons' chisels. As soon as the poor child arrived, the world fell silent."

Something occurred to her, and she sat up straight. The chair hissed.

She glanced at the door. "Speaking of the boy, it's getting late. Where's he gotten off to, I wonder? He's usually home by now." She corrected herself. "He's *often* home by now, and it's damnably cold out there."

Hale settled against the stiff wood back of his borrowed seat. "It's a shame he never got to meet his grandfather. I'm sure Maynard would've been proud."

Briar leaned forward, her elbows on her knees. She put her face in her hands and rubbed her eyes. "I don't know," she said. She straightened herself and wiped her forehead with the back of her arm. She peeled off her gloves and dropped them onto the squat, round table between the chair and the fireplace.

"You don't know? But there aren't any other grandchildren, are there? He had no other children, did he?"

"Not as far as I know, but I guess there's no telling." She leaned forward and began to unlace her boots. "I hope you'll excuse me," she said. "I've been wearing these since six o'clock this morning."

"No, no, don't mind me," he said, and kept his eyes on the fire. "I'm sorry. I know I'm intruding."

"You *are* intruding, but I let you in, so the fault is mine." One boot came free of her foot with a sucking pop. She went to work on the other one. "And I don't know if Maynard would've cared much for Zeke, or vice versa. They're not the same kind."

"Is Zeke . . ." Hale was tiptoeing toward dangerous ground, and he knew it, but he couldn't stop himself. "Too much like his father, perhaps?"

Briar didn't flinch, or frown. Again she kept that poker-flat stare firmly in place as she removed the other boot and set it down beside the first one. "It's possible. Blood may tell, but he's still just a boy. There's time yet for him to sort himself out. But as for you, Mr. Hale, I'm afraid I'm going to have to see you on your way. It's getting late, and dawn comes before long."

Hale sighed and nodded. He'd pushed too hard, and too far. He should've stayed on topic, on the dead father—not the dead husband.

"I'm sorry," he told her as he rose and stuffed his notebook under his arm. He replaced his hat, pulled his coat tightly across his chest, and said, "And I thank you for your time. I appreciate everything you've told me, and if my book is ever published, I'll make note of your help."

"Sure," she said.

She closed Hale out, and into the night. He braced himself to face the windy winter evening, tugging his scarf tighter around his neck and adjusting his wool gloves.

 *Two*

At the edge of the house's corner a shadow darted and hid. Then it whispered, "Hey. Hey, *you.*"

Hale held still and waited while a shaggy brown head peered around the side. The head was followed by the skinny but heavily covered body of a teenaged boy with hollow cheeks and vaguely wild eyes. Firelight from inside the house wobbled through the front window and half shadowed, half illuminated his face.

"You were asking about my grandfather?"

"Ezekiel?" Hale made a safe and easy guess.

The boy crept forward, taking care to stay away from the parted place in the curtains so he couldn't be seen from the home's interior. "What did my mother say?"

"Not much."

"Did she tell you he's a hero?"

Hale said, "No. She didn't tell me that."

The boy made an angry snort and ran a mittened hand up his head, across his matted hair. "Of course she didn't. She doesn't believe it, or if she does, she doesn't give a damn."

"I don't know about that."

"I do," he said. "She acts like he didn't do anything good. She acts like everyone's right, and he emptied out the jail because someone paid him to do it—but if he did, then where's the money? Do we *look* like we have any money?"

Zeke gave the biographer enough time to answer, but Hale didn't know what to say.

Zeke continued. "Once everyone understood about the Blight, they evacuated everything they could, right? They cleared out the hospital and even the jail, but the people stuck at the station—the folks who'd gotten arrested, but not charged with anything yet—they just left them there, locked up. And they couldn't get away. The Blight was coming, and everyone knew it. All those people in there, they were going to die."

He sniffed and rubbed the back of his hand under his nose. It might have been running, or simply numb from cold.

"But my grandfather, Maynard, you know? The captain told him to seal off the last end of the quarter, but he wouldn't do it while there were people inside. And those people, they were poor folks, like us. They weren't all bad, not all of them. They'd mostly been picked up for little things, for stealing little things or breaking little things.

"And my grandfather, he wouldn't do it. He wouldn't seal 'em in to die there. The Blight gas was coming for them; and it'd already eaten up the shortest way back to the station. But he ran back into the Blight, covering his face up as much as he could.

"When he got there, he threw the lever that held all the cells locked, and he leaned on it—he held it down with his own weight, because you had to, to keep the doors open. So while everyone ran, he stayed behind.

"And the last two out were a pair of brothers. They understood what he'd done, and they helped him. He was real sick with the gas, though, and it was too late. So they brought him home, trying to help him even though they knew that if anybody saw them, they'd get arrested all over again. But they did it, same as why Maynard did what he did. 'Cause ain't nobody all bad, through and through. Maybe Maynard was a little bad, doing what he did; and maybe those last two guys were a little good.

"But here's the long and short of it," Zeke said, holding up a finger and pushing it under Hale's nose. "There were twenty-two people inside those cells, and Maynard saved them, every last one. It cost him his life, and he didn't get nothing for it."

As the kid turned to his front door and reached for the knob, he added, "And neither did *we*."

## Three

Briar Wilkes closed the door behind the biographer.

She leaned her forehead against it for a moment and walked away, back to the fire. She warmed her hands there, collected her boots, and began to unbutton her shirt and loosen the support cinch that held it close against her body.

Down the hall she passed the doors to her father's room and her son's room. Both doors may as well have been nailed shut for all she ever opened them. She hadn't been inside her father's room in years. She hadn't been inside her son's room since . . . she couldn't remember a specific time, no matter how hard she tried—nor could she even recall what it looked like.

Out in the hall she stopped in front of Ezekiel's door.

Her decision to abandon Maynard's room had come from philosophical necessity; but the boy's room she avoided for no real reason. If anyone ever asked (and of course, no one ever *did*) then she might've made an excuse about respecting his privacy; but it was simpler than that, and possibly worse. She left the room alone because she was purely uncurious about it. Her lack of interest might have been interpreted as a lack of caring, but it was only a side effect of permanent exhaustion. Even knowing this, she felt a pang of guilt and she said out loud, because there was no one to hear her—or agree with her, or argue with her—"I'm a terrible mother."

It was only an observation, but she felt the need to refute it in some way, so she put her hand on the knob and gave it a twist.

The door drooped inward, and Briar leaned her lantern into the cave-black darkness.

A bed with a flat, familiar-looking headboard was pushed into the corner. It was the one she'd slept in as a child, and it was long enough to hold a grown man, but only half as wide as her own. The slats were covered with an old feather mattress that had been flattened until it was barely an inch or two thick. A heavy comforter flopped atop it, folded backward and tangled around in a dirty sheet.

Beside the window at the foot of the bed there lurked a blocky brown chest of drawers and a pile of dirty clothes that was pocked with stray and unmatched boots.

"I need to wash his clothes," she mumbled, knowing that it would have to wait until Sunday unless she planned to do laundry at night—and knowing also that Zeke was likely to get fed up and do his own before then. She'd never heard of a boy who performed so much of his own upkeep, but things were different for families all over since the Blight. Things were different for everyone, yes. But things were especially different for Briar and Zeke.

She liked to think that he understood, at least a little bit, why she saw him as infrequently as she did. And she preferred to assume that he didn't blame her too badly. Boys wanted freedom, didn't they? They valued their independence, and wore it as a sign of maturity; and if she thought about it that way, then her son was a lucky fellow indeed.

A bump and a fumble rattled the front door.

Briar jumped, and closed the bedroom door, and walked quickly down the hall.

From behind the safety of her own bedroom door she finished peeling away her work clothes, and when she heard the stomp of her son's shoes in the front room, she called out, "Zeke, you home?" She felt silly for asking, but it was as good a greeting as any.

"What?"

"I said, you're home, aren't you?"

"I'm home," he hollered. "Where are you?"

"I'll be out in a second," she told him. More like a minute later she emerged wearing something that smelled less like industrial lubricant and coal dust. "Where have you been?" she asked.

"Out." He had already removed his coat and left it to hang on the rack by the door.

"Did you eat?" she asked, trying not to notice how thin he looked. "I got paid yesterday. I know we're low on cupboard fixings, but I can change that soon. And we've still got a little something left around here."

"No, I already ate." He always said that. She never knew if he was telling the truth. He deflected any follow-up questions by asking, "Did you get home late tonight? It's cold in here. I take it the fire hasn't been up very long."

She nodded, and went to the pantry. She was starving, but she was so often hungry that she'd learned to think around it. "I took an extra shift. We had somebody out sick." On the top shelf of the pantry there was a mixture of dried beans and corn that cooked up into a light stew. Briar pulled it down and wished she had meat to go with it, but she didn't wish very long or hard.

She set a pot of water to boil and reached under a towel for a bit of bread that was almost too stale to eat anymore, but she stuffed it into her mouth and chewed it fast.

Ezekiel took the seat that Hale had borrowed and dragged it over to the fire to toast some of the frigid stiffness out of his hands. "I saw that man leaving," he said, loud enough that she would hear him around the corner.

"You did, did you?"

"What did he want?"

A rattling dump of poured soup mix splashed into the pot. "To talk. It's late, I know. I guess it looks bad, but what would the neighbors do about it—talk nasty behind our backs?"

She heard a grin in her son's voice when he asked, "What did he want to talk about?"

She didn't answer him. She finished chewing the bread and asked,

"Are you sure you don't want any of this? There's plenty for two, and you should see yourself. You're skin and bones."

"I told you, I ate already. *You* fill up. You're skinnier than me."

"Am not," she fussed back.

"Are too. But what did that man want?" he asked again.

She came around the corner and leaned against the wall, her arms folded and her hair more fallen down than pinned up. She said, "He's writing a book about your grandfather. Or he says he is."

"You think maybe he's not?"

Briar stared intently at her son, trying to figure out who he looked like when he made that carefully emotionless, innocent face. Not his father, certainly, though the poor child had inherited the preposterous hair. Neither as dark as hers, nor as light as his father's, the mop could not be combed nor oiled into decent behavior. It was exactly the sort of hair that, when it occurred on a baby, old ladies would fondly disturb while making cooing noises. But the older Zeke grew, the more ridiculous it looked.

"Mother?" he tried again. "You think maybe that man was lying?"

She shook her head quickly, not in answer but to clear it. "Oh. Well, I don't know. Maybe, maybe not."

"Are you all right?"

"I'm fine," she said. "I was just . . . I was looking at you, that's all. I don't see you enough, I don't think. We should, I don't know . . . We should do something together, sometime."

He squirmed. "Like what?"

His squirming did not go unnoticed. She tried to back away from the suggestion. "I didn't have anything in mind. And maybe it's a bad idea. It's probably . . . well." She turned and went back into the kitchen so she could talk to him without having to watch his discomfort while she confessed the truth. "It's probably easier for you anyway, that I keep my distance. I imagine you have a hard enough time living it down, being my boy. Sometimes I think the kindest thing I can do is let you pretend I don't exist."

No argument came from the fireplace until he said, "It's not so bad being yours. I'm not ashamed of you or anything, you know." But he didn't leave the fire to come and say it to her face.

"Thanks." She wound a wooden spoon around in the pot and made swirling designs in the frothing mixture.

"Well, I'm really *not*. And for that matter, it's not so bad being Maynard's, either. In some circles, it works out pretty good," he added, and Briar heard a quick cutting off in his voice, as if he was afraid that he'd said too much.

As if she weren't already aware.

"I wish you'd keep a *better* circle of company," she told him, though even as she said it, she guessed more than she wanted to know. Where else could a child of hers seek friends? Who else would have anything to do with him, except for the quarters where Maynard Wilkes was a folk hero—and not a fortunate crook who died before he could be judged?

"Mother—"

"No, listen to me." She abandoned the pot and stood again by the edge of the wall. "If you're ever going to have any hope of a normal life, you've got to stay out of trouble, and that means staying out of those places, away from those people."

"Normal life? How's that going to happen, do you think? I could spend my whole life being poor-but-honest, if that's what you want, but—"

"I know you're young and you don't believe me, but you have to trust me—*it's better than the alternative*. Stay poor-but-honest, if that's what keeps a roof over your head and keeps you out of prison. There's nothing so good out there that it's worth . . ." She wasn't sure how to finish, but she felt she'd made her point, so she stopped talking. She turned on her heel and went back to the stove.

Ezekiel left the fireplace and followed her. He stood at the end of the kitchen, blocking her exit and forcing her to look at him.

"That it's worth what? What do I have to lose, Mother? All *this*?" With a sweeping, sarcastic gesture he indicated the dark gray home in which they squatted. "All the friends and money?"

She smacked the spoon down on the edge of the basin and grabbed a bowl to dish herself some half-cooked supper, and so she could stop gazing at the child she'd made. He looked nothing like her, but every day he looked a little more like one man, then the other. Depending on the light and depending on his mood he could've been her father, or her husband.

She poured herself a bowl of bland stew and struggled to keep from spilling it as she stalked past him.

"You'd rather escape? I understand that. There's not much keeping you here, and maybe when you're a grown man you'll up and leave," she said, dropping the stoneware bowl onto the table and inserting herself into the chair beside it. "I realize that I don't make an honest day's work look very appealing; and I realize too that you think you've been cheated out of a better life, and I don't blame you. But here we are, and this is what we have. The circumstances have damned us both."

"Circumstances?"

She took a deep swallow of the stew and tried not to look at him. She said, "All right, circumstances and *me*. You can blame me if you want, just like I can blame your father, or *my* father if I want—it doesn't matter. It doesn't change anything. Your future was broken before you were born, and there's no one left living for you to pin that on except for me."

From the corner of her eye, she watched Ezekiel clench and unclench his fists. She waited for it. Any moment, and his control would slip, and that wild, wicked look would fill his face with the ghost of his father, and she'd have to close her eyes to shut him out.

But the snap didn't occur, and the madness didn't cover him with a terrible veil. Instead, he said, in a deadpan voice that matched the empty gaze he'd given her earlier, "But that's the most unfair part of all: *You* didn't do anything."

She was surprised, but cautiously so. "Is that what you think?"

"It's what I've figured."

She snorted a bitter-sounding laugh. "So you've got it all figured out now, have you?"

"More than you'd think, I bet. And you should've told that writer about what Maynard did, because if more people knew, and understood, then maybe some *respectable* folks would know he wasn't a criminal, and you could live a little less like a leper."

She used the stew to buy herself another few bites to think. It did not escape her notice that Zeke must've spoken to Hale, but she chose not to call attention to it.

"I didn't tell the biographer anything about Maynard because he already knew plenty, and he'd already made up his mind about it. If it makes you feel any better, he agrees with you. He thinks Maynard was a hero, too."

Zeke threw his hands up in the air and said, "See? I'm not the only one. And as for the company I keep, maybe my friends aren't high society, but they know good guys when they see them."

"Your friends are crooks," she said.

"You don't know that. You don't even know any of my friends; you've never met any of them except for Rector, and he ain't so bad as far as bad friends go, you even said so. And you should know: It's like a secret handshake, Maynard's name. They say it like spitting in your hand to swear. It's like swearing on a Bible, except everybody knows Maynard actually *did* something."

"Don't talk that way," she stopped him. "You're asking for trouble, trying to rewrite history, trying to shuffle things around until they mean something better."

"I'm not trying to rewrite anything!" And she heard it, the frightening timbre in his freshly broken, almost man-sounding voice. "I'm only trying to make it right!"

She swallowed the last of the stew too fast, almost scalding her throat in her hurry to be done with it, and to quit being hungry so she could focus on this fight—if that's what it was becoming.

"You don't understand," she breathed, and the words were hot on her nearly burned throat. "Here's the hard and horrible truth of life, Zeke, and if you never hear another thing I ever tell you, hear this: It doesn't matter if Maynard was a hero. It doesn't matter if your father was an honest man with good intentions. It doesn't matter if I never did anything to deserve what happened, and it doesn't matter that your life was hexed before I even knew about you."

"But how can it not? If everyone just understood, and if everyone just knew all the facts about my grandfather and my dad, then . . ." Despair crackled through his objection.

"Then what? Then suddenly we'd be rich, and loved, and happy? You're young, yes, but you're not stupid enough to believe *that.* Maybe in a few generations, when plenty of time has passed, and no one really remembers the havoc or the fear anymore, and your grandfather has had time to fade into legend, then storytellers like young Mr. Quarter will have the final word. . . ."

Then she lost her voice from shock and horror, because she suddenly realized that her son had only barely been talking about Maynard at all. She took a deep breath, lifted her bowl up from the table, and walked it over to the basin and left it there. It was too much, the prospect of pumping more water to clean it right then.

"Mother?" Ezekiel gathered that he'd crossed some awful line and he didn't know what it was. "Mother, what is it?"

"You don't understand," she told him, even though she felt like she'd said it a thousand times in the past hour. "There's so much you don't understand, but I know you better than you think I do. I know you better than anyone, because I knew the men you mimic even when you don't mean to—even when you have no idea what you've said or done to startle me."

"Mother, you aren't making sense."

She slapped a hand against her chest. "*I'm* not making sense? You're the one who's telling me wonderful things about someone you never met, building up this great apology for one dead man because you think—because you don't know any better—that if you can redeem *one* dead man you might redeem *another.* You gave yourself away, naming them both in one breath like that." While she had his full attention, before she lost the element of shock that was holding him quiet, she continued. "That's where you're going with this, isn't it? If Maynard wasn't all bad, then maybe your father wasn't all bad either? If you can vindicate the one, then there's hope for the other?"

Slowly, then with stronger rhythm, he began to nod. "Yes, but it's not as daft as you make it sound—no, *don't*. Stop it, and listen to me. Hear me out: If, all this time, everyone in the Outskirts has been wrong about *you*, then—"

"How are they wrong about me?" she demanded to know.

"They think everything was your fault! The jailbreak, the Blight, and the Boneshaker too. But they *weren't* your fault, and the jailbreak wasn't a big ol' act of mayhem and nuisance." He paused to take in some air, and his mother wondered where he'd ever heard such a phrase.

"So they're wrong about you, and I think they're wrong about Grandfather. That's two out of three, ain't it? Why's it so nuts to think they've all been wrong about Levi, too?"

It was exactly as she'd feared, laid out in a pretty, perfect line. "You," she tried to say, but it came out as a cough. She slowed herself down and did her best to calm herself, despite the awful crashing of her son's dangerous, innocent words. "There's . . . listen. I understand why it looks so obvious to you, and I understand why you want to believe that there's something of your father's memory worth saving. And . . . and maybe you're right about Maynard; as likely as not he was only trying to help. Maybe he had that moment, that break when he realized that he could obey the letter of the law or the spirit of it—and he was chasing some kind of ideal, right into the Blight, and into his grave. I can believe it, and I can accept it, and I can even be a little angry about the way he's been remembered."

Zeke made an adolescent squeak of disbelief and held out his hands like he wanted to shake his mother, or strangle her. "Then why haven't you ever said anything? Why would you let them stomp all over his memory if you think he was trying to help people?"

"I told you, *it wouldn't matter*. And besides, even if the jailbreak had never happened, and he'd died in some other, less strange way, it wouldn't have made a difference to *me*. I wouldn't have remembered him any different for any last-minute heroics, and, and, and . . . Besides," she added another fierce defense, "who would listen to me? People avoid me and ignore me, and it's not Maynard's fault, not really. Nothing I could say to defend him would sway a single soul in the Outskirts, because being his daughter is only a secondary curse on my head."

Her voice had crept up again, too close to fear for her own satisfaction. She beat it back down, and counted her breaths, and tried to keep her words in a tight, logical line to match and beat Ezekiel's.

"I didn't choose my parents; no one does. I could be forgiven for my father's sins. But I did choose *your* father, and for *that*, they will never let me rest."

Something salty and bright was searing a deep, angry streak in her chest, and it felt like tears clawing their way up her throat. She gulped them down. She caught her breath and crushed it into submission, and as her son walked away from her, back toward his bedroom where he could close her out, she tagged after him.

He shut the door in her face. He would've locked it, but it had no lock, so he leaned his weight against it. Briar could hear the soft whump of his body pressing a stubborn resistance on the other side.

She didn't yank the knob, or even touch it.

She pressed her temple against a place where she thought his head might be, and she told him, "Try and save Maynard, if that will make you happy. Make that your mission, if it gives you some kind of direction and if it makes you less . . . angry. But please, Zeke, please. There's nothing to retrieve from Leviticus Blue. Nothing at all. If you dig too hard or push too far, if you learn too much, it will only break your heart. Sometimes, everyone is right. Not always and not even usually, but once in a while, everyone is right."

It took all her self-restraint to keep from saying more. Instead, she turned away and went to her own bedroom to swear and seethe.

## *Four*

On Friday morning, Briar rose just before dawn, like always, and lit a candle so she could see.

Her clothes were where she'd left them. She traded yesterday's shirt for a clean one, but she drew the same pair of pants up over her legs and tucked the narrow cuffs into her boots. The leather support cinch dangled on the bedpost. She picked it up and buckled it on, crushing it more tightly around her waist than was strictly comfortable. Once it warmed to her body it would fit her better.

Once her boots were laced and she'd found a thick wool vest to throw over her shirt, she pulled her overcoat down off the other bedpost and slipped her arms through its sleeves.

Down the hall, she didn't hear a sound from her son's room, not even a quick snore or a settling twist in the blankets. He wouldn't be awake yet, even if he was going to school—and he didn't often bother.

Briar had already made sure that he could read all right, and he could count and add better than a lot of the kids she'd seen, so she didn't worry about him too much. School would keep him out of trouble, but school itself was often trouble. Before the Blight, when the city was bustling enough to support it, there had been several schools. But in the aftermath, with so much of the population decimated or scattered, the teachers didn't always stay, and the students didn't get much in the way of discipline.

Briar wondered when the war would end back east. The papers talked about it in exciting terms. A Civil War, a War Between the

States, a War of Independence or a War of Aggression. It sounded epic, and after eighteen years of ongoing struggle, perhaps it was. But if it would only end, then perhaps it might be worth the trouble to head back toward the other coast. With some scraping and saving, maybe she could pull together the money to start over somewhere else, where no one knew anything about her dead father or husband. Or, if nothing else, Washington could become a proper state, and not merely a distant territory. If Seattle was part of a state, then America would have to send help, wouldn't it? With help, they could build a better wall, or maybe do something about the Blight gas trapped inside it. They could get doctors to research treatments for the gas poisoning—and God only knew, maybe even cure it.

It should've been a thrilling thought, but it wasn't. Not at six o'clock in the morning, and not when Briar was beginning a two-mile walk down the mudflats.

The sun was rising slowly and the sky was taking on the milky gray daytime hue that it would never shake, not until spring. Rain spit sideways, cast sharply by the wind until it worked its way under Briar's wide-brimmed leather hat, up her sleeve cuffs, and down through her boots until her feet were frozen and her hands felt like raw chicken skin.

By the time she reached the 'works, her face was numb from the cold but a tiny bit burned from the foul-smelling water.

She wandered around to the back of the enormous compound that hunkered loudly at the edge of Puget Sound. Twenty-four hours of every day it cranked and pumped, sucking rainwater and groundwater into the plant and stripping it, processing it, cleaning it, until it was pure enough to drink and bathe in. It was a slow and laborious procedure, one that was labor intensive but not altogether illogical. The Blight gas had poisoned the natural systems until the creeks and streams flowed almost yellow with contagion. Even the near-constant patter of rain could not be trusted. The clouds that dropped it may have gusted past the walled-up city and absorbed enough toxin to wash skin raw and bleach paint.

But the Blight could be boiled away; it could be filtered and steamed and filtered again. And after seventeen hours of treatment, the water could be safely consumed.

Great wagons drawn by teams of massive Clydesdales took the water out in tanks and delivered it block by block, funneling it into collective reservoirs that could then be pumped by individual families.

But first, it had to be processed. It had to go through the Waterworks facility, where Briar Wilkes and several hundred others spent ten or fifteen hours a day hooking and unhooking brass cylinders and tanks, and moving them from station to station, filter to filter. Most of the tanks were overhead and could be zipped down lines and rails from place to place, but some were built into the floor and had to be shifted from plug to plug like pieces in a sliding puzzle.

Briar climbed up the back steps and lifted the lever arm that secured the workers' entrance.

She blinked at the usual blast of steam-heated air. Over in the far corner, where workers kept company-assigned belongings in cubbyholes, she reached for her gloves. They weren't the heavy wool contraptions she wore on her own time, but thick leather that protected her hands from the superheated metal of the tanks.

She'd pulled the left one all the way down to her wrist before she noticed the paint. On the palm, down the fingers, and across the back knuckles someone had brushed bright streaks of blue. The right glove had been similarly vandalized.

Briar was alone in the workers' area. She was early, and the paint was dry. The prank had been pulled last night, after she'd left for the evening. There was no one present to accuse.

She sighed and shoved her fingers into the other tainted glove. At least this time no one had filled up the interior with paint. The gloves were still wearable, and would not need replacing. Maybe she could even scrub them clean, later.

"It never gets old, does it?" she said to herself. "Sixteen goddamn years and you'd think, someday, the joke might get old."

She left her own wool gloves up on the shelf that used to have her name on it. She'd written WILKES there, but while she wasn't looking it had been crossed out and replaced with BLUE. She'd scribbled over the BLUE and rewrote WILKES, and the game had gone round and round until there was no room left on the ledge for anyone to write anything, but everyone knew who it belonged to.

Her goggles hadn't been bothered; she was thankful for that much. The gloves had been expensive enough, and the company-issued headgear would've cost a week's worth of pay to restore.

All the workers wore goggles with polarized lenses. For reasons no one fully understood, such lenses allowed the wearer to see the dreaded Blight. Even in trace amounts it would appear as a yellowish-greenish haze that oozed and dripped. Although the Blight was technically a gaseous substance, it was a very heavy one that poured or collected like a thick sludge.

Briar strapped the clunky lenses against her face and left her overcoat on a peg. She picked up a wrench that was almost as long as her forearm and stepped out onto the main floor to begin her day of shuffling piping-hot crucibles from slot to slot.

Ten hours later, she stripped off the gloves, peeled away the goggles, and abandoned them on her shelf.

She opened the back metal door to learn that it was still raining, which came as no surprise. She tied her big, round-rimmed hat more closely under her chin. She didn't need any more orange streaks twirling through her otherwise dark hair, courtesy of the nasty rain. With her overcoat fastened tightly across her chest and her hands jammed into the pockets, she set off for home.

The way back from work was almost straight uphill, but the wind was behind her, billowing off the ocean and crashing up the ridges on the edges of the old city. The walk itself was a long one, but a familiar one, and she did it without giving much thought to the wind or the water. She'd lived with the weather so long that it was barely background music, unpleasant but unnoticed, except when numbness settled in her toes and she had to stomp to bring the feeling back.

It was only barely dark when she arrived home.

This pleased her in an almost giddy way. During the winter she was so rarely home before the sky was fully black that it astounded her to find herself scaling the crooked stone steps while there was still a touch of pink between the rain clouds.

Small victory or no, she felt like celebrating it.

But first, she thought, she should apologize to Ezekiel. She could sit him down and talk to him, if he'd listen. She could tell him a few stories, if it came to that. Not everything, of course.

He couldn't know the worst of it, even though he probably thought he did. Briar knew the stories that made the rounds. She'd heard them herself, been asked about them dozens of times by dozens of policemen, reporters, and furious survivors.

So Zeke had certainly heard them, too. He'd been taunted by them when he was small enough to cry in school. Once, years ago, when he was barely as tall as her waist, he'd asked if any of it was true. Did his father really make the terrible machine that broke the city until pieces of it fell into the earth? Did he really bring the Blight?

"Yes," she had to tell him. "Yes, it happened that way, but I don't know why. He never told me. Please don't ask me anymore."

He never did ask for more, even though Briar sometimes wished he would. If he asked, she might be able to tell him something good—something nice. It hadn't all been fear and strangeness, had it? She'd honestly loved her husband once, and there were reasons for it. Some of them must not have been spun from girlish stupidity, and it wasn't all about the money.

(Oh, she'd known he was rich—and maybe, in some small respect, the money had made it easier to be stupid. But it never was *all* about the money.)

She could tell Zeke stories of flowers sent in secret, of notes composed in ink that was almost magical for the way it glittered, burned, and vanished. There were charming gadgets and seductive toys. One time Leviticus had made her a pin that looked like a coat button, but when the filigree rim was twisted, tiny clockwork gears within would chime a precious tune.

If Zeke had ever asked, she could've shared an anecdote or two that made the man look like less of a monster.

It was stupid, she realized, the way she'd been waiting for him to ask. It was suddenly as obvious as could be: She ought to just *tell* him. Let the poor child know that there had been good times too, and that there were good reasons—at least, they'd seemed like good reasons at the time—why she'd run away from home and her strict, distant father and married the scientist when she was hardly any older than her son was now.

Furthermore, the night before she really should've told him, "You didn't do anything *either*. They're wrong about you, too, but there's still time for you to prove it. You haven't yet made the kind of choices that will cripple you for life."

These resolutions buoyed her spirits even more than the early homecoming, and the hope that Zeke might be inside. She could begin on the spot, righting her old wrongs—which were only mistakes of uncertainty, after all.

Her key grated in the lock and the door swung inward, revealing darkness.

"Zeke? Zeke, you home?"

The fireplace was cold. The lantern was on the table by the door, so she took it and fumbled for a match. Not a single candle was lit within, and it irked her that she needed any extra illumination. It had been months since she'd come home and simply parted the curtains for light. But the sun was almost wholly down, and the rooms were black except for the places where her lantern pushed back the shadows.

"Zeke?"

She wasn't sure why she said his name again. She already knew he wasn't home. It wasn't just the darkness, either; it was the way the home felt empty. It felt quiet in a way that couldn't include a boy closed away in his bedroom.

"Zeke?" The silence was unbearable, and Briar didn't know why. She'd come home to an empty house many times before, and it'd never made her nervous.

Her good mood evaporated.

The lantern's light swept the interior. Details crept into the glow. It wasn't her imagination. Something was wrong. One of the kitchen cabinets was open; it was where she kept extra dry goods, when she had them—tinned crackers and oats. It had been raided, and left empty. In the middle of the floor, in front of the big leather chair, a small piece of metal glinted when it caught the edge of the candlelight.

A bullet.

"Zeke?" She tried once more, but this time it was less a question than a gasp.

She picked up the bullet and examined it; and while she stood there, interrogating the small bit with her eyes, she felt exposed.

Not like she was being watched, but like she was open to attack.

Like there was danger, and it could see a way inside.

The doors. Down the short corridor, four doors—one to a closet and three to the bedrooms.

Zeke's door was open.

She almost dropped the lantern and the bullet both. Blind fear squeezed at her chest as she stood riveted to the spot.

The only way to shake it loose was to move, so she moved. She shuffled her feet forward, toward the corridor. Maybe she should check for intruders, but some primal instinct told her there weren't any. The emptiness was too complete, and the echo too absolute. No one was home, not anyone who should or shouldn't be.

Zeke's room looked almost exactly like it had when she'd peeked inside the day before. It looked unclean but uncluttered, by virtue of the fact that he owned so little.

Only now there was a drawer sitting hollowly in the middle of the bed.

There was nothing inside it, and Briar didn't know what it once might've held, so she walked past it and on to the other drawers that remained in their place. They were empty, except for a stray sock too riddled with holes to cover a foot.

He owned a bag. She knew he did; he took it to school, when he deigned to attend. She'd made it for him, stitching together stray scraps of leather and canvas until it was strong enough and big enough to hold the books she could scarcely afford. Not so long ago, he'd asked her to repair it, so she knew he still used it.

And she couldn't find it.

A quick thrashing of the small room failed to turn it up, and failed to reveal any sign of where the boy or the bag might have gone . . . until she dropped to her knees and lifted the edge of the bedspread. Under the bed, there was nothing. But under the mattress, between the frame and the pressed feather pad, something left an odd and geometric bulge. She jammed her hand through the bedding and seized a packet of something smooth that crackled between her fingers.

Papers. A small stack of them, various shapes and sizes.

Including . . .

She turned it over and checked the front, and back, and the fear was so cold in her lungs that she could hardly breathe.

. . . a map of downtown Seattle, torn in half.

The missing half would've indicated the old financial district— where the Boneshaker machine had caused a catastrophic earthquake on its very first test run . . . and where, a few days later, the Blight gas had first begun to ooze.

Where had he gotten it?

Down one side, the map had a tidily torn seam that made her think it had once been part of a book. But the city's small library had never reopened outside the walls, and books were scarce—and expensive. He wouldn't have bought it, but he might have stolen it, or . . .

It smelled funny. She'd been holding it for half a minute before she noticed, and anyway, the smell was so familiar it almost went unremarked. She held the scrap of paper up to her face and sniffed it hard. It might only be her imagination. There was one good way to find out.

Down the hall and into her own room she dashed, and she dug around in her tall, creaky wardrobe until she found it—a fragment of lens left over from the early days, the bad old days . . . the days when the evacuation order was fresh and vague. No one was sure what they were running from, or why; but everyone had figured out that you could see it, if you had mask or a set of goggles with a bit of polarized glass.

At the time, there had been no other test. Hucksters had sold lenses on street corners at ridiculous prices, and not all of them were real. Some were pulled from broken industrial masks and safety eyewear, but the cheaper knockoffs were little more than ordinary monocles and bottle-bottoms.

Back then, money hadn't been an object. Briar's palm-sized piece of tinted lens was real, and it worked as well as the goggles she'd left on a shelf back at the plant.

She lit two more candles and carried them into Zeke's room, and with the light of the lantern added, she held up the scratched bit of transparency and used it to scry the things she'd found in the mattress. And all of them—the map, the leaflets, the shreds of posters— glowed with an ill yellow halo that marked them as clearly as if they'd been stamped with a warning.

"Blight," she groaned. The papers were filthy with its residue.

In fact, the papers were so thoroughly contaminated that there were precious few places from whence they might have come. She couldn't imagine that her son had acquired these strange slips from within the sealed city with its seamless, towering wall. Some of the local shops did sell artifacts the townspeople had evacuated with, but they were often costly.

"Goddamn his stupid friends and their stupid lemon sap," she swore. "*Goddamn every last one of them.*"

She scrambled to her feet and went back to her bedroom again, this time retrieving a muslin face mask. Around her nose and mouth she wrapped and tied it, and she spread the contents of Zeke's mattress out on his bed. The assortment was strange, to say the least. In addition to the map, she found old tickets and playbills, pages pulled out of novels, and clippings from newspapers that were older than the boy was.

Briar wished for her leather gloves. In lieu of them, she used the lone holey sock to touch the papers, sorting them and running her eyes across them—catching her own name, or at least her old name.

AUGUST 9, 1864. Authorities searched the home of Leviticus and Briar Blue, but no insight into the Boneshaker incident was found. Evidence of wrongdoing mounts as Blue remains missing. His wife cannot provide an explanation for the testing of the machine that nearly collapsed the city's foundations and killed at least thirty-seven people, three horses.

AUGUST 11, 1864. Briar Blue held for questioning after collapse of fourth bank on Commercial Avenue, disappearance of her husband. Her role in the events of the Boneshaker calamity remains unclear.

Briar remembered the articles. She recalled trying to muster an appetite for lunch as she skimmed the damning reports, not yet knowing that there was more to her nausea than merely the stress of the investigation. But where had Ezekiel gotten such clippings, and how? All of the stories had been printed sixteen years ago, and distributed in a city that had been dead and closed for nearly that long.

She wrinkled her nose and grabbed Zeke's pillow, tearing off its case and stuffing the papers inside it. They shouldn't have been too dangerous, crammed underneath his bedding; but the more she covered them the better she felt. She didn't want to simply hide them or contain them; she wanted to bury them. But there wasn't any real point.

Zeke still hadn't come home. She suspected that he had no intention of returning home that night.

And that was even before she found the note he'd left on the dining room table, where she'd walked right past it. The note was brief, and pointed. It said, "My father was innocent, and I can prove it. I'm sorry about everything. I'll be back as soon as I can."

Briar crushed the note in her fist, and shook until she screamed out in one frantic, furious blast that no doubt frightened her neighbors, but she cared so little about their opinion that she did it again. It didn't make her feel any better, but she couldn't stop herself from shrieking a third time and then picking up the nearest chair and flinging it across the room—into the mantel over the fireplace.

It broke in two against the stone, but before it had time to tumble into pieces on the floor, Briar was already on her front porch and running down the stairs with a lantern.

She tied her hat back on as she went, and pulled her overcoat tighter as she ran. The rain had mostly stopped and the wind was as harsh as ever, but she charged against it, back down the hill and along the mudflats to the only place she'd ever been able to reliably find Ezekiel on the odd days that he'd stayed gone long enough to make her worry.

Down by the water, in a four-story brick building that was once a warehouse and then a whorehouse, a contingent of nuns had established a shelter for children who'd been left parentless by the Blight.

The Sisters of Loving Grace Home for Orphans had raised an entire generation's worth of boys and girls who had somehow found their way past the gas and into the Outskirts without any supervision. Now the very youngest of the original occupants were getting old enough that they'd soon be compelled to find homes of their own or accept work within the church.

Among the older boys there was one Rector "Wreck'em" Sherman, a lad who was seventeen if he was a day, and who was well known as a distributor of the illegal but much-desired lemon sap. It was a cheap drug—a yellowish, gritty, pastelike substance distilled from the Blight gas—and its effects were pleasant, but devastating. The "sap" was cooked and inhaled for a blissful and apathetic high, until chronic use began to kill . . . but not quickly.

Sap didn't just damage the mind; it turned the body necrotic. Gangrene would catch and sprawl, creeping out from the corners of mouths and eating away cheeks and noses. Fingers and toes would fall away, and in time, the body might fully transform into a parody of the undead "rotters" who no doubt still shambled hopelessly through the walled-up quarters.

Despite the obvious drawbacks, the drug was in high demand. And since the demand was good, Rector was ready with a full assortment of pipes, suggestions, and tiny paper-wrapped packets of lemon sap.

Briar had tried to keep Zeke away from Rector, but there was only so much she could do to restrain him—and, at the very least, Rector did not seem interested in letting Zeke sell or abuse the sap. Anyway, Zeke was mostly interested in the community, the camaraderie, and the chance to fit in with a batch of boys who wouldn't throw blue dye on him or hold him down and write terrible things across his face.

So she understood, but that didn't mean she liked it, and that didn't mean she liked the red-haired beanpole of a boy who answered her loud and impatient summons.

She pushed her way past a nun in a heavy gray habit and cornered Rector, whose eyes were too big and too earnest to be innocent of anything.

"You," she began with a finger aimed high, up under his chin. "You know where my son is, and you're going to tell me, or I'm going tear your ears off and feed them to you, you dirty little poison-pushing wharf kitten." All of it came out without rising into the territory of yelling, but every word was as heavy as a hammer.

"Sister Claire?" he whimpered. He'd retreated as far as he could and there was nowhere left for him to go.

Briar shot Sister Claire a look that would've rusted metal, and returned her attention to Rector. "If I have to ask twice, you will regret it for the rest of your life—however long that may be."

"But I don't know. I don't. I don't know," he stammered.

"But you can guess, I bet, and it would probably be a very *good* guess, and so help me if I don't hear some guesses coming out of your mouth I will do you great and terrible bodily harm, and there isn't a nun or a priest or anyone else in a God-given uniform who will recognize you when I'm finished. The angels will *weep* when they see what's left of you. Now, *talk*."

His frantic stare went wildly back and forth between Briar, the openmouthed Sister Claire, and a priest who had just entered the room.

Briar caught on just in time to keep from punching the boy in the gut.

"I see, all right." He didn't want to talk about business in front of his landlords.

She seized his arm and pulled him forward, saying over her shoulder, "Pardon me, Sister and Father, but this young man and I are going to have a little talk. We won't be but a moment, and I promise, you'll have him back before bedtime." And then, under her breath as she led the kid out into the stairwell, "Kindly keep in mind, Mr. Wreck'em, that I made no promises about your condition when I return you."

"I heard, I heard," he said. He bounced off a corner and tripped over a stair as Briar pulled him down.

She didn't know where she was leading him, but it was dark and quiet, and only a pair of tiny wall lamps and Briar's lantern kept the stairs from being impossible to navigate.

Down by the basement there was a narrow spot behind the steps.

She jerked Rector to a halt and forced him to face her. "Here we are," she told him in a growl made to terrorize a bear. "No one else to hear. You talk, and you talk fast. I want to know where Zeke went, and I want to know *now*."

Rector shuddered and slapped at her hand, trying to peel her fingers off of his slender bicep. But she didn't let go. Instead, she squeezed harder, until he made a sharp whine and rallied enough nerve to twist himself out of her grasp.

"All he wants is to prove that Leviticus wasn't crazy or a crook!"

"What makes him think he can do that? And how could he even begin such a task?"

The boy said, with far more caution than innocence would merit, "He might've heard a rumor from someplace."

"What rumor? From whereplace?"

"There were stories about a ledger, weren't there? Didn't Blue say that the Russians paid him to do something funny with the test?"

Her eyes narrowed. "Levi *said* that. But there was never any proof. And if there *was* proof, you couldn't prove it by me—because he never showed it to anyone."

"Not even you?"

"*Especially* not me," she said. "He never told me a thing about what he was doing in that laboratory, with those machines. He sure as hell never shared any of the money details."

"But you were his wife!"

"That doesn't mean anything," she said. She'd never figured out for certain if her husband had kept so quiet because he didn't trust her, or because he thought she was stupid. It was likely a bit of both.

"Look, ma'am, you must have known Zeke was wondering when he started asking questions about it."

Briar hit the stair rail with her free hand. "He never asked any questions! Never once, not since he was a little boy, has he asked about Levi." And she added, more quietly, "But he'd been asking about Maynard."

Rector was still staring, still cornered, still backed as far away from Briar as he could get. This was the point where he ought to have interjected something helpful, but he stayed quiet until she brought her fist back around and hit the metal rail again.

"Don't," he said, holding out his hands. "Ma'am, don't . . . don't do that. He'll be fine, you know. He's a smart guy. He knows his way around, and he knows about Maynard, so he'll be all right."

"What do you mean by that? He knows about Maynard? Everybody *knows* about Maynard."

He nodded, bringing his hands back down and closer to his chest, ready to defend himself if it came to that. "But Zeke's his grandson, and people will look out for him. Not, well . . ." He stopped himself, and started again. "Not all the people everywhere, but where he's going, what he's doing—the kind of folks he's likely to meet? All those people, they know about Maynard, and they'll look after him."

"All those people *where*?" she asked, and the last word came out with a gulp of anguish, because she knew—even though it was impossible, and crazy. She knew *where*, even though it didn't make any sense at all.

"He's gone . . . He went . . ." Rector lifted his index finger and pointed in the general direction of the old city.

It took every ounce of willpower Briar could summon to keep from cracking the boy across the face; she didn't have enough left over to keep herself from shouting, too. "How would he do that? And what does he plan to do when he gets over the wall and he can't breathe, or see—"

Rector's hands were up again, and he'd found enough nerve to step forward. "Ma'am, you have to stop shouting. You have to stop."

"—and there's no one there but the leftover, locked-in, shambling rotters who will grab him and kill him—"

"Ma'am!" he said loud enough to interrupt, and almost loud enough to get himself kicked. But it stopped her tirade, just for a beat, and it was long enough for him to blurt out, "People live in there!"

What felt like a long stretch of silence followed.

Briar asked, "What did you say?"

Trembling, retreating again, stopping when his shoulders pressed against the bricks, he said, "People live there. Inside."

She swallowed hard. "How many people?"

"Not very many. But more than you might expect. Folks who know about them call 'em Doornails, 'cause they're dead to the rest of the world."

"But how . . . ?" She rocked her head back and forth. "That's not possible; it can't be. There's no air in the city. No food, no sun, no—"

"Hell, ma'am. There's no sun out here, either. And the air, they found a way around that, too. They sealed off some of the buildings and they pump it down from up top—from over the side of the wall, where the air's clean enough to breathe. If you ever hiked all the way around it, you'd see the tubes sticking up on the far side of the city."

"But why would anyone do that? Why go to all the trouble?" And then a horrible thought flickered through her mind and tumbled out of her mouth. "Please tell me they aren't trapped in there!"

Rector laughed nervously. "No, no ma'am. They aren't trapped. They just . . ." He lifted his shoulders into a shrug. "They stayed."

"Why?" she demanded in a short warble of near-hysteria.

He tried again to hush her, patting the air with his hand, begging her for a lower voice and a quieter exchange. "Some of 'em didn't want to leave their homes. Some of 'em got stuck, and some of them thought it'd all blow over."

But he was leaving part of it out; she could tell it from his new burst of nervousness. "And the rest of them?" she asked.

The boy dropped his voice to a harsh whisper. "It's the sap, ma'am. Where do you think it all comes from, anyway?"

"I know it comes from the *gas*," she grumbled. "I'm not a *fool*."

"Never said you were, ma'am. But how do you think people get the gas in the first place? Do you know how much sicksand the Outskirts produce? A lot, that's how much. More than anybody could ever make just from boiling it out of the rainwater."

Briar had to admit, that's how she'd assumed people made the drug—either that, or from the waste cast off by the Waterworks. No one seemed to know what became of the containers of processed Blight resin after it was barreled up to cool. She'd always suspected that it was swiped to be sold on some market or another, but Rector insisted otherwise. "It doesn't come from what you folks cook out of the groundwater at the 'works, either. I've known a chemist or two who got a hand on that mess, but he said you couldn't do anything with it. He said it was useless, just poison."

"And lemon sap is something better?"

"Lemon sap, God," he blasphemed with a sneer of derision. "That's what the old folks call it, sure."

She rolled her eyes. "I don't care what you kids call it, I know what it is when I see it—and I've seen it do worse to people than poison them. If my father were still alive he'd . . ." She didn't know how to finish. "He would've never stood for it," she said weakly.

"Maynard's dead, ma'am. And maybe he wouldn't have liked to know it, I couldn't say, but he's the closest thing to a patron saint that some of us have got."

"It would have driven him mad," she speculated curtly.

It was Rector's turn to ask, "Why?"

"Because he believed in the law," she said.

"Is that all you got? He was your own dad, and that's all you know about him?"

She told him, "Shut your mouth, before I smack it."

"But he was *fair*. Don't you get it? The boys and girls on the street who sell the septic sacks and run 'em, and the thieves, the whores, and the broke and the busted—all of 'em down here who know the hard way how life ain't fair . . . they all believe in Maynard because *he was*."

Briar interrogated Rector on the finer points of Zeke's escape. By the time a larger priest and a greater number of nuns showed up to bully Briar out of the stairwell, she'd learned plenty—none of it reassuring, and all of it leading to one terrifying fact.

Her son had gone inside the walled-up city.

# *Five*

Ezekiel Wilkes shivered at the entrance to the old water runoff system. He stared into the hole as if it might eat him, or as if he wanted it to—because he was having second thoughts about this whole thing. But his third thoughts were insistent. He'd come this far. He only had a few yards to go, through a large tunnel and into a city that had been functionally dead since before he was born.

The lantern in his hand quivered with the chilled shakes of his elbow. In his pocket, a folded, wrinkled map was wadded into a nub. He only carried it as a matter of formality. He knew it by heart.

But there was one thing he didn't know, and it bothered him greatly.

He didn't know where his parents had once lived. Not exactly.

His mother had never mentioned an address, but he was sure they'd lived up on Denny Hill, which gave him a place to start looking. The hill itself wasn't so big, and he knew roughly what the house looked like. At bedtime when he was younger, Zeke's mother had described it to him as if it'd been a castle. If it still stood, it was lavender and cream, with two full stories and a turret. It had a porch that wrapped around the front of the house; and on that porch was a rocking chair painted to look like it was made of wood.

It was actually made of metal, and fitted with a mechanism that connected to the floor. When a crank was wound, the chair would rock itself for the benefit of anyone who was sitting in it at the time.

Zeke found it almost infuriating how little he knew about the man who'd made it work. But he thought he knew where to look for answers. All he had to do was hike through the tunnel and head up the hill to his immediate left, which ought to be Denny Hill.

He wished he had somebody to ask, but there wasn't anybody.

There wasn't anything, except a wafting stink from the heavy fumes of a mysterious gas that still leaked out from the earth inside the wall.

Now was as good a time as any to put on his mask.

He took a deep breath before sliding the harness over his face and securing it. When he exhaled, the interior fogged for a second and then cleared.

The tunnel looked even more distant and unearthly when he viewed it through the mask's visor. It appeared elongated and strange, and the darkness seemed to wobble and twist when he turned his head. The straps of the mask rubbed itchily where they lay over and under his ears. He slipped a finger up underneath the leather and ran it back and forth.

He checked his lantern for the dozenth time and yes, it was full of oil. He checked his bag and yes, it had all the supplies he'd been able to swipe. He was as ready as he was ever going to be, which was only just ready enough.

Zeke turned up the lantern's wick to give himself as much light as possible.

He crossed the threshold, forcing himself past the line between mere night and someplace darker. His lantern filled the interior of the brick-lined, man-made cave with a wash of gold.

He'd meant to leave earlier, in the morning after his mother had gone to the Waterworks. But it'd taken all day to get his supplies together, and Rector had been difficult about the details.

So now it was almost dark outside, and perfectly dark inside.

The lantern cast a bubbled halo that carried him forward, into the unknown. He navigated the crumbled spots where the ceiling had dropped itself in pieces and piles; and he dodged the hanging tendrils of moss that was thicker than seaweed; and he ducked beneath the spiderwebs that dangled, waving, from brick to brick.

Here and there he saw signs of prior passage, but he didn't know if he felt reassured that he was not the first to come this way. On the walls he saw black scuff marks where matches had been struck or cigarettes stubbed out; and he spied tiny, shapeless wads of wax that were too small to work as candles any longer. The initials W.L. were rubbed onto one cluster of bricks. Shards of broken glass glittered between weather-widened cracks.

All he could hear was the rhythmic tap of his footsteps, his muffled breaths, and the rusty hinge of the swinging lantern as it bounced back and forth.

And then there was another sound, one that made him think he was being followed.

He swung the lantern around, but saw no one. And there was no place for anyone to hide—it was a straight shot from the bricks where he stood to the beach. Forward, the way was less clear. As far as he could see, at the very edges of the lantern's reach, nothing but more emptiness waited.

The grade rose. He was going up, very slightly. The open places above him where the bricks had come away did not show any sky because they were covered by earth. The echoes of the small sounds in the tunnel became more smothered and close. Zeke had expected it, but it made him more uncomfortable than he would've thought. He knew that the geography jerked up away from the coast, and that the exposed tunnel wormed a path underneath the city proper.

If Rector was right, at the end of the main pathway the route would split four ways. The leftmost one would lead up to the basement of a bakery. The roof of that building would be a semisafe place to get a handle on his surroundings.

Underground and in the dark, the way seemed to curve left, and then right. Zeke didn't think he'd made a full circle, but he was definitely disoriented. He hoped that he'd still be able to pin down Denny Hill when he broke the surface.

After what felt like miles—but was surely only a fraction of that—the way widened and fractured as Rector had promised. Zeke took the hole on the far left and followed it another hundred feet before it terminated in a total dead end—or so he thought, until he backtracked slightly and found the secondary passage. This new corridor did not appear crafted, but dug. It did not look reinforced or secure. It looked temporary, spontaneous, and ready to fall.

He took it anyway.

The walls were more mud than stone or brick, and they were filthy wet. So was the floor, which was mostly a mash of decomposing sawdust, soil, and plant roots. It bit down on his boots and tried to hold him, but he slogged forward and finally, at the end of another twist and on the other side of another turn, he found a ladder.

With a skip and a jump he extricated himself from the gummy muck and seized the ladder hard. He lifted himself out and up, and into a basement so thickly dusted that even the mice and roaches left tracks on every surface. And there were footprints, too—quite a number of them.

At a rough glance he counted maybe ten sets of feet that had passed this way. He told himself that it was good, that he was glad to see that other people had survived the trip without trouble, but in truth it made him queasy. He'd hoped, and partly plotted, to find an empty city filled with mindless perils. Everybody knew about the rotters. Rector *had* told Zeke about the quiet societies that kept underground and out of sight, but mostly Zeke hoped to avoid them.

And, footprints . . . well . . .

Footprints implied he might run into other people at some point.

As he surveyed the room and determined that it held nothing of value, he resolved to be on his most careful behavior. While he climbed the stairs in the corner, he vowed to stick to the shadows and keep his head down, and his gun ready.

Really, he liked the thought of it. He enjoyed the prospect of being one boy against the universe, on a grand and dangerous adventure—

even if it was only going to last a few hours. He would move like a thief in the night. He would be as invisible as a ghost.

On the first floor, all the windows were boarded and covered, reinforced and braced from corner to corner. A counter with a splintered glass cover rotted along the wall, and a set of old striped awnings lay forgotten in a pile. Stacks of rusting pans cluttered a broken-down sink, and a dilapidated cash box was scattered in pieces across the floor.

He found a ladder propped in an empty pantry. At the top of the ladder a trapdoor had been left unlocked. He pushed against it with his hand, his head, and his shoulder, and it opened away from him. In a moment, he was on the roof.

And then there was something cold and hard pressed against the back of his neck.

He froze, one foot still on the ladder's top step.

"Hi there."

Zeke replied, without turning around, "Hello yourself." He tried to keep it low and growly, but he was scared and it came out at a higher pitch than he'd hoped for. In front of him he saw nothing but the corners of an empty rooftop; as far as the visor and his own peripheral vision could tell him, he was alone except for whomever was behind him with the very cold-barreled gun.

He set the lantern down with all the precision and caution he could muster.

"What are you doing up here, boy?"

He said, "Same as you, I reckon."

"And what exactly do you think *I'm* doing?" his interrogator asked.

"Nothing you'd like to get caught at. Look, let me alone, will you? I don't got any money or anything." Zeke slowly stepped out of the hole, balancing carefully, with his hands held uselessly aloft.

The cold, circular chill of something hard and dangerous didn't leave the exposed patch at the base of his skull.

"No money, eh?"

"Not a penny. Can I turn around? I feel stupid standing here like this. You can shoot me just as easy if I'm facing you. I'm not armed or nothing. Come on, let me loose. I didn't do nothing to *you*."

"Let me see your bag."

Zeke said, "No."

The pressure came harder against his neck. "Yes."

"It's just papers. Maps. Nothing worth anything. But I can show you something neat if you'll let me."

"Something neat?"

"Look," Zeke said, trying to wriggle himself away by inches and not succeeding very well. "Look," he said again, trying to buy time. "I'm a peace-abiding man, myself," he exaggerated. "I keep Maynard's peace. I keep it, and I don't want any trouble."

"You know a bit about Maynard, do you?"

"Well, I ought to," he grumbled. "He was my granddad."

"Get *out*," said the voice behind him, and it sounded more honestly impressed than dubious. "No, you ain't. I'd have heard about you, if you were."

"No, it's true. I can prove it. My mom, she was—"

The interrogator interrupted, "The Widow Blue? Now, come to think of it, she *did* have a boy, didn't she?" He fell silent.

"Yeah. She had *me*."

Zeke felt the cold circle against his neck slide, so he took a chance and stepped away—still keeping his hands in the air. He turned around slowly, and then dropped his hands with an exasperated yelp. "You were going to shoot me with a bottle?"

"No." The man shrugged. It was a glass bottle with the remnants of a black-and-white label stuck raggedly to its side. "I never heard of anyone getting shot with a bottle. I just wanted to make sure."

"Make sure of what?"

"That you understood," he said vaguely, and sat down against the wall with a sliding, slumping motion that implied he was reinstating the position he'd held when Zeke had interrupted him.

The man was masked as a matter of necessity, and he was wearing at least one fatly knitted sweater and two coats—the outer one of which was a very dark blue, or maybe black. A row of buttons pocked the front, and a pair of dark, oversized pants lurked beneath it. His boots were mismatched: One was tall and brown; the other was shorter and black. At his feet lay an oddly shaped cane. He picked it up and gave it a twist, then set it in his lap.

"What's wrong with you?" Zeke demanded. "Why'd you scare me like that?"

"Because you were there," he said, and there didn't seem to be any smirk or smugness behind it. "And why were you, anyway?"

"Why was I what?"

"Why were you there? I mean, why are you here? This ain't no place for a boy, even if you are Maynard's. Shit, it might be a worse place for you, if you run around firing off claims like that, whether they're true or not. You're lucky, I guess," the man said.

"Lucky? How you figure?"

"You're lucky it's me who found you, and not somebody else."

"How was that lucky?" Zeke asked.

He wiggled the bottle that still swung from his hand. "I didn't stick you up with anything that'd hurt you."

Zeke didn't see anything on the man that might have actually hurt him, but he didn't mention it. He picked up his lantern again, adjusted his bag, and scowled. "It's a good thing for you I didn't have my gun out."

"You've got a gun?"

"Yeah, I do," he said, standing up straighter.

"Where is it?"

Zeke patted the bag.

"You're an idiot," said the seated man with the bottle and the bulky clothes. Then he brought the mouth of the bottle up to the edge of his mouth, where it knocked loudly against his gas mask.

He gazed sadly at the bottle and swirled its last few drops around in the bottom.

"I'm an idiot? My momma has an expression about a pot and a kettle, you jackass."

The man looked as if he were about to say something ungallant about Zeke's mother, but he didn't. He said, "I don't think I caught your name, kid."

"I didn't offer it."

"Do so now," he said. There was a hint of menace underlying the command.

Zeke didn't like it. "No. You tell me yours first, and I'll think about telling you mine. I don't know you, and I don't know what you're doing here. And I . . ." He fumbled with his bag until he'd pulled his grandfather's old revolver out. It took about twenty seconds, during which the man on the roof didn't bother to budge. "I have a gun."

"So you do," the man said. But he didn't sound impressed this time. "And now you've got it in your hands, at least. Ain't you got a belt? A holster?"

"Don't need one."

"Fine," he said. "Now what's your name?"

"Zeke. Zeke Wilkes. And what's yours?" he demanded.

Inside his mask, the man grinned, presumably because he'd gotten the boy's name before giving away his own. Zeke could only see the smile because of the way his eyes crinkled behind the visor. "Zeke. Wilkes, even. Can't say I blame you for dropping the color, kid." And before Zeke could complain or retort, he added, "I'm Alistair Mayhem Osterude, but you can join the rest of the world in calling me Rudy, if you want."

"Your middle name is Mayhem?"

"It is if I say it is. And if you don't mind my asking, Zeke Wilkes, what the hell are you doing inside this place? Shouldn't you be in school, or at work, or something? And better yet, does your momma know you're here? I hear she's a real firecracker of a lady. I bet she wouldn't like it if she knew you done took off."

"My mother's working. She won't be home for hours, and I'll be home by then. What she don't know won't hurt her," he said. "And

I'm wasting time here talking to you, so if you'll excuse me, I'll be on my way."

He stuffed the gun back into his bag and turned his back on Rudy. He breathed slowly and evenly through his mask's filters and tried to remember exactly where he was, and exactly where he was trying to go.

Rudy asked, from his spot up against the wall, "Where you going?"

"None of your business."

"Fair, and all right. But if you tell me what you're looking for, I might be able to tell you how to get there."

Zeke walked to the edge and looked down, but he didn't see anything through the thick, sticky air. His lantern revealed nothing except more of the tainted fog in all directions. He said, "You could tell me how to get to Denny Hill."

And Rudy said, "I could, yeah." Then he asked, "But where on Denny Hill? It wraps around this whole area. Oh. I get it. You're trying to go home."

Before he could think to argue or be vague, Zeke said, "It ain't home. It never was. I never saw it."

"I did," Rudy told him. "It was a nice house."

"Was? Is it gone now?"

He shook his head, "No, I don't think so. As far as I know it's still standing. I only meant that it's not nice no more. Nothing inside here is. The Blight eats up paint and fixings, and makes everything go yellow-brown."

"But you know where it is?"

"Roughly." Rudy untangled his legs and stood, leaning on his cane and wobbling. "I could get you there, easily. If that's where you want to go."

"That's where I want to go." He nodded. "But what do you want for helping me?"

Rudy considered his response, or maybe he only waited for his head to clear. He said, "I want to go looking through that house. Your pa was a rich man, and I don't know if it's been cleaned out good or not, yet."

"What's that supposed to mean?"

"Exactly what it sounds like," Rudy almost snapped. "These houses, and these businesses—nobody owns them no more, or at least nobody's coming back inside after them. Half the people who used to live here are dead, anyhow. So those of us who are left, we . . ." He hunted for a word that sounded less direct than the truth. "Scavenge. Or we salvage, anyway. We ain't got much choice."

Something about the logic sounded wrong, but Zeke couldn't put his finger on it. Rudy was looking to bargain, but Zeke didn't have anything to counter with. This might be the perfect opportunity, if he played it right. He said, "I guess that's fair. If you take me to the house, you could take some of the things you find left there."

Rudy snorted. "I'm glad to have your permission, young Mr. Wilkes. That's mighty big of you."

Zeke knew when he was being made fun of, and he didn't care for it. "Fine, then. If you're going to act like that, maybe I don't need a guide at all. Maybe I can find it on my own. I told you, I've got maps."

"And a gun, yes. I believe you mentioned it. That makes you a big man ready to take on the Blight, and the rotters, and all the other outlaws like myself. I'd say you're all ready to go." He sat down on the roof's edge as if he'd changed his mind.

"I can find it on my own!" Zeke insisted, too loudly.

Rudy made a hushing motion with his hands and said, "Keep it low, boy. I'm telling you for your own good, and for mine. Keep your voice low. There are worse things out here than me by a long shot, and you don't want to meet any of them, I *promise*."

## *Six*

There were two ways past the seamless wall that contained the downtown blocks of Seattle. Anyone wishing to breach the barrier could go over it, or under it. According to Rector, Zeke had gone under it.

Rector didn't know everything Zeke had brought with him on the trip, but he was pretty sure Zeke had taken some food, some ammunition, and his grandfather's old service revolver, which he'd stolen from the drawer in Maynard's bedside table where it'd been sitting unused for sixteen years. He'd also taken a few of Maynard's small things for bartering purposes: a pair of cufflinks, a pocket watch, a bolo tie. Rector had helped him procure a battered old gas mask.

One of the last things Rector had said before Briar had been thrown out of the orphanage was, "Look, I bet you a dollar he'll be out again in ten hours. He has to be. The mask won't protect him any longer than that, and if he doesn't find his way to safety, he knows to turn around and come out. You've got to wait just a little bit longer. Wait until later tonight, and if he doesn't come back—*then* worry about him. He's not going to die in there, he's *not*."

As she walked away from the orphanage in the dark, drizzling rain, Briar wanted to scream, but she needed the energy to walk. She was exhausted from the worry and rage, and she tried to tell herself that Zeke was prepared.

He hadn't just climbed the wall and dropped down into the city center, filled with hordes of staggering rotters or roving gangs of criminals. He'd taken precautions. He'd taken supplies. There was always a chance he'd be all right, wasn't there? Ten hours of time in a mask, and if he didn't find safety he'd turn around and leave. He wasn't stupid enough to stay. If he could find his way in, he could find his way out.

The entrance he'd used was down by the ocean, by the water-runoff pits, almost hidden by the battered rocks that shielded the drainage way from the pounding of the surf. It had never occurred to Briar that the old sewage lines might still go all the way up, under-neath, and into the city. They'd been part of the underground system that collapsed and was later gated up just in case. But Rector had in-sisted that the remnant population on the other side had cleared the debris that the Boneshaker had left in its wake, that the gate could be opened with less trouble than it looked.

Ten hours ought to be up by nine o'clock, give or take.

Briar made up her mind to wait it out. It wouldn't do her any good to go home—she'd only worry herself into a frenzy—and it wouldn't be a good idea to go after him, not yet. If she went in now, there was a fair chance she'd get inside just as he was getting out, and then they'd miss one another and she still wouldn't know what had become of him.

No, Rector had been right. The only thing to do was wait. There wasn't so much time left, anyway—only a few hours.

It was plenty of time to hike out to the other edge of the sound and crawl over the rocks, around the thigh-deep tidal pools and past the jagged crags of cliff that hid the abandoned runoff system from the settlements on the Outskirts.

Night had settled down hard and wet, but Briar was still dressed for work, and wearing boots that were tough enough to protect her feet and flexible enough to let her toes feel their way over the rocks. The tide was out—and thank God for that—but the ocean spray still came in on the wind. She was nearly soaked by the time she rounded the last uneven strip of sand and stone and saw the seaweed-draped mecha-nisms that once had lifted and lowered the pipes out of the ocean.

And there, buried partly by the accumulated years of gravel, shells, and driftwood, lay the cracked brick cylinder that led back under the city streets.

Bleached by the ocean and the rain, worn by storms and battered by incoming waves, the tube was decrepit. It looked like it might collapse if Briar touched it; but when she leaned a hand against it and pushed, it did not move or settle.

She ducked her head underneath the overhang and let the lantern lead her. It still had oil enough for many hours, and she wasn't worried about anything short of drowning or a downpour putting it out. But inside the coal-black extra-night of the tube's interior, its glow felt weak and small. The sphere of light cast by the flame only traveled a few feet.

Briar listened as hard as she could, straining to hear anything other than the faint rush of water coming and going and the incessant drip of mist and rain slipping through where the bricks had broken.

This was as close to the city as she'd been since before Zeke was born.

How far was it? Half a mile at most, though surely it would feel longer and more strenuous, doubled over in a crouch and hunkering uphill in the darkness. Briar tried to imagine her son, lantern in one hand and gun in the other. Would he hold the gun? Or would he holster it?

Did he even know how to use it, if he needed to?

She doubted it. So perhaps he'd brought it to trade—and that was smart, she thought. If his grandfather was a folk hero, then small articles of clothing, personal effects, things of that ilk—they'd be valuable enough to buy information, perhaps.

Farther inside the tunnel, she found a patch of moss-covered wall that was more dry than not, and she sat down. With the back of her hand she rubbed a spot on the bricks. She put the lantern there and wiggled it until she was sure it would stay upright. She leaned back, trying not to feel the chill and damp of the curved wall through her coat; and although she was frightened, and angry, and cold, worried to the point of being ill, she toppled into a rough-dreamed doze.

And then she was awake.

Hard.

Her head jerked and she knocked the back of her skull against the concave bricks.

She was confused and stunned. She didn't remember nodding off, so the jolt awake was a double shock. It took her a moment to figure out where she was and what she was doing there, and another to realize that the world was shaking. A clump of bricks rattled loose and dropped beside her, almost shattering the lantern.

Briar grabbed it and jerked it into her hand before another patch of shaken stone collapsed on it.

Inside the tunnel the echo was deafening, and the sound of crumbling bricks and falling bits of wall sounded like a war being waged inside a jar.

"No, no, no," she swore and struggled. "Not now. Not now, dear God, not *now*."

Earthquakes were common enough, but bad ones weren't so frequent; and there, inside that narrow, low space of the old sewage system it was hard to gauge the ferocity of this one.

Briar stumbled out of the tunnel and back into the night, and she was shocked to see how close the tide had crept up to her waiting place. She didn't have a watch, but she must've been asleep for several hours and it must be after midnight.

"Zeke?" she yelled, just in case he was inside and trying to find his way out. "Zeke!" she screamed over the rumbling roar of the shifting sands and the shaking coastline.

Nothing answered but the heavy splashes of shattered waves, jostled out of alignment and dropped onto shore. The tunnel wobbled. Briar wouldn't have believed that anything so big could wobble as easily and lightly as a child's toy, but it did, and it crinkled down upon itself—and upon the vintage apparatus that had once held it up and steady.

Together the bulk of it swayed and dropped, folding flat as suddenly as a house of cards.

A plume of dust rose, only to be squashed by the ambient moisture.

Briar stood stunned. Her legs adjusted with the rolling earth and she stayed upright; and she tried to tell herself a thousand and one good things that would keep her from panicking.

She thought, *Thank God I'm outside*, because she'd been in a bad quake once or twice before and it was far more terrifying when the ceiling threatened to drop, and she whispered frantically, "Zeke wasn't in there. He didn't come out yet, or he would've seen me. He wasn't in the tunnel when it fell; he wasn't in the tunnel when it fell."

This meant that he was still inside, somewhere—either dead or safe.

If she didn't believe he was safe, she would have started crying, and crying wasn't going to get her anywhere. Zeke was inside the city and now he was stuck there.

Now it was not a matter of waiting.

Now it was a matter of rescue.

And there was no way under anymore, so Briar would have to go over.

The sand was still rumbling, but it was starting to settle, and she didn't have time to wait for a perfect path. While the rocks clacked faintly together and the low, ugly buildings of the Outskirts rattled in their foundations, she jammed her hat back harder on her head, hoisted her lantern, and began to climb the mudflats.

Two ways past the wall, over and under—that's what Rector had said.

Under wouldn't work. Over would have to suffice.

Perhaps the wall could be climbed, but it couldn't be climbed by Briar. Perhaps the wall had a secret ladder or a hidden set of stairs, but if that were the case then Zeke would've gone that way instead of ducking underground.

Over could only mean one thing: an airship.

Traders who made their way out to the coast came over the mountains when they could. It was dangerous, yes—the air currents were unpredictable and the altitude made breathing a dreadful chore; but scaling the passes on foot was deadly and time-consuming, and it required wagons or pack animals that must be maintained and protected. Airships were not a perfect solution, but to certain entrepreneurs, they looked much, much better than the alternative.

But not at this time of year.

February meant frigid rain on the coast. Over the mountains there would be snow, and storms, and astounding gusts of air that could bat a zeppelin like a kitten with a leaf.

The only airships flying in February were run by smugglers. And as soon as Briar realized this, something else became clear: No legitimate businesspeople would ever bring a valuable airship over the Seattle wall—not so close to the acidic, corrosive Blight that pooled within it.

But now she knew something else about the toxic gas.

It was *valuable*.

Chemists needed the gas to make lemon sap. The gas came from inside the city. Airships went over—or past—the wall on a regular basis, even during the worst parts of the year. And just like that, two obvious thoughts collided in her head, leading to an equally obvious conclusion and, finally, to a logical course of action.

A secondary tremor followed the initial quake, but it passed quickly. As soon as the land was stable again, Briar Wilkes began to run.

On the way home she passed debris in the street and people crying or shouting at each other, standing on the cobblestones in their nightclothes. Here and there, something that had fallen over had caught fire. Off in the distance, the clanging chimes of makeshift fire brigades were sounding as the blocks awakened into disarray one by one.

No one noticed or recognized Briar as she dashed, lantern in hand, up the steep hills and around the wide places where big things had fallen and blocked the way. The quake hadn't felt so bad to her, down on the beach, but the earth was funny sometimes and it moved inconsistently. It hadn't been nearly so bad as the . . .

*And in her memory, the shocking, jolting, bashing fury of the Boneshaker machine was moving underneath her again, tearing down basement walls and gutting the underground, pummeling the rocks and digging, blasting, destroying everything it touched.*

. . . *She wasn't the* only one thinking it, she knew. Everyone thought of it, every time another quake wiggled the land.

She wasn't worried about her father's house; it had withstood worse. And when she got there, she wasn't even relieved to find it standing without any obvious damage. Nothing short of finding Zeke on the porch could have slowed her down.

She burst in the door and into the cold, dry interior that was every bit as empty as she'd left it.

Her hand stopped at the knob to her father's room.

There was a brief instant of hesitation, a resistance to the breaking of long-established habit.

Then she seized the knob and shoved it.

Inside, all was dark until she brought the lantern around. She left it on the bedside table and idly noted that the drawer was still open from where Zeke had stolen the old revolver Rector had mentioned. She wished he'd taken something else. The gun was an antique that had belonged to Maynard's father-in-law. Maynard himself had never used it and it probably didn't even work, but, of course, Zeke wouldn't have known that.

Again she felt that stab of regret, and she wished she'd told him more. Something. Anything.

When she got him back, then.

When she got him home, she'd tell him anything he wanted to know—any story, any fact. He could have it all if he'd just make it home alive. And maybe Briar had been a terrible mother, or maybe she'd only done the best she could. It didn't matter now, when Zeke was in that toxic, walled-up city where undead Blight victims prowled for human flesh and criminal societies lurked at the bottom of rigged-up homes and cleaned-out basements.

But for all the things she'd botched, screwed up, lost, forgotten, lied about, or misled him on . . . she was going in there after him.

With one hand on each door's handle, she whipped Maynard's huge old wardrobe open and stood before it, a determined frown planted firmly on her face. Its false bottom lifted up when Briar popped her thumb down into a hole.

Something tight and heavy squeezed in her stomach.

There it all was, just like she'd left it years before.

She'd tried to bury these things with Maynard. At the time, she couldn't have imagined ever wanting or needing them. But the officers had come and dug him up, and when they returned his body, it had been stripped of the things she'd used to dress him.

Six months later Briar had come home to find them in a bag, sitting in front of the door. She never did find out who'd returned them, or why. And by then, Maynard had been in the ground too long to disturb him a second time. So the artifacts of his life, the things he wore every day, had gone back into their private drawer underneath the floor of his wardrobe.

One by one she withdrew the items and set them on the bed.

The rifle. The badge. The hard leather hat. The belt with its big oval buckle, and the shoulder holster.

His overcoat hung like a ghost in the back of the four-footed closet. She grabbed it and pulled it out into the light. Black as the night outside, the wool felt trench was treated with oil to resist the rain. Its brass buttons were tarnished but securely stitched, and inside one of the pockets Briar found a pair of goggles that she'd never known he owned. She tore off her own coat and clawed her way into his.

The hat should have been a little too big, but she had a lot more hair than Maynard did, so it all worked out. The belt was too long and the ornate MW buckle was huge, but she threaded it through the loops of her pants, yanked it tight, and locked the big metal plate low on her belly.

In a back corner of the wardrobe was a plain brown trunk stuffed with ammunition, rags, and oil. Briar had never cleaned her father's Spencer repeater, but she'd watched him do it a thousand times, so she knew the motions. She sat on the edge of his bed and copied them. When it was fresh enough that it gleamed in the low, runny lantern light, she picked up a tube of rimfire cartridges and thumbed the contents into the rifle.

At the bottom of the plain brown trunk, she found a cartridge box. Though the trunk's lid had gathered fifteen years of dust, the contents appeared sound, so she took the box of additional ammunition and stuffed it into a satchel she spotted lying under the bed.

To the cartridges she added her father's goggles, her old gas mask from the evacuation days, her pouch of tobacco, and the sparse contents of a coffee jar she kept behind the stove, which amounted to about twenty dollars. It wouldn't have been that much if she hadn't just been paid.

She didn't count it. She already knew it wouldn't get her very far.

As long as it got her inside the city, it would do. And if it wouldn't, she'd think of something else.

Through the curtains in her father's bedroom, the sun was on the verge of rising—and that meant she would be late for work, had she intended to go. It'd been ten years since she'd missed a day, but on this occasion they'd have to forgive her or fire her, whichever they preferred.

But she wasn't coming in.

She had a ferry to catch—over to Bainbridge Island, where the airships docked and fueled for legitimate business. If the smugglers with their contraband didn't also originate from the island across the Sound, then surely one of them could point her in the right direction.

She dumped the rifle into the holster that slung over her back, shrugged her way into the satchel, and closed her father's wardrobe. Then she closed his house, and left it dark and empty.

## *Seven*

By the time Briar reached the ferry, daylight was as full as it was going to get. The sky was coated in a mold-gray film, but there was sun enough filtering through the clouds that she could see a tree-covered island across the water.

Here and there a dome-shaped thing would rise above the trees. Even at this distance, she could see the airships docked and waiting for crews or cargo.

The ferry creaked and dipped when she stepped onto it. There were few other passengers at such an early hour, and she was the only woman. Wind swept off the waves and tugged at her hat, but she held it down, low over her eyes. If anyone recognized her, no one bothered her. Maybe it was the rifle, and maybe it was the way she stood, feet apart with her hands on the rail.

Maybe nobody cared.

Most of her fellow passengers were sailors of one kind or another. Folks on this island either worked the airships or the boats at the pier, because when an airship unloaded on the island, some other means of transport had to take it over the water and into town.

It had never occurred to her to wonder why there were no airship docks any closer to the Outskirts, but now she did wonder, and she could make a guess or two. The rambling, sketchy conclusions she drew bolstered her hopes that they kept away from the public eye for shady reasons. As far as she was concerned, the shadier the better.

After over an hour of bobbing awkwardly across the tide, the creaky, white-painted ferry tied itself to the docks on the far shore.

Side by side the landing areas were pressed up against one another—the wooden piers with their brittle armor of barnacles down at the water line, and the cleared-out lots with great iron pipes that jutted up, out, and back down deep into the earth. A dozen airships in varying states of repair and quality were moored to the pipes, affixed via sets of brass lobster-claw clips as big as barrels.

The ships themselves came in assorted designs. Some were little more than hot air balloons with baskets held up low and close to the balloon's underbelly; and some were more impressive, with buckets that looked like the hull of a water-running vessel—but built onto a hydrogen tank and propelled with steam thrusters.

Briar had never been to Bainbridge. Unsure of where to start, she stood in the middle of a landing where even the tradesmen were only just beginning to bustle. She watched as the crews arrived and as men shifted cargo from bucket to cart, and then from cart to boat.

The process wasn't smooth, but it managed to move the incoming products from air to water in a quickly clicking cycle.

Before long, one of the smaller airships gave a lurch, and two crewmembers slid down the mooring ropes to disengage the docking clips. The clasps unhinged and swung free, and the men scrambled back up the ropes into the bucket. From there, they reeled the clips up to the vessel's edge and hung them around the exterior.

An older man in a captain's hat paused near Briar to light a pipe.

She asked him, "Excuse me, but which of these ships is going closest to the Seattle wall?"

He gave her a knobby-browed glare over the pipe, summing her up as he sucked at the stem. He said, "You're on the wrong side of the island for that kind of question, missy."

"What's that mean?"

"It means you should take that road there." And he used the pipe to point at a muddy, flattened trail that disappeared back through the trees. "Walk as far as it'll take you. You might find someone who can answer you better."

She hesitated, her arm on her satchel because she felt the need to hold something. Another airship was unlocking itself from the pipework dock, and a new one was hovering over the lot. On the side of the airborne ship she saw a name painted, and then she realized it was a company name, not a ship name.

"Ma'am," the man called to her.

Briar returned her attention to him and caught the way his gaze flicked from her belt buckle to her eyes.

He continued. "The island's not that big. It won't take you long to find your way over to the . . . *alternate* commercial row, if that's what you're looking to do."

She thanked him, considered the muddy stretch of semi-road, and said, "You're very kind."

He replied, "No, but I do my best to be fair."

Someone nearby called a name, and the man in the hat responded to it with a wave and a nod. Briar looked at the trail again and noticed that no one else was walking it.

She wasn't sure if nonchalance or outright sneaking was called for, so she tried to meld the two into a quiet retreat that took her up a slight hill and out to the overgrown path with its deep ruts.

The tops of the ruts were drier. She tiptoed across them and up through the trees, out of sight of the docks. The woods had never been a comfortable place for Briar: she was a city child born and bred, and the wide-trunked walls of bark and brush made her feel small and anxious, as if she were trapped in a fairy tale with wolves.

She tripped up the way, trying hard to keep her heels from sticking in the thick, wet surface. As she scaled the rolling landscape the trail became wider and clearer, but she still saw no one else coming or going along it.

"But it's early yet," she said to herself.

The trees were higher the farther back she wandered, and the forest was thicker the deeper she hiked into the heart of the island . . .

which was why she didn't realize she'd found another set of airship docks until she was nearly in their midst.

She stopped herself fast and retreated back onto the trail only to realize that it had all but ended behind her. And she was no longer alone.

Three broad airmen stood smoking off to the side of a clearing. They all stopped smoking their pipes to stare at Briar, who was wholly uncertain of how to proceed but determined not to show it. She split a casual examination between the mottled airships and the three quiet, startled men.

Most of the ships were anchored to trees, tied like horses. The trees were fully stout enough to stand the weight, and they bore it with the odd creak or crack, but none of the ships sprung loose or failed. These ships were of a different sort, less glossy and less uniform than the ones at the main dock. They were not so much manufactured as cobbled together from bits and pieces of other, sturdier, larger vessels.

Over to the side of the airships, the smallest smoking man looked roughly like any given one of Briar's coworkers, pale and a little dirty, in baggy clothes and a leather apron that had a pair of long leather gloves sticking out of the pockets.

The middle man was a mulatto with long hair braided into coiled ropes and pulled back in a scarf. He was wearing a fisherman's sweater with a tall, folded neck that tucked up under his dense, dark beard.

The remaining smoker was the best-dressed of the three, a coal-black Negro in a sharp blue jacket with bright brass buttons. A pink scar ran from the corner of his mouth nearly back to his ear, which was festooned with a row of small gold hoops that jangled when he started to laugh at the sight of her.

The laugh began as a low, rumbling chortle and worked its way into a full-belly guffaw that his fellow smokers shortly joined him in.

"Hey there, lady," the darkest man said, between hastily caught breaths. He had an accent that came from somewhere over the mountains, and to the south. "Are you lost?"

She waited out the height of their shared hilarity, and when they were reduced to wheezes she said, "No."

"Oh," he said with a lift of his eyebrow. "So you've come to Canterfax-Mar on purpose, then, eh? I could not tell you the last time we had such a lady in our midst."

"What's that mean?" she asked.

He shrugged and pursed his wide lips. "Only that you appear ready for business of a different sort. What is it you want from us here, at our lost little dock? Your mind is set on something firm, I can see that now."

"I need a ride. I'm looking for my son. Can you help me?"

"Well, ma'am, that depends," he said. He left his companions and came forward to meet her. She could not tell if he was trying to be intimidating, or if he only meant to see her closer; but he was more ominous than she'd expect for his size. He was no taller than her father had been, but his shoulders were wide and his arms were as thick as logs beneath the sleeves of the woolly blue jacket. His voice was low and loud, and it sounded almost wet inside his chest.

Briar did not back away or down. She did not move even to shuffle her feet. "What does it depend on?"

"Any number of things! For one, I must know where you wish to be, and how far you mean to go."

"You do?"

"Of course I do. This ship over here is mine. You see her? The *Free Crow*, we call her, and she is a little bit stolen, a little bit bought, and a great bit made . . . but oh, she can *fly*."

"She's a very fine ship," Briar said, because it seemed appropriate, and because the ship was indeed impressive. There was a mark on its side; she could see the edge of it and almost read it.

The captain saved her the trouble of squinting. "It says CSA because that is where the body of the bird was first created, in the Confederate States. I might have intercepted her, and put her to a better use. In days like these, in this time of war and adventure, I say the initials mean, 'Come See America,' for that is what I intend to do."

"This isn't quite America, yet."

"All of this is America in one way or another. Did you know the entire continent is called after an Italian mapmaker? And anyway, your corner of the map will make a fine state one day. It'll happen," he assured her. "With patience, when the war ends."

"When the war ends," she repeated.

He was looking at her closely now, standing in front of her and peering hard at her hat, then at the badge that she'd stuck on the side of the belt. After a thorough appraisal, he said to her, "I don't think you represent any rule or government. I never heard tale of a woman of the law, though that looks real." He pointed at the badge. "And I know who it references. I know what that symbol means."

He pointed at the buckle with its large, ornate MW.

"I don't know if ol' Maynard is guarding your knickers or anything else, but you're wearing the sign, plain as can be, so me and my men are forced to believe you've not come for trouble."

"No," she assured him. "I don't want to find any trouble, and I don't want to make any. I'm only trying to find my son, and I don't have anyone to help me, so I came here."

The captain unfolded his arms and offered her a handshake. He said, "Then perhaps we can do business. But tell me first, since you haven't told me yet, where is it you mean to go, that you need services from the island's back side?"

"Seattle," she said. "I need to go over the wall, into the city. That's where my son went."

He shook his head. "Then your son is dead, or damned."

"I don't think he is. He got inside; he just can't get out."

"Got inside, did he? And how'd he do that? We've seen no boy come out this way."

"He went under, through the old sewage runoff."

"Then he can find his way back out the same direction!"

Briar was losing his attention. He was backing away. She tried not to sound too frantic when she said, "But he can't! The earthquake last night—you must've felt it. It collapsed the old tunnel, and there's no way underneath anymore. I have to get inside and get him out. I *have* to, don't you understand?"

He threw his hands up and almost walked back to his fellows, who were whispering between themselves. Then he faced her again and said, "No, I don't understand. There's no breathing the air in there, you know that, don't you? There's nothing in there but death."

"And people," she interjected. "There are people in there too, living and working."

"The scrappers and Doornails? Sure, but they've been there years, most of them, and they've learned how to keep from getting eaten or poisoned. How old's your son?"

"Fifteen. But he's smart, and stubborn."

"Every mother swears it of every son," he argued. "But even if you get inside, how you going to get him out? You going to climb? You going to dig?"

She confessed, "I haven't gotten that far in my planning yet, but I'll think of something."

The mulatto man behind the captain put aside his pipe and said, "Next gas run's going in less than a week. If she can live that long, she can catch a rope out."

The captain whirled around. "Now don't you go encouraging her!"

"Why not? If she can pay, and if she wants to dip into the city, why won't you take her?"

The captain answered Briar, although she wasn't the one who'd asked the question. "Because we aren't equipped to do a gas run right now. Our two best nets got snagged on the tip of the tower last trip, and we're still patching them up. And so far, I haven't heard any mention of paying anything, so I'd hate to assume that our surprise guest is a wealthy widow."

"I'm not," she admitted. "But I have a little money—"

"To talk us into a gas run that doesn't net us any gas, you'll need a lot more than a little money. I'd love to help a lady, but business is business."

"But . . . ," she asked, "is there anyone else who might fly?"

"Anyone dumb enough to fly up to the walls? I don't know." He shoved his hands in the pockets of that Union-blue coat. "I couldn't say."

Again the mulatto spoke. He said, "There's Cly. He's dumb for a pretty woman, and he respects the Maynard peace."

Briar wasn't sure whether to be flattered or offended, so she chose instead to be hopeful. "Cly? Who's he? Can I talk to him?"

"You can talk to him." The captain nodded. "And ma'am, I do wish you well in your search for your mad little son. But I ought to warn you, it's a devilish place inside. It's no place for a woman, or a boy."

"Point me at this Cly," she said coldly. "I don't care if it's no place for a dog or a rat, it's going to have a woman in it before sundown, so help me God. Or Maynard," she added, remembering what Rector had said.

"As you like." He offered her his arm, and Briar wasn't sure if she should take it, but she did so anyway. As long as everyone else was playing nice, she'd play nice, too. She didn't know how much help she needed from these people, so it was worth her time to be pleasant even when it frightened her.

The captain's forearm felt every bit as dense as it looked, straining at the seam of the coat. Briar tried to keep her fingers from fluttering out of nervousness, but it wasn't like a handshake where she could squeeze and make her position known a little more firmly.

The captain patted her nervous hand, and said, "Lady, so long as you wear Maynard's mark and respect our peace, we're bound to respect yours. There's no need to fret."

"I believe you," she said, and it might or might not have been true. "But I have more things to fret about than your proximity, I promise you."

"Your son."

"My son, yes. I'm sorry, you didn't mention your name, Captain . . . ?"

"Hainey. Croggon Hainey," he told her. "Captain for short. Captain Hainey for long. Crog, in passing."

"Captain, yes. I do thank you for the assistance."

He grinned to display a row of shocking white teeth. "Don't thank me yet. I've done nothing but treat you as I'm bound to. My fellow friend and airman may or may not give you any further assistance."

Crog led her between the creaking, swaying airships that moored themselves in the wider paths between the massively thick trunks. They bobbed against their leashes and bumped gently against the treetops, brushing their undercarriages with evergreen boughs and bird nests.

The nearest of them was a slapdash affair that looked wholly improvised and yet thoroughly solid. If anything, it looked too heavy to fly. It boasted a steel-plated, canoe-shaped basket the size of a rich man's living room and a pair of gas tanks as big as a poor man's wagon. Riveted, stitched, bolted, and tied together, it loomed over the clearing where it was held by three long, fat ropes.

A rope ladder trailed on the ground, dangling from the bottom of the ship's underside. Beside it, in the shade of the strangely shaped craft, a man sat in a folding wooden chair. In the crook of his arm rested a bottle of whiskey. The bottle rose and fell against his chest as he breathed, and if it weren't for the goggles over his eyes, it would have been obvious that he was stone asleep.

Crog stopped a few yards away from the almost-snoring man and said in a rumbling whisper, "Ma'am, allow me to introduce Captain Andan Cly. And there above his thick-boned head you'll see his ship, the *Naamah Darling*. Wake him with kindness, and—if possible—at a distance."

"Wait, you're not going to—"

"Oh no. You're the one who wants the favor. You can nudge him awake for it. Best of luck to you, ma'am. And if he won't take you, the best I can offer is a trip in three days, at our next gas run. Or, if he lets you ride and drop, then you can look for the *Free Crow* on Tuesday, docked at the Smith Tower. It don't cost me a thing to pull you out, though you might think to bring me a present if I do."

He pulled her fingers off his arm, and until he picked at them she hadn't realized she'd been clenching at his sleeve. "Thank you," she told him. "And I do mean it, *thank you*. If you lift me out on Tuesday, I'll find a way to pay you. I know of places, and things inside the city. I'll make it worth your while."

"Then I'll be the one thanking *you*, ma'am."

He disappeared back through the maze of trees and ropes and hovering ships while Briar tried not to cringe at the presence of the man underneath the *Naamah Darling*.

Andan Cly was not precisely slumped, and not precisely seated in the wood-slat chair. His light brown hair was cropped so close that he appeared almost bald, and his ears sat high on his skull. The left one was pierced with three silver studs. The right one remained plain. He was wearing a dirty undershirt and a pair of brown pants that cuffed down into boots.

Briar thought that surely he must be too cold to sleep, but as she crept towards him she felt the temperature rise. By the time she stood in front of him, she was almost sweating—and then she realized that he'd positioned himself underneath the ship's boilers, which were steaming themselves into a fully heated state.

She didn't step on a twig or tap her foot against a rock. She didn't move, only stared, but it was suddenly enough to bring him awake. Nothing signaled this change of state except a sharpening of his posture, and then a sleepy finger that lifted his goggles until they sat on his forehead.

"What?" he asked. The question was not specifically a demand or complaint, but it sounded like it could've been either.

"Andan Cly?" she asked, and added, "Captain of the *Naamah Darling?*"

He grumbled, "Speaking. To who?"

It was Briar's turn to ask, "What?"

"Who am I speaking to?"

"I'm . . . a passenger. Or I want to be. I need a lift, and Captain Hainey said I should talk to you." She left out the rest of what Crog had said.

"Did he?"

"Yes."

He twisted his head left, then right, and all the joints in between cracked loudly. "Where do you want to go?"

"Over the wall."

"When?"

"Now," she said.

"Now?" He drew the bottle out of the crook in his arm and set it down on the ground beside the chair. His eyes were a clear, vibrant hazel that almost looked like copper, even in the half-lit shade of his ship. He stared at her, not blinking nearly often enough for her comfort.

"My son; he ran away," she condensed the story. "He's gone into the city. I have to go in after him."

"You've never been in there, then?"

"Not since the wall went up, no. Why do you ask?"

"Because if you'd ever been inside, you'd know better than to think some kid's in there alive."

She met his glare blink for blink and said, "*My* son might be. He's smart, and he's prepared."

"He's an idiot," Andan corrected her. "If he went inside."

"He's not an idiot, he's only . . . uninformed." She settled on the truest word, even though it hurt her to say it out loud. "Please, listen. Help me. I've got a mask, and if I can get inside I can find my way around all right. Crog said he'd pick me up on Tuesday—"

"You think you'll live till Tuesday?"

"Yes. I do."

"Then you're an idiot too. No offense."

"You can offend me all you like if you'll take me over the wall."

He made half a smile as if he meant to laugh at her, but the upward swing of his lip lost its momentum. "You're serious. And stubborn. But you'll need more than that"—he pointed at the rifle—"and Maynard's mark if you want to stay in one piece down there."

"But if I respect the peace—"

He cut her off. "Then *some* of the other people you meet inside will respect the peace, too. But not all of them will. There's a madman named Minnericht who runs part of the city, and big quarters of Chinese folks who might or might not be friendly to a strange white woman. And your friends the crooks will be the least of your problems. Have you ever seen a rotter? A real hungry one?"

"Yes. I saw them during the evacuation."

"Aw." He shook his head. While his head moved his eyes stayed casually locked on her belt buckle. "Those things? They weren't hungry. Not yet. The ones who've been starving inside for fifteen years, they're the problem. And they move in packs."

"I've got plenty of ammunition." She patted the satchel.

"And an old repeater too, I see. That'll be useful. But eventually you'll run out of shot, and if the rotters don't get you, Minnericht's men will. Or the crows might. There's no telling with those damn birds. But let me ask you a question."

"Another one?"

"Yes, another one," he said crossly. He aimed one long finger at her midsection and said, "Where did you get *that*?"

"This?" From reflex, she grasped the buckle and looked down at it. "It . . . why?"

"Because I've seen it before. And I want to know where you got it."

"That's no business of yours," she argued.

"I guess it isn't. And it's no problem of mine if you don't get over the wall to look for your kid, Mrs. Blue."

For a moment, she couldn't breathe—she could only swallow. The fear clutched her throat and she couldn't speak, either. Then she said, "That's not my name."

He said back, "Well, that's who you are, aren't you?"

She shook her head a little too hard and said, "No. Not since the wall went up. It's Wilkes. And my boy, he's a Wilkes too, if you've got to assign a name to him." The rest came spilling out too fast, but she couldn't stop it. "He thinks his father was innocent because you're right, he's a little bit of an idiot, but he's gone in because he wants to prove it."

"Can he prove it?"

"No," she said. "Because it isn't true. But Zeke, you've got to understand, he's just a boy. He don't know any better, and I couldn't sell him on it. He had to go see for himself."

"All right." He nodded. "And he knows about Maynard's mark, and he found a way inside. He went under, I guess?"

"He went under. But the earthquake we had last night—it flattened the old runoff tunnel. He can't get out that way, and I can't get in. Now will you take me over the wall, or won't you? If you won't, then say so, because I've got to go ask someone else."

He took his time answering her. While he decided, he looked her up and down in a way that wasn't altogether offensive, but wasn't too flattering, either. He was thinking about something, and thinking about it hard; and Briar didn't know what it was, or how he'd guessed so easily, or if Maynard could help her now.

"You should've started with that," Andan said.

"With what?"

"With how you're Maynard's girl. Why didn't you?"

She said, "Because to claim him as my father marks me as Blue's widow. I didn't know if the cost would outweigh the benefit."

"Fair enough," he said. And he stood.

It took him a few seconds. There was a lot of him to stand.

By the time he was on his feet, underneath the belly of the *Naamah Darling,* he stood taller than any man Briar had ever seen in her life. Seven and a half feet from toes to top and thickly muscled, Andan Cly was more than simply huge. He was terrifying. He was not an attractive man to begin with, but when his plain, workman looks were combined with his sheer size, it was all Briar could do not to run.

"You afraid of me now?" he asked. He pulled a pair of gloves out of his pockets and stretched them over his huge hands.

"*Should* I be afraid of you?" she asked.

He snapped the second glove into place and bent over to pick up his bottle. "No," he told her. His eyes shifted to her buckle again. "Your daddy used to wear that."

"He wore a lot of things."

"He didn't get buried in all of them." Andan held out his hand to her and she shook it. Her fingers rattled around in the cavern of his grasp. "You're welcome aboard the *Naamah Darling*, Miss Wilkes. Maybe I'm doing wrong in taking you—it might not be the right way to pay an old debt, since I'm a little scared I'm going to get you killed—but you're going to get inside one way or another, aren't you?"

"I am."

"Then best I can do is get you ready, I suppose." He kicked a thumb up at the boilers and said, "The thrusters will be hot before long. I can take you up and over."

"For . . . for an old debt?"

"It's a big old debt. I was there in the station, when the Blight shut down the world. Me and my brother, we carried your dad back home. He didn't have to do it." He was shaking his head again. "He didn't owe us a thing. But he let us out, and now, Miss Wilkes, if you won't have it any other way . . . I'm going to let you in."

# *Eight*

Zeke reluctantly followed Rudy's orders; he shut his mouth and listened. Down below, somewhere on the street, he thought he heard something shuffle or scrape. But he saw nothing, and he wondered if Rudy was only trying to scare him. "I don't see anything," he said.

"Good. If you see them, it's probably too late to get away from them."

"Them?"

Rudy said, "Rotters. You ever seen one?"

"Yes," Zeke lied. "I seen plenty."

"Plenty? Where've you seen plenty, over there in the Outskirts? I doubt you've ever seen one or two together, and if you have, then I'm a liar and that's fine. But in here, there's more than one or two. We've got them in packs, like dogs. And by Minnericht's best count, there are at least a few thousand of them—all crammed together inside this place with nowhere to go and nothing to eat."

Zeke didn't want to let Rudy see him shudder or worry, so he said, "Thousands, huh? That's a lot. But who's Minnericht, and how long did it take him to count them all?"

"Don't get smart with me, you little bastard," Rudy said, and he tipped the bottle toward his mouth again in that futile gesture that wanted a drink and couldn't have it. "I'm just trying to be the good guy and lend you a hand. If you don't want it, then you can jump off the building and play tag with the walking dead and see if I give a damn. Here's a hint: I won't."

"I don't care!" Zeke almost shouted again, and when Rudy jumped off the ledge Zeke jumped too, backward and almost back down the hole where the ladder had led him onto the roof.

Rudy shoved his heavy-looking cane up underneath Zeke's chin and said, "Shut your mouth. I won't ask you twice because I won't have to. You make a stink and bring out the rotters, and I'll push you into the street myself. Make trouble for yourself, if that's what you're going to do, but leave me out of it. I was just enjoying the peace and quiet when you came along, and if you wrench that up for me, I'll have your head off for it."

Without taking his eyes off Rudy, Zeke fumbled with his bag, trying to retrieve his gun. With a fast flip of his wrist, Rudy used his cane to pick the strap off Zeke's shoulder and knock the whole bag to the floor.

"This isn't the Outskirts, junior. You act like a fool out there, maybe someone takes a switch to you or pops you in the jaw. You make problems in here, and you'll be rotter shit before dawn."

"It's a long way till dawn tomorrow," Zeke gasped against the cane's tip, which was still shoved against his neck.

"You know what I mean. Now are you going to keep it down, or is this going to get ugly?"

"It's already ugly," Zeke gasped again.

Rudy withdrew the cane and scowled about it. He dropped its tip back onto the floor and leaned against it, propping himself up on that one hand, balanced on the top of that cane. In his other hand he still held the bottle, even though it was all but empty.

"I don't know why I even bothered," he grumbled, and backed away. "Do you want to go see that house, or not?"

"I *do*."

"Then if you want to live long enough to set eyes on it, you're going to travel on my terms, do I make myself clear? You're going to keep your voice down and your mouth shut unless I tell you it's all right to talk, and you're going to stay close. I'm not pretending, and I'm not trying to scare you when I say it's dangerous down there—and

I don't think you'll survive an hour by yourself. You can try it if you like and I won't stop you. But you'll be better off to stick with me. It's up to you."

Zeke picked up his bag and hugged it while he tried to decide. There were many things about the situation that he did not like.

First of all, he had little patience for being told what to do by anyone, much less a stranger who appeared to be inebriated and looking to become further inebriated at the nearest opportunity. Second, he had deep-seated doubts as to why this man who'd initially greeted him with threats of bodily harm might be moved to help. Zeke didn't trust Rudy, and he didn't believe much of what Rudy had told him.

And furthermore, he didn't like him.

But when he looked out over the side of the roof and saw only the swirling, billowing air the color of soot and rotting citrus, and when he looked up at the taller buildings and saw the gold-glittering eyes of a hundred wary black birds watching back . . . he reconsidered his stance on going it alone.

"Those birds," he said slowly. "Have they been there all this time?"

Rudy said, "Sure." He tipped his bottle upside down and dumped the contents over the side of the building—then set the glassware aside. "They're the gods of this place, insomuch as anything is."

Zeke scanned the ledges, windows, and architectural lips where the blue-black feathers and glass-beaded eyes glistened against the watery light of the new day. "What's that supposed to mean?"

Rudy walked to the nearest small bridge and climbed up onto the ledge beside it. With a wave, he suggested that Zeke follow. He said, "They're everywhere, and they see everything. Sometimes they're helpful, and sometimes they attack you—and you never know which, or why. We don't understand them, and we're not sure we like them. But"—he shrugged—"there they are. You coming or not?"

"I'm coming," Zeke said, though for a moment he made no move to follow.

Something was working against his feet, and he didn't know what it was until the building beneath him started to quiver. "Rudy?" Zeke asked, as if this was something the other man was doing, and he ought to stop it.

The shaking went harder and faster, and Rudy said, "Earthquake. It's an earthquake, kid—that's all. Hang on."

"To what?"

"To anything."

Zeke retreated from the hole in the roof and ducked down in the corner near where Rudy was crouching and holding onto the edge, waiting. Zeke waited too, clinging to himself and to the wall, praying that it didn't get any worse and that the place he knelt would continue to stand.

"Just wait it out," Rudy said. He didn't sound perfectly confident, but he didn't sound surprised, either. He braced his body against the bricks and even put out a hand to hold Zeke down.

Zeke didn't think that it made him any safer, but he was glad to have Rudy there all the same. He took Rudy's hand and used it to pull his way closer to the man and the wall. When the rumbling ruckus peaked, the boy closed his eyes, because he did not know what else to do.

"First quake?" Rudy said conversationally. He didn't release his squeeze on Zeke's hand and arm, though.

"First real one," the boy said. His teeth knocked together when he tried to talk, so he crushed his mouth shut.

And it was over, as quickly as it had begun. That's not to say that the knocking, breaking waves of motion stopped in a perfect moment; but they tapered sharply and then fizzled to a wobble, and then a faint shudder.

The whole thing had lasted perhaps two minutes.

Zeke's legs felt like pudding. He tried to pull himself up, and using the wall and Rudy's arm, he succeeded enough to stand. His knees nearly folded, but he locked them. He stood up straight and waited, knowing that the rushing noise and the jostling floors might return at any second.

They didn't.

The noise had dwindled, and where it was once a full-on roar he could now hear only the crackling of old bricks settling and the patter of loosened masonry hitting the pavement.

"That was . . . ," Zeke said. "That was . . ."

"That was an earthquake, that's all. Don't make a mountain out of a shaky little molehill."

"I've never been in one like that before."

Rudy said, "And now you have. But that one wasn't so bad. Maybe it just felt worse because you're all high up. Anyway, we ought to get running. There's always a chance that the shaker knocked the tunnels up, and we might have to improvise a path. We'll see."

He patted himself down, checking his cane and straightening his overcoat. Then he said, "You can leave the lantern here. In fact, I recommend that you do so. We've got lights scattered everywhere, and you'll just lose that one or leave it someplace. Besides, we're going to have to hit street level soon, and it'll only draw the kind of attention that we most definitely do not want."

"I'm not leaving my lantern."

"Then put it out. I'm not asking you, boy. I'm telling you that I won't take you down there until you let that go. Look, stick it over there in the corner. You can pick it up on your way back home."

Zeke reluctantly complied, leaving the lantern stashed in the nearest corner and covering it with some scraps he found there. "You don't think anyone'll take it?"

"I'd be astounded," Rudy said. "Now come on. We're burning daylight, and we haven't got any to spare down here. It's not a short jaunt over to your parents' old place."

Zeke carefully scooted onto the ledge to follow. He worried about a man with a limp tackling the fragile bridge, but the odd assortment of boards and strips of scrap creaked and held beneath their collective weight.

Zeke was glad he couldn't see very far below, but he couldn't stop himself from asking, "How far up are we?"

"Just a couple of stories. We'll go up higher before we go lower, so I hope the heights don't bother you."

"No sir," Zeke said. "I don't mind the climbing."

"Good. Because we're going to do plenty of it."

They stalked across the bridge and up against a window next door. The wood seemed to dead-end against it, but when Rudy shoved a lever, the window opened inward and they both stepped inside, into darkness that was profound and wet—just like the bakery when Zeke had first let himself into the city's interior.

"Where are we?" he whispered.

Rudy struck a match and lit a candle, although technically the sun was still up. "As I understand it? We're in hell."

## Nine

When Andan Cly said "now," he actually meant, "When the rest of the crew returns"; but Cly assured Briar that the delay would be no longer than an hour—and anyway, if she could scare up a better offer she was welcome to take it. He invited Briar up to the cabin and told her to make herself at home, though he'd appreciate it if she didn't touch anything.

Cly stayed outside, where he busied himself with the checking of gauges and the fiddling of knobs.

Up the rough rope ladder and through the porthole, Briar climbed into a compartment that was surprisingly spacious, or perhaps it only looked that way because it was nearly empty. Huge, flaccid bags hung from the ceiling on tracks that lowered and adjusted with pulleys; and in the edges at the stern and bow there were barrels and boxes crammed to the ceiling. But in the middle the floor was free, and hurricane lamps hung on hinges like ship lanterns from the crossbeams and from the high spots up on the walls where they were unlikely to be rocked or jostled. Inside them, she could see small bulbs with fat, yellow-glowing wires instead of flames. She wondered where Cly had gotten them.

Over on the right side, farthest from the ladder, there was a short set of wooden slat steps built against the wall.

Briar climbed those, too. At the top, she found a room packed with pipes, buttons, and levers. Three-quarters of the wall surface was made of thick glass that was cloudy in places, scratched, scraped, and dinged from the outside. But there weren't any cracks in it, and when she flicked her nail against it the sound it made was more of a thud than a clink.

At the main control area there were levers longer than her forearm and bright buttons that flickered on the captain's console. Pedals arched out of the floor to foot level, and hanging latches descended from the overhead panels.

For reasons she could not explain, Briar felt the sudden, fearful certainty that she was being watched. She held still, looking forward out the front window. Behind her, she heard nothing—not even breathing, and no footsteps, nor the creak of the wooden stairs—but even so she was positive that she was not alone.

"Fang!" Cly called from outside.

Briar jumped at the shout, and turned around.

A man stood behind her, so close he could've touched her if he'd tried.

"Fang, there's a woman in there! Try not to scare her to death!"

Fang was a small man about the same size as Briar, and slender without looking fragile or weak. His black hair was so dark it shone blue, shaved back away from his forehead and drawn into a ponytail that sat high on the top of his skull.

"Hello?" she tried.

He didn't respond, except to slowly blink his angled brown eyes.

Cly's big head poked up from the portal in the floor. "Sorry about that," he said to Briar. "I should've warned you. Fang's all right, but he's just about the quietest son of a bitch I ever met."

"Does he . . . ," she began, and then feared it might be rude. She asked the man in the loose-fitting pants and the mandarin jacket, "Do you speak English?"

The captain answered for him. "He doesn't speak anything. Someone cut out his tongue, but I don't know who or why. He understands plenty, though. English, Chinese, Portuguese. God knows what else."

Fang stepped away from Briar and placed a cloth satchel down on a seat off to the left. He pulled an aviator's cap out from the bag and put it on his head. There was a hole cut out of the back of the hat so that he could thread his ponytail through it.

"Don't worry about him," Cly emphasized. "He's good people."

"Then why is he called Fang?" Briar asked.

Cly scaled the steps and began crouching. He was too tall to comfortably stand in his own cabin. "As far as I know, that's his name. This old woman in Chinatown, down in California—she told me it means honest and upright, and it doesn't have anything to do with snakes. I'm forced to take her word for it."

"Out of the way," demanded another voice.

"I *am* out of the way," Cly said without looking.

From below came another man, grinning and slightly fat. He was wearing a black fur hat with flaps that came down over his ears, and a brown leather coat held together with mismatched brass buttons.

"Rodimer, this is Miss Wilkes. Miss Wilkes, that's Rodimer. Ignore him."

"Ignore me?" He feigned affront as he failed to feign disinterest in Briar. "Oh, I should dearly pray that you wouldn't!" He seized one of Briar's hands and gave it a dry and elaborate kiss.

"All right, I won't," she assured him, reclaiming her hand. "Is this everyone?" she asked Cly.

"This is everyone. If I carried anyone else we wouldn't have room for cargo. Fang, see about the ropes. Rodimer, the boilers are hot and ready to spray."

"Hydrogen check?"

"Topped off over in Bradenton. Ought to be good to go for another few trips."

"So the leak's patched?"

"Leak's patched." Cly nodded. "You," he said to Briar. "You ever flown before?"

She admitted that she hadn't. "I'll be all right," she told him.

"You'd better. Any spills are your own, and you clean them up. Fair deal?"

"Fair deal. Should I sit down somewhere?"

He scanned the narrow cab and didn't see anything that looked comfortable. "We don't usually take passengers," he said. "Sorry, but there's no first-class in this bird. Pull up a crate and brace yourself if you want to see outside, or"—he waved an enormous arm toward a small, rounded door at the back of the craft—"there's sleeping spots in the back area, just hammocks. Not one of them is fit for a lady, but you can sit there if you want. Do you get sick from moving?"

"No."

"I'd ask that you be damned sure before you get too comfortable back there."

She cut him off before he could say any more. "I don't get sick, I said. I'll stay out here. I want to see."

"Suit yourself," he said. He grabbed a heavy box and pulled it over the floor until it was next to the nearest wall. "It'll be an hour before we get to the wall, and then it'll take half again that long to set up for the drop and catch. I'll try to set you down someplace . . . well, there's no place *safe* in there, but—"

Rodimer sat up straight and jerked his head around to look at Briar. "You're going *inside*?" he asked in a voice too deliberately melodic for a man his size and shape. "Good God almighty, Cly. You're going to dump the lady off behind the wall?"

"The lady made a very persuasive case." Cly watched Briar from the corner of his eye.

"Miss Wilkes . . . ," Rodimer repeated slowly, as if the name hadn't meant anything to him when he'd heard it spoken; but upon replaying it in his head, he suspected that it was important. "Miss Wilkes, the walled city is no place for—"

"A lady, yes. That's what they tell me. You're not the first to say it, but I'd very much prefer that you've said your last on the subject. I need to get inside, and I *will* get inside, and Captain Cly is being kind enough to assist me."

Rodimer closed his mouth, shook his head, and returned his attention to the console under his hands. "As you like, ma'am, but it's a damned shame, if you don't mind my saying so."

"I don't mind you saying so," she said. "But there's no need to hold my funeral yet. I'll be out again, come Tuesday."

Cly added, "Hainey's offered to pull her out on his next run. If she can hold out that long, she'll be all right with him."

"I'm not comfortable with this," Rodimer grumbled. "It's not right, leaving a lady in the city."

"Maybe not," Cly mumbled as he took his seat. "But when Fang gets back we're taking off, and she won't be making the return trip with us unless she changes her mind. Pull the front lift, will you?"

"Yes sir." The first mate reached forward and tugged one of the levers. Somewhere above, something heavy disengaged one thing and connected with another. The clank from the shift echoed down into the cabin.

The captain squeezed a handle latch and tugged a shift bar toward his chest. "Miss Wilkes, there's a cargo net on the wall behind you, fixed to the surface. You can hang on to that, if you need to. Wrap your arms through it, or however works best. Make yourself secure."

"Will it be . . . will it be a rough ride?"

"Not too bad, I don't think. The weather's quiet enough, but there are air currents around the walls. They're high enough that the wind off the mountains comes breaking around them. Sometimes we get a little surprise."

Fang manifested in the cabin with the same scary silence as before. This time Briar knew not to gasp, and the mute Chinese man did not give her any further scrutiny.

A slight shift in the tilt of the floor signaled the start of motion. Against the exterior hull, tree branches scraped a high-pitched tune as the *Naamah Darling* began to rise. At first it seeped slowly upward of its own volition, unpowered by any steam or thrust, but lifted by the hydrogen in the lumpy inflated tanks above them. There was no real shaking or swaying, only a faint sense of rising until the airship cleared the treetops and floated above them, drifting higher, but not with any urgency or speed.

The whole operation was quieter than Briar expected. Except for the creaking of ropes, the stretching of metal joints, and the sliding of empty boxes across the floor downstairs, there was little sound.

But then Cly pulled a wheel-like column into his lap and flipped three switches along its side. Then the cabin was filled with the rushing hiss of steam being shifted from boilers into pipes, and down to the thrusters that would steer the vessel between the clouds. With the steam came a gentle lurch, east and up, and the *Naamah Darling* again offered moans, screeches, and groans as she lifted herself into the sky.

Once airbound, the ship moved smoothly with a forward drift augmented by the periodic burst of the steam thrusters. Briar rose from her seat at the edge of the cabin and came to stand behind the captain so she could see the world outside and below.

They weren't so high that she couldn't distinguish the boats and ferries that trudged along the water; and when they crossed the line between water and land, Briar could tell which blocks were which, and even determine the streets. The Waterworks compound was flat and spread unevenly across the shoreline. The low hills and sharp ridges had houses perched on them, leaning into them; and here and there great horses towed the water carts from district to district, making the weekly deliveries.

She looked for her own house, but did not see it.

Before long, the Seattle wall loomed in front of them, curved, rough, and gray above the Outskirts neighborhoods. The *Naamah Darling* floated closer to it, and then past it, and began a course around it.

Briar almost asked, but Cly anticipated her concern. "This time of year," he told her, "proper transport ships on legitimate business don't go so close to the city. Everyone takes the northern pass around it, up over the mountains. If we look like we're going to dip inside, it'll be noticed."

"And then what?" she asked.

"Then *what* what?"

"What if you're noticed, I mean? What would happen?"

Fang, Cly, and Rodimer all exchanged glances that told her plenty.

She answered on their behalf. "You're not sure, but you don't really want to find out."

"More or less," Cly said over his shoulder. "The sky isn't regulated like the roads, not yet. The time will come, I'm sure—but for now, the only governing force in the air is distracted with the war back east. I've seen a couple of official ships, here and there, but they looked like fugitive war vessels to me. I don't think they were out to police anyone, or anything. We've got plenty more to fear from other sky pirates, if you want the truth."

"Fugitive war vessels . . . like Croggon Hainey's ship?" she asked.

"Like that one, yes. I'm not sure what kind of favor he did himself, stealing a toy from the losing side, but—"

"They haven't lost *yet*," Rodimer interjected.

"They've been losing for a decade. At this point, it'd be better for everyone if they'd find a nice quiet spot to surrender."

Rodimer pushed a pedal with his foot and used the back of his hand to flip a switch. "It's a wonder the Confederate States have held out this long. If it weren't for that railroad . . ."

"Yeah, I know. If it weren't for a million things they'd have been smashed up ages ago. But they ain't been yet, and God knows how much longer they'll dig in their heels," Cly complained.

Briar asked, "What do you care, anyway?"

"I don't, much," he told her. "Except that I'd like to see the country incorporate Washington, and I'd like to see some American money up here—maybe clean up that mess in the city somehow. There isn't any more Klondike gold, if there ever was to start with, so there's not enough local money to make them care, otherwise." He flicked his hand at the window to his right, at the wall. "Somebody ought to do something about it, and Christ knows nobody down there has got half an idea of how it ought to get fixed."

The first mate's head bobbed in a semi-shrug. "But we make an all right living off it. Lots of people do."

"There are better ways to earn livings. More decent ways." Cly's voice carried a funny threat, and neither Briar nor Rodimer pursued the subject further.

But Briar thought she understood. She changed the subject. "What were you saying about sky pirates?"

"I didn't say anything about sky pirates except that they happen. But not so much around here, not usually. There aren't too many shippers with nerve enough to duck down far into the gas. The way some of us look at it, we're doing the Outskirts a favor by taking some of it away. You know, that gas is still coming up out of the hole. It's still filling up that wall, like a big old bowl. What we skim off the top is only helping." ·

"Except for what it gets turned into," Briar said.

"That's not up to me, and it's not my problem," Cly replied, but he didn't sound mad at her about it.

She didn't answer him because she was tired of arguing. "Are we almost there?" she asked instead. The *Naamah Darling* was slowing down and coming to a settled position, hovering above a segment of wall.

"We're there. Fang?"

Fang rose from his seat and disappeared down the wooden steps. A few seconds later there was a sound of large things rolling or shifting, and then there was a dip and a jump as the ship found its balance. When the ship stopped bobbing, Fang reappeared in the cabin. He was wearing a gas mask and leather gloves so thick that he could scarcely move his fingers.

He nodded at Cly and Rodimer, who nodded back. The captain said to Briar, "You've got your own mask, don't you?"

"I do."

"Put it on."

"Already?" She reached into her satchel and heaved it out. The buckles and straps were clunky and tangled, but she unfastened them, straightened them, and held the thing up to her face.

"Yes, already. Fang's opened the bottom bay doors and anchored

us to the wall. The gas is too heavy to rise very fast up here into the
ship, but it'll waft its way through the cabin once we get moving."

"Why are you anchored to the wall?"

"To keep us stable. I already told you about the air currents. Even
when it's quiet, there's always a chance a gust will grab the ship and
throw her down into the bad blocks. So what we do is anchor with a
rope that's a few hundred feet long. Then we shove off like it's a boat
leaving a pier, over the city proper." He unbuckled himself out of his
seat and pushed the wheel away from his knees. The captain stood,
stretched, and remembered not to stand up straight just in time to
keep from cracking his forehead against the window.

"Then," he said, "we'll lower the empty bags and yank the thrusters
into full drive. The thrusters will send us shooting back towards the
wall, dragging the sacks behind us—and they'll fill right up, fast as can
be. The extra power will lift us up higher, because like I said, the gas is
heavier than you think. We'll need the boost to get all the way into the
air again."

Briar held her mask just over her face, strapped onto her skull but
propped up above her eyes so she could talk. "So basically you drift
out over the gas, drop the bags, and slingshot yourself back out of the
city."

"Basically," he said. "So you have until we finish drifting. Then
I'm going to hold you out over one of the air tubes. You're going to
have to either climb down it or slide down it. I'd recommend a combination of the two. Hold your hands and feet out to slow your fall.
It's a long way down, and I don't have any idea what you're going to
find at the bottom."

"No idea at all?" She was holding the mask up, unwilling to shut
herself off from the rest of them by affixing it to her face.

He scratched at the side of his head and tugged a big black mask
down over his nose and mouth. As he tightened the straps and worked
it into position, his voice changed to a loudly muffled whisper. "I
guess if I drop you down a tube, the odds are good you'll wind up in
an air pump room. But I don't know what those look like. I've never

seen one up close and personal. I know that's how they bring down the good air, though—such as it is."

Rodimer had jammed his own mask over his roundish face, leaving only Briar unprotected. She could smell the Blight already, strong and bitter below her, and she knew she ought to cover up, so she did.

But the mask was awful. It fit, but not very well. The seal around her face sucked itself into a tight groove, and the mask startled her with its weight as it hung from her forehead and her cheeks. She adjusted the straps over her hair, trying to keep them from painfully pulling the strands. Inside the mask it smelled like rubber and burned toast. Every breath was a little hard to draw, and it tasted a little bad.

"What's that, an old MP80?" Cly asked, pointing at the mask.

She bobbed her head. "From the evacuation."

"It's a good model," he observed. "You have any extra charcoal filters for it?"

"No. But these two were never used for long. They should be all right."

"They'll be all right for a while. A whole day if you're lucky. Wait a minute." He reached under the console and pulled out a carton filled with round discs of assorted sizes. "How big are yours?"

"Two and three-quarters."

"Yeah, we've got some of those. Here, take a few. They're not very heavy, and they might do you good in a pinch." He selected four and checked them against one another, and against what light came through the windshield. Satisfied that they were sound, he thumbed them over to Briar. While she inserted them into her satchel, Cly continued. "Now listen, this won't hold you for the next few days—I don't have enough to set you up that way. You're going to have to find some sealed spots with air in them. And they're down there, I know they are. But I couldn't tell you how to find them."

Briar fastened her bag again, knocking the chin of her gas mask on her collarbone when she looked down. "Thank you," she said. "You've been very kind, and I appreciate it. When I'm down there, I mean to go home—I mean, back to my old home, for all that I didn't

live there long. I know where there's money, real money, and all kinds
of . . . I don't know. What I'm saying is, I'll make a point to find some
way to repay you."

"Don't worry about it," he said, and his voice was unreadable there
inside the mask. "Just stay alive, would you? I'm trying to repay a favor
here myself, but I won't consider it an even score if you go inside and
die."

"I'll do my best," she promised. "Now point me to the way out,
and let me go find my son."

"Yes, ma'am," he said, and pointed back down the steps. "After
you."

It was tough to climb down with the mask knocking against every
other rung; and it was hard to see through the round, heavy lenses
that cut off all Briar's peripheral vision. The smell was already driving
her mad, but there was nothing to be done about it, so she tried to
pretend that she could see just fine, and she could breathe just fine,
and that nothing was clenching her head in a viselike grip.

Down in the cargo hold Fang was unlatching the blocks that served
as brakes for the big bags on their tracks. Rodimer worked from the
other end of the room, gathering the deflated, rubber-treated sacks in
his arms and pulling them along the track, drawing them over to the
open bay door.

Briar shuffled carefully to the edge of the squared-off hole and
peered down into the gas. There was nothing to see, and it shocked
her.

The window in the floor revealed a brownish fog that swirled and
puffed, obscuring all but the highest building peaks. There was no
sign of the streets or blocks below, and no hint of any life except for
the occasional caw of a distant black bird with a bitter grudge.

But as she looked longer, Briar saw tiny details here and there, between the briskly stirred clouds. The edges of a totem pole peeked
through the gas and vanished. A church's steeple punctured the ugly
fog and was lost.

"I thought you said there were breathing tubes, or . . ."

And then she saw it. The ship was parked alongside it, so she wouldn't have seen it by staring down and out, only at an angle. The tube was a bright, cheery yellow and frosted with bird manure. It swayed back and forth, but mostly stayed steady, bolstered by a strange and fragile-looking framework that was fastened around it like a bustle under a skirt. Briar couldn't see what this framework was fastened to, but it was secured against something under the clouds of fog—perhaps rooftops, or the remains of trees.

The tube's exit end was lifted up above the tainted air. It was big enough to accommodate Briar and possibly a second person at the same time.

She craned her neck to see it, trying to find the top.

"We've still got to rise a little," Cly said. "Give it a minute. We'll climb another few feet, and then we'll be close enough for you to dive. The gas is dense. It'll push us up a little farther before we load."

" 'Dive,' " she repeated, trying not to choke.

The world was spinning beneath her, bleak, blind, and bottomless. And somewhere, hidden within it, her fifteen-year-old son was lost and trapped, and there was no one to go down there and get him except for his mother. But she had every intention of finding him, and hauling him out on the *Free Crow* in three days' time.

Focusing on this goal and swearing that it was a strict eventuality did little to calm the throbbing horror of her heart.

"Having second thoughts?" Rodimer asked. Even through his gas mask Briar thought she heard a note of hope in the question.

"No. There's no one else to get him. He doesn't have anyone else." But she couldn't tear her eyes away from the murky vortex beneath the ship.

As the *Naamah Darling* rose, pushed above the gas foot by foot, the air tube came into clearer focus. From the greater height Briar could see hints of other tubes jabbing up through the disgusting cloud. They waved like the antennae of giant insects hiding in the haze, pinned together with sticks and slowly bobbing against the nasty currents, but remaining always upright.

And then they were above the lip of the tube, just barely—just enough that Briar could grab it. She reached out a hand, down through the open bay, and she wrapped her fingers around the edge.

The tube felt rough to the touch, but strangely slick. Briar thought it might be burlap coated with wax, but through the thick lenses of the mask she couldn't see well enough to guess any better. The tube was ribbed with hoops of wood to keep its shape, and these ribs bulged at four-foot intervals, giving the tube the appearance of a segmented worm.

Finally the ship was as high as it was going to get, and the tube's mouth was just beneath it.

The captain said, "Now or never, Miss Wilkes."

She took a deep breath, and it hurt—drawing the air, forcing it past the filters and into her chest. "Thank you," she told him again.

"Don't forget: When you get over the side, spread out to slow your way down."

"I won't forget," she said. She tossed a parting nod at Rodimer and Fang both, and grasped the tube's edge.

Cly walked around the square bay door. He twisted his wrist in a cargo net and used it to hold himself steady. "Go on," he told her. "I've got you."

Although he wasn't touching her, she could feel him there behind her, arms out, unwilling to let her fall where she shouldn't. Then his free arm swung to hold her elbow.

She leaned against him while she lifted her leg and sent it over the lip of the tube. With a short lurch she left the *Naamah Darling* and the support of the helpful captain and fell a few feet until she was straddling the tube's wall. Briar snapped her arms and legs tight around it, clinging to it tightly.

She closed her eyes, but opened them again, because it was better to see even if the view nauseated her. The tube was not as steady as it seemed, and it dipped, weaved, and bobbed. Even though the motions were slow, they were impossibly high above the earth. Every fraction of an inch one way or another was enough to take her breath away.

Over on the *Naamah Darling*, three curious faces peered out through the bay.

They were still close enough, and the captain was long-limbed enough, that if she were to reach out and beg, they could pull her back on board. The temptation was almost more than she could stand.

Instead, one shaking finger at a time, she peeled her death grip free of the tube and sat up enough to pivot her hips and bring her second leg over the edge. She paused there for a moment, as if she were entering a bathtub. Then, with one last look over her shoulder—too quick to change her mind—she pitched forward into the deep black interior of the fresh air apparatus.

The shift from grim, watery daylight to full-on night was sudden and loud.

She did her best to hold her arms and legs out to slow her fall, but she quickly realized that she'd have to use one hand to hold the mask as she toppled down, lest it be ripped off by the sheer force of the scrambling slide. That left two legs and one arm for ballasting duty. Three being less stable than four, Briar clattered and tumbled, sometimes headfirst, sometimes knock-kneed and toes-first, down the yellow tube with its hard wood ribs.

She couldn't see anything, and everything she felt was hard, damp, and whooshing past. As she toppled, a new and separate sound became louder and louder. It was hard to single it out over the clattering calamity of her descent, but there it was, a windy sound—in, out, in, out—as if some great monster waited openmouthed and breathing at the bottom.

She could sense that she was nearing that bottom, though she couldn't explain how she knew. Still, she made a final, desperate push to brake her body's battering drop: head upright, feet down, right arm out, both knees locked.

She finally dragged herself to a halt when her feet snared on a wider, thicker rib than the ones she'd plummeted past. The air sucked violently at her clothes, and then reversed its direction—coughing hard and long, pushing up and out. Briar thanked heaven she wasn't wearing skirts.

After a ten-second blast the current reversed, and then came shoving back out again.

She could see nothing in the ink-dark hole under her feet, but between the enormous gasping breaths of the tube she heard machinery grumbling and large metal parts clicking together.

The air came and went with whistling moans, inhaling and exhaling Briar's hair, her coat, her satchel. Her hat trailed above her head like a balloon, anchored by the ties that fastened it under her chin, over the mask.

She couldn't stand there forever, but she couldn't see where a farther fall might bring her. A series of clanks like the fastening and rolling of huge gears sounded in time with the breathing: close, but not dangerously close, she didn't think. And at that point, all danger was relative.

On the air current's intake stroke, she scooted one foot away from the rim and braced her back against the tube. Her foot felt around, examining the darkness by touch. She found nothing, so she lowered herself a bit more. Her arms strained against her body's weight, even when the air tube's outtake gasp tried to lift and expel her.

She let herself down another few inches, until she was hanging with her shoulders and chest level with the last sturdy rib, the toe-points of her boots dangling down over nothing, and finding nothing. By now she could reach the more substantial rib with her fingertips, so she unlocked her elbows and let herself droop down a few inches more.

There.

Her feet scraped against something soft. The investigating motion of her swinging boots pushed it aside, only to land again on something else soft and small. Whatever she was fondling with the bottoms of her feet, it was resting on something firm, and that knowledge was enough to let her exhausted hands release their grip.

She fell, only briefly, and landed on all fours.

Under her hands and knees, small things broke with a hundred muffled snaps, and when the air tube exhaled again, she felt light fluttering bits of debris rise into her hair. They were birds, dead ones— some of them long dead, or so she guessed from the brittle beaks and decayed, dismembered wings that flapped with the shifting air. She was deeply glad she couldn't see.

Briar wondered why the birds didn't explode out through the tube every time the air flow shifted, but by exploring with her hands and feeling the gusting gasps, she thought that perhaps they had only collected there, out of reach of the tube's main drawing and exhaling force. This was confirmed when she tried to rise and knocked her head against a ledge.

Her stopping place was only a shielded corner where detritus could accumulate. She held out her hands, crouched to keep from hitting her head again, and searched for the chamber's boundaries.

Her fingertips stopped against a wall. When she pressed against this wall it gave a little, and she realized it wasn't made of brick or stone. It was thicker than canvas, more like leather. Perhaps it was fashioned from several layers fused together—she couldn't tell. But she leaned on it, and continued searching with her hands, up and down, seeking a seam or a latch.

Finding nothing of the sort, she pressed her head against the barrier and was almost certain she heard voices. The wall was too thick or the sound too distant for her to gather a language or any distinct words, but yes, there were voices.

She told herself that it was a good sign, that yes, there were people there inside the city and they lived just fine—so why not Zeke, too?

But she couldn't bring herself to knock or cry out, not yet. So she held her ground, littered as it was with the corpses of long-dead winged things, and strained to learn more about whatever might wait on the other side. She couldn't stay there in the feathered graveyard forever. She couldn't pretend that she was safe. So she had to act.

At least she'd be out of the dark.

She balled her hands into fists and struck at the dense, slightly pliable wall. "Hello?" she yelled. "Hello, can anyone hear me? Is there anyone out there? Hello? Hello—I'm stuck inside this . . . thing. Is there any way out?"

Before long, the grinding apparatus of the inhaling, exhaling machine slowed and stopped, and then Briar could hear the voices better. Someone had heard her, and there was excited chattering on the other side of the wall, but she couldn't tell if the chatterers were angered, or pleased, or confused, or frightened.

She smacked her fists on the barrier again and again, and she continued her loud, insistent plea until a line of light cracked to life behind her. She swiveled, crushing a small carcass underfoot, and held her hand up to her mask. Narrow though it was, the ribbon of white seared her eyes as if it were the sun.

The silhouette of a nearly naked head was outlined and backlit.

A man's voice rattled something hurriedly, and incomprehensibly. He waved his hand at Briar, urging her to come out, come out. Come out of the hole where the dead birds gather.

She stumbled forward, toward him, her arms extended. "Help me," she said without shouting. "Thank you, yes. Just get me out of here."

He seized her hand and pulled her out into the light of a room filled with carefully controlled fires. She blinked and squinted against the sudden brightness of coals and a haze of smoke or steam, turning her head left and right, trying to see all the corners that the mask cut off from her vision.

Behind her and to the left, there was a huge set of bellows—a giant's version of what might sit beside an ordinary fireplace. The bellows were attached to an elaborate machine with gears that had teeth as big as apples; and there was a crank to move the gears, presumably to pump the bellows. But the crank itself was folded against the side of the machine, resting there as if it were only a secondary means of moving the device.

Off to the side, a massive coal furnace with a smoldering-hot interior seemed the more likely power source. Its door was open, and a

man with a shovel stood beside it. Four tubes of assorted materials
and designs came and went from the mighty bellows: the yellow slide
through which Briar had descended, a metal cylinder that connected
to the furnace, a blue cloth tube that disappeared into another room,
and a gray one—once perhaps white—that vanished back into the
ceiling.

All around Briar the voices asked questions in a language she
didn't speak, and from every direction hands squeezed at her, touching her arms and her back. It felt like a dozen men, but it was only
three or four.

They were Asian—Chinese, she guessed, since two of the men had
partially shaved heads with braids like Fang's. Covered with sweat,
wearing long leather aprons that protected their legs and bare chests,
the men wore goggles with tinted lenses to shield their eyes from the
fires they worked.

Briar tore herself away from the men and retreated into the nearest corner that did not hold a furnace or an open bowl of flame.

The men advanced, still speaking to her in that tongue she could
not decipher, and Briar remembered she had a rifle. She whipped it
off her back and aimed it at the first man, and the next one, and the
third—back and forth—and at the next two men who entered the room
to see what the commotion was about.

Even through the charcoal filter in her mask, she could sense the
soot choking the air. It smothered her, even though it couldn't really
be smothering her, could it? And it watered her eyes, though it couldn't
really reach them.

It was too much, too sudden—the masked and chattering men
with their fires and their shovels, their gears and their buckets of coal.
The darkness in the closed, claustrophobic room was oppressive and
bright around the edges from the white-hot coals and the yellow
flames. All the shadows jerked and twitched. They were sharp and terrible, and they looked violent against the walls and the machinery.

"Stay away from me!" Briar shrieked, only barely thinking that
they might not understand her, or even be able to hear her very well

through the mask. She brandished the rifle, swinging it and jabbing it at the air.

They held up their hands and retreated, still talking rapidly in spits and bursts. Whether or not they spoke English, they spoke gun.

"How do I get out of here?" she demanded, on the off chance that someone understood her language better than he could communicate in it. "Out! How do I get out?"

From the corner, someone barked a single-syllable reply, but she couldn't hear it clearly. She quickly turned her head to glimpse the source and saw an elderly fellow with long white hair and a beard that came to a scraggly, pale point. A white film covered his eyes. Briar could see, even in the orange-and-black fever of the bellows room, that he was blind.

He raised a thin arm and pointed to a corridor between a furnace and a machine the size of a cart. She hadn't seen it before. It was only a black sliver as wide as a drawer, and it seemed to be the only means of entry or exit.

"I'm sorry," she said to him. "I'm sorry," she said to the rest of them, but she didn't lower the rifle. "I'm sorry," she said again as she turned herself sideways and dashed for the hallway.

Into the narrow space she ran. After a few feet something slapped against her face, but she burst past it and kept jogging madly, into a better-lit walkway pocked with candles shoved into crannies. She glanced over her shoulder and saw long strips of rubber-treated cloth hanging down like curtains, keeping the worst of the smoke and sparks out of the brighter thoroughfare.

Here and there she saw slotted windows to her left, covered and stuffed with more treated cloth, papers, pitch, and anything else that might insulate and seal out the awful gas outside.

Briar was panting inside the mask, fighting for each lungful of air. But she couldn't stop, not when there might be men chasing her, not while she didn't know where she was.

It did look familiar, she thought. Not *very* familiar—not an oft-visited place, but a location she might've seen once or twice under better circumstances, and brighter skies. Her chest hurt, and her elbows ached a little from the bruising descent through the waving yellow tube.

All she could think was *out*: where the exit might be, where it might lead her, and what she might find there.

The hallway opened into a large room that was vacant except for barrels, crates, and shelves stocked with all manner of oddities. There were two lanterns, too, one at each end of a long wooden counter. She could see more clearly in there, except for the cutoff edges of her peripheral vision.

Listen as hard as she might, she couldn't hear anyone following behind her; so she slowed down and tried to catch her breath while she glared from corner to corner at the boxes with their stenciled labels. It was hard, though, to gather her calm. She forced the air through the filters and dragged it through her mouth in a demanding, drawn-out gasp, but there wasn't enough to satisfy, no matter how much she fought. And she didn't dare remove the mask, not yet—not when her goal was to find her way out into the streets, into the thick of the gas. She read the labels on the boxes like the words were a mantra.

"Linen. Processed pitch. Eight-penny nails. Two-quart bottles, glass."

Behind her there were voices now, maybe the same ones and maybe different ones.

A big wood door with glass cutout panels had been buttressed and sealed with thick black patches of pitch. Briar shoved her shoulder against it. It didn't budge, not even to squeak or flex. To the door's left, there was a window that had received similar treatment. It was covered with sheets of thin wood that had been thoroughly sealed around its edges and along its seams.

To the right of the door there was another counter. Behind it, there were stairs leading down into yet more darkness, with yet more candles glimmering above them.

Even around the ambient swish and press of the mask moving

against her hair, Briar could hear footsteps. The voices were getting louder, but there was nowhere else to run or hide. She could go back into the corridor stuffed with onrushing Chinamen, or she could head down the stairs and take her chances with whatever may wait at the bottom.

"Down," she said into the mask. "All right, down."

And she half stumbled, half skipped down the crooked, creaking stairwell.

*Ten*

Down through the old hotel next door to the bakery, Zeke followed Rudy and his one dim candle. Once they got to the basement they took another tunnel lined with pipes and brickwork. They were going lower—Zeke could feel the grade declining by feet at a time. The descent seemed to take hours. He finally felt compelled to ask, "I thought we were going up the hill?"

"We'll get there," Rudy told him. "It's like I said, sometimes you've got to go down in order to go up."

"But I thought it was mostly houses where they lived. My mother said it was just a neighborhood, and she told me about some of their neighbors. We keep going underneath all these big places—these hotels and things."

"That wasn't a hotel we just went through," Rudy said. "It was a church."

"It's hard to tell from the underside of it," Zeke complained. "When do we get to take off these masks, anyway? I thought there was supposed to be clean air down here someplace. That's what my buddy Rector told me."

Rudy said, "Hush. Did you hear that?"

"Hear what?"

They stood together, perfectly still, under the street and between a tunnel's worth of walls that were wet with mold and muck. Above, a skylight of glass tiles allowed enough light to see down into the corridor, and Zeke was astonished to conclude that it must already be morning. These skylights dotted the underground chambers, but between them there were places where the darkness overcame everything, creating nooks where the tunnels were as black as ink. Rudy and Zeke stepped between these patches of darkness as if the shadows made safe places, where no one could see them and nothing could touch them.

Here and there, a drip of water would ping and splash its way to the earth. Up above, there was sometimes a rattle of something moving far away, out of reach. But Zeke heard nothing closer.

"What am I listening for?" he asked.

Rudy's eyes narrowed behind his visor. "For a second there, I thought someone was following us. We can take our masks off soon. We're working our way—"

"Along the hill. Yeah. You said."

"I was *going to say*," Rudy growled, "that we're working our way toward a part of town where there's a little action. We've got to cut through it, and when we do, we'll hit the sealed quarters. And then you can take off your mask."

"So people still live there, at the hill?"

"Yes. Sure they do. Yes," he said again, but his voice died away and he was listening again for something else.

"What's wrong? Are there rotters?" Zeke asked, and started fumbling for his bag.

Rudy shook his head and said, "I don't think so. But something's wrong."

"Someone's following us?"

"Hush up," he said fiercely. "Something's wrong."

Zeke saw it first, the deliberate outline that flowed away from the nearest shadowed patch where nothing could see and nothing could touch them. It did not move so much as it formed, from a vague shape approximately his own size into something with edges—something with clothes, and the white-sharp glint of a button catching the light from the next skylight over.

It came into focus from the shoes up; he detected the curve of boots and the crumpled wrinkles of slouched pants and flexed knees straightening as if to stand. The cuffs of a jacket, the seams of a shirt, and finally a profile that was as jarring as it was distinct.

Zeke's breath caught in his throat, and it was warning enough for Rudy to swivel on his one good heel.

The boy thought it was strange, the way his guide lifted the cane again like it was a weapon; but then he pointed it at the shape against the wall and squeezed some mechanism in its handle. The resulting explosion was every bit as loud, violent, and damaging as any gunshot Zeke had ever heard—which was admittedly not too many.

The shattering clatter of sound and lead rocked the corridor, and the profile ducked away. "Goddammit! Fired too fast!" he swore.

Rudy flipped a lever on his cane with his thumb and pumped it, then aimed again, searching the darkness for the intruder, who had not fallen. Zeke did his best to hide behind the other man as he aimed this way, and that way, and forward, and to each side.

Zeke was breathless and half-deafened by the firearm's concussion. "I saw it!" he squealed. "It was right there! Was that a rotter?"

"No, and hush your mouth! Rotters don't—"

He was cut off by a whistling clink and the sound of something sharply metal carving a sudden, forceful slot into mushy bricks. Then he saw it, beside Rudy's head. A smallish blade with a leather-wrapped handle had landed very close—so close that, given a second or two to ooze, Rudy's ear began to slowly bleed.

"Angeline, that's you, ain't it?" he barked. And then he said lower, "And now I see you better, and if you move, I'll ventilate your insides, I swear to God. Come on out, now. You come out here where I can see you."

"What kind of fool do you take me for?" The speaker had a strange voice and a strange accent. Zeke couldn't place either one.

Rudy said, "The kind of fool who'd like to live another hour. And don't you get all uppity with me, Princess. You shouldn't have worn your brother's buttons if you planned to fight in the dark. I can see the light shining on them," he told her. No sooner were the words out of his mouth than the jacket shimmered and dropped to the ground.

"Son of a bitch!" Rudy shrieked and swayed with his cane. He grabbed Zeke and yanked him backward, into the next black patch where no downward dripping sunlight drizzled.

They hunkered there together and listened for footsteps or motion, but heard nothing until the other unseen speaker said, "Where are you taking that boy, Rudy? What are you going to do with him?"

Zeke thought she sounded as if she were hoarse, or as if her throat had been somehow wounded. Her voice was gummy and harsh, like her tonsils were coated in tar.

"That's no concern of yours, Princess," he said.

Zeke tried not to ask, but he couldn't stop himself from wondering aloud, "Princess?"

"Boy?" said the woman. "Boy, if you've got a lick of sense you'll let that old deserter be. He'll take you no place good and no place safe."

"He's taking me home!" Zeke insisted to the dark.

"He's taking you to your death, or worse. He's taking you to his boss, hoping to trade you for favors. And unless you live down under the old train station that never was, then you're not going home no time soon, no how."

"Angeline, you say another word and I'm going to shoot!" Rudy declared.

"Do it," she dared. "We both know that old stick won't hold more than two rounds at once. So take another shot. I've got blades enough to turn you into a colander, but I won't need that many to slow you down permanent."

"I'm talking to a princess?" Zeke asked again.

Rudy cuffed him across the mouth with something firm and bony wrapped in fabric—Zeke figured it was an elbow, but he couldn't see and he had to assume. His mouth began to seep blood between his teeth. He clutched his face and mumbled every bad word he knew.

"Walk away, Angeline. This ain't no concern of yours."

"I know where you're going, and that boy doesn't. That makes it my concern. You sell your own soul if that's what you've got in mind, but you don't drag nobody else down with you. I won't have it. I especially won't have you leading that boy down into no-man's-land."

"That boy?" Zeke said through his fingers. "I've got a name, lady."

"I know. It's Ezekiel Blue, though your momma calls you Wilkes. I heard you telling him, up on the roof."

Rudy all but shouted, "I'm looking out for him!"

"You're taking him to—"

"I'm taking him someplace safe! I'm just doing what he asked!"

Another knife hissed through the darkness, from shadow to shadow, and it landed close enough to Rudy that he yelped. Zeke didn't hear it connect with the wall behind them. A second knife followed close behind, but it smashed against the bricks. Before a third could join it, Rudy fired, but aimed up instead of out by accident or surprise.

The nearest support beam splintered, crumbled, and fell . . . and the earth and brick wall came tumbling down behind it.

The cave-in spread for yards in each direction, but Rudy was already on his feet and using his cane to drag himself forward. Zeke clung to the man's coat and followed blindly toward the next light up ahead—the next patch where the lavender glass let the sky glow underground.

They scrambled and scuttled forward, and the ceiling sank behind them, putting half an acre of dirt and stone between them and the woman who'd hollered from inside the darkness as black as a grave.

"But we just came this way!" Zeke protested as Rudy hauled him onward.

"Well, now we can't go the other way, so we'll backtrack and drop back down. It's fine. Just come on."

"Who was that?" he asked breathlessly. "Was she really a princess?" Then, with a note of honest confusion he augmented the question. "Was she really a 'she'? She sounded like a man. Kind of."

"She's old," Rudy told him, slowing his pace as he checked over his shoulder and saw only the blockage behind them. "She's old as the hills, mean as a badger, and ugly as homemade sin."

He paused beneath the next patch of purple sky and examined himself, and it was then that Zeke saw all the blood. "Did she get you?" he asked. It was a stupid question and he knew it.

"Yes, she *got* me."

"Where's the knife?" Zeke wanted to know. He stared at the gruesome slit cut into the shoulder of Rudy's coat.

"I pulled it out, back there." He reached into his pocket and removed the weapon. It was sharp, and flush with gore. "No sense in throwing it away. I figure if she tosses it at me, and I catch it, it's mine to keep."

Zeke agreed. "Sure. Are you all right? And where are we going now?"

"I'll live. We're taking that tunnel over there." Rudy pointed. "We came out that one, on our way. The princess has screwed up our course, but we'll do all right going this way. I just wanted to avoid the Chinamen if I could help it, that's all."

The boy had so many questions, he couldn't decide which one to queue up first. He started with his original one, "Who was that lady? Was she really a princess?"

Rudy grudgingly answered, "She's no lady; she's a woman. And I guess she's a princess, if you think the natives have any claim to royalty."

"She's an *Indian* princess?"

"She's an Indian princess same as I'm a well-respected, highly decorated lieutenant. Which is to say, she could make a case for it . . . but at the end of the day, she *ain't*." He poked at his shoulder and grimaced—with anger more than pain, Zeke thought.

"You're a lieutenant? For what army?" he asked.

"Guess."

At the next interlude of light, Zeke stared hard at Rudy's clothes and again noted the dark blue fossils of a uniform. "Union, I guess.

What with the blue and all. And you don't sound like no Southern man I've ever heard, anyway."

"Well, there you go," he said idly.

"But you don't fight with them no more?"

"No, I don't. I think they took plenty out of my hide before spitting me out. How do you think I got the limp? Why do you think I walk with the cane?"

Zeke shrugged and said, "Because you don't want to look like you're armed, but you want to be able to shoot people anyway?"

"Very funny," he said, and he actually sounded like he might be smiling. After a pause that implied he'd given Zeke all the reaction he was planning, he continued. "I took some cannon shrapnel to my backside at Manassas. Tore up my hip but good. They let me go, and I never looked back."

But Zeke was remembering what Angeline had called him, and he pressed the subject. "Then why did that lady call you a deserter? Did you really desert?"

"That *woman* is a lying whore and a killer, too. She's as crazy as can be, and she has some weird feud going on with a man I sometimes work for. She wants to kill him, but she can't, and it makes her mad. So she takes it out on the rest of us." He reached into a nook on the wall and pulled out a candle, then struck a match and explained, "No skylights down this one, not for a bit. We don't need much light, but we'll need a little."

"What was it like?" Zeke asked, changing the subject as much as he was willing to. "Fighting in the war, I mean?"

He grumbled, "It was war, you dumb kid. Everybody I liked got killed, and most of the folks I'd just as soon have shot made it out with medals on their chests. It wasn't fair and it sure as hell wasn't any fun. And Jesus knows it's been going on way too long."

"Everybody says it can't last much longer." Zeke parroted something he'd heard someplace else. "England is talking about pulling its troops out of the South. They might've broke the blockade a long time ago, but—"

"But it's coming back, a little bit at a time," Rudy agreed. "The North is choking them slow, and it's harder on everybody this way. I've got a lot of wishes about it, but you know what they say. 'If wishes were horses, then beggars would ride.'"

Zeke looked confused. "I've never heard that before in my life, and I'm not sure I even know what it means."

"It means that you could spit in one hand and wish in the other, and we all know which hand'll fill up quicker."

He took the candle and held it high, almost high enough to char the wood-beam ceiling above them. All around them the world was wet and bleak. Above them, feet were randomly running here and there, or nowhere in particular. Zeke wondered about the feet, and if they belonged to rotters or to other people, but Rudy didn't seem to know—or if he did, he didn't want to talk about it.

Instead he continued talking about the war. He said, "What I'm saying is, if that general of theirs, that Jackson fellow, had died at Chancellorsville like they thought he was going to—then that would've taken a few years off this thing, and the South would've gone down to its knees that much sooner. But he recovered after all, and he's kept them in the game on that front. That bastard might be blind in one eye, missing an arm, and too scarred-up to recognize on the street, but he's a mean tactical man. I'll give credit where it's due."

He took another turn, this one to the left, and up. A short stack of steps led into another, more finished tunnel—one with skylights, which prompted him to blow out his candle and stash it against the wall. He continued, "And then, of course, if we'd managed to pull that first cross-country railroad up to Tacoma instead of letting it take the southern route, they wouldn't have had such a good transportation system, and that would've knocked another few years off the time they could hold on."

The boy nodded and said, "All right, I get it."

"Good, because what I'm trying to tell you is, there are reasons the war has lasted as long as it has, and most of those reasons have got nothing to do with how hard the South's been fighting. It's been chance, and circumstance. The fact is, the North has a whole lot more people to throw at the fighting, and that's all there is to it. One day, and maybe one day soon, we'll see an end to it."

After a pause, Zeke said, "I hope so."

"Why's that?"

"My mother wants to go east. She thinks it'll be easier for us, once the war's over. Easier for us there than here, anyway." He kicked at a stray crumb of brick and shifted his shoulders underneath his bag. "Living out here is . . . I don't know. It ain't good. It can't be too much worse than someplace else."

Rudy didn't answer right away. But then he said, "I can see why it might be hard for you, and for her, sure. And I've got to wonder how come she didn't take you away when you were smaller. Now you're nearly a man, and you'll be able to leave on your own if it comes to that. I'm almost surprised you haven't taken off to try your hand at soldiering."

Zeke shuffled his feet, and then picked up a steadier pace as Rudy sped up to climb an uncomfortable grade. "I've thought about it," he admitted. "But . . . but I don't know how to get back east, and even if I did manage to catch a dirigible or get on board a supply train, I wouldn't know what to do with myself once I got there. And besides . . ."

"Besides?" Rudy glanced back at him.

"Besides, I wouldn't do that to her. She's sometimes . . . she's sometimes a little mad and sometimes she's real closemouthed, but she does the best she can. She's tried real hard to do right by me, and she works real hard to keep us both fed. That's why I got to hurry this up. I've got to find what I came for and get the hell out of here."

Up ahead, Zeke thought he could hear the chattering patter of conversation—but it was too far away to make any sense to him. "What's that?" he asked. "Who's talking? Should we be quiet now?"

"We should always be quiet," Rudy said. "But, yeah. Those are Chinamen. We'll avoid them if we can."

"And if we can't?"

Rudy's only answer was to start reloading as he limped along. Once he'd locked his weapon into position, he switched back to using it as a cane. He said, "You hear that, up there? That whooshing noise, like a big gust of wind coming and going?"

"I sure do."

"Those are the furnace rooms and the bellows. The Chinamen work them; they're the ones who keep the air down here good and clean, as far as it ever gets good and clean. They pump it down here from up top, by these big ol' tubes they made. It's loud, hot, and dirty, but they keep it up anyway, Christ knows why."

Zeke guessed, "So they can breathe?"

"If they wanted to breathe, all they'd have to do is go someplace else. But they don't. They stay here, and they keep the air pumped down to the sealed blocks, and before long, you'll be able to pull that mask off. I know these things aren't none too comfortable, and I'm real sorry. I thought we'd be in a safe zone by now, but that goddamned bitch had to . . ." He didn't finish the thought, but he rubbed at his shoulder. The bleeding had stopped and gone tacky as it dried.

"So you don't like them, and we can't trust them?"

Rudy said, "That's the long and short of it, yes. It don't make a lick of sense to me why they just don't go home to their women and children. I can't figure out why they've stuck around as long as they have."

"Their women and . . . so it's all a bunch of men?"

"Mostly, but I hear they've got a boy or two inside now, and maybe a couple of old women who wash clothes and cook. How that happened, I couldn't tell you—'cause they sure aren't *supposed* to be here. There was a law, years ago. It kept them from bringing their families here from China. Those folks breed like rabbits, I swear to God, and they were taking over the west. So the government figured it'd be an easy way to keep them from getting settled. We don't mind having them here to work, but we don't want to keep them."

Zeke had some questions about why that might be, but he got the feeling he shouldn't ask them, so he didn't. Instead he said, "All right. I guess I understand. But if they left, who'd pump the clean air?"

"Nobody, I guess," Rudy was forced to admit. "Or somebody else would. I assume. Minnericht would pay somebody, probably. Hell, I don't know."

There was that name again. Zeke enjoyed the consonants in it, the way they rattled around on his tongue when he said it. "Minnericht. You never did tell me who that is."

"Later, kid," Rudy said. "Keep hushed up for now. We're coming up close to Chinatown, and the men here, they don't want anything to do with us. And we don't want anything to do with them. We're going right around the other side of their furnace room. It's loud in there, but those sons of bitches have ears like an eagle has eyes."

Zeke strained to hear. He could catch, yes, there in the background—muffled by the earth around them and the streets above them—a huffing, puffing sound that was too large and slow to be breathing. And the chattering he'd heard . . . as they drew closer, he knew why he couldn't make it out. It was a language he didn't understand, and the syllables meant nothing to him.

"This way. Come on."

The boy kept close to his guide, who seemed at times to be flagging. "Are you all right?" Zeke whispered at him.

And Rudy said, "My shoulder hurts, that's all. And my hip hurts too, but there's not shit to be done about it right now. This way," he repeated his mantra. "Come on."

"If you're hurt, can you really take me up to Denny—"

"I said, *come on.*"

Around the main rooms they sneaked, taking corridors that ran parallel or underneath the rattling factory sounds of the working men. "Not much farther," Rudy told Zeke. "Once we reach the other side, we'll be home free."

"To get to the hill?"

"That's what I told you, wasn't it?"

"Yes sir," Zeke murmured, though he hadn't felt from the changing earth that they were headed up at any point—not really. They'd been sliding down, deeper and farther than he'd thought he ought to be traveling. They'd been tracking lower, and along the ocean shore wall instead of deeper into the city's center.

But now he felt trapped and he did not know what other course to take, so he would follow, he figured. He'd follow until he felt too threatened to do anything else. That was the whole of his plan.

Rudy held up a finger to the end of his mask, and held out the hand holding the cane as if he meant for Zeke to freeze and be silent. An urgency in the gesture successfully held the boy in place while he waited to understand what peril waited around the corner.

When he craned his neck to see, he was downright relieved. A young Chinese man stood hunched over a table that was stacked with lenses, levers, and tubes. His back was to the corridor's entrance where Zeke and Rudy stood. His face was pointed down, hovering intently over something the two intruders couldn't see.

Rudy's hand made a ferocious thrust that told Zeke to hold his position, and not to leave it upon pain of death. It was amazing, how much he could convey with just a few fingers.

Zeke watched Rudy reach into his pocket again and pull out the knife that the princess had thrown into his arm. The blade was no longer wet, but under the dried blood it flashed in Rudy's hand.

The man at the table was wearing a long leather apron, and his back looked hunched. He wore glasses and was bald as an apple except for that long ponytail. He might be old enough to be someone's father, somewhere. As Zeke looked the man over, it dawned on him that this man might be uninterested in doing anyone any harm.

But it did not dawn on him in time to say anything. He'd later wonder: Even if he'd thought to call out . . . would he have done so?

But he didn't think.

Rudy slipped up behind the smaller man, seized him, and wiped the sharp edge of the blade across his throat as Rudy's good arm covered the other man's mouth. The Chinese man struggled, but the assault had been swift.

In their fight, they swirled and pirouetted like two men waltzing. Zeke was astonished by how much blood there was. It looked like gallons, gushing in a crimson cascade from a cut that ran from earlobe to earlobe. As the men swayed and spun, they flung it in a fountain's spray and doused the lenses, levers, and tubes.

Zeke slumped down the wall, his back braced against the door frame and his hands over his own mouth to keep it quiet. When he pressed there, he remembered the bruising punch of Rudy's elbow and a fragile patch on his gums began to bleed again.

He thought for a moment that he could taste the copper-orange pouring of blood that stained the man's leather apron and the floor, leaving smeared and smudged footprints from board to board, but then remembered that it was only his own pain, in his own mouth.

Knowing this did not change his macabre impression, and it made him feel no less like throwing up.

But he was wearing a mask, and to take it off would mean certain choking death. So he swallowed the impulse, and the bile, and suppressed the need to eject some terrible taint from his body.

And then, as the corpse fell limp in Rudy's grasp, and Rudy kicked it underneath the table where the Chinaman had so recently worked, Zeke noticed that he had worn no mask.

"He . . ." Zeke gagged on his own fluids.

"Don't get all soft on me now, boy. He would've handed us over as fast as he would've said, 'Hello.' Get yourself together. We've got to get out of here before anyone notices what we've done."

"He . . ." The boy tried again. "Wasn't . . . didn't have . . . isn't wearing . . ."

"A mask?" Rudy caught on. "No, he wasn't. And we'll pull ours off soon enough. But not yet. We might get chased topside before our trip is over." As he dashed a lurching escape down the next door over, he whispered, "It's better to have them and not need them, then need them and not have them."

"Right," Zeke said, and he said it again in order to have something in his mouth other than vomit. "Right. I'm . . . I'm following you."

Rudy said, "Attaboy. Now stick close."

## Eleven

At the bottom of the stairs Briar stumbled into a mostly empty room with a floor that was sinking below its original foundation. It sagged and dipped, a foot or more at the room's center and a few inches along its edges. Down there, coal was stashed in big mining carts that had been wheeled directly to their location through a tunnel cut into the brick.

The tunnel was surprisingly well lit, and since no other logical direction presented itself, Briar pushed past the carts with their black-dusted cargo.

There were no tracks in the tunnel, but the floor had been packed hard and paved with stones in places, so the carts could be rolled—possibly with the aid of machinery, or so Briar inferred from the scattered chains and cranks that were anchored in the walls and floors.

From beam to beam, long segments of knotted rope were strung up high, and, from the rope, glass lanterns hung in steel cages.

As if it were a trail of bread crumbs, Briar followed the rope as fast as she could push herself. She still held Maynard's rifle out and ready to be lifted or fired, but it mostly swung underneath her arm as she ran. She saw no other people coming or going, and if the Chinamen were following her, they were doing so quietly. Nothing like the rumbling rush of feet echoed behind her, and nothing like voices, coughs, or laughter chimed out from her destination.

Perhaps fifty yards down the line, under the row of whichever businesses occupied the block, the tunnel split into four directions, each one covered by the same long leather or rubber-treated flaps that had curtained the hallway outside the bellows room.

She pushed the flaps aside a tiny crack, just enough to peer past them.

Two directions were lit; two were dark. One of the bright corridors resonated with an argument. The other was quiet. She hastily took the quieter lit passage and hoped for the best. But in another twenty feet, the passage dead-ended against an iron gate that could've held back a herd of elephants.

The gate stuck up out of the ground where its pilings had been buried somewhere far below, and deeply, for more than mere appearance. It leaned out at a determined angle, intended to repel some astonishing force with the pointed tips of its topmost pikes. On the other side of the leaning gate Briar saw a tight wooden wall wrapped with barbed wire. The timbers looked as if they'd once been on the ground, functioning as railroad ties, but there was a horizontal latch where an immense wooden arm could be levered up and out—and as Briar looked more closely, she could see cracks where a door was cut, or pressed, or jammed into place.

She grasped at the gate, feeling along its bars until her fingers fumbled at a lifting lock. It wasn't fastened, only slipped into place so it was easy to move.

She gripped the latch and pulled, but the door didn't budge.

So she pushed. It groaned forward, and a gust of air puffed into the underground chamber. Briar didn't need to smell the gas through the mask or look through her fragment of polarized lens to know it was there.

On the other side, she found a set of stone stairs. The stairs led up and out, but no farther down.

She didn't give herself time to change her mind or look for another way through the situation. Up on the street she could get her bearings. She flattened herself sideways and squeezed past a wooden door onto the stairwell. She used her backside to push the door shut and lifted the rifle again, forcing her hands to steady and her attention to focus, because here she was, in Seattle proper. Inside the wall, with the terrible things that were trapped within it, and terrible people, too, for all she knew of it.

The rifle made her feel safer. She squeezed it hard and silently thanked her late father for his taste in firearms.

Up the steps she couldn't see a thing except for a sharp rectangle of hard ash gray, and it wasn't even the gray of the sky. It was the permanent dusk imposed by the height of the wall, its shadow blocking out even the weak, drizzling sunlight that came for a few hours each day during the winter.

"What street is this?" Briar asked herself. Her own voice wasn't much more comfort than the rifle. "What street?"

Something was odd about the door, she thought, but it didn't occur to her until she was past it that there had been no external latch, knob, or even a lock. It was a door designed to keep people out unless they had the permission of those already secured there.

It almost gave her a flash of panic, knowing that now, even if she needed to, she could not retreat. But retreat wasn't part of the plan, anyway.

The plan was *up*. The plan was to reach the street, scout for street markers, acquire her bearings, and then set out for . . .

Where? Well. There was always home.

The house on the side of the hill hadn't been home for very long, only a few months; and since she now knew there were people inside the wall, she could safely bet that the house had been raided for the bulk of its valuables. But there might be something useful remaining. Leviticus had made so many machines, and he'd hidden so much of his best and favorite devices in tricky, closed-off rooms that might've gone overlooked.

And besides—she knew nothing of Ezekiel's plans except that he'd wanted to see his father's laboratory and hunt for exonerating evidence there.

Did Ezekiel even know where the house was located?

Briar rather thought that he didn't; but then again, she'd also thought he couldn't get inside the city, and she'd been quite wrong on that point. He was a resourceful boy; she had to give him that. Her wisest course of action might be to simply assume that he'd succeeded.

While she lurked at the bottom of the chipped stone stairs, down in the darkness as if she were sitting in a well, Briar slowly caught her breath and found her psychic footing. No one shoved the door open and discovered her. Not a sound reached her ears—not even the clanging racket of the machine works in the building at her back.

It might not be so bad.

She leaned one booted toe forward and placed it quietly on the nearest stair. The second step was climbed with equal slowness and silence. While her mask-impaired side vision permitted it, Briar watched the door behind her shrink as she rose.

She'd heard stories about the rotters, and she'd seen a few of them in the first days after the Blight broke, but how many could possibly be left inside the city? Surely at some point they would die, or fail, or decay, or simply succumb to the elements. They must be in terrible shape, and weak as kittens if they still crawled or shambled.

Or that is what she told herself as she climbed.

Bending her knees to crouch, she kept her head below the crest of the stairwell until the last possible moment, and then she craned her neck to see without exposing herself to whatever might wait above.

More dark than bright, the city was not quite so bleak that she'd need a light, but it wouldn't be long before the tar-thick shadows of the walls and the roofs would cast the whole scene into early midnight.

The street crumbled at Briar's eye level, slick and muddy from rainwater and Blight runoff. Its bricks split and spread. The whole surface was uneven and lumpy, and it was littered with debris. Carts sprawled overturned and broken; the mostly dismembered and long-decayed corpses of horses and dogs were scattered into piles of sticky bones, loosely connected by stringy, green-gray tissue.

Briar swiveled her head slowly left, then right. She couldn't see far in any direction.

Between the dimness and the concentrated, thickened air, no more than half a block could be discerned at once. Which way the streets ran, there was no telling. North and south, east and west, none of it meant anything without the sun to guess it by.

Not even the faintest gust of air ruffled Briar's hair, and she couldn't hear the water, or the birds. Once upon a time there had been birds by the thousands, most of them crows and seagulls, all of them loud. Together the tribes had made a mighty racket of feathers and clacking calls, and the silence without them was strange. No birds, no people. No machines or horses.

Nothing moved.

Leading with her left hand, Briar crept up and out of her hole on leather-soled feet that didn't make a sound to disturb the disturbing silence.

Finally she stood out in the open, close against the building beside the stairs.

The only sound was the rustle of her own hair against the straps and sides of the face mask, and when she quit moving, even that faint tickle of noise ceased.

She was standing on an incline, and she could see a place downhill where the incline increased sharply—dropping off and out of sight. At the edges of the drop-off, there were stalls filled with empty bins. And off to the side, and up, as Briar explored the scene with her eyes, she saw the remains of a half-toppled sign and an enormous clock without any hands.

And this must be . . . "The market. I'm near Pike Street."

She almost said it aloud, but then merely mouthed the observation. The street made a dead end at the market, and on the other side of the market was the Sound—or it would've been, if the wall hadn't cut the shoreline away from it.

The building at her back must face Commercial Avenue, the street that once ran alongside the ocean and now ran alongside the wall.

For the next few blocks, any of the streets that paralleled Pike would take her in roughly the direction she'd chosen.

She hugged close to the building, aiming rifle and eyes up and down the street as she shuffled sideways. Breathing inside the mask hadn't become any easier, but she was growing accustomed to it and there was no alternative, anyway. Her chest was sore from the extra effort her muscles were making to inflate and deflate her lungs, and down at one corner of her left eyepiece, the view was getting foggy from condensation.

Heading uphill ever so slightly, she worked her way away from the wall, which she couldn't even see. Briar knew that its tall blank shadow reached up into the sky, but it vanished from view far sooner and it was easy to forget, especially when she'd turned away from it.

Through her head ran endless calculations. How far was she from the lavender house on the hill? How long would it take to reach it if she ran? If she walked? If she skulked like this, squeezing between the tendrils of low-lying, stinking fog?

She flexed her cheek, trying to shake the condensation and make it gather or roll.

It didn't work. The vapor clung to the mask.

She sighed, and a second sigh gave it a funny echo.

Confused, she shook her face. It must have been a trick of the straps, or the way the device fit around her forehead. It could've been her hair, brushing against the exterior. It might've been her boots, scraping unexpectedly against a jagged paving stone. The sound could've come from anywhere. It was so quiet, anyway. Hardly a sound at all, really.

Her feet wouldn't move. Neither would her arms, or her hands, locked around the rifle. Even her neck would barely turn, lest she re-create the noise, or fail to. The only thing worse than hearing it again would be hearing it again and knowing it hadn't come from her own careful movements.

So slowly that even her long coat didn't tap itself against her legs, Briar retreated, feeling with her heels, praying that there was nothing behind her. Her heel found a curb, and stopped there.

She stepped up onto it.

The sound came again. There was a whistle to it, and a moan. It was almost a hiss, and it could've been a strangled gasp. Above all, it was quiet, and it seemed to have no source.

It whispered.

Briar tried to place the sound, and she decided, now that she'd heard it again and could be certain she hadn't imagined it, that it came from somewhere to her left, down toward the wall. It was coming from the street stalls where nothing had been bought or sold in almost sixteen years.

The whisper rose to a hum, and then stopped.

Briar stopped too—or she would have, if she hadn't already. She wanted to freeze herself further, to make herself inaudible and invisible, but there was nowhere to hide—not in her immediate range of vision. The deep old stalls were behind her. All the doors were barred with boards nailed tight around them, and all the windows had likewise been covered. The corner of a stone building pressed against her shoulder when she leaned away from the market.

The noise stopped.

This new kind of quiet was even more frightening than the old kind, which was simply empty. Now it was worse, because the foggy, cluttered landscape was not merely silent. Now it was holding its breath, and listening.

Briar removed her left hand from the rifle and reached backward until she touched the corner. Finding it, and feeling it, she guided herself to the far side of the building. It was no real protection, but it put her out of the market's line of sight.

The mask was squeezing tight around her face. The condensation on one side was driving her to distraction, and the smell of rubber and toast clogged her throat.

She needed to sneeze, but she chewed on her tongue until the feeling passed.

Around the corner, the whispered wheeze rustled through the calm.

It halted, then began again, louder. And then it was joined by a second hacking gasp, and a third, and then there were too many to count.

Briar wanted to crush her eyes closed and hide from the noises, but she couldn't even take a moment to peer around the side of the building to see what was making the cacophony, because it was escalating. There was nothing she could do but run.

The middle of the road was mostly clear, so she took it, weaving between the overturned carts and leaping past slabs of earthquake-loosened walls that had collapsed into the road.

Silence was no longer an option.

Briar's feet smacked against the bricks and her rifle slapped up and down on her hip as she charged downhill, even though she'd meant to go the other direction. She couldn't run uphill; she didn't have enough air to struggle any harder. So down, then. Down the hill but not—she thought in a flickering moment of hope—strictly the wrong direction. She was running alongside the wall, and alongside the water behind it. Commercial would go down, yes—but it flanked the hill all the same and she could follow it as far as she needed.

She risked a glance, and then a second glance, and then she stopped trying, because she'd been terribly, terribly wrong—and they were coming in *fast*.

Those two quick looks had told her everything she needed to know: Run, and for heaven's sake, don't stop.

They were not quite on her heels. They were rounding the corner in a loping, ludicrous hobble that was shockingly fast despite the awkward gait. More naked than clothed, and more gray than the proper color of living flesh, the rotters pressed a rollicking lurch that tumbled in a wave. They rolled forward, over everything, past everything, around everything that might have otherwise slowed them down.

Without fear and without pain, they beat their ragged bodies against the litter in the street and bounced away from it, not deterred and not redirected. They smashed through water-weakened wood and stomped through the corpses of animals, and if any other rotters tripped or fell they crawled a vicious assault over the bodies of their own.

Briar remembered all too well those first sad, shambling people who'd been poisoned by the Blight. Most of the victims had died outright, but a few had lingered—and they'd groaned, and gasped, and consumed. They had no other thoughts beyond consuming, and they wished for nothing but fresh, bloody flesh. Animals would suffice. People were preferred, insomuch as the rotters had any preference for anything.

And right then, they had no preference for anything but Briar.

The first time she'd taken a backward look, she'd seen four. The second time, a half moment later, she'd seen eight. God only knew how many were on her tail by the time she'd reached the next road down.

She stumbled over a curb and hit the walkway running.

In passing, she saw a line of tall letters engraved into the surface of the sidewalk, but she was moving too quickly to read it so she didn't know which cross street she'd passed. It didn't matter. The cross street was heading up the hill, and she never would have made it.

Her air was already too low, from even such a short and incline-assisted flight. Her throat was burning from the stress of it, and she had no idea how long she could continue. Her slim lead shrank as she dodged and ducked through the fog.

A narrow iron pole zipped past her vision, followed closely by a second one.

It was a ladder for a fire escape, or so she realized only when it was entirely too late to grab it and begin climbing.

She couldn't decide if the missed opportunity was just as well or not. It might only exhaust her further, trying to rise so drastically above the fray; but then again, it might have saved her. Could the rotters follow her up?

The gargling gasps of their furious hunger hit closer to Briar's ears, and she knew they were gaining ground. It wasn't only that they were quick. It was that she was slowing, and there was nothing she could do to move herself harder. Try as she might, she couldn't pant or puff, and there was only so much escaping she could do.

The mist never parted, but it thinned in spots and thickened in others. For one revealing second the side of another building came into view and another iron ladder blinked into range.

Briar almost didn't see it. The fog at her left eye nearly hid it.

She didn't have time to reconsider or weigh the pros and cons; she just seized the ladder, jerking herself to a stop against her own inertia. She locked her hands around the ladder's legs and pulled with all her weight.

Her feet kicked against the wall and against the bottommost rungs, then they caught footing enough to scramble up one step.

The closest rotter missed her boots, but snagged her father's duster and gave it a yank.

Briar's gloved hands slipped and skidded on the rungs, but she clamped down hard and held her position. She wrenched her arms up under the rusty bars and anchored herself so she could kick, and kick she did. She couldn't hope to harm the things, but she could push them back or break their fingers—anything to force them to let go.

She couldn't rise with the rotter's weight dragging on the coat, so they hung there, suspended, as the rest of the horde swarmed in for the kill.

Briar swung her body back and forth, trying to shake the thing loose. Its elbows and skull thunked dully against the wall and made a little twanging echo when they hit the metal ladder.

Finally, some magically lucky combination of kicks and shakes cast the beast down to his fellows. The other rotters tried to step on him to give themselves more reach as they grabbed with their bony, chewed-looking hands, but Briar was high enough that they couldn't reach her unless they scaled the rungs.

But could they?

She didn't know, and she didn't look. She only climbed, one hand up, one foot up. Other hand up, other foot up. Soon she was beyond the grasp of even the tallest, longest-armed monstrosity. But there was no stopping, not yet. Not when the shaking and rattling of the ladder suggested that yes, they would follow—or, if not follow, they would pull the ladder off the wall and bring her back to them. As far as the rotters were concerned, there was no such thing as a "hard way."

Bolts on either side of Briar's head began to squeal as they split and tugged away from their moorings.

"Oh God," she gasped, and might've used worse language if she'd had any breath to do so. Up ahead, the ladder's destination was obscured by the yellowish stain of the fog. It might end in ten feet, or in ten floors for all Briar knew.

Ten floors were not an option. She'd never make it.

The ladder swayed and popped with a terrifying jolt, and one supporting rail gave way. Before she could be swung out over the street, Briar slapped a hand down on the nearest window ledge and hung on—her grip split between the wide stone sill and the remaining leg of the ladder. The ladder was swaying and bending, and she would not have it long.

Under her arm, the rifle clattered against the sill.

She braced as much of her weight as she dared on the wobbling rungs, let go of the sill, and swung the rifle around hard. It exploded through the glass, and Briar barely had enough balance to hang on as she leaped toward the window.

Her leap failed, and only her right leg made the catch.

Splinter-sharp shards dug into the underside of her leg, but she ignored them and tightened her thigh to pull herself closer to the window.

Locked that way, half inside and half outside, she brought the rifle around and pointed it down. One bald and deeply scarred head reared into view, and Briar thanked God that she'd loaded the gun while she had the chance.

She fired. The head split and exploded, and bright brown bits splattered against her gas mask. Until the bloody flecks of bone slid down her lenses, she hadn't known that the thing had made it so close.

Right behind the first rotter was a second, pushing its way higher.

It didn't get very far. Its left eye burst into a watery splatter of brains and bile and it fell away, leaving one of its half-decomposed hands behind it, still clinging to the rung. The third rotter was farther down the ladder, and it took Briar two shots to knock it away: The first grazed the thing's forehead, and the second one caught it in the throat and broke the important bones that held its head in place. The jaw dropped down and fell off just as the head lolled back and snapped free.

Rotter number three's downward fall forcibly removed number four from the climb, and rotter number five's face shattered when a bullet went up its nose.

More were coming, but the ladder was cleared. Briar took the brief respite to haul herself into the broken window. Small slivers of glass still stung in her leg, but there was no time yet to remove them, not when more rotters were figuring out the joy of climbing.

She braced herself from the inside and reached out with her rifle, not firing again but using it as a lever against the half-ruined bolts that held the iron structure in place. One side was already gone, and the second one screeched and stretched as she worked the rifle back and forth, wiggling the old bolts loose until they abandoned their moorings. Slowly, but without any real protest, the ladder came leaning away from the building until the angle was too steep to hold it anymore, and it collapsed.

Rotters six through eight went down with it, but did not stay down, and there were more behind them.

They writhed and raged below, three stories below by Briar's count.

She retreated from the window and tried to catch her breath—which was a permanent activity, now; then she twisted herself around to pick at the glass that had lodged in her leg.

She winced as she smoothed the back of her pants. She hated to expose any skin to the Blight, but she couldn't feel the damage without removing her gloves. She pulled the right one free and did her best to ignore the slimy wet air.

It could've been worse.

She didn't find anything bigger than a sunflower seed. There was hardly any blood, but the broken fabric let the Blight irritate the scratches, and it stung more fiercely than it should have. If she'd had bandages, or wraps, or any other stray and clean piece of fabric she would've wrapped the minor injury. But she had nothing, and there was nothing to be done except to make sure it was free of glass.

This having been established, she took a moment to examine her surroundings.

She had not landed in the top floor of anything, as the staircase at the far wall demonstrated; and at one point in time her stopping place had almost certainly been a hotel. On the floor in front of the window there was a great smattering of broken glass, some of which had landed on a battered old bed with a brass headboard that had gone a nastily tarnished brown. A half-broken nightstand crouched against a wall, two drawers out on the floor, and a basin with a broken pitcher had fallen over in the corner.

The floor creaked when she stepped across it, but the noise was no worse than the rumbling havoc outside, where more rotters were collecting, having been drawn by the cries of the others. Eventually they would break their way in, more likely than not; and eventually the filters in Briar's mask would clog, and she'd suffocate.

But Briar could worry about these things later. For the moment, she was safe. Or at least, she was safer than she had been a handful of moments before. Her definition of "safe" was increasingly flexible.

Looking out the window, she could see an intersection below, where Commercial met some other thoroughfare coming down the hill. Rotters swarmed over the spot on the corner where the street's name would be marked. It didn't matter which one it was; it didn't matter that she hadn't caught the engraving in the ground to tell her more precisely. The streets were impossible now. Perhaps they'd been impossible for sixteen years. But she'd given it a go, and it had been her best effort. She'd been quiet and she'd been careful, and it hadn't been enough. So this was it, then. The streets were navigated the same as the wall.

Over or under. It would cost too much to go straight *through*.

Briar went to the stairwell and pushed aside the door that had dropped from its hinges. Surely it went up no more than another floor or two. She'd go up, first, and see what it looked like from there.

Inside the stairwell it was purely and perfectly dark. The noise of the rotters outside was muffled until it was almost absent, and she could almost forget they were out there, loudly waiting and demanding her bones.

But not quite. Their arguments vibrated in her ears and tugged at her attention, no matter how hard she tried to push them out. Behind her eyes she remembered too clearly the peeling, gray fingers that had clung disembodied to the ladder—persistent to the very last.

Her composure was returning, and with it, her breathing was slowing as she paced herself, scaling the stairs with a measured speed that let her body catch up and adjust.

At the top of the stairs she found a door that opened onto the roof; and on the roof were a few signs of recent life. A broken pair of goggles had been kicked into a corner. A discarded bag had been crumbled and left to soak in a puddle of tar and water. Footprints smudged in coal crossed here and there.

She followed the footprints to the roof's edge. They disappeared on the ledge, and she wondered if the rooftop pedestrians had jumped or fallen. Then she saw the next building over. It was a taller structure by one full story, and there was a window on perfect parallel with the spot where she stood. This window had been boarded over with two doors that had been pieced together to form one much longer plank; and this plank was fastened up against the other building—left there like a drawbridge, to be lowered or raised depending on the necessity and danger.

Below, one of the rotters had followed her around to the far side. It looked up with a revolting moan, and soon it was joined by more undead with similar intentions. In a matter of minutes, the whole building would be surrounded by them.

As far as Briar could tell, the other building was wholly unoccupied. The windows were boarded or blank, with thin, sloppily drawn curtains and nothing moving on the other side of them.

She might have better luck downstairs. She'd emerged in the city through the underground, so underground might be the best way to travel.

Not very far away, and directly beneath her, something splintered and broke. The moans increased in their intensity, from added numbers and fresh agitation.

Briar reached for her satchel and hastily reloaded. If the rotters had breached the building, she might have to shoot her way through them on the way to the basement.

Her hands paused as they held the canister of shells, but only briefly.

If she went downstairs and they came behind her, she'd be trapped there.

She recommenced loading the rifle, and fast. Trapped downstairs, trapped upstairs. The differences were small, and she was damned either way. Better to keep her gun ready and her options open.

The cacophony escalated, and Briar wondered if she hadn't already lost the option of seeking a subterranean escape. She locked the cartridges into place and took another look over the edge.

On the street the swarm gathered and clotted. The number of rotters had at least tripled, more than making up for the small handful she'd dispatched on her way up the hotel's exterior.

She did not see anyplace where they'd found entry. They did not disappear one by one or even in clumps to resume their pursuit; instead they flung themselves at the bricks and the boards, but made no progress.

Again there came a crashing noise and the telltale shattering of damp wood.

Where was it? And what was causing it?

The rotters howled and staggered. They also heard the breaking commotion and sought its source, but they were unwilling to leave Briar, who felt very much like a bear that had been treed.

"*You, up on the Seaboard Hotel! Are you wearing a mask?*"

The voice shocked her worse than the rotters had. It burst out loud and hard, with a tinny edge that made it sound both foreign and loud. The words carried up from somewhere below, but not all the way down in the street.

"*I said, hey up there—you on the Seaboard. You on the roof. Have you got a mask or are you dying?*"

Briar hadn't seen any indication that this was the Seaboard, but she couldn't imagine who else the voice could be addressing. So she answered, as loud as she could, "Yes! I've got a mask!"

"*What?*"

"I said, I've got a mask!"

"*I can hear you, but I can't understand you for shit—so I hope that means you've got a mask! Whoever you are, get down and cover your goddamned ears!*"

She looked frantically back and forth across the small sea of rotters, seeking the source of the instructions. "Where are you?" she tried to shout back, and it was ridiculous because she knew that wherever the speaker was, he'd never catch the question over the roiling symphony of the undead on the street.

"*I said,*" the low voice with the metallic edge repeated, "*get down and cover your goddamned ears!*"

Across the road, looking out from another broken window in another broken building, Briar glimpsed motion. Something bright and blue glimmered sharply, then winked out—only to be followed by a brighter light and a high-pitched, whirring hum. The hum carried up through the Blight and whistled past her hair, delivering a determined warning directly into her brain.

She didn't need to be told a third time.

She ducked, flinging herself into the nearest corner and throwing her arms up over her head. Her elbows clenched tight around her ears and muffled them, but it wasn't enough to keep out the needle-sharp wheedling of the electric whine. She pulled up her satchel and wrapped it around her skull, and she was still holding that position, facedown against the tar paper and bricks, when a blast pulsed through the blocks with a gut-turning pop that lasted far too long to be the report of a gun.

When the worst of the shattering, thundering audio blow had dissipated, Briar heard the almost-mechanical voice gargle out another set of instructions, but she couldn't hear it and she couldn't move.

Her eyes were jammed shut, her arms were locked around her head, her knees were fixed in place beneath her body, and she couldn't budge any of them. "I can't," she whispered, trying to convey, "I can't hear you," but her jaw was stuck, too.

*"Get up now! GET UP, NOW!"*

"I can't. . . ."

*"You have about three minutes to get your ass up and get down here before the rotters get their bearings back, and when that happens, I'm going to be gone! If you want to stay alive in here, you need me, you crazy bastard!"*

Briar muttered, "Not a bastard," at the distinctly masculine tirade. She tried to focus her irritation and turn it into a motive to move. It worked no better and no worse than the screamed demands with their monstrous inflections.

Joint by joint she unfixed her arms and legs, and she stuttered to her knees.

She dropped to them again in order to retrieve the rifle, which had slid down off her shoulder. Heaving that shoulder to retrieve the strap, she once again forced her boots up underneath herself. Her ears were ringing with that horrible sound, and with the horrible cries of the man down on the street—he wouldn't stop yelling, even though she'd lost her capacity to understand him. She couldn't stand, walk, and listen at the same time, not so shaken as she was.

Behind her, the door to the stairwell was still open, sagging on its latch.

She fell against it, and nearly fell down the subsequent steps. Only her momentum and her instinct for balance kept her upright and moving forward. Her body swayed and tried to tumble, but the longer she remained on her feet, the easier it became to stay that way. By the time she'd reached the first floor she was almost running again.

Down in the lobby, all the windows were covered and it was darker than midnight except for the spots where slivers of the dim afternoon light leaked drably through the cracks. As Briar's eyes corrected themselves to account for the dark, she saw that the desk was covered with dust and the floor was crisscrossed with more black footprints.

There was a big front door with a massive plank across it.

Briar yanked it up and rattled the door's handles.

The panic she felt was amazing. She would've sworn that she'd exhausted her store of manic fear, but when the door wouldn't budge she felt another surge. She shook it and tried to yell through it, "Hello? Hello? Are you out there?"

Even to her own ears the cry was garbled. No one on the other side could possibly hear it, and it was stupid of her, anyway—she should've gone back downstairs and risked another ladder. Why had she gone all the way to the ground floor? What had she been thinking?

Her head was humming with leftover pain and her eyes were swimming with static.

"Help me, please, get me out of here!"

She beat the door with the butt of her rifle, and it created a magnificent racket.

Seconds later, another racket met it from the other side.

*"What the hell's the matter with you? Should've gone down the outside!"* the shouty voice accused.

"Tell me about it," she grumbled, relieved to hear the other person even though she didn't know if he planned to help her or kill her on sight. Whoever he was, he'd gone to trouble enough to make contact, and that was something. Wasn't it?

She said, louder, "Get me out of here!"

"*Get away from the door!*"

Having learned her lesson about responding fast, she sidestepped her way around the hotel's front desk. A new and catastrophic crash bowed the front door inward, but didn't break it. A second assault cracked the thing's hinges, and a third took it clear off the frame.

An enormous man hurtled through it, then dragged himself to a stop.

"*You—*" He pointed and stopped himself midthought. "*Are a woman.*"

"Very good," Briar said, wobbling out from behind the desk.

"*All right. Come with me, and do it fast. We haven't got a minute before they start reviving.*"

The man with the tinny voice was speaking through a helmet that gave his face the shape of a horse's head crossed with a squid. The mask ended in an amplifier down front, and it split into two round filters that aimed off to either side of his nose. The contraption looked heavy, but then again, so did the man who was wearing it.

He wasn't fat at all, but he was nearly as wide as the doorway— though the effect was enhanced by his armor. His shoulders were plated with steel, and a high, round collar rose up behind his neck to meet the helmet. Where his elbows and wrists bent, makeshift chain mail functioned as joints. Across his torso, thick leather straps held the whole thing taut and close.

It was as if someone had taken a suit of armor and made it into a jacket.

"*Lady, we haven't got all night,*" he told her.

She began to say that it wasn't night, yet, but she was winded and worried, and irrationally glad for the company of this heavily armed man. "I'm coming," she said. She stumbled and knocked against his arm, then righted herself.

He didn't grab her to help, but he didn't push her away, either. He only turned around and headed back out the door.

She followed. "What was that *thing*?" she asked.

"*Questions later. Watch your step.*"

The street and walkways were littered with the tangled, twitching, growling bodies of rotters. Briar's first steps took trouble to avoid them, but her escort was outpacing her, so she abandoned the approach and moved from corpse to corpse without regard for where her feet might land. Her boots broke arms and stomped through ribcages. Her heel landed too close against a dead woman's face and scraped down her skull, dragging a sheet of flaky skin with it and leaving the flesh wiped upon the stones.

"Wait," she begged.

"*No waiting. Look at them,*" he said, as he too disregarded the quivering rotters.

Briar thought it was a ridiculous instruction. She couldn't help but look at them; they were everywhere—underfoot and down the road, flattened against curbs and leaning against bricks with their tongues lolling and their eyes fluttering.

But she thought she understood the armored man's meaning. Animation was returning to their limbs. Their jerking hands moved harder, and with more deliberation. Their kicking feet were twisting and turning, trying to work themselves up to a standing position. Every second that passed, they gathered their wits—such as they were—or at least gathered their intuitive sense of motion.

"*This way. Faster.*"

"I'm trying!"

"*That's not good enough.*" He threw back a hand and seized her wrist. He yanked her forward, lifting her as lightly as a toddler over another stack of restless, prone rotters.

One of the gruesome things held up a hand and tried to grab Briar's ankle.

She kicked at its twiggy arm but she missed, because the man in the mask shifted his grip on her wrist and pulled again, past one last clump of bodies where a rotter was sitting up and moaning, trying to rouse its brethren.

"*All right, it's a straight shot now,*" the man said.

"A straight shot to what?"

"*To the underground. Hurry. This way.*"

He indicated a stone-faced structure adorned with the mournful statues of owls. A legend across the front door declared that the place had once been a bank. The front door was nailed shut with the remains of shattered shipping crates, and the windows were covered with bars.

"How do we—?"

"*Stay close. Up, then down.*"

Around the side there were no helpful fire escapes with dangling ladders, but when Briar looked up she could see the underside of a rickety balcony.

The man in the steel jacket pulled an ugly hooked hammer out from his belt and tossed it up. It trailed a long hemp rope behind it, and when it snagged somewhere above, the man yanked on the rope and a set of stairs unfolded. They clanked down with all the loud, rhythmic grace of a drawbridge descending too quickly.

He caught the bottom stair and strained to hold it low. It hung at Briar's waist level.

"*Up.*"

Briar nodded and slung her rifle over her back, freeing both hands for climbing.

It wasn't fast enough to suit the man, who reached up with one broad palm and heaved it against her rear. The added jolt boosted her enough to fasten both hands and both feet securely onto the structure, so she wasn't prepared to make any complaints about the ungentlemanly gesture.

Her body's weight was pendulum enough to hold the stairs in a hovering position over the street. When the man's weight joined hers, the whole structure creaked and jerked, but held steady. The folding stairs did not wish to hold them both, and they made their displeasure known with every ominously squeaking step.

Briar tuned it out and climbed, and the stairs rose up underneath her like a seesaw as the man behind her caught up to her heels.

He patted at the back of her boot to get her attention. *"Here. Second floor. Don't break the window. It lifts out."*

She nodded and hauled herself off the steps, onto the balcony. The window was barred but not blockaded. Down at the bottom, a wooden latch had been affixed. She pried it up and the window popped out of its frame.

The man joined her on the balcony, and the steps bounced up behind him. Having lost their counterweight, the springs that dropped and lifted it coiled back into place and remained firm, holding the stairs beyond the reach of even the tallest rotters with the longest arms.

Briar lowered her head, turned herself sideways, and wiggled inside.

The armored man squeezed himself in after her. Much of the urgency had drained away from him; once he was above the rotters and safely inside the old bank building, he relaxed and took a moment to adjust his accoutrements.

He unhooked his armor and stretched his arms, and cracked his neck from side to side. The clawed hammer with the rope required rewinding, so he twisted it between his palm and his elbow until it made a loop, and then he clipped it back onto his belt. He reached into a holster over his shoulder and set aside a tube-shaped device that was longer than his thigh. It was shaped like a huge gun, but the trigger was a brass paddle and there was a grate across the barrel that was not altogether different from the grate in his mask.

Briar asked, "Is that what made the noise? The one that stunned the rotters?"

*"Yes, ma'am,"* he said. *"This is Dr. Minnericht's Doozy Dazer, or plain old 'Daisy' for short. It's a mighty piece of equipment and I'm proud to call it mine, but it has its limitations."*

"Three minutes?"

*"Three minutes, give or take. That's right. The power supply's in the back end."* He pointed to the handle, wrapped with tiny copper pipes and slender glass tubes. *"It takes forever to charge the thing back up again."*

"Forever?"

*"Well, about a quarter of an hour. Depending."*

"On what?"

He said, *"Static electricity. Don't ask me any more than that, because I don't know the particulars."*

She politely admired the blasting device. "I've never seen anything like it. Who's this Dr. Minnericht?"

*"He's an ass, but sometimes he's a useful ass. So now I have to ask, who are you and what are you doing here, in our fine and filthy city?"*

"I'm looking for my son," she dodged the first half of his question. "I think he came here yesterday; he came up through the old water runoff tunnels."

*"Tunnels are closed,"* he said.

"Now they are, yes. Earthquake." She leaned against the windowsill and sat there, too exhausted to bother with too many words. "I'm sorry," she said, and she meant it for a variety of reasons. "I'm so . . . I knew about the city—I knew it was bad in here. I knew, but . . ."

*"Yeah, it's that 'but' that'll kill you if you're not careful. So you're looking for your boy."* He checked her up and down. *"How old are you?"* he asked outright, since he couldn't see her face very well behind her mask.

"Old enough to have a son who's dumb enough to come in here," she countered. "He's fifteen. Have you seen him?"

*"He's fifteen—that's the best description you got?"*

"How many random fifteen-year-old boys can this place possibly get in a week?"

The man shrugged. *"You might be surprised. We get a lot of stragglers from the Outskirts coming in here, looking to steal or barter, or learn how to process the Blight for sap. Course, most of 'em don't live too long."*

Even through her visor, the man saw Briar's eyes narrow.

He quickly added, *"I don't mean your kid didn't make it; that's not what I'm saying. He only got here yesterday?"*

"Yesterday."

"*Well, if he's lived this long he might be all right. I haven't seen him, but that doesn't mean he ain't here. How'd you get inside?*"

"I hitched a ride with a sky captain."

"*Which one?*"

"Look." She stopped him with a worn-out wave of her hand. "Can we talk? Can we do this somewhere else? I need to get out of this mask," she pleaded. "Please, is there somewhere I can breathe? I can't breathe."

He took her face in his hand and turned it this way and that, examining her mask. "*That's an old model. A good model, sure. But if your filters are clogging up, it don't matter how good it is. All right. Let's go downstairs. We've got a sealed pod here in the bank, and a connector to the underground roads.*"

The man led her downstairs, not holding her hand or dragging her, but waiting when she lagged behind.

At the entrance to the main hallway, where there were no windows to let in any light, an oil lantern had been left beside the door. The man took it, set it alight, and held it up to brighten the way to the basement.

While Briar watched his big, bobbing back stomp through the halls and down the stairs, she told him, "Thank you. I should've said so sooner, but thank you, for helping me out down there."

"*Just doing my job,*" he said.

"So you're the Seattle welcome wagon?"

He shook his head. "*No, but I keep my eyes open for noisy newcomers like yourself. Most of the kids, they slip in easy and keep their mouths shut. But when I hear gunshots and things breaking, I've got to come take a look.*" The lantern's flame wavered. He shook the light to swirl the oil. "*Sometimes it's somebody we don't want here and don't need here. Sometimes it's a little woman with a big gun. It's something new every day.*"

At the first floor there was a door with all its loose bits sealed by pitch—and treated leather flaps around every crack.

"*Here we go. When I open the door, you move quick and get inside.*" He handed her the lantern. "*I'll be right behind you. We just try to keep the door shut, if you get my meaning.*"

"Got it," she said, and took the lantern.

From a pants pocket he withdrew a ring with a dozen black iron keys. He picked the one he wanted and pushed it through a rubber seal where Briar wouldn't have thought to put a lock; but he turned the key and a mechanism clicked, and the door loosened when he bent his elbow.

"*Count of three. One, two . . . three.*" He tugged the latch and the door sucked outward with a pop.

Briar sidestepped her way into more darkness, and as promised, the man in the armor darted in behind her, then swiped the door back into its seal and locked it behind them.

"*A little farther,*" he said.

He took the lantern again and led the way, through some leather and rubber flaps hanging down in strips, and down another short corridor. The corridor ended in a strange-looking door that looked more like a cloth screen than an ordinary barricade. It was fitted with the same treated flaps around its edges to create the seal that the other underground doors all shared; but this one was porous.

Briar pushed her ear to the door and she could feel air moving through it.

"*Look out. And same rules as before—be quick. One, two . . . three.*"

He didn't need to unlock anything this time. The door slid sideways on a track, retreating into the wall with a squeak of its seals.

She jumped around it and into the next chamber, where candles were slowly melting down to stumps upon a table. Around the table six unoccupied chairs were pushed up close, and behind them there were more crates, more candles, and another corridor with the rustling leather curtains she'd come to expect.

The man wrestled with the door and finally snapped it into position.

He crossed to the far side of the room, where he began to remove his loosened armor. *"Don't take off the mask quite yet. Give it a minute,"* he said. *"But make yourself at home."* The plated arm sheaths clattered as he folded them and set them down on the table. His tubular noise gun—Daisy—also sounded heavy when he plunked it down beside the protective garment.

*"You thirsty?"* he asked.

She said, "Yes," in a dry whisper.

*"We've got water down here. It isn't very good water, but it's wet. Got plenty of beer, too. You like beer?"*

"Sure."

*"Go ahead and take off the mask now, if you want. Maybe it's just superstitious of me, but I don't like to whip mine off until I've had the filter door closed for a minute."* He reached inside one of the crates labeled STONEWARE and pulled out a mug. In the corner was a fat brown barrel. He popped the lid off and dipped out a mug full of water.

He put it down in front of Briar.

She gave the water a greedy look, but the man hadn't removed his mask yet, and she didn't want to go first.

He caught on and reached for the straps that held the elaborate contraption around his head. It slid down to his chest with a sliding scrape of leather being stretched and loosened, revealing a plain, wide face that was neither kind nor unkind. It was an intelligent face, with wild brown eyebrows and a flat nose, plus a pair of full lips that were smashed close against his teeth.

"There you go," he said of his own reveal. "No prettier, but a damn sight lighter."

Without the mechanical mask's assistance, his voice was still low, but perfectly human.

"Jeremiah Swakhammer, at your service, ma'am. Welcome to the underground."

 *Twelve*

Rudy shuffled in a loping, lopsided walk that was faster than it looked. Through the crushing, smelly pressure of the mask Zeke wheezed and puffed to keep up; he struggled to suck in air through filters that had grown somewhat clogged since he'd first entered the city, and he fought with his own skin as it was pulled, stretched, and rubbed raw by the unyielding seal around his face.

"Wait," he breathed.

"No," Rudy replied. "No time to wait."

He shambled on. Behind them, Zeke was certain he heard a new, rising commotion that came from anger, or grief. He heard the cacophony of consonants and unfamiliar vowels and the shouting, howling, screaming agreement of other voices from other men.

Zeke knew they'd been discovered—or, as he told himself, that Rudy's violence had been discovered. But Zeke hadn't done anything wrong, had he? The rules were different here, weren't they? And all's fair in war and self-defense, wasn't it?

But in the back of his mind a small foreign man with glasses was bleeding and confused, and then dead for no reason at all except that he'd once been alive.

The tunnels seemed more winding and the darkness seemed more oppressive as he tagged along behind his guide, whom he viewed with increasing suspicion. He even found himself wishing the princess would come back, whomever she was. Maybe he could get a question or two in edgewise. Maybe she wouldn't throw knives at him. Maybe she wasn't dead.

He hoped she wasn't dead.

But he could still hear, when he thought about it, the rumbling thunder of the ceiling and walls folding in upon themselves and filling all the air space between them, and he wondered if she'd been able to escape. He consoled himself by remembering that she was old, and no one gets to be that old without being smart and strong. It gave him an odd pang, one that he couldn't place as he watched the hobbling escape of the man in front of him.

Rudy turned around and said, "You coming, or not?"

"I'm coming."

"Then stick with me. I can't carry your ass, and I'm bleeding again. I can't do everything for the both of us."

"Where are we going?" Zeke asked, and he hated the sound of the begging that he heard from inside his mask.

"Back, same as before. Down, and then up."

"We're still going up the hill? You're still taking me to Denny Hill?"

Rudy said, "I told you I was, and I will. But there ain't no direct way between two spots in this city, and I'm real sorry if I'm not making the trip as spotless as you'd like. Forgive me, for Chrissake. I didn't plan to get stuck with a knife or nothing. Plans change, junior. Detours happen. This is one of them."

"This is?"

"Yeah, this is. Right here," Rudy said, stopping beneath a skylight and pointing at a stack of boxes topped precariously with a ladder. Where the ladder terminated against the ceiling, a round door was locked into place. "We're going up. And it might be bad, I'm warning you now."

"All right," Zeke said, even though it wasn't all right, not even a little bit. He was having trouble breathing—more trouble with every passing footstep, because he could not catch his breath and there was nowhere to rest.

"Remember what I told you about the rotters?"

"I remember." Zeke nodded, even though Rudy was facing away from him and didn't see it.

"No matter how terrible you've got them pictured," Rudy said, "seeing them is twice as bad. Now you listen." He turned around and wagged his finger in Zeke's face. "These things move fast—faster than you'd think, to look at them. They can run, and they bite. And anything they bite has to get cut off, or else you die. Do you understand?"

Zeke confessed, "Not really."

"Well, you've got about a minute and a half to wrap your head around it, because we're going up before those vicious old slant-eyes catch up and kill us just for standing here. So here's the rules—keep quiet, keep close, and if we're spotted, climb like a goddamned monkey."

"Climb?"

"You heard me. Climb. If the rotters are motivated enough they can scale a ladder, but not easily, and not very fast. If you can reach a windowsill or a fire escape, or even just a bit of overhanging concrete . . . do it. Go up."

Zeke's stomach was swishing and filled with lava. "What if we get separated?"

"Then we get separated, and it's every man for himself, boy. I hate to put it that way, but there you have it. If I get picked off, you don't come back for me. If I see you get picked off, I ain't coming back for you. Life's hard. Death's easy."

"But what if we just get split up?"

Rudy said, "If we get split up, same rule: Go up. Make your presence known from whatever rooftop you reach, and if I can, I'll get you. So really, the number one point is, don't get far from me. I can't protect you if you take off like a lunatic."

"I'm not going to take off like a lunatic," Zeke sulked.

"Good," Rudy said.

Back down the corridor the sounds were rising again, and maybe coming closer. If Zeke listened hard he could track an individual voice or two, lifted in rage and sounding ready to retaliate. Zeke felt absolutely sick, both for watching a man die and for knowing he'd had some part in it, even if he'd only stood by and not known what to do. The more he thought about it, the worse he felt; and the more he thought about a city above that was packed with gangs of the lurching undead, the worse he felt about that, too.

But he was in it now, and up to his eyeballs. There was no going back, at least not yet. Frankly, he had no idea where he was anymore—and he couldn't have left the city on his own accord if he wanted to.

So when the sealed doorway unfastened with a giant gasp, he followed Rudy up through it and into a street that was every bit as bleak and unforgiving as the tunnel below it.

Ezekiel did just like Rudy had told him.

He stayed close, and he stayed quiet. It was easy to do, almost; the silence above was so alarmingly complete that it was easier to keep it than to break it. Once in a while a pair of wings would catch the sky overhead and flap hard, and fast, up above the Blight that filled the walls. Zeke wondered how they did it—how they survived, breathing the poisoned air as if it were the cleanest spring day.

But he didn't get a chance to ask.

Instead, he almost cuddled up against the injured man who led him onward, and he copied everything he did. When Rudy pressed his back up against a wall and scooted himself along it, Zeke did likewise. When Rudy held his breath and listened, Zeke did the same, choking himself inside the mask and hanging onto every bit of oxygen. He used it up and waited for more until he saw stars flickering across his visor, and then he breathed because he had to.

He couldn't see more than a few yards in any given direction. The Blight had a density to it, and a color that was somewhere between shit and sunflowers. It was not quite fog, but it was some toxic kin, and it blocked their view as surely as any low-lying cloud.

Around the edges of Zeke's clothes—at his wrists where his gloves didn't meet the sleeves, and around his neck where his coat didn't close all the way—he began to itch. The urge to rub it was tough to fight, but when Rudy caught him dragging his wool-clad knuckles back and forth, he shook his head and whispered, "Don't. It'll make it worse."

The buildings were shapeless stacks in different squared-off heights, and their windows and doors were either broken altogether or boarded and reinforced. Zeke assumed that the boarded-up first floors indicated safe places, more or less, and that if he needed to, he could perhaps get to relative safety if he could find a way inside one. But that was easier to speculate than accomplish. He saw fire escapes here and there—great ironwork tangles of stairs and rails that looked as fragile as doll furniture; and he thought he could climb them if he had to, but then what? Could he break a window and let himself down that way?

Rudy had said there were lights, stashed along the way.

And here was Zeke, already plotting ways to get away from him.

It surprised him to realize that this was what he was doing. He knew no one else in the city at all, and he'd only seen two other people—one of whom Rudy had murdered outright. The other one had tried to murder Rudy. So if Zeke was trying to assign the benefit of a doubt, he supposed that a fifty-fifty shot of getting murdered was a good-enough excuse to get proactive. But that didn't make it feel any better.

As he towed along in Rudy's wake, he wondered again about the Chinese man. The contents of his stomach threatened an escape attempt.

No. He wouldn't have it. Not in the mask. Not when he couldn't take it off, not without dying. Forget it.

He willed his belly to settle down, and it did.

Rudy ambled forward, his back hunched and his shoulder cringing. He led the way with his cane, which—as Zeke now knew—held only two shots. And what were two shots against a slavering pack of rotters?

He'd no sooner thought of them than he heard, somewhere close, a softly grunted moan.

Rudy froze. Zeke froze behind him.

Rudy's head swung left to right, up and down, seeking some obvious escape or path.

*Rotters?* Zeke mouthed, but inside his mask Rudy couldn't see the lips forming the question, so he didn't answer.

Another moan joined the first, like a question added to a conversation. It came with a different timbre and a more jagged edge, as if the mouth that made it was no longer complete. After the groans came the footsteps, tentative and slow and so perilously nearby that the fear felt like a boot on Zeke's chest.

Rudy spun around and grabbed Zeke's mask, pulling it close to his own and whispering as softly as he could manage. "This road." He waved a hand at the nearest intersection and pointed down to the right. "Several blocks. Big tower—white building. Climb up to the second floor. Break what you have to."

Rudy closed his eyes for a full second and then opened them again. He added, "Run for it."

Zeke didn't know if he could run for anything. His chest was as tight as if it were wrapped in ropes, and his throat felt like it was wearing a noose tied from a scarf. He looked down the road Rudy indicated and saw almost nothing but a slow, sloping grade that he was nearly certain must dip farther away from the hill he wanted.

Through his head a parade of memorized maps flipped a page at a time, reassuring him that this was the wrong way—but could he run uphill? Where would he go to escape, if not to this tower that Rudy had told him about?

Panic was filling his mask and blinding him, but it didn't matter. The groans, moans, and shuffling steps were coming closer, and he was confident that soon, very soon, they'd be upon him.

Rudy took off first. Bum hip or no, he could run, but he couldn't run quietly.

At the slapping of his feet the moans took on a higher, keening pitch, and somewhere in the depths of the fog a press of bodies began to organize. They began to assemble. They began to hunt.

Zeke panted, trying to draw in enough breath to catch himself up or calm himself down. He pointed himself down the hill and took a last look over his shoulder. Seeing nothing but the swirling, grasping fog, he took heart. And he ran.

The streets under his feet were uneven and split, from the earthquake or simply from time and terrible wear. He tripped and recovered, stumbled and caught himself on his hands—which bruised and bumped, but worked like reflexive spiders and threw him back up to his feet. Then he ran some more.

Behind him in the fog he could hear them coming in a rushing tide.

He did not look. He focused hard on the shrugging, pushing figure of Rudy—who was moving ahead, gaining speed, though Zeke didn't know how. Perhaps the older man was more accustomed to wearing the suffocating masks, or perhaps he was not as crippled as he seemed. Regardless, he was closing in on the white building that rose up suddenly out of the murky air.

Fog crashed against it like waves, as if it were a boulder in the ocean and the tide had come in to stay.

As soon as Zeke could see it, he was nearly on top of it—and this was a problem. He had no idea how to reach the second floor. He didn't see a fire escape or a set of stairs. He only saw the front entrance—huge tarnished bronze doors that had been barricaded with split logs and chains.

His forward momentum was uncontrollable and unstoppable until he slapped his hands against the structure and forced himself to a halt. The force of his collision ached and stung against his already battered hands, but he used them to feel his way around the boarded windows and their intricate frames, where the stonework wasn't covered with boards or sheets of metal.

Looking around, he saw no sign of his guide. "Rudy!" he squeaked, too frightened to yell and too frightened to keep silent.

"Here!" Rudy called from someplace out of sight.

"Where?"

"Here," he said again, much louder because he was right beside Zeke. "Around the side, come on. Hurry up, they're coming."

"I hear them. They're coming from—"

"Everywhere," Rudy said. "That's right. Feel that?" He took Zeke's hand and pushed it up to a ledge somewhere around chest-height.

"Yeah."

"Up, boy." He threw his cane over the side and hauled himself up after it, then began to crawl even higher with the aid of an improvised ladder. Zeke could see it, once he knew where to look: It was made of boards and bars bolted directly into the stone.

But it wasn't so easy for him to get up to that point. He was shorter than Rudy and not as strong; and he was gagging from lack of air and the stink of rubber mixed with leather in every breath he drew.

Rudy reached back and grabbed Zeke's arm, yanking him bodily up onto the ledge and then pivoting the boy to aim him at the ladder built into the wall. "How fast can you climb?" he asked.

Zeke's only answer was to scale the wall like a lizard. Once he knew where the handholds were, he trusted them to hold because there was no time to test them one by one. He wedged his feet against the boards and wormed his hands around the bars and climbed. Rudy came up behind him, moving slower. Though he acted comfortable enough in a straight stretch, rising was hard on his hip, and he groused and grunted with every step.

"Wait," he wheezed, but Zeke didn't see the point. He saw a window with a small balcony—and it looked promising.

"Is this where we get off?"

"What?" Rudy cocked his head up and his hat tipped back, nearly falling away.

"This window. Is this—"

"Yeah, that's it. Go on, I'm right behind you."

A bar like the handle on an oven crossed the window and looked like a logical place to grab. Zeke seized it and yanked; it squeaked and budged, but not enough. He yanked it again and the window popped outward from its frame—almost casting Zeke off balance, and off the balcony.

"Careful, junior," Rudy admonished. His hands reached the balcony, and he rested while Zeke navigated the window.

Below them the streets had gone darker—not with shadows, but with pressing, groaning bodies that clotted together like a thickening soup. When Zeke looked down he could not distinguish the rotters individually, but he could discern a hand here, and a head there. The dirty air blanketed them and blurred them.

"Ignore them," Rudy said. "Get inside so we can get these damn masks off. I can't stand this thing another minute."

Zeke couldn't have agreed more if he'd tried. He lifted one leg and dropped it down on the other side, into the interior of the white-walled building. The other leg followed, and he was inside.

Rudy fell in behind him, folding up and rolling to a rollicking halt. He stayed flat on his back for a moment, breathing harder than the mask would let him. "Shut the damn window, boy. You're letting the Blight inside."

"Oh, sure." Zeke wrestled the window back into position. It was harder from the far side, where waxed flaps of stiffened fabric lined the edges to form a seal. But he closed it, and it sucked itself back into place. "Can I take the mask off now?"

"No, not now. Not on this floor, not unless you want to get good and sick, good and fast. Let's go downstairs. You can take off your mask down there, and we can find our way back to the tunnels, no problem."

"Back to the tunnels? And back up the hill?" Zeke asked, knowing that he was asking Rudy to lie and not really caring. He only wanted to remind him of the promise, even if his guide had no intention of keeping it.

"To the hill, sure. We can get there from here. But not by going up any farther. This damn tower is too far away from anything, so there aren't any bridges or walkways connecting it to any other building. And even if there were, we'd have to keep wearing these things."

Zeke tugged at the seals on his mask, and scratched at the raw skin he found there. "I *do* want to take this off."

"Then let's go downstairs. If I can find the damn stairs," Rudy said, sitting up and rubbing at his own mask's edges.

"If you can find them?"

"It's been a while since I've been in here, that's all." He drew up his cane and used it to lever himself upright. He teetered back and forth. He steadied.

The boy gazed around the room, with its unboarded windows and air that was somewhat clearer than the stuff outside. Scattered around the room were ghostly shapes that turned out to be furniture covered with drapery. Zeke poked at one and felt the arm of a chair underneath, and then he inferred the shape of a couch and a table. When he looked up, he saw the skeleton of a chandelier—a piece that surely was beautiful once, but now was missing its crystals. "Where *are* we?" he asked.

"We're in . . ." Rudy swung around and surveyed the premises. "Somebody's room? Or it used to be, maybe. I don't know. We're in the Smith Tower, at any rate."

"Why's it called that?"

"Because it was built by a guy named Smith," he answered dryly. "You know what a typewriter is?"

"Yeah," Zeke responded. "Maybe."

"All right. You ever hear of Smith Corona?"

He said, "Oh sure, yeah. The guns."

"No, that's Smith and Wesson. This tower was built with typewriter money. Watch where you're stepping, kid. Parts of the floor aren't finished yet, and there aren't any rails on the stairs. This place wasn't done being built when the Blight hit. It's mostly solid, but here and there you've got to keep an eye out."

"Is it tall?"

"The tower? Yeah, it's tall. It's the tallest building anyplace for miles, even though the last couple of floors aren't up yet."

Zeke said, "I want to go upstairs. I want to look out over the city from the top." He didn't add, "So I can figure out where I am, and how much you've been lying to me."

Rudy's eyes narrowed behind his visor. "I thought you wanted to see the hill?"

"I do want to see the hill. I want to see it from up there. Are the other floors sealed up?"

"Most of them are," Rudy admitted. "Just this one's not, because it's how everybody gets inside. If you go up or down, you can pull the mask off, but if you go all the way up you'll have to shove it back on. The airships like to dock up there, and the dock ain't sealed-up space or anything. And it's a whole lot of stairs, kid. Are you sure you want to hike it?"

"You think you can keep up with me?" Zeke said, trying to make it a light challenge. He wanted to test his guide, and maybe wear him out a little if he could. He'd already figured out that he might need to run, and if it came to that, he'd need to outrun more than the limping man. He'd have to get out of the way of that cane.

"I can keep up with you," Rudy said. "Go out there, to the main hallway. There should be a lantern around the corner." He tossed him a box of matches and said, "Light it up."

Zeke found the lantern and made it bright. Rudy came to stand beside him. He said, "You see that curtain over there?"

"The black one?"

"That's the one. It's a seal—silk covered with tar. There's a bar down there at the bottom; it weighs it down and holds it steady. Slide it out and we can move the curtain." He leaned on his cane and watched while Zeke followed instructions, then said, "Now hop through fast. I'm behind you," and he was.

Zeke reset the bar and they were smothered in darkness except for the lantern, which did its best to hold a cheery glow. "Let's go down to the end, and then we'll pop these things off."

"Can we breathe in here?"

"Probably, but I ain't chancing it. I like to put a pair of seals between me and the Blight if I can help it." Rudy took the lantern and followed the carpeted hallway to its terminus, then squeezed himself between another set of flaps. After a few seconds, only his left hand with the cane remained out where Zeke could see it. Rudy extended his finger and crooked it, meaning the boy should slip through, too.

On the other side of the seal there was light, though, it was gray and sickly.

Rudy's mask was already off by the time Zeke pushed himself through the slot. Seeing the other man breathe freely made Zeke desperate to do likewise. He ripped his mask off and sucked in the foulest-tasting air he'd ever inhaled, but it was beautiful because it came without a fight.

Happily he gasped himself back to life. "I can breathe! It stinks in here like shit, but I can breathe!"

"Even the freshest stuff smells like sulfur and smoke up here," Rudy agreed. "Down below it's not so bad, but the air up here gets stale because there's nowhere for it to go. At least underground we force it to move."

Zeke examined his mask and saw that his filters were changing colors. "I need new filters," he observed. "I thought these were supposed to work fine for ten hours?"

"Son, how long you think you've been down here? That long, at least, I'll tell you that much for sure. But that's nothing to panic about. Filters are a penny a pound in the underground since that big old negro robbed a Confederate supply train last spring. And if you find yourself running low, there are sealed tunnels all over the place in this part of town. Remember the rule, though: Put two seals between you and the Blight if you can."

"I'll remember," Zeke said, since the advice seemed sensible.

Off in some unseen corner of the enormous, unfinished tower, both travelers heard a pinging crash. It echoed from loud to soft, and dissipated in the distance. Zeke demanded, "What was that?"

"Damned if I know," Rudy said.

"It sounded like it was coming from inside."

Rudy said, "Yeah, it did." He tightened his grip on his cane and lifted it up off the floor so it'd be ready to fire, should the moment require it.

A second scuttling sound followed the first, and it was more unmistakable this time. It was the sound of something falling down the stairs behind them.

"I don't like this," Rudy grumbled. "We got to get back down."

"We can't!" Zeke whispered fiercely. "That noise came from downstairs! We'd be better off going up!"

"You're an idiot. We head up, and we get trapped wherever the stairs run out."

The argument ended there, because a different sound from a different direction blew louder and stranger up above. It was the sound of machinery and force; it was the swish and rattling sway of something huge coming close—all too quickly.

"What's that—?"

Zeke couldn't finish the question. From outside and above, an enormous airship with a billowing, flapping basket and hard metal tanks crashed against the side of the tower and bounced into another structure, then returned for a second broken landing. Windows shattered and the whole world heaved, just like it had when the earth quaked hours before.

Rudy jammed his mask back on over his face and Zeke did likewise, even though the act made him want to cry. Rudy ran to the stairs even as the building shuddered beneath their feet, and he commanded, "Down!"

And so he began to half run, half stumble downward into the darkness.

Zeke didn't have the lantern anymore, and he didn't know what had become of it. The hustling retreat of Rudy beating a rambling flight was as noisy as the beating air and the banging ship that assaulted the walls. But when Zeke reached the stairs and the rocking blackness sought to undermine him, he fought it.

And he began to climb up.

And then there was more darkness than what he started with, and it was collapsing toward him, rushing like water, or earth, or the sky itself.

*Thirteen*

Briar downed first the one mug, then a second one filled with water. She asked about the beer.

"Do you want some?"

"No. I just wondered why it was an option."

Swakhammer served himself a taller mug filled with sour-smelling ale and pulled up a chair across from Briar. He said, "Because it's easier to turn Blight-bitter water into beer than it is to purify it. Distilling makes for a nasty brew, but it won't kill you or turn you rotty."

"I see," she said, and it made perfect sense. But she couldn't imagine swilling the urine-yellow beverage except under the most dire of circumstances. Even at a distance, it had a scent that would peel paint.

"It takes some getting used to," he admitted. "But once you do, it's not so bad. And you know, I never did catch your name."

"Briar," she offered.

"Briar what?"

She gave fast consideration to inventing a new identity, and discarded the idea just as quickly. Her experience with the *Namaah Darling*'s captain and crew had been an encouragement. "It was Wilkes," she said. "And now, it's Wilkes again."

"Briar Wilkes. So that makes you . . . all right. No wonder you were keeping it to yourself. Who let you down here—Cly?"

"That's right. Captain Cly. He's the one who dropped me down, on his way elsewhere. How'd you know?"

He took another swallow of beer and said, "Everybody knows how he escaped the Blight. It's no secret. And he's not the worst sort of guy. Not the best, but definitely not the worst. I trust he didn't give you any trouble?"

"He was a perfect gentleman," she said.

He smiled, revealing a bottom row of teeth that fit together strangely. "I find that tough to believe. He's a big son of a gun, ain't he?"

"Enormous, yes, though you're no small fry yourself. You gave me a hell of a scare, bursting in like that. As if your voice weren't awful enough in that mask, it makes you look like a monster, too."

"It does! I know it does. But it keeps me breathing better than that old contraption you were wearing, and the suit keeps the worst of the rotter bites from landing. They'll eat you up whole, if they can catch you and bring you down." He rose to refill his drink and stayed standing, striking a thoughtful pose with one arm folded and the other holding the mug. "So you're Maynard's girl. I thought you looked familiar, but I wouldn't have placed you if you hadn't said anything. And that makes your son who's missing—"

"Ezekiel. His name's Ezekiel, but he goes by Zeke."

"Sure, sure. And Zeke is Maynard's grandson. You think he's making a point to tell people about it?"

Briar nodded. "He must be. He knows it might help him here, and he doesn't realize—not fully, I don't think—how it could also hurt him. Not that he's Maynard's, I mean. About his father."

She sighed and asked for more water. While Swakhammer refilled the mug, she said, "It's not his fault. None of it's his fault; it's all mine. I should've told him . . . God. I never told him anything. And now he's on this mission to root through the past and see if he can find anything that's worth having."

Another mug of stale water landed on the table in front of her. She took it, and drank down half its contents.

"So did Ezekiel come here looking for his father?"

"Looking for him? In a way, I suppose. He thinks he can prove his father was innocent if he can find proof that the Russian ambassador paid to have the Boneshaker tested before it was ready. He came here wanting to find the old laboratory, so he could hunt for some way to clear Levi's name." Briar drank the rest of the water. Swakhammer offered her more, but she waved her hand to tell him no.

"Can he do it?"

"I beg your pardon?"

"Can he do it? Can he prove Blue was innocent in the Blight affair?"

She shook her head and almost laughed. "Oh no. Oh God no, he can't. Levi was as guilty as Cain." Almost immediately, she wished she hadn't said that last part. She didn't want her new companion to ask any questions, so she hurriedly added, "Maybe, deep down, Zeke knows it. Maybe he only wants to see where he came from, or see the damage for himself. He's only a boy," she said, and she tried hard to keep the exasperation out of her words. "Heaven only knows why he ever does anything."

"He never knew his dad, I guess."

"No. Thank God."

Swakhammer leaned against the back of the chair across from Briar. "Why would you say that?"

"Because Levi never had a chance to corrupt him or change him." That wasn't all she could say, but it was all she could muster for this stranger. "I keep thinking, maybe one day this war back east will end— and then I can pack him up and head somewhere else, where nobody knows about either one of us. That would be better, wouldn't it? It can't be any worse than being here."

"Being here's not so bad," he argued with a sardonic grin. "Just look at this palace!"

"It *is* bad, and you know it as well as I do. So why do you stay? Why would you live here—why would anybody?"

Swakhammer shrugged and finished his beer. He chucked the mug back into a crate and said, "We all got our reasons. And you can make it down here, if you want to. Or if you have to. It's not easy, but it's not easy anyplace, anymore."

"I suppose you're right."

"Anyway, there's money to be made. There's freedom, and plenty of opportunity if you know where to look."

"From what? From how?" Briar asked. "From looting the old rich places? One day, that money will run out. There's only so much you can steal and sell inside the walls, or so I'd think."

He shifted on his feet. He said, "There's always the Blight. It's not going anywhere, and no one knows what to do about it. If you can't turn a buck off the sap, then it really *isn't* any use to anyone."

"Lemon sap kills people."

"So do other people. So do dogs. So do angry horses, and diseases, and gangrene, and birthing babies. And what about the war? You don't think the war back east kills people? I promise you this—it kills them by the score, and it kills more of them than the Blight does. More by thousands, I bet."

Briar shrugged, but it wasn't a dismissal. "You've got a point, I'm sure. But my son isn't going to die in childbirth, or in war—not yet, at least. At the moment, he's much more likely to sicken himself to death with that stupid drug, because he's only a child, and children do stupid things. And please understand, I'm not accusing you of anything. I understand how the world works, and I know plenty about doing what you must in order to get by."

"I don't owe you an explanation."

"I'm not asking you for one. But you seemed mighty ready to offer one in self-defense."

He pushed at the chair and gave her a look that was almost a glare, but wasn't quite. "That's fine. As long as we understand each other."

"I think we do, yes." She rubbed at her eyes and scratched at her thigh, where the little cuts from the window were itching like mad; but least they weren't bleeding anymore.

"You hurt?" Swakhammer asked, eager to change the subject.

"Just a few cuts. It wouldn't be so bad except for the gas rubbing in it. You don't have any bandages around here, do you? I'll need some for decency's sake, if nothing else. My pants are going to come apart before long, so I could use a needle and thread, too."

His crooked-toothed smile warmed its way back onto his face. "Sounds like you need a secretary, or a nice hotel. I'm afraid I can't give you much along those lines, but now that I've decided where to take you, I think we can get you patched up."

Briar didn't like his phrasing. "What do you mean by that? Where are you going to take me?"

"You've got to understand," he said. He shouldered his armor and stuffed his mask up under his arm. "This is a . . . well, let's call it a controlled community. It's not for everyone, and we like it just fine that way. But every now and again, someone drops down off an airship or wriggles up from down by the water, wanting to make a change. People get the idea that there's something valuable in here, and people want to get their fingers in that pie." He cocked his head at her mask, and at the bag and rifle that were sitting on the table beside her. "Get your stuff together."

"Where are you taking me?" she asked more urgently, wrapping her fingers around the gun.

"Sweetheart, if I was going to do you any trouble, I would've taken that away." He pointed at the Spencer. "I'm going to take you to your daddy's place. Sort of. Now come on. It's afternoon now and it's getting dark, and it gets even worse out there when it's dark. We're walking underneath the really bad parts, but this time of day, everybody and their brother is dropping down into the tunnels."

"Is that bad?"

"It might be. As I was going to tell you, before you distracted me, we've got plenty of problems down here already. That's why we have to watch the new folks so closely. We don't need any more trouble than we already got."

Briar felt somewhat refreshed, but not much reassured by the conversation's faintly sinister turn. She shouldered the rifle, slipped herself through the strap of her satchel, and stuffed the mask inside it. Her father's old hat fit much better without the mask, so she put the hat back on rather than tie it to her satchel.

She told him, "All I want to do is find my son. That's it. I'll find him, and get out of your city."

"I think you underestimate the trouble a woman like you can cause without even trying. You're Maynard's girl, and Maynard is the closest thing to an agreed-upon authority down here."

She blinked hard. "But he's *dead*. He's been dead for sixteen years!"

Swakhammer pushed aside a leather curtain and held it for Briar, who was now more reluctant to let him follow her. But there was no graceful way around it. She took the lead, and he dropped the curtain behind them both, casting the corridor into darkness except for his lantern.

"Sure he's dead, and it's a good thing for us. It's hard to argue with a dead man. A dead man can't change his mind or make new rules, or behave like a bastard so no one will listen to him anymore. A dead man stays a saint." He tapped her on the shoulder and handed her the lantern. "Aim this over here so I can see."

As if he'd forgotten something, he held up a finger that asked her to wait. He ducked back through the curtain and reappeared a few seconds later, chased by the smell of smoke.

"Had to put out the candles. Now bring that up close."

Next to the leather curtain a long iron rod was propped against the wall. Swakhammer took it and threaded it through a series of loops at the bottom of the leather curtain.

"Are you . . ." Briar wasn't sure how to ask the question. "Locking the curtain?"

He grunted half a laugh. "Just weighing it down. The more barriers we keep between the undersides and the topsides, the better the air stays; and when the bellows kick on and off, they blow these curtains all over the place."

She watched him work, paying close attention. The mechanics of it all fascinated her—the filters, the seals, the bellows. Seattle used to be an uncomplicated trading town fed and fattened by gold in Alaska, and then it had dissolved into a nightmare city filled with gas and the walking dead. But people had stayed. People had come back. And they'd adapted.

"Is there anything I can do to help?"

"Just hold the light. I've got it." The curtains were anchored and bound by the rod, and he jammed the rod's end into a groove beside the doorjamb. "That takes care of that. Now let's go. Keep the light if you want. Go straight up here, and take the right fork, if you would, please."

Briar wandered through the damp, moss-covered hallway that rang with the distant, perpetual drip of water. Sometimes from above, a thud or a jangling clank would sound, but since her escort paid the noises no attention, she did her best to tune them out too.

"So, Mr. Swakhammer. What did you mean when you said we were going to . . . to my father's?" She looked over her shoulder. The jagged lantern light gave the man's face a hollow, haggard appearance.

"We're going to Maynard's. It used to be a pub, down on the square. Now it's the same as everything else here—dead as a doornail—but down in the basement there's a crew of folks who keep the place running. I figure we'll try that first because, well, for one thing you're going to need some better filters and maybe a better mask. And for another, if your boy was out here telling people he's Maynard's grandson, the odds are good that someone would've brought him there."

"Do you think so? Really? But he was trying so hard to find his way back to Levi's house."

The corridor opened into a three-way split. "Take the middle," Swakhammer told her. "The question is, does the kid know where the house is?"

"I don't think he does, but I might be wrong. If he doesn't know, then I can't imagine how he'd begin to start looking."

"Maynard's," he said with confidence. "The pub is both the safest place he could end up, and the most likely place he'd end up."

Briar tried not to let the lantern shake when she asked, half to herself and half to her companion, "What if he's not there?"

He didn't answer at first. He sidled up next to her and gently took the lantern away, holding it up higher and out as if he were looking for something. "Ah," he said, and Briar saw the street name and the arrow painted on the wall. "Sorry. For a minute there, I thought we'd gotten turned around. I don't come out this way often. Mostly, I stick closer to the square."

"Oh."

"But listen, as for your boy, if he's not at Maynard's . . . well, then he's not at Maynard's. You can ask around, see if anyone's seen him or heard about him. If nobody has, then at least you're spreading the word—and that can only help him. Folks down at Maynard's, when they hear they've got flesh and blood to the old lawman lost or wandering here in the city, they'll move hell, high water, or Blight-wash to find him, just to say they've seen him."

"You're not just saying that to make me feel better?"

"Why would I bother?"

Above them something heavy fell, and the pipes that ran along the walls shuddered in their posts.

"What was that?" Briar demanded. She skidded closer to Swakhammer and resisted the urge to ready her rifle.

"Rotters? Our boys? Minnericht testing some new toy? There's no telling."

"Minnericht," Briar repeated. It was the third time she'd heard the name. "The same man who made your . . . your Daisy?"

"That's him."

"So he's a scientist? An inventor?"

"Something like that."

Briar frowned. "What's that supposed to mean?"

"He's a man with many toys, and he's always unveiling new ones. Most of his toys are dangerous as hell, though a few of them are kind of fun. He does little mechanical things sometimes, too. He's an odd bird, and not always a friendly one. You can say it out loud, if you want."

"Say what out loud?" She stared straight ahead, into the damp, faintly noxious distance.

"What you're thinking. You're not the first person to notice it—how much Minnericht sounds like your husband."

"My *former* husband. And I wasn't thinking that," she lied.

"Then you're a damn fool. There's not a man down here who hasn't wondered about it."

"I don't understand what you're getting at," she protested, though she was deathly afraid that she *did*. "Seattle wasn't a huge city, but it was big enough to have more than one scientist living here, I bet. Or this Minnericht might've come from someplace else."

"Or he might be old Levi, dressed up different and wearing a new name."

"He isn't," she said so quickly that she knew it must sound suspicious. "My husband is dead. I don't know who this Minnericht may be, but he's not Levi, I can promise you that."

"Down this way." Swakhammer urged her toward a darker path that ended in a ladder. The ladder disappeared into another brick-lined tunnel. "You want to go first, or do you want me to?"

"You can go first."

"All right." He put the lantern's wire handle in his teeth, leaned his head forward, and descended with the light almost singeing his shirt. "How?" he asked from down below.

"How what?"

"How do you know Minnericht isn't Leviticus? You sound pretty certain, Widow Blue."

"If you call me that again, I'll shoot you," she promised. She set her feet on the rungs and climbed down after him.

"I'll keep that in mind. But answer my question: How do you know it ain't him? Far as I know, no one ever found Blue's body. Or if anyone did, no one announced it."

She hopped down off the last rung and stood up straight. At her full height, she barely came up to his shoulder. "Nobody found him because he died here in the city at the same time so many other people did, and no one was willing to come back to look. Rotters probably got his body, or maybe it's just decayed away to nothing. But I'm telling you, he's as dead as a stone, not down here living inside these walls that are all his fault. I can't imagine why you'd even wonder such a thing."

"Really? You can't imagine?" He gave her a smirk and shook his head. "Yeah, it's real hard to imagine . . . one crazy scientist makes crazy machines and destroys a whole city, and then as soon as the dust settles, there's a crazy scientist making crazy machines."

"But surely someone has actually seen Minnericht? Everyone knew what Levi looked like."

"Everyone knew what Blue looked like, sure. But no one knows about Minnericht. He keeps his face covered and his head down low. There's a girl who used to lurk down here, Evelyn somebody. He used to have a good time with her, every now and again, before she got herself too junked up on the Blight and started to turn."

He looked down at Briar and said quite pointedly, "That was a few years ago, before we had a good idea of how to breathe down here. It took some trial and error, it did, and this is a place where only the strong survive. And Evie, she just wasn't strong. She got sick and started slipping, so the good doctor shot her in the head."

"That's . . ." Briar couldn't think of a response.

"That's plain old practicality, is all. We've got plenty of rotters shambling around; we didn't need one more hanging about. Point is," he tried again, "before she went down, she told folks she'd got a look at his face, and it was all scarred up—like he'd been burned, or like something else bad had happened to him. She said he almost never took off his gas mask, even when he was underside here in the safer places."

"Well, there you go. He's just an unfortunate man who's hiding some scars. There's no reason to assume the worst."

"No reason to assume the best, either. He's a madman, sure as your husband was. And he's got the same knack for building things, and making things work." Swakhammer seemed on the verge of saying something else. "I'm not saying that's who he is, for sure. I'm just saying that lots of people think he *might* be."

Briar sneered. "Oh, come on. If you folks really thought he was Blue, you'd have dragged him into the street and fed him to the rotters by now."

"Mind your step," he told her, indicating with the sweep of the lantern the way the tunnel was broken up into an uneven floor. "And it didn't come to us all of a sudden—how we got thinking this stranger might not be such a stranger. It happened real gradual, over a couple of years. One day two folks who'd been thinking about it in private shared their thoughts, and from then on out, it was a runaway rumor that nobody could stop."

"I could stop it."

"Maybe you could; maybe you can't. If you're that sold on taking the trouble, I'd like to see you try it. Last few years, the old doctor's been more trouble than he's worth down here—useful instruments aside." He patted at the Daisy and shook his head. "He does good work, but he does bad things with his good work. He's got a bit of passion for being in charge."

"You said yourself, nobody's in charge down here except a man who died sixteen years ago."

He grumbled, "I didn't say that *exactly*. Come on. Not much farther, I swear. Can you hear it?"

"Hear what?" Even as she asked the question, she could hear strains of music. It wasn't loud and wasn't too melodic, but it was distinct and cheerful.

"Sounds like Varney's playing, or trying to play. He can't pound out a song worth a damn, but he's doing his best to learn. There was an old player piano in Maynard's, but the mechanism inside it rotted out. A few of the boys rigged it up so you could play it like a regular instrument. The poor machine hasn't been tuned since before the walls, but you can probably hear that for yourself."

"I'm surprised you're comfortable with that much noise. I'd think you'd spend your days staying quiet. The rotters seem to have good ears."

"Oh, they can't hear us so well when we're down here. The sound travels underground more than it carries up there." He cocked his head at the ceiling. "And even if they do get a hint of what we're up to, they can't get at us. Maynard's—well, most of the old square, really—is reinforced like nobody's business. It's the safest part of what's left, I'll tell you that much."

She was reminded of Zeke, and again she offered a silent prayer to anyone listening that perhaps the boy had found his way to the fortress within the fortress. "And if we're lucky, we'll find my son there."

"If we're lucky indeed. Is he the resourceful sort?"

"Yes. Oh God, yes. Too much so for his own good."

The music was brimming up louder, spilling out around the edges of a round door that had been sealed on both sides. Swakhammer picked at the flaps and fumbled for a latch.

Briar spied a mark on the door. It was geometric and sharp, a zig-zagged line that reminded her of something. She pointed at it and asked, "Mr. Swakhammer, what's that? What does that mark mean?"

"What, don't you recognize it?"

"Recognize it? It's only a jagged line. Does it mean something?"

He reached out for her and she almost backed away out of reflex, but she held still while he poked at her belt buckle. Using one finger, he tipped it up so she could stare down at it and see for herself. "It's your own daddy's initials, that's all. It marks this place as a safe spot, for people who'll keep the peace."

"So it is," she murmured. "And don't I feel like a dummy."

"Don't feel too silly about it. The poor quality of Willard's hand-writing is a thing of legend. Stand back, if you don't mind. These doors are sealed from both sides, just in case." And he pulled the latch, tugged the door, and leaned on it to hold it open.

"In case of what?"

"In case there's a breach. In case the bellows fail, or the cleared-out spots upstairs are busted open and contaminated. Just in case, that's all. Around here, anything's possible."

She stepped through the door, and she believed him.

## Fourteen

Except for the fact that there were no windows, the establishment looked every bit like a thousand others that operated aboveground. A big bar made of wood and brass hulked against the far wall, and behind it a cracked mirror had been installed. It brightened and reflected the warm-looking room, doubling the clustered candles alight on every square, squat table—and contributing a fractured luster to the scene.

At the piano a gray-haired man in a long green coat sat on a stool and banged away at the keys, each one of them yellowed like old teeth. Beside him, a large-boned woman with only one arm tapped her foot in time to the tune he was struggling to produce; and at the bar, a thin man served up a sickly yellow substance that must be the disgusting beer.

Three men sat at the bar, and six or seven more were scattered throughout the tavern, seated here and there—except for a fellow who was sitting unconscious on the floor beside the piano. Something about the mug in his hand and the drool on his chin suggested he'd passed out there, not fallen victim to some more exciting event.

At the sight of Swakhammer, several patrons tipped a mug in a passive greeting; but upon seeing Briar, the place fell silent except for the determined, simple tune.

Even the music stopped when the one-armed woman noted the newcomers.

"Jeremiah," she said in a cigarette-rough voice. "Who've you got there?"

From the look of anticipation on the faces of Maynard's patrons, Briar was able to guess many things. She was trying to frame a gentle way of disappointing them when Swakhammer did it for her.

"Lucy," he said to the barwoman—and by telling her, he told the room, "she's not that kind of visitor."

"Are you sure?" asked one of the men at the bar. "She's prettier than the usual crew."

" 'Fraid so." He turned to Briar and said, with a note of apology in his voice, "Once in a while, working girls find their way down here. They can make a fortune in a week, but you know how it is. They've got to be pretty desperate to give the walls a try."

Briar said, "Oh."

Swakhammer said, "All right then, let me make an introduction or two. That's Lucy O'Gunning over there at the bar. She's in charge of the joint. Going around the room, that's Varney on the stool; Hank on the floor by the piano; Frank, Ed, and Willard at the bar; Allen and David at the far table; Squiddy and Joe over there playing cards; and down front there's Mackie and Tim. I think that's everybody."

Then he said, "Everybody, this is Miss Briar Wilkes."

A sudden hum of low-pitched chatter filled the room, but Swakhammer kept talking. "She got a ride from your friend and mine, Captain Cly, and thought she'd visit our fair and fine vacation destination here inside the walls—and I couldn't think of a better place to begin than here at the spot named for her daddy. She's got a few questions she'd like to ask, and I hope you'll all be good enough to treat her nice."

No one rose or offered any objections or accusations, so Briar dove headlong into the point of her visit. "I'm looking for my son," she blurted. "Has anybody seen him? His name is Ezekiel, and he'll be going by Zeke. Zeke Wilkes. He's only fifteen, and he's a smart kid aside from the stump-stupid idea to come in here. I was hoping maybe someone here had seen him. He's . . ."

No one interrupted her with helpful information. She kept talk-ing, and with every word she became more certain of what the out-come would be, but that only made her ramble longer.

"He's about as tall as me, and thin as a rail. He's got a few of his grandfather's things; I guess he meant to barter them, or use them as proof of who he is. He would've gotten here yesterday sometime. I'm not sure exactly when he left, but he came up through the water runoff system before it collapsed in last night's quake. Have any of you . . ." She met a few eyes, but none of them held a yes. She had to ask anyway, so she did. "Have any of you seen him?"

No one spoke, or blinked.

"I thought—that is, Mr. Swakhammer said—that maybe someone would've brought him here, since Zeke is who he is. I thought . . ."

They didn't need to answer. She knew the answer, but she wished someone would reply, anyway. She hated being the only one talking, but she was going to keep going until someone stopped her.

Lucy finally did. She said, "Miss Wilkes, I'm real sorry. I haven't seen hide nor hair of him. But that don't mean he's come to harm. There's more than one sealed spot here in the walls where he might've holed up and taken rest."

Briar must've looked closer to tears than she hoped, because the older woman came forward, adjusting her shawl. "Honey, you've had a hard day, I can already tell it. Let me get you a drink and sit you down, and you can tell us the whole thing."

She nodded and choked on the lump that was swelling in her throat.

"I shouldn't," she began to argue. "I need to keep looking for him."

"I know you do. But give us a minute or two to freshen you up and get you some clean filters, and you can tell us all about it. And maybe we can help you out. Let's see. Has Jeremiah there offered you any beer?"

"Yes, but no; no thank you. And I already have some extra filters; I just haven't had a chance to use them."

Lucy led Briar up to the nearest empty barstool and positioned her there.

Frank, Ed, and Willard all hopped seats until they were hovering right at Briar's elbows; and behind her, she could hear the scraping of chairs being pushed and abandoned. The remaining occupants of the bar all crowded in close, too.

Lucy used her only arm to shoo them away, or at least back; and then she went behind the counter and poured some beer despite the woman's refusal. "Take it," she told her, setting a mug down in front of her. "It smells like horse piss with a sprig of mint, but any port in a storm, wouldn't you say? Well, we don't have any port, so drink this down, dear. It'll warm you up and wake you up."

Varney, the man from the piano, leaned forward and said, "Mostly she tells us it'll put hair on our chests."

"Get back to your keys, you old coot. You're not helping." Lucy reached for a bar towel and wiped up a splash of wayward beer.

Briar wondered about the glove Lucy wore on her sole remaining hand. It was brown leather and it reached up to her elbow, where it was held in place by a series of tiny buckles and straps. There was stiffness in Lucy's fingers, and a faint clicking sound as they squeezed the towel and flapped it open.

"Go on," Lucy insisted. "Give it a try. Won't kill you, I promise—though it might give you a case of the sneezes for a minute. It does that to lots of people, so don't feel funny if it happens."

Not encouraged, but not willing to be rude to the moon-faced woman with the fluffy, graying curls, she sniffed at the beer and steeled herself for a sip. It became apparent at a whiff that a mere sip would gag her, so she seized the handle and jerked the mug to her mouth, swallowing as much as she could in one forced gulp. She tried not to think about what the beverage might do to her stomach.

The woman behind the bar smiled approvingly and patted Briar's shoulder. "See? There you go. Awful as can be, but it'll make you feel better. Now, baby," she urged, "tell ol' Lucy how she can help."

Again, and without meaning to, through eyes that watered from the burn of the beer, Briar was looking at Lucy's hand. Where her other arm ought to have hung, her dress sleeve had been stitched shut and pinned to her side.

Lucy caught her looking and said, "I don't mind if you stare—everybody does. I'll tell you all about it in a bit, if you want to hear it, but right now I want to hear about what *you're* doing here."

Briar was almost too miserable to speak, and the addition of the beer had constricted her throat until she could scarcely manage a sound. "This is all my fault. And if anything horrible has happened to him, that's all my fault too. I've done so many things wrong, and I don't know how to fix any of it, and . . . and . . . are you bleeding?" She cocked her head and scrunched up her forehead as a drip of greasy red-brown fluid splattered onto the bar.

"Bleeding? Oh no, sweetheart. That's just oil." She flexed her fingers, and the knuckles popped with a tinny clack. "The whole thing's mechanical. It gives me a little leak, every so often. Didn't mean to distract you, though. Go on. All your fault, I heard—and I'm prepared to argue, but I thought I'd let you finish."

"Mechanical?"

"Clear up to here," she said, indicating a spot an inch or two down from her elbow. "It's bolted onto my bones. But you were saying."

"That's *amazing.*"

"That's not what you were saying."

Briar said, "Well no, it's not. But your arm is amazing. And . . ." She sighed, and took another long drink of the terrible beer. Her whole body shuddered as the brew went down to sour in her stomach. "And," she repeated, "I'd said all I meant to say. You heard the rest of it. I want to find Zeke, and I don't even know if he's alive. And if he's not—"

"Then it's all your fault, yes. You mentioned. You're being awfully hard on yourself. Boys disobey their parents with such great regularity that it's barely worth a comment; and if yours is talented enough to rebel in such grand fashion, then you ought to consider it a point of

pride that he's such a sharp lad." She leaned forward on her one elbow, laying her mechanical forearm down on the bar. "Now tell me,
you don't really think—do you—that there's anything you could've
done to keep him out of here?"

"I don't know. Probably not."

Someone behind Briar gave her back a friendly pat. It startled her,
but there was nothing salacious about the gesture so she didn't flinch
away from it. Besides, this was more friendly human contact than
she'd had in years, and the pleasantness of it smoothed the keen, guilty
edge of her sorrow.

"Let me ask you this, then," Lucy tried. "What if you'd given him
all the answers to every question he ever asked. Would he have liked
those answers?"

"No, he wouldn't have," she confessed.

"Would he have accepted them?"

"I doubt it."

The barwoman sighed in sympathy and said, "And there you go,
don't you? One day, he'd have gotten a bee in his bonnet about the
old homestead, and he'd have come poking about regardless. Boys
are boys, they are. They're useless and ornery as can be, and when
they grow up they're even worse."

Briar said, "But this particular boy is *mine*. I love him, and I owe
him. And I can't even find him."

"Find him? But baby, you've barely got looking! Swakhammer,"
she turned to him and demanded, "how long have you been dragging
this poor woman through the undersides?"

He swore, "I brought her here first thing, Miss Lucy. I sorted her
out real quick, and—"

"You'd better have sorted her out real quick. If you'd brought
Maynard's girl anywhere else, *or to anyone else*," she said with em-
phasis that made Briar divinely uncomfortable, "I'd have tanned your
hide till it glowed in the dark. And don't you tell me you had to figure
out who she was. I knew as soon as she showed her face in here, and
you did too. I remember that face. I remember this girl. It's been . . .

my word, it's been . . . well, it's been a long time, and a hard time, to be sure."

The chorus behind her murmured agreement. Even Swakhammer mumbled a "Yes, ma'am."

"Now finish your beer, and we'll talk turkey."

It was even harder to suck down the fearsome brew when she was trying so hard not to cry, and the subsequent gulps didn't slide down any easier than the first one.

"You're being so very kind," she said. Between the beer and the throttling, fist-sized lump in her throat, it came out garbled. She added, "I'm sorry, please forgive me. I'm not usually so . . . I'm usually more . . . I'm not used to this. It's like you said, it's been a hard day."

"More beer?"

Much to Briar's surprise, the mug was empty. It was baffling stuff, and she almost certainly shouldn't have replied, "More, all right. But only a bit. I need to keep myself steady."

"This'll keep you steady—or anyway, it won't make you too sloppy, too fast. What you need right now is a moment to sit and talk and think. Let's come on together now, boys." She waved for the bar's occupants to come in closer and pull up seats. "Right now I know you think you've got to run out and get looking, and I don't blame you. But listen to me, baby, there's *time*. No, don't look at me like that. One way or another, there's time. Let me ask you this, did he come with a mask?"

She took another hard swallow and found that the beer wasn't so bad on its second full dose. It still made her mouth taste like the bottom of a restaurant sink, but with practice, it became easier to drink. "He did, yes. He made preparations."

"All right, that would buy him half a day. And it's been more than half a day, so that means he's found a spot to hole up and hunker down."

"Or he's dead already."

"Or he's dead already, fine." Lucy frowned. "Yes, that's a possibility.

Either way, there's nothing you can do for him right at this moment except pull yourself together and make a plan."

"But what if he's trapped somewhere, stuck and needing a rescue? What if he got pinned down by the rotters, and his air's running out, and he's—"

"Now see, don't go getting yourself all worked up like that. It's no help to him, or to you. If you want to think that way, then sure, we can think that way. What if he *is* trapped up someplace and needing a hand? How are you going to find that place? What if you go running off to the *wrong* place, and leave him stranded?"

Briar grimaced down into the mug and wished that the woman weren't making so much sense. "Fine. Then what do I do to get started?"

If Lucy'd had two hands, she would've clapped them together. As it was, she thwacked her clockwork fist down on the counter and declared, "Excellent question! We start with you, of course. He got inside through the water runoff tunnels, you said. Where was he going?"

She told them about the house, and about how Zeke wished to prove his father's innocence by finding proof of the Russian ambassador's interference, and how she did not know if the boy had any idea where the house was located.

Even though Swakhammer had heard most of it already, he stood quietly in the background and paid attention to the story again, as if he might learn something new on the second hearing. He loomed behind the bar, and in front of the fractured mirror. He was all the more ferocious when she could see him from all sides.

When Briar had finished catching them up on everything she could think of, a jittery silence fell in Maynard's.

Varney broke it by saying, "The house you lived in with Blue, that was up the hill there, wasn't it? Up off Denny Street."

"That's right. If it's still standing."

"Which one?" someone asked. Briar thought it might've been Frank.

"The lavender one with cream-colored trim," she said.

The one Swakhammer had called Squiddy asked, "Where was his laboratory? Downstairs?"

"In the basement, yes. And it was huge," she recalled. "I swear, it was as big as the whole house aboveground, almost. But . . ."

"But what?" Lucy asked.

"But it was so badly damaged." Despite the warming numbness of the alcohol, her anxiety spiked once more. "It's not safe down there. Parts of the walls fell down, and there was so much glass everywhere. It looked like an explosion in a goblet factory," she said more quietly.

The memory distracted her with its immediacy. The machine. The destruction downstairs when she'd run there, terrified and searching frantically for her husband. The smell of wet earth and mold; the raging hiss of steam pouring from cracks in the Boneshaker's body; the stink of burning oil and the wire-sharp taste of metal gears grinding themselves into smoke.

"The tunnel," she said out loud.

"I beg your pardon?" Swakhammer said.

She repeated, "The tunnel. Er . . . Varney, is that right? Varney, how did you know which house was ours?"

He fired a wad of tobacco into the spittoon at the end of the counter, and answered, "Used to live up that way myself. Lived with my son, a few streets over. Used to joke about how it ought to be painted blue instead of that purple color."

"Did anyone else here know about the old house? Where we lived, it wasn't a secret, but it wasn't the most common knowledge in the world, either." No one replied, so she concluded, "Right. Basically, nobody knows. But what about the money blocks?"

Lucy raised an eyebrow. "The money blocks?"

"The money blocks, the bank blocks, yes. Everybody knows where those are, right?"

Swakhammer said, "Oh yeah. You can't miss 'em. It's that section over on Third where there's no block at all anymore, just a big hole in the ground. Why? What are you thinking, Miss Wilkes?"

"I'm thinking that the hole got there because . . . oh, we all know *why*. It was the Boneshaker engine; even Levi admitted that much. But after he ran the thing down there, and after the bottom dropped out of the bank blocks, he drove it back home. As far as I know, the Boneshaker is still sitting underneath the house, parked in what's left of that laboratory."

She pushed the mostly empty mug of beer aside and tapped her fingertips on the counter.

"Let's say Zeke can't find the house because no one knows where it is. But he *does* know about what happened with the Boneshaker. He'd have no trouble finding the bank blocks because, like you said, everybody knows where *those* are—and if he could get down in the hole with a light . . . he might think he's got an easy way to find the house."

Lucy lifted the other eyebrow, then dropped them both into a worried look.

"But dearest, those tunnels haven't held up—not all this time. They're just dirt, and dug out with a machine. These days, they're more collapsed than whole. Hell, if you go wandering up the hill, here and there you can see the spots where the tunnels have dropped into sinkholes—eating up trees and walls, and parts of buildings, sometimes. And then there was the quake last night. No, he couldn't have gone too far, not through those tunnels."

"I don't disagree," Briar was quick to say. "But I don't know if any of that would occur to Zeke. I bet you he'll try it. He'll try it, and he'll feel like a genius for it. Hmm."

"Hmm?" Varney echoed.

"He has maps, I think," she told him.

Then she said to Lucy, and therefore to the room, "I found papers in his bedroom, and I think he's got a map or two. I don't know how useful they'll be, and I don't know if they marked out the banks, or the money district, or anything like that. Could you tell me, is there anyone over there—in that part of the city—who Zeke might've asked for help? You said Maynard's isn't the only sealed place inside the walls. Didn't you? You've carved out these places down here."

She looked around at the underground bar and added, "I mean, look at Maynard's. You've done something incredible here. This is as good as anything I've seen in the Outskirts. When I found out people lived here, I didn't understand why. But now I do. You've turned a place of peril into a place where people can live in peace—"

And at that moment, a low-pitched buzz sounded a dull alarm, and everyone in the bar transformed in perfect sync.

Swakhammer pulled a pair of gigantic pistols out of his holsters and spun the cylinders to make sure they were loaded. Lucy reached under the bar and retrieved a modified crossbow. She flipped a latch and the contraption opened; she placed it upside down on the counter and slammed her mechanical arm upon it, and the weapon affixed itself to her wrist with a hard click. Even white-haired Varney with his fragile-looking limbs was bracing himself for trouble. He lifted up the piano's lid and retrieved a pair of shotguns, which he held ready—one under each armpit.

"Is that thing loaded?" Lucy asked, jerking an eyebrow at the Spencer.

It was still on Briar's back, but she retrieved it and held it ready. "Yes," she said, though she couldn't remember to what extent it still held ammunition. How many shots had she fired on the windowsill? Had she reloaded it afterward? Surely it had a few rounds left.

Briar asked Swakhammer, since he was standing closest, "What's going on? What does that noise mean?"

"It means trouble. Not sure what sort. Maybe bad, maybe nothing."

Squiddy held up a brass canister that looked like a shoulder-mounted cannon and said, "But it's best to be ready for bad."

Lucy added, "It's hooked up to a trip wire down the west entrance—the main door, that is. The way you came inside. Jeremiah guided you past the alarm; you probably didn't see it."

And then the buzz was joined by a whistling moan that everyone recognized all too well, coming from the chamber beyond the sealed space of the bar.

"Where's your mask, baby?" Lucy asked. She didn't take her eyes off the front door.

"In my bag. Why?"

"In case we get flushed out, and there's nowhere to go but up." She might have been ready to say more, but a heavy collision knocked against the door and nearly broke it down. More moaning came from the other side, rising in anticipation and excitement, and gaining volume. Briar put on her mask.

Lucy said to Swakhammer, "How's the east tunnel?"

He was already there, examining the passageway via slats in an oblong door behind the piano. "Uncertain," he replied.

Allen asked, "What about the upstairs block? Is that way safe?"

Above them there came a splintering crash, then a loud stumble of decomposing feet rumbled on the floors of whatever lay upstairs. No one asked again if it might be safe.

Varney pointed his guns at the straining door and said, "We have to go *down*."

"Wait," Lucy told him.

Swakhammer returned from the piano corner door to the west tunnel entrance, dragging a railroad tie behind him with one hand and shoving his mask over his head with the other. Squiddy ran to his side and picked up the dangled end of the squared-off log, and between the men they lifted it and shoved it against the door, into a set of slots that held it flush there. Almost immediately, a clattering crack echoed through the bar, accompanied by the splintering stretch of wood that might not hold. The new brace was straining; the brass and steel fittings that lifted it up were leaning away from their mounts.

"What can I do to help?" Briar asked.

Lucy said, "You've got a gun."

"*And she can shoot it*," Swakhammer vouched as he dashed toward the back of the room, where he picked up a metal bar and used it to pry up a section of the floor in a big square sheet. Varney took over and propped it with his hip. Swakhammer returned to stand back-to-back with Lucy, his guns aiming at the west tunnel door.

"There you go," Lucy told her. "You can take a defensive position and shoot for the head of anything that makes it through that door. Nothing else will slow them down."

"East tunnel's no longer uncertain," Frank declared as he whipped the door shut and dropped a metal bar down to latch it. It shut with a crash that sounded in time with another hard push from the other side of the main entrance.

"The subbasement's intact!" Swakhammer declared. "Do we hold the fort or bail? It's your call, Ms. Lucy."

"It's *always* my goddamned call," she swore.

"It's your goddamned bar."

She hesitated, and the front door shattered in slow motion, giving way from the middle beam outwards. "Frank, you said—"

"East way's blocked, ma'am."

"And that way." She cringed as one full door slab cracked and a festering eyeball appeared behind it. "It's hopeless, ain't it?"

Briar lifted the rifle up to her shoulder, squinted, and fired. The eyeball vanished, but in a moment, another one took its place.

Lucy said, "Nice shot. But God knows how many more are behind him. We've got to bail. Bloody goddamn hell. I hate cleaning up after those things. All right. Yes. Everybody out. Varney, you hold the door. Swakhammer, up front. Everybody else, down the hatch behind the bar. You too, Miss Wilkes."

"No. I'm staying with you."

"Nobody's staying. We're all going to run for it." Without looking over her shoulder, Lucy said, "The rest of you bastards had better have one foot in the tunnel and the other on a banana peel. When I turn around, I don't want to see a soul except for Varney holding up the lid."

Briar chanced a look and saw the scuffle that matched the scrambling sounds behind her. Frank, Ed, Allen, and Willard were gone, and Varney was half kicking, half shoving the still-groggy Hank down the hole.

"All clear," Varney announced as Hank fell to the bottom with a yelp.

"Good," Lucy said. But then a whole chunk of wood came smashing out of the door frame and into the bar, and three waving, stinking, grasping hands came reaching through it, prying and yanking at the other boards that stood between them and the emptying room. "After you, Miss Wilkes."

Swakhammer swore loudly and turned his attention to the door behind the piano. "*Behind you!*" he warned.

Briar said, "Mr. Swakhammer, I've got plenty in front of me!" and she fired again.

Swakhammer ran to the east tunnel door and leaned against it, pressing his back firmly and digging his feet into the wood-grained floor. The east entrance was failing every bit as fast as its western counterpart.

"*We can't stay like this!*" he said, and ripped himself away as the first writhing, twisting fingers tried to drill themselves past his armor. He whirled around and cocked the pistols, and fired them at the door with less aiming than Briar had summoned. The blasts hit as much wood as rotter, loosening the barrier even more. A foot broke through the bottom beam and kicked back and forth as if feeling around for something.

"Go!" Briar shouted, preparing the rifle again and firing at anything that wiggled behind the broken places in the doors.

"You first!" Lucy ordered.

"You're closer!"

"All right!" she agreed. Lucy threw herself around the bar's edge and dove for the hole in the floor.

When Briar heard a definitive dropping of the one-armed woman down to some lower corner below, she turned just in time to see Swakhammer's masked face only feet away from hers, and coming in quick.

He seized her arm and grabbed it so fast, and so hard, that she almost shot him by accident; but she lifted the rifle with her unencumbered hand and towed it behind her like a kite as Swakhammer dragged her down to the hole.

The doors broke one after another; the western main entrance and the east tunnel collapsed inward, and a flood of reeking, broken bodies came cascading into the interior.

Briar saw them in snatched glimpses. She didn't slow and didn't hesitate, but she could look, couldn't she? And they were coming with a speed she could scarcely believe from corpses that could hardly hold themselves together. One was wearing half a shirt. One was wearing nothing but boots, and the parts of its body that would otherwise be covered had come sloughing off—revealing gray-black bones underneath.

"*Down,*" Swakhammer insisted. He jammed his hand onto the top of her head, and she ducked to follow the shove of his palm.

She almost fell, mirroring Hank's sloppy toppling; but at the last moment her hand snared the top rung and she swung down in a gangly slide, knocking her knees against the walls and the ladder edges. She stopped at the bottom and slipped, then regained her footing. Her naked hand splashed down onto the floor and she hoped her gloves were in her coat pockets. Otherwise, she didn't know where they'd gone off to.

A hand lifted her by the elbow, and in the darkness she saw Frank's concerned face above her. "Ma'am," he said. "You all right?"

"Fine," she told him, rising to her feet and moving away just in time to keep from getting landed on by Swakhammer, who dropped down into the deeper chamber with a stomp and a splash.

He reached up and locked his hands around the underside handles. "*Lucy,*" he said, and he didn't need to say anything else.

She was already there, her mechanical fist cinched around a trio of steel bars that could've been anything before they were used as braces. Lucy passed them up to Swakhammer one at a time, and he held on tight with one hand while he threaded the bars through the handles with his other one.

From above, fleshless fingers picked angrily at the cracks, but there was no outer hole and Swakhammer had brought the crowbar down below. As a last gesture of defiance and security, he jammed the prying device into a handle and let it serve as an extra brace.

While the hands and feet of the dead things stomped and scratched above, Briar tried to scan the tunnel's atmosphere and figure out where she was. Surely this was the deepest she'd ever been beneath the world, below a basement and down into the bowels of something else—something lower and wetter. This place was not like the finished, brick-lined tunnels that Swakhammer had led her through in order to get to Maynard's; this was a hole dug beneath a solid place, and it unnerved her. It reminded her of another hole beneath another solid place. It made her think of a spot beneath her former home where a catastrophe machine had burrowed its way out into the world, and back again.

It smelled the same, like wet mud and moss, and decomposing sawdust. It stunk like something unfinished and not yet born.

She shivered and clutched herself and her Spencer close, but the warmth of the freshly fired rifle didn't do much to penetrate her coat. All around her, the others huddled together. Their discomfort fed hers, until she was so nervous that her teeth were rattling together.

Finally the trapdoor was as secure as it was going to get, and Swakhammer's bulky shadow stood under the noisy roof. He said, "*Lucy, where're the lanterns at? We still got some down here?*"

"We got one," she said. Briar didn't like the sound of her voice when she shaped that last word, like there was something faulty about it.

"What's wrong?" she asked.

Lucy said, "There ain't hardly any oil in it. I don't know how far it'll get us. But, here, you take it, Jeremiah. You've got your tinder-strike, don't you?"

"*Yes, ma'am.*"

The object in his hand was about the size of an apple, and he struggled with it: His large, gloved fingers were too dull to move it.

"Here," Briar said. She pulled off her mask and shoved it back in her satchel, and she reached out to take the thing. "Tell me what to do with it."

He handed it over and said, "*Don't take that mask off yet, missy. We're going up before we're going back down.*" Then he pointed at a thumb-shaped switch. "*Press that down. No, faster. Harder. Shove it with your fingers.*"

She tried to follow his instructions and, after four or five attempts, a splatter of sparks caught a thick, charred wick and the flame illuminated the tiny crowd. "Now what?"

"*Now you give it back to me, and you put your mask back on like I told you. Lucy, you need help with yours?*"

"Don't be a dummy, boy. I've got it under control," the barkeep said. With her one arm she pulled a folded face-covering out from under her skirt and flapped it open. To answer the question on Briar's face she said, "This is one of Minnericht's experiments. It's lighter than what you've got and it works real good, but it doesn't work for very long. I won't have an hour with these skinny filters. Mostly I keep it tucked in my garter for emergencies."

"Will an hour be enough?" Briar asked.

Lucy shrugged, and she popped the mask over her eyes and chin with a move that couldn't have been smoother if she'd had two arms. "One way or another. We'll find some candles stashed before that's up."

As all around her the other residents of the tunnel produced and donned masks, Briar joined the movement and reapplied her own. "I hate this thing," she complained.

"Nobody loves them," Varney assured her.

"Except Swakhammer," Hank said. He still sounded tipsy, but he was awake and on his own two feet, so his condition was significantly improved. "He loves *his.*"

The armored man cocked his head to the left and agreed. "*Sure. But let's be honest: Mine looks amazing.*"

Lucy said through her compressed cotton and coal filters, "Who says men aren't vain?"

"*I never said it.*"

"Good. So I don't have to call you a liar. You men and your *toys.*"

"Please," Briar interrupted. The closeness of the quarters made her restless, and the wet chill was seeping into her clothes. "What do we do now? Where do we go? Mr. Swakhammer, you said up and then out."

"*That's right. We'll have to come back and clean up Maynard's later.*"

She frowned inside her mask. "Then we're going to another safe spot? A safer spot, I mean. Maybe I should take off now and see about finding Zeke."

"*Oh no you don't. Not with those things swarming, and not on old filters. You'd never make it, crack shot or no. We'll head for the old vault and regroup there. Then we'll talk about clearing the topside and taking on the bank blocks.*"

"Bossy old bastard, aren't you?" she huffed.

"*Yet quite reasonable,*" he said, without having taken any offense.

Willard lifted the lantern, and Swakhammer adjusted the glass. Soon the whole tunnel was alight with a weak orange glow as wet as juice.

Moisture glistened off the incomplete walls, and Briar was only somewhat reassured to see support columns rearing up from the earth and disappearing into the ceiling—the underside of Maynard's floor. Shovels lounged against the walls and were almost consumed by them; the digging tools sank into the muddy surface and jutted against carts. From the carts, Briar's eyes followed the scene down to the tracks beneath them, and then she realized that this was a deliberate place—not simply some cooling cellar.

"What's going on here?" she asked. "You've been clearing this out, haven't you?"

Lucy answered. "Always deeper, dear. Always deeper. For things just like this, you see? We can't go up, not really. We don't have the materials, or the wherewithal, or any safe means of doing so. These walls bind us inside as surely as they hold the world at bay. So if we need to expand—if we need to make more safe places, or create new roads—we have to go down."

Briar stretched her chest to take a deep breath inside her mask, and she grimaced at the musty gray taste of the air she drew. "But don't you ever worry? Like you're undermining the whole place—like it might all come collapsing down?"

From the back of the group Frank said, "Minnericht," as if it explained everything.

Swakhammer said, "*He's a goddamned monster, but he's brilliant. The plans are his. He's the one who laid it all out and told us how to pull the dirt away without hurting the building. But we stopped doing it about six months ago.*"

"Why?" she asked.

"*Long story,*" he said, and he didn't sound like he meant to expound on the subject. "*Let's move.*"

"To where?" Briar demanded, even as she fell into step behind him.

"*To the old vault, I said. You'll like it. It's closer to the bank blocks. We'll get out and take a look around. Maybe we'll see if your boy's been there.*"

"Closer?"

"*Right at the edge of it. We're headed for the old Swedish Trust— the only one that didn't go under. What happened was, the foundation was undermined by the Boneshaker; and the big metal vault was too heavy for the floor. So it sank. And we use it as a front door.*" He lifted the lantern up high and looked back over his shoulder. "*We got everybody?*"

"We got everybody," Lucy confirmed. "Keep moving, big man. We're right behind you."

In some places the way widened so far that the light from the wiggling flame couldn't penetrate its edges; and in some areas the going was so tight that Swakhammer had to turn himself sideways to squeeze through.

Briar trundled along behind him in the middle of the pack, tracking that weak yellow light and chasing its shadows from inside her miserable mask.

# *Fifteen*

"Wake up. Wake up, boy. You alive, or are you dead?"

Zeke wasn't sure who was talking, or if he was the one being spoken to.

His jawline itched all the way up to his ears—that's what he noticed first. The skin felt burned, like he'd gone and laid down on a stovetop. Next, he noticed the weight on his belly, the uneven pressure of something heavy and hard. Then he felt a pain jabbing at his back, where he was lying against something uneven and possibly sharp.

And someone was shaking him, wiggling his head back and forth and fighting for his attention.

The room smelled funny.

"Boy, you wake up now. Boy, don't you play dead. I can see you breathing."

He couldn't figure out who the speaker was. Not his mother. And not . . . Rudy, whose name made him start and almost drag himself straight to horrified consciousness. Remembering was the tricky part, and the awful part. Suddenly he knew where he was, approximately.

He opened his eyes, and did not exactly recognize the face above his.

Almost androgynous with age, the face belonged to a woman, Ezekiel decided. She was old enough to be his grandmother, he was certain, but it was hard to be more precise by the light of her lantern. Her skin was a shade or two darker than his own, the color of a good suede tobacco pouch or the hair of a deer. The jacket she wore had belonged to a man, once. It was cut to fit someone bigger, and her pants were rolled and cinched to keep them from falling down. Her eyes were a pure dark brown like coffee, and they were framed with graying eyebrows that jutted from her forehead like awnings.

Her hands moved like crabs, fast and stronger than they looked. She squeezed the sides of his face.

"You're breathing, ain't you?"

"Yes . . . ma'am," he told her.

He wondered what he was doing on his back. He wondered where Rudy was. He wondered how he'd gotten here, and how long he'd been there, and how he was going to get home.

The fluffy gray brows above him furrowed. "You didn't take in no Blight, did you?"

"Couldn't say, ma'am." He was still lying, still wondering. Gazing up at her and too dazed to do anything but answer a direct question.

She stood upright, and only then did Zeke realize that she'd been crouched beside him. "If you'd taken any inside you, you wouldn't be able to smart off. So I say you're fine, unless you've broken something I can't see. Have you broken anything?"

"Not sure, ma'am."

"Ma'am. Aren't you a funny thing." It wasn't a question.

"Not trying to be funny," he mumbled, and tried to sit up. Something large and flat was blocking the way, and when he wrapped his fingers around it to push it aside, he realized it was a door. "Why is there a door on top of me?"

"Boy, that door done saved your life, it did. You wore it like a shield, all the way down the stairs. It kept you from getting crushed like you oughta have. What happened, see, is that an airship hit the tower. It crash-landed, you might say, right against the side. If it'd hit any harder, it could've broken through the cleaned-up floors all together, and then you'd have been one dead little boy, wouldn't you?"

"I suppose so, ma'am. Ma'am?" he asked.

"Stop calling me ma'am."

"All right, ma'am," he said from habit, not orneriness. "I'm sorry. I only wondered if you were the princess we met down in the tunnels. Are you the princess?"

"You call me Miss Angeline. That's name enough for me, boy."

Zeke said, "Miss Angeline. I'm Zeke."

He flexed his legs to kick the door away from him, and he sat up. And with her help he stood, but without her help he would've slumped right back down to the floor again. Stars and foam gushed across his eyes, and he couldn't see a thing for all the brilliant black light in his head. The sparkles throbbed in time to a vein on his temple.

He pulled himself together and thought that this was how it felt to faint; and then he thought that Princess Angeline had arms stronger than just about any man he'd ever met.

She was holding him, lifting him up and propping him against a wall. She said, "I don't know what became of your deserter. He deserted you, too, I reckon."

"Rudy," Zeke said. "He told me he didn't desert."

"And he's a liar, too. Here, take your mask back. The air in here ain't so good; some of the windows broke upstairs and the bad air's leaking inside. You're back down in the basement now, and it's better here than some other places, but all the seals are shot."

"My mask. My filters are getting all stuffy."

"No they ain't. I cut two of mine down and stuck 'em in your slots. You'll be all right again for a while—plenty long enough to get out of town, anyway."

He complained, "I can't get out of town yet. I came here to go up Denny Hill."

"Boy, you ain't no place near Denny Hill. It's like I tried to tell you down in the Rough End tunnels, old Osterude wasn't running you back home. He was running you down to the old devil they call Dr. Minnericht, and Jesus Christ knows what would happen to you then, but I don't. Zeke," she said more softly, "you've got a momma outside, and if you don't get yourself home, she's gonna worry herself something awful. Don't you do that to her. Don't you make her think she's lost her child."

A flash of pain quickened her face, and for a moment it looked like stone.

"Ma'am?"

The stone flexed and fell away. "It ain't right, to do a mother like that. You got to get yourself home. You already been gone all day—a whole day—and it's past nighttime again, practically morning. Come with me now, won't you?" She held out her hand and he took it, for lack of knowing what else to do. "I think I've scared you up a quick passage back to the Outskirts."

"Maybe, maybe that's best," he said. "I can always come back later, can't I?"

"Sure enough, if you want to get yourself killed. I'm trying to do you a kindness, here."

"I know, and I thank you," he said, still uncertain. "But I don't want to leave, not yet. I don't want to go until I've seen the old house."

"You're in no shape for that, young man. None at all. Look at you, all banged-up head and torn-up clothes. You're lucky you ain't dead. You're lucky I came after you, meaning to pull you away from that old devil with his fire-breathing cane."

"I liked his cane," Zeke said, and he reluctantly accepted the return of his mask. "It was neat. Helped him walk, and helped him defend himself, too. After the war where he got hurt—"

She cut in. "Osterude didn't get hurt in no war. He ran away from it before he had time to get blowed up. He hurt his hip when he fell down drunk a couple years ago, and now he sucks down opium, whiskey, and yellow sap to keep it from hurting him too much. Don't you forget this, boy—he ain't your friend. Or maybe he *weren't* your friend, I don't know if the slide done killed him or not. I can't find him, no how."

"Are we in the basement?" Zeke changed the subject.

"That's right, just like I told you. You slid back all the way down when the ship crashed into the tower, like I said."

"A ship crashed into the tower? Why'd it do that?" he asked.

"Well it wasn't on purpose, you silly thing. I don't rightly know *why*. Brink's a pretty good captain, but I don't recognize the ship he's flying now. It must be new, and maybe he ain't used to running it yet. They must've had a little accident, that's all—and now they're up there, fixing the damage before they take off again."

His eyes adjusted to the lantern light and he realized, with some difficulty, that she was holding something stranger than a regular, oil-based device. "What's that?"

"It's a lantern."

"What kind?"

"A good and bright one, that the rain won't likely put out," she said. "Now get yourself up, boy. We need to get you up a few floors to the tower's top, where the ship's hanging tight. It's a piecemeal, hodgepodge of a pirate's thing called the *Clementine*. And just so you know"—she lowered her voice—"when I said that the captain's flying a new ship, I didn't mean it's a brand-new craft. I mean, like as not he *stole* it."

"And you're just gonna hand me over to him?" Zeke grumbled. "I don't like the sound of that—pirates dropping me over a wall."

But she insisted, "They won't give you no guff. I've bought 'em off good, and they know me too well to hurt you once I've taken their word. They won't treat you too softly, but they won't hurt you none worse than you're already battered."

Alternately motherly and general-like, the princess ushered him into the rubble of the stairwell and told him, "Come on, now. The way upstairs is more clear than it looks. Everything dumped out at the bottom, same as you."

Zeke didn't know how to feel as he followed her spry, sidestepping climb. There was absolutely no light except for the peculiar white gleam of Angeline's lantern, even when they scaled a flight or two and he could see through the empty, unfinished floors how black the night was on the other side of the windows. It was dark, and so late that it'd become early.

"I left her a note, but . . . my mother's going to kill me."

The princess said, "That all depends on timing. The trick is, you've got to be gone long enough that she stops being mad, but starts to worry . . . but you don't want to make her worry too much, otherwise she'll tip back over to anger."

Zeke smiled in his mask as he rose behind her. "You must have kids of your own."

She did not smile back. Zeke knew because he did not hear an up-turned twitch of her mouth when she hesitated on the next debris-littered stair and kept walking. She said, "I had a daughter once. A long time ago."

Something in her tone kept Zeke from following up with any polite inquiries.

He huffed and puffed up after her, marveling at her energy and strength; and he found other inappropriate things to wonder and sti-fle. He was desperate to ask how old she was, but he bit that question back only by asking instead, "Why do you dress like a man?"

"Because I feel like it."

"That's weird," he said.

She replied, "Good." And then she said, "You can ask the other question if you want to. I know you're wondering. You wonder it so loud I can almost hear it. It's like listening to the crows outside."

Zeke had no idea what any of that meant, but he wasn't about to directly ask how long she'd walked upon the earth, so he came at it sideways. "How come there aren't any young people here?"

"Young people?"

"Well, Rudy's old enough to be my dad, at least. And I saw some Chinamen, but most of them looked that old or . . . even older. And then there's . . . you. Is everyone down here . . ."

"Old?" she finished for him. "Keeping in mind that your idea of old and my idea of old are two different things, you've noticed rightly. And sure enough, there's a reason for it. It's an easy reason, and you could think of it yourself if you tried hard."

He pushed a toppled beam up out of his way so he could walk

past it instead of climb under it. "I'm a little busy for thinking," he told her.

"Well ain't that something. Too busy for thinking. Busy is when you ought to think the fastest. Otherwise, how you expect to last down here any longer than a flea lasts on a dog?" She paused on a landing and waited for him to catch up to her. Lifting the lantern and looking up and down, she said, "I hear them up there, the men on the ship. They aren't real sweet, not any given one of them, but I think you'll be all right. You're willing to think on the fly, aren't you?"

"Yes, ma'am."

"All right, then tell me now, while we walk, why there aren't hardly no kids like you down here."

"Because . . ." He recalled Rudy's mention of the Chinese men and why they had no women. "There aren't any women here. And women usually take care of kids."

She pretended to be offended, and said, "No women? I'm a woman if ever you saw one. We've got women down here."

"But I meant *young* women," he babbled, and then heard how wrong it was. "I meant, younger women than . . . I meant, women who might have babies. I know there aren't no Chinese women. Rudy said so."

"Well, what do you know? Rudy told you the truth about something. He was right there, yes. There ain't no Chinawomen here in the city, or if there are, I ain't seen them. But I tell you what, I know of at least one other woman who lives down here. She's a one-armed barkeep named Lucy O'Gunning, and one arm or many, she'll break down doors or men or rotters. She's a tough old bird," Angeline said with no small trace of admiration. "But saying that, I should also say, she's old enough to be my daughter. And she's old enough to be *your* mother—or maybe even your grandmother. So keep thinking, boy. Why aren't there any young folks here?"

"Give me a hint," he begged, chasing after her, up the next clogged and dusty flight of stairs. He didn't know how many they'd scaled, but he was tired and he didn't want to climb any farther. It didn't matter. She wasn't slowing down, and she was the one with the light, so he tagged along behind.

"You want a hint, all right. How long ago did the walls go up?"

"Fifteen years," he said. "Give or take a couple of months. Momma said they were finished on the day I was born."

"Is that so?"

"That's how I heard it," he swore.

And he began to think of how many years fifteen was, if you weren't a baby to start with. He thought about how old his mother had been—barely twenty, fifteen years ago. He tried, speaking slowly as he worked to breathe against his mask and his exhaustion, "Most of the folks in here, have they been here all this time?"

"Most of them, yep."

"So if they were grown men—and women," he added fast, "in their twenties and thirties . . . now they're all in their thirties and forties, at least."

She stopped and swung the light around, nearly clapping him in the forehead. "There you go! Good boy. Good thinking, even while you're panting like a puppy." After a thoughtful pause she added, "I hear there's a couple of boys down in Chinatown, brought inside by their dads or uncles. Orphans, some of them might be. I don't know. And Minnericht, since that's what he calls himself—he's been known to bring down a younger crew once in a while. But you got to understand, most people who didn't start out down here . . . they can't get used to it. They don't stay long. I can't say as I blame them."

"Me either," he said, and he wished hard for three wishes—the very first of which would send him home, should the universe be so kind. He was worn out, and nauseous from the filtered, stinking air, and his skin was smudged raw around all its edges. The face of the murdered Chinese man kept flitting through his mind when he shut his eyes, and he didn't want to be anywhere near the body—not even within the same city walls.

"Soon," Angeline promised him.

"Soon?"

"Soon, you'll be out and on your way home."

His eyes narrowed behind his visor and he said, "Can you read people's thoughts or something?"

She said, "No. But I read people pretty good."

Zeke could hear a background hum then, above him and off to the left—the banging din of tools against steel and the hoarse swearing of unhappy men in protective masks. Every now and again the building would quiver as if it'd been struck again, and each of these shocks made Zeke grab for the wall to steady himself. Rudy was right about two things. There were no women in Chinatown, and there were no rails in the unfinished tower.

"Miss Angeline?" he broached, and around the next corner the world grew a few shades lighter, or he thought it did.

"What is it?" she asked. "We're almost there. See? The windows are more broken, and what's left of the moonlight's coming inside. We're right up close to where they crashed against the side of this old place."

"That's fine. I was just wondering. Rudy wouldn't say, and you haven't mentioned—who's this Dr. Minnericht you've both been talking about?"

The princess didn't quite stop, but she jerked and shuddered, like she'd seen a ghost or a murder. Something in her posture tightened and coiled. She looked like a skinny-armed clock wound up too tight and ready to break.

She said, "That ain't his name."

And she turned around to him, again almost hitting him with her lantern, for she didn't know how close he trailed in her wake. Even inside the mask her face was a shadowbox of canyons and peaks; her hawk's-beak nose and deep-set, slightly slanted eyes made a map of someone's anger.

With her free hand she grabbed Zeke's shoulder and pulled him close, until the warm white light was almost a burn against his face. She shook him and pulled him near, and she said, "If something goes wrong, perhaps you ought to know—we're in his land, in this part of the city. If hell comes for us with a handbasket and a one-way ticket and you don't make this ship, or if you fall, and if he finds you, you may as well be prepared for him."

Upstairs the men were swearing louder, speaking in English with a world's assortment of accents. Zeke tried not to hear them, and tried not to see the cavernous wrinkles in the princess's leather face. But he was transfixed by her rage, and he couldn't move, even to disentangle his stare from hers.

"He's no doctor, and he's no German—though that's the name he's taken. No Hessian, no foreign man and no local man, either. That's what he likes to say," she said. And then she started as if something new and horrible had occurred to her.

Her eyes caught fire and she hissed, "Whatever he tells you, whatever he says, he's no native of this place and no man he ever claimed to be. He'll never tell you the truth, because it's worth his trouble to lie. If he finds you, he'll want to keep you—and the more I think of it, the more I'm sure that'll be his way. But nothing he tells you is true. Assume that, and you'll survive an encounter with him, as likely as not. But . . ." She withdrew, and the boiling fear in her face cooled to a small, simmering pot.

"But we'll just have to make sure that doesn't happen," she said, and patted him on the head, ruffling his hair and making the straps on his mask tug at his irritated skin. "So let's get you upstairs, onto that ship."

She released him and, smiling again, took the lead up one more interminable flight of stairs until the top came and fresh air spilled into the stairwell.

Ezekiel had to remind himself that the air wasn't really fresh. It was just cold, and it came from outside. But that didn't mean anything, and it surely didn't mean he could yank his mask off—though he would've given anything to do so. He was shaken by Angeline's tirade and unsettled by the rough, noisy men who worked on the floor above.

The princess led the way with her light, and she saluted the airship men with a swear word that made Zeke laugh.

They turned to watch the old woman glow with her wild, white lamp and the skinny, ruffle-haired boy behind her.

Zeke saw five of them, scattered around the room doing such useful things as patching holes and swinging mallets against bent bolts protruding from the hull of a ship so big that the boy couldn't see the end of it. Only one small part of the hull had crammed itself against the row of windows, which had been broken into dust by the impact of the ship's collision.

The *Clementine* had either stuck there or forcibly docked there, and Zeke didn't know the difference—or if it mattered.

Lashed against the wall's support beams, the floating ship was drawn almost inside the building, where the five men worked on its more battered parts. A large hole was coming closed under the sweaty, leaning force of a man with a crowbar the size of a small tree, and a tall white man in a dark orange mask was restringing a web of ropy nets.

Two of the five saluted the princess back with more profanity. One of them looked like he might be in charge.

His hair was bright red under the straps of his mask, and his wide, burly body was marked with elaborate inkwork and scars. On one arm, Zeke spied a silver-scaled fish; and on the other he saw a dark blue bull.

Angeline asked him, "Captain Brink, you almost ready to fly off again?"

"Yes, Miss Angeline," he replied. "Once this split in the hull is all smoothed shut, we'll be able to take off and take a passenger or two. This your friend?"

"This is the boy," she said, dodging the implication, if there was one. "You can set him down anyplace outside, just take him outside. And on your next pass-through, I'll give you the rest of what I promised."

He adjusted his mask while he looked Zeke up and down, like a horse he was thinking about buying. "That's fine with me, ma'am. But just so you know, our next pass-through might be some ways off. We're in a bit of a rush to get going, and get going far."

"Why's that?" she asked.

"Just chasing the market," he answered vaguely. Then he said, "Nothing for you two to worry about, no problem. Boy, you come on inside. Angeline, you sure you don't need a wing out of the city?"

"No, Captain, I don't. I've got business to attend to here. I've got a deserter to shoot," she added under her breath, but Zeke heard her.

He asked, "You're not really going to shoot him, are you?"

"No, probably not. Like as not, I'll pin him." She said it offhandedly and watched the airmen work their repairs. She said to Brink, "This don't look like the last ship of yours I saw."

He'd picked up a mallet and was beating down another pinched plate. He stopped and told her, "Matter of fact, she's new. You're a sharp-eyed woman to notice."

"And her name's *Clementine*?"

"That's right. Named after my momma, who ain't lived long enough to see it fly."

She said, "That's sweet of you," but there was doubt in her words, for all she tried to keep Zeke from hearing it.

He whispered, "Is something wrong?"

"No," she did not whisper back. "It's all fine. I know these fellas," she assured him. "That there is Captain Brink, as you've done guessed by now. Beside him there's his first mate, Parks; and over there with the nets is Mr. Guise. Ain't that right?"

"That's right," the captain said, without looking over his shoulder. "And the two you don't recognize are Skyhand and Bearfist. They're brothers. I picked them up in Oklahoma, last time we kicked through there."

"Oklahoma," Angeline echoed. "You two brothers of mine?" she asked them.

Zeke frowned. "You've got brothers you don't know?"

"No, you dumb boy," she said without any real venom. "I wondered if they was native, like me. Or maybe what tribe they hailed from."

But neither of the men answered. They kept working, elbows-deep in a boiler-shaped engine that was blackened at one end and steaming ominously from the other.

Brink said, "They aren't out to disrespect you, Miss Angeline. Neither one of them speaks English too good. I don't think Duwamish would be clear to 'em either. They work as hard as mules, though, and they know their way around machinery."

Under the straps of their masks Zeke could see dark, straight hair. Their forearms were browned, but it might have only been ash or soot that darkened them. Still, he could see they were Indians like Miss Angeline. Neither of the men looked up, and if they knew they were being discussed, they didn't care about it any.

Zeke asked Angeline, very quietly, "How well do you know these guys?"

"We're all acquainted."

The captain said, "Anyway, we'll be able to lift off in a few minutes." Zeke thought he sounded like a man who was trying not to sound agitated.

First Mate Parks glanced out the window, or he tried—but of course his ship was in the way. He exchanged a look with the captain, who made rushing gestures as if everyone ought to hurry.

He asked, "How close are we to done?"

Mr. Guise, a meaty man in rolled-up pants and an undershirt, said, "Done enough to fly now, I think. Let's load up and hit the sky."

Princess Angeline was watching the scene with worry, which she painted over with optimism when she caught Zeke looking at her and saw that the worry was catching. She said, "It's time. And it's been nice to meet you, Zeke. You seem like a nice enough boy, and I hope your mother doesn't beat you too bad. Get on home now, and maybe I'll see you again sometime."

For a moment Zeke thought he was in for a hug, but the princess didn't squeeze him. She only walked away, back down to the corridor, where she disappeared down the stairs.

Zeke stood awkwardly in the midst of the windblown room with the broken windows and the battered warship.

Warship.

The word fluttered through his brain, and he didn't know why. The *Clementine* was only a dirigible, patchwork and piecemeal stuck together to make a machine that could fly across the mountains to move cargo of any kind. So perhaps, he told himself, there was some segment of something rougher built into that matte black hull.

He asked the captain, who was stuffing his tools into a cylindrical leather bag big enough to hold another man, "Sir? Where should I—"

"Anywhere's fine," he answered hastily. "Princess paid your way, and we won't do wrong by her. She's an old lady, for sure, but I wouldn't double-cross her. I like my insides right where they are, thank you much."

"Erm . . . thank you, sir. Should I just . . . go inside?"

"Do that, yeah. Stay close by the door. The way things are going, we'll probably have to kick you out a little higher up than we'd like."

Zeke's eyes went huge. "You're just going to . . . throw me out of the ship?"

"Oh, we'll put a rope around you first. We won't let you splat too hard, all right?"

"All right," Zeke said, but he didn't think the captain was joking, and he was going weak with fear.

Just like Angeline's worry was contagious, the impatience and nervousness of the swiftly working crew was knocking against the boy's psyche, too. Something about their movements had become even more frenetic and hurried when Angeline had left the room, lending Zeke the impression that they'd been putting on a front for her. He didn't like it.

Jammed against the building's side and wedged quite firmly in place, a portal in the hull had been propped open for the crew mem-

bers to come and go. Zeke pointed at the portal and the captain nodded at him, encouraging him to let himself inside.

"But don't touch anything! That's a direct order, kid, and if you
disobey it you'd better grow wings before we take air. Otherwise I'll
leave out the rope," he promised.

Zeke held up his hands and said, "I hear you, I hear you. I won't
touch anything. I'm just going to stand inside, right here, and . . ." He
realized that no one was listening to him, so he stopped talking and
stepped gingerly through the portal.

The interior of the ship was bleak and cold, and not completely
dry; but it was brighter than Zeke would've expected, scattered
throughout with small gas lamps that were mounted to the walls on
swinging arms. One was broken, and its pieces were ground into the
floor.

He straightened and peered from corner to corner, being careful
to keep his hands from even brushing past the complicated controls
and dangling levers. His mother used to have an expression about
avoiding even the appearance of evil, and he stuck to it quite firmly as
a matter of self-preservation.

The cargo hold was open and gaping. When Zeke poked his head
inside he saw boxes stacked in the corners, and bags hanging from
the ceiling. His old buddy Rector had told him a little bit about the
way Blight was collected for processing, so he could guess what the
bags were for; but the boxes weren't labeled in any way, and he had
no idea what they might contain. So the *Clementine* wasn't moving
gas; it was moving some other cargo instead.

Outside someone loudly dropped a wrench.

Zeke leaped back as if he'd been struck, though no one was near
him and no one seemed to notice that he'd left the doorway where
he'd been ordered to stand. He retreated quickly and planted himself
beside the portal, where Mr. Guise and Parks were carrying their
tools back inside. Neither man gave him a second look, though the
captain complained when he tried to follow them. "You're staying
there, aren't you?"

"Yes sir, I am."

"Good lad. There's a strap above your head. Hang onto it. We're shoving off."

"Now?" Zeke peeped.

Mr. Guise pulled a jacket off the back of a chair and shrugged his shoulders into it. "Twenty minutes ago would've been better, but now will work."

"It'd better," Parks complained. "They'll be on our tail any minute," he said. Then he saw Zeke out of the corner of his eye, and stopped himself from saying more.

"I know," the captain agreed with whatever abbreviated thought had been on Parks's tongue. "And Guise is off by about forty minutes. Damn us all for blowing the hour's head start."

Parks gritted his teeth so hard that his jawline, visible outside his mask, was as sharp as granite. "It's not my fault the thrusters were marked wrong. I wouldn't have hit the goddamned tower on purpose."

"No one said it was your fault," Brink said.

"No one had *better* say it, either," Parks growled.

Zeke laughed nervously and said, "I'm not, that's for sure."

Everyone ignored him. The Indian brothers came on board and immediately began yanking the portal shut. The rounded door stuck, then succumbed to the force of four arms pulling and popped itself into place. A wheel on the door was spun and locked, and everyone assumed a position in the crowded, cluttered deck.

"Where are the goddamned steam vents?" Mr. Guise threw up his fingers and flexed them into a fist.

"Try the left panel," the captain urged.

Mr. Guise sat down in the main chair and it swiveled and rocked. He braced his feet down beneath the console and tried to draw the chair closer to the control panel, but it wouldn't budge.

Zeke retreated against the wall and leaned there, his hand tangled in the strap that hung down above his head. He caught one of the Indian brothers—he didn't know which one—looking at him, so he said, "You uh . . . haven't been flying this ship long, have you?"

"Shut that kid up," Parks said without turning around. "I don't care how you do it, but shut him up or I'm going to shut him up."

The captain glowered back and forth between Zeke and Parks, and he settled on Zeke, who was already blabbering, "I'll be quiet! I'll shut up, I'm sorry, I was just, I was only, I was making conversation."

"Nobody wants your conversation," Mr. Guise told him.

The captain agreed. "Just keep your mouth closed and you'll be fine, and I won't have to answer to that deranged old lady. Don't make us throw you out without a net or a rope, boy. We'll do it if we have to, and I'll tell her it was an accident. She won't be able to prove otherwise."

Zeke had already assumed as much. He made himself as small as he could, crushing his bony back against the boards and trying hard not to choke on his own fear.

"You got that?" the captain asked, looking him straight in the eye.

"Yes sir," he breathed. He wanted to ask if he could remove the mask, but he didn't want to take the risk of angering anyone else. He was pretty sure that any given man on board would've shot him in the head as soon as told him "hello."

The mask's seals scrubbed against his skin, and the straps constricted his skull so hard he thought his brain would come out his nose. Zeke wanted to cry, but he was too afraid to even sniffle, and he figured that was just as well.

Mr. Guise fumbled with a row of buttons, smashing them almost randomly, as if he didn't know what any of them did. "There's no release latch for those miserable clamps. How are we supposed to disengage from the—"

"We're not docked like normal," Parks told him. "We're smashed against the tower. We'll go outside and pry the thing out ourselves, if we have to."

"We don't have time. Where's the grapple release? Is there a kit for it over there? A lever or something? We got the hooks to deploy for stability; how do we call them back to disengage?"

Brink said, "Here, maybe this?" He leaned over his first mate and stretched one pale arm out to grab a lever and tug it.

The sound of something clacking outside relieved everyone inside. "Did that do it? Are we loose?" Mr. Guise demanded, as if anyone knew any better than he did.

The ship itself answered them, shifting in the hole it'd broken into the side of the half-built tower. It settled and listed to the left and down. Zeke felt less like the *Clementine* had disengaged than that it was falling out of place. The boy's stomach sank and then soared as the airship tumbled away from the building and seemed to freefall. It caught and righted itself, and the dirigible's lower decks quit rocking like a grandmother's chair.

Zeke was going to throw up.

He could feel the vomit that he'd swallowed after watching the Chinaman's murder. It crept up his throat, burning the flesh it found and screaming demands to be let out.

"I'm going to—" he said.

"Puke in your mask and that's what you're breathing till we set you down, boy," the captain warned. "Take off your mask and you're dead."

Zeke's throat burbled, and he burped, tasting bile and whatever he'd last eaten, though he couldn't remember what that might have been. "I won't," he said, because saying the words gave his mouth something to do other than spew. "I won't throw up," he said to himself, and he hoped that he gave that impression to the rest of the men, or that they could ignore him, at least.

A left-facing thruster fired and the ship shot in a circle before stabilizing and rising.

"*Smooth*," the captain accused.

Parks said, "Go to hell."

"We're up," Mr. Guise announced. "We're steady."

The captain added, "And we're out of here."

"Shit," said one of the Indian brothers. It was the first English

Zeke had heard from either of their mouths, and it didn't sound good.

Zeke tried to stop himself, but he couldn't.

He asked, "What's going on?"

"Jesus," Captain Brink blasphemed with one eye on the rightmost window. "Crog and his buddy have found us. Holy hell, I figured it'd take him a little longer. Everybody, buckle down. Hang on tight, or we're all of us dead."

## Sixteen

Swakhammer shined his lantern at a pile of broken and buried crates that had been stacked haphazardly and left to wobble and sink. It seemed to be the only way forward.

"*Me first,*" he said. "*We ought to be far enough away from Maynard's that maybe we'll miss the worst of the swarm. Those things are relentless. They'll try to dig through the floor until their hands wear off, and the louder they get, the more of their number they'll draw.*"

"Away from us," Briar mumbled.

"*Here's hoping. Let me take a look around up there and make sure.*"

He lifted one big leg to stomp on the bottom crate and it sank a couple of inches, squishing down into the muck. Once the crate had stopped drooping, he brought the other leg around and climbed slowly up the rickety pile. A set of reinforcing metal bands peeled back with a splintering scrape that was louder than gunfire in the muffled underground.

Everyone cringed and held silent and still.

Lucy asked, "Do you hear anything?"

Swakhammer said, "*No, but let me look.*"

Briar shuffled and lifted her boot up out of the muck, but she was forced to put it right back where it had been sinking. There was no place sturdy enough to stand without feeling the slow, sticky draw of the wet earth. "What are you looking for? More rotters?"

"*Uh-huh.*" He pressed the back of his shoulder against the trapdoor and locked his knees. "*East way was plugged up with them. We've gone east underneath 'em, but I don't know if we've gone east enough to miss the back end of the swarm. Everybody quiet now,*" he said. The crates groaned beneath him and the mud slurped terribly at the cheap pine corners, threatening to bring the whole stack down. But the structure held, and Swakhammer strained to move himself quietly—and to lift the door without making a noise.

"Well?" Hank asked, a little too loudly.

Lucy shushed him, but she looked up at the armored man and her eyes asked the same question.

"*I think it's clear,*" he said. He did not sound convinced, but the huddled crowd below heard no hint of shuffling, scratching, or moaning, either, so the silence was taken as a good sign.

Swakhammer lowered the door again and addressed the group as softly as his altered voice would permit. "*We're at the apothecary's on Second Avenue, right underneath old Pete's storage cellars. As far as I know, there's no connecting space between this basement and Maynard's. Lucy, you know how to get to the Vaults from here, right?*"

"From here it ought to be one block down, and one block right."

"*Good. Now listen—Miss Wilkes—there aren't any down-drops between here and there, so stick close and run like hell if it comes down to it.*"

"Down-drops?"

"*Entrances to the underground. Secured places. You know. Once we get outside, we're stuck outside until we reach the Vaults. That's the closest and safest place around here, outside of Maynard's. And there's no going back to Maynard's for another day or two at soonest.*"

"Goddamn," Lucy grumbled. "And I just got it cleaned up again after last time."

"*Don't worry about it, Miss Lucy. We'll put it back together for you. But for now, we need to head down and stay down until we can sort out how the rotters found their way through so fast.*"

"No," Briar shook her head. "No, I can't hunker down anywhere. I've got to find my son."

Lucy put her hard, clicking hand down on Briar's arm. She said, "Honey, the Vaults are as close to your boy as we're likely to get, if you think he's seeking the way to the Boneshaker. Listen, we'll head over there, and maybe we'll find someone who's seen him. We'll ask, and we'll pass the word around. But you've got to stick with us if you want to keep yourself in one piece long enough to find him."

Briar wanted to argue, but she bit the protest back. She nodded over at Swakhammer as if to tell him she agreed, and he accepted the gesture enough to lift the lid and push himself through.

One by one the fugitives from Maynard's scaled the unsteady stack of crates and chairs, and one by one they emerged from the mildew-dank underworld and up into the basement of an old apothecary's place.

Swakhammer's lantern light was fluttering, on the verge of going out altogether, when Frank and Willard scared up a pair of candles in time to spread the glow out farther. They broke the candles in two to make the room brighter with extra flames, but Lucy gave a word of caution.

"Keep the candles up high, folks. These old crates are packed with munitions stuffed in sawdust. All it takes is one spark on a batch that ain't soaked, so keep 'em close. We got everyone?" she asked.

Hank said, "Yes, ma'am." He was the last one up, and the trapdoor dropped down behind him.

"Everyone's masks all secured?"

Nods went around the circle. Buckles were tightened, straps were cinched, and lenses were adjusted into place. Briar checked her satchel and pulled her hat on over the mask. She slung the Spencer over her shoulder. In her pockets she found her gloves, and she thanked heaven for them. If she was going outside, she didn't want any skin exposed.

While Swakhammer tiptoed up the basement staircase and tried his hand at the door's latch, Briar worked the gloves on over her filthy fingers.

He unbarred the door and held a pistol out and ready, up next to his chest. The door swung out a few inches and he jammed his head into the crack. Looking left, and looking right, he concluded that the way was clear and announced this to the small crowd downstairs.

*"Hurry up, stay quiet, and keep your heads low. The windows aren't covered up too good. A rotter who's paying enough attention can take a peek inside. Don't give them anything to see."*

He let himself all the way into the shop, up into the back room, and out of the way so that others could follow behind him. *"Come on. Hurry up. That's right, everybody—go on past me now and I'll watch the rear. We're going to go out the side door. See it? It's behind the counter. Try to keep yourself below the counter line, and I want all the candles out. I know we just lit them up, but I didn't know the windows were uncovered and we can't take a chance up here. We'll be spotted faster than we can run. So put them out, and stick 'em in your pockets. We'll want them later. Are we ready?"*

"Ready," said a chorus of whispers, choked by mask filters and nervousness.

*"Come on, then,"* Swakhammer said.

Lucy went first. Swakhammer brought up the back of the single-file line and guarded it with pistols drawn, the Daisy bouncing against his back.

Briar kept her body curled in a crouch as she shuffled—hunched, bent, and half-blind from the darkness—through the boarded-up store with its dusty windows smeared with grime.

Within the store there was almost no light. Swakhammer had abandoned the lantern, and all but one candle had been snuffed and stored. That last candle was kept close and dim at Lucy's chest, and it cast almost no illumination. But here and there, Briar could see smashed countertops that collected the dripping moisture of a building no longer in good repair. The wood of the floor and the window frames was warped with the sodden air and perpetual acidic, gnawing teeth of the ever-present Blight.

*"Lucy, you got that door?"* he breathed, barely any quieter than his normal voice.

She bobbed her head and wrapped her mechanical hand around the big wooden brace that shut it from the inside. She leaned her head against the door and said, "I don't hear anything."

"*Good. Make way. I'm coming through.*" He shimmied sideways and hunkered up to the front of the line, and Lucy stepped aside so he could lead the way.

He looked back at the assembled crew, said, "*Worse comes to worst . . . ,*" and cocked his head at the Daisy, just sticking up over his shoulder. "*But let's keep it softer than that if we can. Just two blocks.*"

"Two blocks," Briar echoed. She swallowed hard, and told herself that she was making progress. She was getting closer. She was headed toward the neighborhood where her son might have gone, and that was a step in the right direction.

Swakhammer took Lucy's candle and drew the door inward. The whole line of people behind him retreated half a step at a time, giving him room.

Outside the world was perfectly black.

Briar could've guessed that much from the inky interior of the apothecary's shop, but she'd assumed that the debris-cluttered windows and the filthy glass might make a grim illusion. She hadn't realized how late the day had become. "It's night," she breathed with some amazement.

Lucy reached over and squeezed Briar's shoulder. "It takes some getting used to," she whispered back. "Being underneath, it's hard to tell the time; and God knows the days are short enough during the winter. Come on, sweetheart—it's still Saturday, technically anyhow. Onward and upward. Over at the Vaults, maybe somebody will know about your boy. But first, we've actually got to get there. One thing at a time, right?"

"One thing at a time," she agreed.

Swakhammer extinguished the last candle with a reluctant pinch of his leather-gloved fingers against its wick. As he drew the door wide enough to let himself out, Briar held her breath and waited for the night to try to kill them all.

But nothing happened.

Swakhammer hustled the group out the door and pulled it closed behind them, making sure that only the smallest click announced the seal. Then he turned back and growled so low that he could scarcely be heard, "*Hold close. Hold hands if you can stand it. We're going one block north and one block west. Miss Wilkes, you and that repeater should bring up the rear. Don't be too quick to shoot. No noise if possible.*"

Her hat brushed against the stone storefront as she nodded, and that was all Swakhammer needed to hear. He could barely see her, but she hadn't objected. Briar retreated to the back of the line and pulled the Spencer off her shoulder, so she could hold it poised and ready to fire.

In line behind Hank, who was seemed on the verge of falling asleep where he stood, Briar tried to keep watch on both directions at once. But Hank fell behind and lost his place, and Briar shoved him back into position.

He was dragging, and she couldn't afford to be dragged. She didn't know where she was going, not really—and certainly not at night, in the dark, when she could not see the shifting forms of her companions. She could not see the sky above, not even the yellow tubes that she knew must sprout up into the air; and only if she squinted through the smudged lens of her cumbersome old mask could she detect the jagged outlines where the rooftops and spires of the crumbling buildings stood black against the clouds above them.

But she couldn't look long. Hank was sliding back down, knocking his skinny shape against the walls.

She caught him with one hand, and propped him up with the rifle while she tried to steady him. *Stupid goddamn drunk*, she thought, but she didn't say it out loud. She used all her weight to hold him in a semistanding position.

"What's the matter, Hank?" she asked, pushing and shoving, and using her own limbs as crutches to keep him on his feet.

He groaned in response, but it didn't tell her anything except that he'd had too much of the miserable yellow beer and now it was hurting him. She wished she could see to help, but it was hard to see, and harder to help when he swatted her hands away and rolled himself along the wall.

"*Hush up back there!*" Swakhammer ordered, the metal in his voice cutting the hiss to a whistling demand.

"I'm trying to keep him—," Briar started to say back, and stopped herself. "Hank," she whispered to him, instead. "Hank, get yourself together. You've got to walk. I can't carry you."

He moaned again and seized at her hand.

She thought he meant to use it to push himself forward, and that was fine; she helped nudge him that way, back into his spot in the frightened, shuffling queue. But the moan stuck in her mind and it itched there, as if it ought to be telling her more than she'd heard at first.

Hank stumbled again and she caught him again, letting him lean on her shoulder as he ambled along. One foot kicked against the other and he crumpled to the ground against the curb, dragging Briar down with him.

She clutched at his hand and he clutched back. To the others, whose footsteps were scraping onward and away, she called out, "Wait!" in the loudest whisper she dared.

A jostling stop signaled that she'd been heard.

"What is it?" Lucy asked. "Where are you, honey?"

"Back here, with Hank. There's something wrong with him," she said down into his hair, for his face was pressed against her collarbone.

Lucy swore. "Hank, you idiot old drunk. If you get us killed, I swear, I'm going to kill you." As she spoke, the volume of her hushed recriminations rose in time with the impatient patter of her approaching feet. Some stray spark of light—some wayward, determined moonbeam or reflection from a window—kicked against an exposed bit of Lucy's metal arm and glinted there, revealing her position.

Briar only half saw it. Her attention was elsewhere, caught in the straps that bound the head of a hungover man with little sense of self-preservation.

"Wait," she said to Lucy.

Lucy said, "I heard you baby, I'm right here."

"No. Not what I meant. Wait—stay back." She could feel it when she ran her palm against his head; she could detect the fractured buckle and the dangling, unfastened strap that should've held his mask firmly against his face.

He was wheezing. His head knocked lightly against her body and there was a rhythm to it that didn't sound like breathing. Tighter and tighter he squeezed at her hand, and then at her arm, and then at her waist as he tried to draw her nearer.

Briar resisted. She used the rifle to pry him off her and away.

Lucy crouched down close and tried to grab him. She said, "Hank, don't tell me you're so soggy you're getting fresh with our guest."

But Briar grabbed the clockwork arm before Lucy could land a grip. "Don't," she said. She stood up and pulled Lucy back, too. "Don't, Lucy. His mask has come off. He's been breathing it."

"Oh Jesus. Oh Jesus."

"*What's going on back there?*"

"Go *on*," Lucy said. "We'll catch up to you."

"*Forget it*," Swakhammer said, and a rustling of armor suggested he'd reversed his course.

She insisted, "We're right behind you. Get the rest of them under." Lucy said that last part quickly, because Hank was standing and straightening.

Briar could see him too, the way his body's shadow reluctantly hauled itself upright and shuddered. "It's too fast," she said to herself, or maybe to Lucy. "It shouldn't change him so fast. It ought to take days."

"It *used* to take days. It doesn't anymore."

They were paralyzed as long as Hank only stood, and did not make a move toward them. Briar breathed through the mask, "Lucy, what do we do?"

"We have to put him down. Sorry," Lucy said to him, or at least Briar hoped it was to the fresh and retching rotter who reached out with bony, angry hands.

Briar used her elbow to knock the swinging rifle back into her hands. Although she could barely see even the fuzziest shape of the thing that once was Hank, she listened for his next gurgle and aimed for it.

The blast hit him and knocked him down. She didn't know if it'd killed him. She didn't care—and Lucy seemed to approve.

The barkeep seized Briar by the gun and drew her forward, and away. In only a few feet they collided with the wall they'd been hugging as they fled the apothecary's shop, and they hugged it again together, their panting gasps revealing far too much of their location.

Farther down the block, Swakhammer was doing his best to prevent an outbreak of full-on chaos. He held the crew together and pressed them firmly against the building with his own body and said, just loud enough for Lucy and Briar to hear, *"Here's the corner. Follow it around to the right."*

"I know," Lucy said, no longer whispering, her voice tinged with frustration and fear.

*"Hush up!"* Swakhammer told her, but his own vibrating words were creeping up as well.

"It don't matter. They hear us now," Lucy complained, and still towing Briar by the warm gun, she led the way along the block. "Keep going, you big old bastard. I'll bring up the rear with Miss Wilkes."

*"Lucy—"*

"*Run*, iron man. Stop arguing with me, and we'll do the same," she puffed.

New moans coughed through the city night. They fed on one another, alerted by the noise and driven by their insatiable hunger for more meat—and they gathered, unhindered by the lack of light.

Lucy jerked on Briar's gun and pulled her toward the corner, where the clattering retreat of Swakhammer and the other denizens of Maynard's could be heard above the racket. They were getting farther ahead by the moment, but Lucy acted like she knew where she was going, so Briar let her lead.

Only two blocks, they'd said; but these must be the longest blocks in the universe, and the rotters had caught their scent, or their trail, or whatever thread by which they tracked their prey.

Briar wrestled her way out of Lucy's grip and said, "Not the gun. Might need it."

"Take the apron ties. Stay with me."

She wormed one hand's fingers between the linen strips until her grip was assured. She said, "Got it. Go. How much farther?"

Lucy didn't answer; she only pushed forward.

The corner. Briar felt it against her shoulder and side when she crushed herself against it, bobbing along in Lucy's wake. Lucy yanked Briar to the right and followed the wall in this new direction, and along this new street they could hear it louder—the stomping, insistent footsteps of the rest of their party.

"They're getting away," Briar panted. "Are *we*?"

Lucy said, "Sort of," and then slammed directly into an inrushing pod of rotters.

Briar yelped and Lucy swung her marvelous mechanical hand into the fray, using it to bludgeon any hapless head that made it within reach. She brained one beast against the wall and punched the sinuses free from another before Briar could get her gun propped and fired— and when she did squeeze off a shot or two, she had no idea if she was hitting anything important.

"Careful!" Lucy shouted, not because she was far away but because she'd just had a rifle discharge next to her head.

"Sorry!" Briar gave a hearty tug on the Spencer's lever and fired again at the clot of bodies. She'd dropped Lucy's apron ties and was on her own, but Lucy wouldn't let her get lost.

She cranked the lever again and prayed for another round in the magazine, but there was no time to fire it.

Lucy wrapped her arm around Briar's waist and lifted her up, over, and past two fallen rotters—but something held onto Briar's hand. She felt a surge of terror that was every bit as bad as the first time she'd ever heard that shaky, deathlike warble from a corpse's throat.

"It's got me!" she shrieked.

"No it hasn't!" Lucy said as she swung that cannon-thick arm around and clapped it down on a brittle, flaking head that was as empty as a cup. The head shattered and Briar's heart gave a horrified squeeze when she realized that the rotter had been holding her by its teeth.

She gasped, "Lucy! Lucy, it—I think it hurt me!"

"We'll look later," she said under her breath. "Take the ties again, doll. I'm going to need this arm. It's all I've got."

Briar did as she was told, and once again she trailed behind Lucy like a kite on a string. She could feel more than she could see the way Lucy used her arm like a battering ram and she used her weight to chug forward like a steam engine.

The streets were blacker than the ocean at midnight and Briar thought she might throw up at any second, but she held herself together long enough to hear, "*Over here, you two!*"

"Fire the Daisy!" Lucy commanded. "Fire it, or we're finished over here!"

"It's warming up!"

Lucy griped, "Muddy *shit*! I hate that stupid gun. Never works when—" A rotter swept its reach at her breasts and she battered it across the temple. It toppled down off the curb. "When you need it," she finished.

They were close enough to their destination that Swakhammer heard them.

"*It works great!*" he insisted. "*It just takes a second! Now, ladies, cover 'em up!*"

Briar didn't feel like she had the maneuvering room to obey, but she heard the warning hum from the enormous gun. As the sound bomb fired, she released Lucy's ties and grabbed her own head with one arm and Lucy's with the other, since Lucy couldn't cover both ears at once. Then Briar buried her uncovered ear against Lucy's breast.

The women imploded together, dropping to the ground and huddling while the wave shook the world around them. All the grasping hands fell away, and when the worst of the blast had faded into a memory of shaking, breaking air, Swakhammer's rolling steel voice began the countdown.

Briar and Lucy staggered to their feet, quivering in their shoes. Both were disoriented, but Lucy said, "This way, I think."

And with a crack and a snap, a red-white burst of light illuminated the crowded, dirty blocks with a glow that was almost blinding. *"No need for dark or quiet now, is there?"* Swakhammer said as he charged toward them, sizzling flare in hand. *"You all right?"*

"I think so," Lucy said, despite what Briar had told her.

Swakhammer took Briar's hand and Lucy's arm and hauled them forward, stumbling, tripping over their own feet and the limbs of dead things that quivered where they'd fallen. "This is . . ." Briar's boot caught on something squishy. She kicked free so she could run again. "The longest two blocks . . ." Her heel slipped against something wet and sticky. "Of my life."

*"What?"*

"Never mind."

*"Mind the step."*

"What step?" Briar asked.

*"That one. Watch it. Going down."*

She saw it then, because it was right underneath her. A square of hard yellow light burned down inside the earth, at the bottom of a stairwell gap lined with bags full of something heavy and muffling, like sand. Briar leaned against them and used them to steady herself as she descended, but Lucy stuck to the middle. Something was wrong with her arm: Even in the half-light and the frantic motion of escape, Briar could see that it was leaking fluid and ticking oddly.

Her own hand throbbed, and she shuddered to think of pulling off the glove. She didn't want to know, but she needed to know—and fast. If the rotter had bitten through the dense material, there wasn't much time.

She skipped awkwardly down the cracked stairs and almost fell at the bottom, where the room leveled out. It was so bright down there, after the absolute darkness of the streets above; for a moment she could barely see anything except for the hot, sizzling glare of the furnace by the far corner.

"We lost Hank," Lucy said.

Swakhammer didn't require any further exposition. He reached up for the double doors that might've marked a storm cellar, and he turned a crank beside them. Slowly, the doors ratcheted inward; then, with a loud drop they banged down into place. A waxed strip of fabric snapped along the seam where the doors' edges met. Once he'd secured it, he reached for a great crossbeam that leaned against the stairs. He lifted it up and set it into place.

*"We got everybody else?"*

"I think so," she told him.

Briar's eyes squinted, and adjusted. And yes, everyone else was present—bringing the count of room occupants to about fifteen. In addition to the crew from Maynard's, a handful of Chinamen crossed their arms and whispered beside the furnace.

For a terrible second, Briar was afraid that she'd returned to the place where she'd first landed, and these must be the same men she'd threatened with her Spencer; but her reason returned, and she realized that, no—she was quite a ways off from the market, and from the first furnace room where she'd descended down the dirty yellow tube.

Coal dust floated in dark puffs, and a sucking, whooshing gush of air dragged itself through the room as the bellows began pumping beside the furnace, forcing fresh air down through another tube and out into the underground.

At first, Briar hadn't seen the bellows or the tube, but yes, there they were. Just like in the other room, though the furnace was smaller here, and the mechanisms that moved the powerful devices looked different somehow. They were familiar in a strange, unsettling way.

Swakhammer saw her staring at the furnace and answered her un-spoken question. "*The other half of the train engine wasn't any good. Someone dumped it at the fill down by the water. We dragged it in here and now it's a big old bastard of a stove, ain't it? Nothing in the under-ground can cook a batch of steam faster.*"

She nodded. "Genius," she said.

"Tell me about it." Lucy sat down heavily on a thick wood table at the edge of the fire's reach. She used the light to inspect her arm, which she could no longer control with any real skill. It jerked and lunged against the top of her thighs when she rested it there to try to assess the damage. A thin, pissing stream of lubricant shot out over her skirt and stained it. "Son of a bitch," she said.

Varney, who had been wholly silent since leaving Maynard's, came to sit beside her. He took her arm in his hands and turned it over, looking at it from one angle after another. "You busted it up, huh? It's heavy as hell, I guess. And look, you lost the crossbow."

"I know," she said.

"But we'll fix it up, don't worry. It's dented in, right here. And right here," he added. "And maybe a line's broke. But we'll fix it up and it'll be good like new."

"Not tonight," she said. Her fist shot open, then crushed closed of its own volition. "It'll have to wait." She turned to one of the China-men and addressed him in his own language.

He nodded and ducked out through one of the passages—returning seconds later with a belt. Lucy accepted it and handed it to Varney. "Truss me up, would you, darling? I don't want to hurt no-body tonight, not without meaning to."

While Varney fashioned a binding sling to hold the broken arm against her, Lucy gestured with her chin, indicating Briar. "It's time now, baby. Better sooner than later."

Swakhammer pulled his mask off and stuffed it in the crook of his elbow. He said, "What are you talking about?"

"Hank bit her. Or one of them did, right on the hand. She needs to pop that glove off and let us look."

Briar swallowed hard. "I don't know if it was Hank or not. I don't think it went through. It's bruised me up good, but I don't think—"

"Take it off," Swakhammer ordered. "Now. If it broke skin, the longer you wait, the worse it'll be to fix." He stepped toward her and reached for her hand, but she drew it away, clutching it up to her breasts.

"Don't," she said. "Don't. I'll do it. I'll check it."

"That's fine, but I'm going to insist on seeing for myself." There was no anger in his face, but there was no room for negotiation, either. He loomed up beside her and opened his arms as if he'd opened a door and was offering to let her go first. His fingers pointed at the old engine furnace, where the light was brightest and the heat was most intense.

"Fine," Briar said. She took herself over to the edge, as close to the warmth as she could stand it; and she knelt down against a soot-stained stair to remove her mask and her hat. Then—using her teeth to tug at the wrist strap—she pulled off her glove.

She stared at the back of her hand and saw a half-moon of blue-red bruising on the flesh below her smallest finger. Holding the hand up close, and turning it to best catch the light, she peered at it hard.

"Well?" Swakhammer demanded, taking her hand into his own and flipping it up so he could see it, too.

"Well, I think it's all right," she said. She did not jerk her hand away. She let him look, because she wanted his opinion—even if she deeply feared it.

The whole room stopped breathing—except for the bellows. They gusted and gasped, and the yellow tube between the furnace and the table shuddered with the intake and outrush of air.

Swakhammer said, after a pause, "I think you're right. I think you lucked out. Those must be some good gloves." He released a big breath he'd been stashing in his chest and let go of her hand.

"They're good gloves," she agreed, so relieved that she couldn't think of anything else to add. She cradled her hurt hand and shifted her weight so she could sit on the step instead of kneeling there.

Willard joined Varney at Lucy's side. He said to no one in particular, "It's a shame about Hank. How'd we lose him?" The question wasn't broken or grieving, but it wasn't happy. It was more than merely curious.

"His mask," Lucy supplied. "Wasn't on him good. It got loose, and he took in too much Blight."

Willard said, "I suppose it happens."

"All the damn time. But he was too drunk to be careful, and you see now what it gets you. Will, help me with this mask, will you, man?" Lucy changed the subject. She twisted her neck and tried to convince her hand to work, but it only fluttered against her sternum. "Help me take it off."

"Yes, ma'am," he said. He reached behind her, unbuckled her mask, and pried it off her skull. Then he tackled his own. Soon everyone was barefaced again.

The Chinamen hung back by the furnace, dark eyed and patient, waiting for their work space to empty again. Swakhammer noticed first, the way they lingered with unspoken impatience. He said, "We should get out of their way. These bellows need to run another two hours yet before the downside's fresh enough to last the night."

He gave a duck of his head that wasn't quite a bow and wasn't quite a nod, and he said a few words in another tongue. He didn't say the words smoothly or quickly, as if they were sharp in his mouth, but Briar gathered that it was an expression of thanks and a request for pardon.

The leather-aproned, smooth-faced Chinamen appeared to appreciate the effort. They smiled tightly and bobbed their heads back, failing to conceal their relief as the group evacuated down a secondary tunnel.

Varney and Willard stayed close on either side of Lucy, and Swakhammer led the way with Briar beside him. The rest of them—Frank, Ed, Allen, David, Squiddy, Joe, Mackie, and Tim—brought up the rear. They marched together in silence, except for Frank and Ed, who were grousing about Hank.

Frank said, "It's horseshit, is what it is. And turnabout's fair play. We ought to go to the edges of the station and turn a few rotters loose down there, at Minnericht's own front door."

Ed agreed. "We could go in through the Chinese quarters. They'd let us, I bet. They'd let us if we told 'em what we were up to."

"And the airmen who hang down at the fort, over by the tower. We could see if any of them are game to raise a little ruckus," Frank proposed.

But Lucy hushed them from the front of the line. "Knock it off, you two. Don't you go dragging other folks into your harebrained schemes. Nobody's going down to the station. Nobody's tempting fate, or rotters, or the doctor. We don't need any more trouble."

Briar thought it was Mackie who quietly complained, "Well how much trouble do we have to swallow before we say it's enough?"

Lucy said, "More than *this*." But she didn't put much weight behind it.

Mackie mumbled a final word. "I'd like to see how he feels about rotters in his own parlor, biting on his own friends." He might've said more, but Lucy stopped and turned around and stared him down until he closed his mouth.

With rounded walls and sealed, sucking doors that opened and closed like dirty airlocks, the corridor drifted gently down and over to the left.

"These are the Vaults?" Briar asked.

Swakhammer said, "Not exactly. There's only one real vault, but the name stuck. The rest of what's back here is mostly where people .sleep. Think of it as a big apartment building, turned upside down. Not that many folks live here, really. Most of the people that do live inside the walls have taken up residence at the edges—near Denny Hill, where the nice old houses have big, deep basements."

"That makes sense," she observed.

"Yeah, but there are drawbacks to living that far off the beaten path; I mean, if you need anything, it's a tough hike down here to the core. Hell, you know what I'm talking about. Just now we got a man killed going two short blocks. Try picking your way down eight or nine. But people do it."

"Why?"

He shrugged. "The accommodations are a lot nicer. See what I mean?" He leaned on a latch and opened a metal-banded door with a sealed-up window. "It's not exactly clean, and not exactly comfortable, but it's pretty much secure."

"That's what I thought about Maynard's."

Swakhammer made a dismissive flap with his hand and said, "Down here we've got those guys." She assumed he meant the China-men. "They've got the situation under control. If there's trouble, they know what to do. Anyway, here's your room, Miss Wilkes."

She craned her head to look inside and saw exactly what he'd promised: a somewhat clean, somewhat comfortable-looking space with two beds, a table, a washbasin, and three steaming pipes that ran along the far wall.

"Look out for those pipes," he added. "They keep the room warm, but you don't want to touch them. They'll burn your skin right off."

"Thanks for the warning."

"Briar, darling," Lucy said as she maneuvered her way to the front of the line. "I don't want to impose on your privacy, but I'm in a bit of a pickle here with this busted arm. Usually I don't need much assistance, but I'd appreciate yours this evening."

"That's fine. We girls need to stick together, don't we?" She understood a little too well why a woman might not want a man to be her extra hands, even if those men were the well-meaning sort with only the best of intentions.

Briar let Lucy go inside first, and as she settled her bottom on the edge of the bed, Swakhammer had one more set of useful instructions. "There are privies down at the end of the hallways, usually on the left. They don't lock too good, and they don't smell too great either, but there you go. Water can be found back towards the China-men. They keep it in barrels right outside the furnace-room doors. Anything else you need to know, Lucy can probably fill you in."

"That's fine," she told him, and as he trooped away with the rest of the men tagging behind him like ducklings, she closed the door and went to sit on the other bed.

Lucy had leaned herself over so that her head rested on the flat, musty pillow. "I don't need so much help, really," she said. "I just didn't want to spend the night surrounded by those silly old boys. They want to help, but I don't think I could stand it."

Briar nodded. She picked at her bootlaces and wiggled her feet out of the shoes, then went to sit beside Lucy to help her do the same.

"Thank you dear, but don't worry about it. I'd rather leave them on for now. It's easier to let 'em stay than to get 'em back on tomorrow. And tomorrow I'm going to get this old thing tuned up." She shifted her shoulder in an attempt to lift the arm.

"As you like," Briar said. "Is there anything else I can do for you, then?"

Lucy sat up and pushed the covers aside with her rear end. "I think I'm fine for now. By the way, I'm real glad about your hand. I'm glad you get to keep it. It's a sad and aggravating thing to lose one."

Briar said, "I'm glad too. That was awful fast, how Hank turned. What happened to make it go so much quicker?"

Lucy rolled her head back and forth, settling down onto the pillow. "I couldn't tell you for sure, but I could give you a guess. All the Blight down here, it gets thicker and thicker each year. You used to be able to see the stars at night—but not anymore, just the moon if it's good and bright. You can't see the Blight itself exactly, but you know it's there, and you know it's collecting up inside the walls. One of these days," she said, scooting back in the bed so she could lean against the headboard and prop herself and the pillow up enough to talk, "you know what's going to happen, don't you?"

"No. What do you mean?"

"I mean, these walls are just a bowl—and a bowl can only hold so much. The Blight is coming up from underground, ain't it? Pouring more and more into this sealed-up shape. The gas is heavy, and for now, it stays down here like soup. But one day it's going to be too much. One day, it's going to overflow, right out there to the Outskirts. Maybe it'll overflow and poison the whole world, if you give it enough time."

Briar retreated to her own bed and unfastened her waist cinch. Her ribs burned without it, suddenly struck by its absence and almost missing the constriction of it. She rubbed at her stomach and said, "That's a grim way to look at it. How long you think it'll take before it comes to that?"

"I don't know. Another hundred years. Another thousand years. There's no telling. But down here, we're figuring out how to live with it. It isn't perfect, but we do all right, don't we? And one day maybe the rest of the world will need to know how we do it. Even if I'm thinking about it too big—even if it doesn't come to that—I can promise you this: One day before long the Outskirts are going to be swimming in this mess too. And all those folks outside these walls are going to need to know how to survive."

*Seventeen*

The *Clementine* swooped away from the tower with all the grace of a chick learning to fly, and Zeke's lurching stomach sent a mouthful of vomit up into his cheeks. He swallowed it back down with an eye-watering gulp and clung to the strap that did nothing except give him something from which to dangle.

He stared at the strap, trying to concentrate on anything but the acid against his teeth and the whirlpool in his belly. It was a belt, he thought. Someone had buckled it and slung it over a brace beam to make a holding spot. The buckle was brass with a lead backing, and on the plate's front it said CSA.

As the ship dipped, bobbed, and fired off at top speed to a place above the Blight-fogged streets, Zeke thought of Rudy and wondered if he'd deserted from the Union army or not. He thought of a war back east and wondered what a Confederate belt was doing serving as a holding strap in a . . . and again, the word manifested in his brain . . . in a *warship*.

And that gave him something else to consider, apart from the lava-hot taste in his mouth.

Above the console he saw storage panels with hooks that looked like they could hold weapons, and a square drawer that said MUNI-TIONS on it. Toward the back of the ship, there was a large door with a spinning vault wheel like one you'd see in a bank. Zeke presumed it must be the cargo hold, since a cargo door might have a sturdy lock on it as a matter of general principle, but a wheel like that? And he couldn't help but notice the way the floors, walls, and seals around that giant door were reinforced.

"Oh God," he whispered to himself. "Oh God." He curled himself up as tightly as he could, into the smallest ball of Zeke he could fashion, lodged there in the curve of the ship's wall.

"Incoming, starboard!" shouted Mr. Guise.

"Evasive maneuvers!" Parks either ordered or declared, though the captain was already on top of it.

Brink tugged violently on an overhead apparatus and a set of levers popped down from the ceiling. He tore at one trapezelike apparatus and the airship's gas tanks hummed so loudly they nearly shrieked.

"We're running too hot!" Parks advised.

Captain Brink said, "Doesn't matter!"

Out of the front windows that wrapped halfway around the oval interior, Zeke saw the horrifying specter of another ship—a smaller ship, but still plenty big—barreling down headlong against the *Clementine*.

"They'll pull up," Mr. Guise murmured. "They'll have to pull up."

Parks yelled, "They aren't pulling up!"

"We're out of time!" the captain shouted.

"What about *evasive maneuvers*?" Parks asked with a note of mockery.

"I can't get the goddamned thrusters to—" The captain quit explaining himself and slammed his elbow on a switch as big as his fists.

The *Clementine* bolted upright like a nervous deer, pitching its contents and crew backward, and sideways, and up; but the impact wasn't altogether averted. The second ship clipped it soundly, and there was a terrible squeal of metal and ripping fabric as the great machines grazed one another in midair. Zeke thought his teeth were going to vibrate out of his gums, but they miraculously stayed in place. And in a few seconds, the ship righted and seemed on the verge of escape.

"We're up!" declared the captain. "Up—do you see them? Where'd they go?"

All eyes were plastered on the windshield, scrying every corner for a sign of their attackers. Parks said, "I don't see them."

Mr. Guise griped, "Well, we couldn't have just *lost* them."

Parks breathed in slow, steady gulps and said, "It's a smaller ship they're chasing us with. Maybe they shouldn't have hit us. Maybe their boat couldn't take the damage."

Zeke's ice-white knuckles refused to unlock from the belt, but he craned his head to see out the window, and he held his own breath because no amount of calming talk could keep it steady. He'd never been much of a praying kid, and his mother hadn't been much of a churchgoing woman, but he prayed hard that wherever that other ship had gone, it wasn't coming back.

But the sound of Parks saying, "No, no, no, no, *no!*" did not reassure him.

"Where?"

"Down!"

"Where? I don't see them!" the captain argued.

And then another righteous crash rocked the ship and sent it teetering through the air. Zeke's belt broke and his body dropped to the floor, then rolled to the wall and back down to the middle of the deck again. He scrambled and struggled to crawl forward. Given the inertia of the ship's sway, the first thing he could snag was the vault-style wheel on the cargo hold door. He tangled himself in it as deeply as he could.

Somewhere below, a plate of steel was stretching and splitting, and rivets were flying loose as hard and fast as bullets. Somewhere to the side, a thruster was spitting and hissing, making sounds that no working thruster ought to.

Somewhere in front of them, the Blight was smudging the landscape—and it took Zeke a moment to realize that he could see the Blight directly in front of him because the ship was fully facing down, soaring toward a collision with whatever was underneath the pea-soup air. "We're going to crash!" he shrieked, but no one heard him.

The swelling back-and-forth of the crew's conversation occupied them all, and not even the boy's screams could distract them.

"Left thruster!"

"Disabled, or stuck, or . . . I don't know! I can't find the stabilizer pad!"

"This idiot bird might not have one. Right thrust, air brakes. Jesus Christ, if we don't pull up soon, we're never pulling up at all."

"They're coming back for another round!"

"Are they crazy? They'll kill us all if they drive us to ground!"

"I'm not sure they care—"

"Try that pedal—no, that other one! Kick it, and hold it back—"

"It's not working!"

"We're coming up on—"

"Not fast enough!"

Zeke closed his eyes and he felt them stretching, pushing back in his eye sockets from the pressure of their descent. "I'm going to die here, or I'm going to die down there, on the ground, in an airship. This isn't what I meant . . . ," he said to himself, for no one else was listening. "This isn't what I meant to do. Oh, God."

The airship's underside dragged itself along a new surface, one that was rougher and made with bricks, not metal; and the dusty, pebbled sound of stones crushed along the ship and rattled to the ground. "What'd we hit?" Parks asked.

"Wall!"

"City wall?"

"Can't tell!"

The ship was spinning in an uncontrolled orbit that knocked it against hard things here and sharp things there, but it was slowing and then it was rising—so suddenly that the immediate lift and leap brought more bile into Zeke's mouth. He spit a little spray against his visor.

Then the ship stopped with a pitiless shrug, like the yank of a dog's leash.

Zeke fell off the wheel lock and went facedown onto the floor.

"Tethered," the captain said grimly. "Damn us all, they've locked us."

Someone stepped on Zeke's hand and he yelped, but there was no time to complain. A demanding knock was beating a drum-tune against the main portal. It was the sound of someone big and very, very angry. Zeke pulled himself up and scuttled away, back to his cubby by the cargo door. He hunkered there while the captain and his crew pulled out guns and blades.

They abandoned their buckled seats and tried at first to hold the door shut, but it had been damaged before when the *Clementine* had hit the Smith Tower, and now it was barely affixed to its hinges. Shoulders shoved and feet braced, but whoever was on the other side was heavier or more determined. Inch by inch, the door came peeling away.

Zeke had nowhere to go and nothing to contribute; he watched from the floor as a coal-black arm reached through the opening on one side and a burly white one burst through from the left. The black arm caught Parks by the hair and beat his head against the frame, but Parks used his knife to cut at the hand until it retreated, bleeding— only to swipe inside again a moment later with a blade of its own.

The larger arm on the other side could've belonged to a giant, or one of those amazing gorillas Zeke had once seen in a circus. Though it wasn't covered in hair, it was longer than any arm the boy had ever personally set eyes upon; and he shuddered to consider the man who might wield it.

The white arm dipped down, took hold of the nearest boot, and pulled. Mr. Guise went dropping to the floor, where he kicked against the arm, the door, and everything else. The monstrous hand retreated for less than a second and reappeared holding a revolver, which it fired straight through the bottom of Mr. Guise's foot.

Up through the boot the bullet blew, not stopping there but searing in a straight line through Guise's thigh, and up into the soft flesh of his forearm. He howled and fired his own gun at the door, at the arm, at anything moving on the other side.

But the bullets wouldn't penetrate the plated doors, and the giant hand appeared unharmed.

The door caved in another half a foot, denting beneath the force of the men who pushed against it. The captain left his spot at the door to come to the vault. He kicked Zeke out of the way, bruising the boy's leg and ribs as he cast him aside and spun the wheel to open the hold.

"Hold that door!" he commanded. His officers were doing their best, but Guise was bleeding and Parks had a nasty smash that looked like the skin of a rotting fruit on his forehead.

The burly Indian brothers braced their backs against the dented door and held their ground against the encroaching raiders.

On the other side of the bridge, an escape hatch opened with the creak of hinges that were not often used. Zeke watched the captain sling himself outside the ship, clinging to it and crawling along it like a spider, until he'd disappeared and the opened door showed nothing but a square of Blight-poisoned sky. He could hear the man's feet and knees beating against the exterior of the craft as he climbed along it, seeking the hijacking hooks and trying to yank them out by hand.

Zeke couldn't imagine it, being up above the earth, heaven knew how high, and scaling a ship's exterior with no harness, no ropes, no guarantee that anything soft was waiting below. But the captain's hand-holds and footholds sounded like small gongs across the ceiling and around the back.

Parks hollered, "What's he doing?" Zeke could scarcely hear him, for his ears were still ringing with the percussion of the shots fired in such a close space.

"Their hooks!" Mr. Guise said, though he was breathless with pain and trying to daub at his wounds while he pressed his back against the door. "He's freeing them."

Zeke wanted to help, but he had no idea how to do so; and he wanted to run, but there was nowhere to go except into the sky and down to the ground, which would surely receive him in pieces.

Beside Mr. Guise, a sharp-pointed bowie knife had fallen out of someone's reach. Zeke slid a foot across the floor to grab it and pull it close. When no one objected to this action, he pulled it into his hands and clutched it up to his chest.

With a tearing sort of tin-can rip, something came loose and the ship gave a gut-swabbing heave.

The door that stood between the crews of the *Clementine* and the attacking ship slammed shut, and almost slammed clear out into the sky because there was nothing on its other side; the other craft had rebounded, and they had fallen apart from one another.

"Got it!" Brink shouted, though he could barely be heard inside the belly of the airship.

The other ship's crewmembers yelped. Someone might have fallen out as the ships swayed apart from one another—Zeke didn't know, and could not see.

"Get away from that door!" Mr. Guise hollered, and scooted himself away from it, back over to his chair, which he could scarcely pull himself up to reach.

The door was bent in all the wrong ways, and it wasn't going to hold. The final hinge gave way to the weight of the steel slab. With a tiny squeal, the door dropped to the city below.

Everyone listened, and counted seconds until they heard it land.

Zeke counted almost to four before the crash echoed up from the streets. So they were high up, still. Real high up.

The captain came swinging down into the door on the far side of the cargo hold. He shut the door, sprinted back to the cockpit, and took his seat, despite the teetering angle and missing door that exposed the whole cabin to the stinking sky. "Out of here," he gasped, fully out of breath and quivering from exertion. "*Now.* If we can't get over the wall, we're done for."

Parks leaned over the slumping form of Mr. Guise and pulled a lever, then stretched his foot over the slouching body to push a pedal. It was the wrong pedal, or maybe the right one. The ship bounced up, and with a hearty half-roll, it dislodged Zeke from his defensive position by the wheel lock.

He bumped, sprang, and toppled over to the open door.

Without dropping his knife, Zeke lashed out with one hand to seize the frame, or the hinge, or anything else he could catch; but the ship was listing up and there was no helping hand to assist him. The twisted, split hinge cut a gash into his palm too deep to allow him to hold his position—swinging half out of the deck, half out in the air— and by reflex and terror he let go.

He fell.

. . . And smashed against something hard much sooner than he'd expected, even in his fear-addled state.

And then the giant hand Zeke had seen before grabbed onto his arm with the crushing force of a cabinetmaker's vise.

Zeke's head swam with adages about frying pans and fires.

He couldn't decide whether or not to struggle, but his body de-cided for him—even though there was nothing beneath his feet but sickly air. He kicked and fussed, trying to twist against the grip of the enormous fingers.

"You stupid kid," growled a voice that matched the hugeness of the hand. "You don't *really* want me to let go, do you?"

Zeke grumbled something back, but nobody heard it.

The big hand reeled him up, to the very edge of the other ship's deck.

The boy tried hard not to gasp, lest he suck in any more vomit off the mask's visor. Holding him up by the wrist was the biggest man he'd ever seen, or even heard of. He was crouching in order to fit in the opening where the door of his own ship had been pushed aside— it did not open out on hinges, but slid from side to side on a track. The man's mask was a close-fitting model without a large breathing apparatus. It made him look bald, and something like a snub-faced dog.

Behind the big man, Zeke heard voices bickering unhappily.

"They disengaged! The son of a bitch disengaged us! By hand!"

"So the thief's a tricky bastard; we knew that already."

"Get this ridiculous bird up in the air! Get it up, right this moment! My ship is leaving me moment by moment, and I will not lose it, do you hear me? I will not lose my ship!"

The big man turned his attention from the wriggling boy to say, over his shoulder, "Hainey, you've already lost your goddamned ship. We tried, all right? We'll try again in a bit."

"We'll try again *now*," insisted a thick voice from deeper within the cabin.

But another voice, higher and almost prissy, argued, "We can't try again now. We're hobbling, you big jerk."

"And we'd better get rising!"

"We're not rising, we're sinking."

Over that same shoulder, shaped like a mountain range, the big man said, "Rodimer's right. We're hobbling, and we're sinking. We've got to set down, or we're going to crash."

"I want my goddamned ship, Cly!"

"Then you shouldn't have let somebody *steal* your goddamned ship, Crog. But I might have a hint about where it's gone off to." He looked again at Zeke, still held up over the empty, swirling fog that settled like scum at the bottom of the city below. "Don't I?"

"No," Zeke said. It almost sounded like he was sulking, but he was just choking and aching from being held up so oddly and breathing through vomit-clogged filters. "I don't know where they took the ship."

"What an unfortunate tune you're singing," the man said, fluttering his wrist as if he meant to fling Zeke out into the ether.

"Don't!" he begged. "Don't! I don't know where they took it!"

"You were sitting on the crew, weren't you?"

"No! I was only hitching a ride out of the city! That's all! Please put me down; put me down *inside,* I mean. Please! You're hurting my arm. You're hurting—you're hurting me."

"Well I ain't trying to give you a massage," he said, but his tone had changed. He swung Zeke inside as effortlessly as if he were moving a kitten from basket to basket, and all the while he stared at him strangely.

He pointed a finger as long as a bread knife straight between Zeke's eyes and said, "Don't you move, if you know what's good for you."

"Shoot the little bastard if he won't talk!" demanded the most irate of the voices in the cabin.

"Put a lid on it, Crog. He'll tell us something in a few minutes. Right now we've got to put this bird down before she falls down." He slung the side door shut on its track and reclaimed a very large seat in front of a very large windshield. He looked back at Zeke to say, "I'm not playing with you, boy. I saw you dropped your knife, but you'd better not be hiding anything else, anyplace. I want to talk to you in a few minutes."

Zeke crouched on the floor and rubbed at his aching arm and flexed the sore muscles in his neck. He griped, "I don't know nothing about where they were going with the ship. I only just done got on it, not an hour before. I don't know *nothing*."

"Nothing? Really?" he said, and Zeke assumed from the largest chair—and from the way the others let him do all the speaking—that he must be this ship's captain. "Fang, watch him, will you?"

From the shadows, a slender man whom Zeke had not yet seen took a gliding step forward. He was Chinese, with a pilot's gas mask pulled over a ponytail; and he wore the mandarin jacket that was common to his kind. Zeke swallowed hard, partly out of guilt and partly from abject fear.

"Fang?" he squeaked.

The Chinaman did not nod, or blink, or flinch. Even as the ship swayed unhappily downward, drooping through the sky, he did not stumble. It was as if his feet were rooted to the spot, and he was as level and smooth as water in a tilting vase.

Zeke said, to himself since no one else seemed to be listening, "I was only trying to get out of the city. I was only—"

"Everybody hang on," the captain suggested, more than ordered. It was a good suggestion, because the ship was beginning to spin slowly in a downward spiral.

"Air brakes malfunctioning," someone said with forced and deliberate calm.

The captain asked, "Any function at all?"

"Yes, but—"

The ship skimmed a building with a sickening screech of metal against brick. Zeke heard the popping shatter of windows breaking all in a row as the hull dragged itself through their frames on the way down.

"Thruster on, then."

"Right one's being fussy."

"Then we'll screw ourselves into the ground when we land; that's fine. *Just do it.*"

Roaring filled Zeke's ears. He wished for something to hold, but found nothing. He crouched hard against the floor and spread himself out, trying to grasp or lock his feet around anything he found. In the process he inadvertently kicked Fang, who didn't appear to care and barely moved.

"Going down, folks," the captain said calmly.

The dark-skinned man in the blue coat—Crog, Zeke gathered—said, "Two in one day! Goddammit!"

The giant replied, "If I'd known you were so lucky I'd have never given you a lift."

The ground was coming up fast. Every time the ship's semicontrolled orbit swung to a certain point the earth would appear in the window—and it promised a very hard stop at the bottom.

"Where's the fort?" the captain demanded. For the first time he sounded flustered, maybe even on the edge of afraid.

"Six o'clock."

"From which . . . ? From where . . . ?"

"Over *there.*"

"I see it," he said suddenly, and yanked at a lever above his head. "I hope nobody's down there."

The man in the first mate's chair said, "If anyone's there, they've heard us coming. If they haven't got out of the way yet, it's no one's fault but their own." He might have been on the verge of adding more, but that's when the ship began to stop in earnest, lurching almost belly-up until nothing but sky filled the windows in front of the captain and his crew.

Zeke was certain he was going to vomit again and there would be no stopping it, except that he didn't have time. The earth caught up to the bottom side of the ship. It landed hard and almost bounced, but instead it got stuck in a groove and started to drag a trench that began at one wall and continued for another fifty yards until the whole contraption was tugged to a stop by the turf inside a compound.

When the world stopped rocking and the ship stopped—almost like it'd been parked on its side—Zeke staggered to his feet and clutched his head.

Something warm filled his glove, and he knew without looking that it was blood. He could feel the slit in his skin, jagged and throbbing. He knew it must look terrible, and perhaps it *was* terrible. Perhaps he'd killed himself by crashing his skull against the wall, or the door, or whatever he'd hit as the ship had perform its warbling descent. Wouldn't that be a thing for his mother to hear? That her son had died in an airship crash, somewhere inside the walled city, where he had no business being and no excuse for his carelessness.

He tried to feel resigned about it, but he mustered self-pity and searing pain instead. His feet refused to fasten to the floor underneath him. He staggered, one arm smashed against his bleeding head and one hand held out to steady or ballast himself, or maybe search for an exit.

The ship had landed with a serious list to the left, which had crushed the side entryway through which Zeke had entered. The lot of them were effectively trapped.

Or so he thought, until the ship's bottom hatch fell open a promising crack.

## *Eighteen*

Lucy's smile faded into a tight line that had a question to ask. "Let me ask you something, if that's all right."

Briar said, "By all means." She worked her sore hand under dusty covers. They smelled clean, but old—as if they were kept in a cupboard and rarely used. "If I get to ask one next."

"Absolutely." Lucy waited for a piercing fuss of steam from the pipes to quiet itself, and then she lined up her words with care. "I don't know if Jeremiah's said anything to you about it or not, but there's a certain man down here. We call him Dr. Minnericht, but I don't rightly know if that's his given name or not. He's the man who made me this arm."

"Mr. Swakhammer might've mentioned him."

She wormed herself more deeply into her own blanket and said, "Good, good. He's a scientist, this doctor. An inventor who turned up down here not long after the wall went up. We don't know where he came from, exactly, and we don't know what's wrong with him. He always wears a mask, even in the clean air here underneath, so we don't know what he looks like. Anyway, he's real smart. He's real good with mechanical things like this." She jiggled her shoulder again.

"And the tracks, and the Daisy."

"Yes, those things too. He's quite a fellow. He can make something out of nothing, like nobody I ever heard of before." She added one more word, a word that strongly pointed at a question Briar had no intention of answering. "Almost."

Briar turned over on her side and leaned on her elbow. "Where are you going with this, Lucy?"

"Oh come on, now. You're not dumb. Don't you wonder?"

"No."

"Not even a little bit? It's a hell of a coincidence, isn't it? There's a lot of talk down here that it might be—"

Briar said flatly, "It's not. I can promise you that."

And Lucy's eyes lowered, not with fatigue but with cunning that gave Briar a pang of paranoia. The barkeep said, "That's a big promise, coming from a woman who's never even seen our terrible old doctor."

She almost snapped, "I don't need to see him." But instead she said slowly, measuring every word against Lucy's eager eyes, "I don't know who this Dr. Minnericht is, but he can't be Leviticus. For all Levi was a wicked old fool, he was a wicked old fool who would've come for me if he'd been alive all this time. Or, if not for me, he'd come back for Zeke."

"He loved you that much?"

"Love? No. Not love, I don't think. Possessiveness, maybe. I'm just one more thing that belongs to him, on paper. Zeke is one more thing that belongs to him, in blood. No." She shook her head. She uncrooked her elbow and lowered herself against the mattress, smushing the feather pillow and flattening it with her cheek. "He'd never let it stand. He would've come for us whether we wanted him to or not."

Lucy digested this, but Briar couldn't read the conclusion from the other woman's face. "I suppose you knew him better than anybody."

Briar agreed. "I suppose I did. But sometimes, I don't think I ever knew him at all. It's like that sometimes. People fool you. And I was a fool, so it was easy for him."

"You were just a girl."

"Same difference. Same result. But now it's my turn. I get to ask a question."

"Hit me," Lucy said.

"All right. You don't have to answer if you don't want to."

"That's fine. There's nothing you can ask that'll embarrass me."

"Good. Because I'd be lying if I said I wasn't wondering about your arms. How'd you lose them?"

Lucy's smile came back. "I don't mind. It's not a secret, anyhow. I lost the right one during the running time—when all of us were leaving because if we didn't go, we'd die, or worse.

"I was on the far side of the square, closer to the city dump than to the nice hill you lived on. Me and my husband, Charlie, we kept up a place where people used to come—mostly men. The old wharf rats and fishermen in their oiled coats, the prospectors with their tin pans banging together on their backs . . . They came for the food. I'm sorry, I should've said so first thing—it wasn't a cathouse or anything. We had a little bar, smaller than Maynard's and about half as nice.

"We called it the Spoiled Seal, and we did all right with it. We served mostly brew and spirits, and fish poached or fried in sandwiches. We kept the place, just the pair of us—me and Charlie—and it wasn't perfect, but it was fine."

She cleared her throat. "So sixteen years ago this big old machine came crashing down from the hill, burrowing under the city. You know that part. You know the things it broke, and you probably know better than anyone whether or not the Boneshaker brought the Blight. If anyone knows, *you* know."

Briar said softly, "But I *don't* know, Lucy. So I guess nobody does."

"Minnericht thinks he does," she said, temporarily shifting the subject. "He thinks the Blight has something to do with the mountain. He says that Rainier's a volcano, and volcanoes make poison gas, and if they don't spew it out, it stays underground. Unless something breaks through and lets it out."

Briar thought it was as good a theory as any, and she said so. "I don't know anything about volcanoes, but I guess I'd believe that."

"Well, I don't know. That's just what Dr. Minnericht said. Maybe he's a crackpot, but there's no telling. He made me this arm, so I owe him something, for all he's made things difficult, too."

"But you and Charlie," Briar prompted her. She didn't want to hear any more about Minnericht, not quite yet. The very letters of his name made her queasy and she didn't know why. She knew he wasn't Leviticus, even though she couldn't tell Lucy how she knew. But it only mattered so much; the man might as well have been Levi's ghost, if people still believed in him.

Lucy said, "Oh yes. Well, the Blight ate its way through town and it was time to run. But I was at the market picking up supplies when the order went out, and the panic hit us good. And Charlie was out at the Seal. We'd been married ten years, and I didn't want to leave him, but the officers made me. They picked me up and threw me out of town like I was a drunk taking up space on the sidewalk.

"They were already putting up walls, those treated linen ones with the wax and oil. Those didn't work too great, but they worked better than nothing, and workers were hammering the frames together. As soon as I could, a couple of days after the biggest part of the panic, I put on a mask and ran right on past them—back down to the Seal and to Charlie.

"But when I got there, I couldn't find him. The place was empty and the windows were broken out. People had thrown things inside and were stealing. I couldn't believe it—stealing at a time like that!

"So I came inside and called his name over and over, and he answered from the back. I climbed around the counter and stormed into the kitchen, and there he was, all bit up and covered with blood. Most of the blood wasn't his. He'd shot three of the rotters who'd tried to bring him down—you know how they do, like wolves on a deer—and he was alone with their bodies, but he was so bit up. He was missing an ear and part of his foot, and his throat was half tore out."

She sighed and cleared her throat again. "He was dying, and he was turning, too. I didn't know which one he was going to do first. We didn't understand back then, so I didn't know that I shouldn't get down close to him. His head was nodding all loose-like, and his eyes were drying up, going that yellow-gray color.

"I tried to pull him up, thinking maybe I'd rush him over to the hospital. It was a stupid thing to think. They'd closed everything up by then, and there wasn't anywhere to go for help. But I got him up onto his feet. He wasn't a big man, and I'm no tiny woman myself.

"Then he started fighting me; I don't know why. I like to think that he knew it was the end, and he was trying to help keep me safe by pushing me away. But I fought his fighting me. I was as determined as hell to take him away and get him safe. He was equally determined to stay.

"We fell together, landing against the counter, and when I got him back up again, he was gone. He'd started moaning and drooling— with all those bites on him, the poison had worked its way inside him.

"That's when it happened. That's when he bit me.

"He only got my thumb, and he barely broke the skin, but it was enough. I knew he was gone then, even more than when his eyes had gone nasty and his breath had turned stale like a dead animal on the street. Charlie would've never hurt me." She cleared her throat again, but she wasn't crying. Her eyes stayed dry, glittering in the candle-light.

The pipes whistled again, and she used it as an excuse to pause. She continued with, "I should've killed him. I owed him that kindness. But I was too afraid, and I've hated myself for it ever since. Anyway, it's all done now, or left undone, and there's no fixing it. Point is, I ran out to the Outskirts and found a church where they let me lie down and cry."

"But the bite."

"But the bite," Lucy said. "Yes, the bite. The bite took to rotting, and the rot took to spreading. Three of the nuns held me down and a priest did the first amputation."

Briar cringed. "The *first*?"

"Oh, yes. The first one didn't take enough. They only took my hand, right at the wrist. The second time they came back with the saw and they took it above the elbow, and then the third time I lost it all the way up to the shoulder. That did the trick, at least. I nearly died from it, each time. Each time the wound was red and hot for weeks, and I wished the sickness would just take me, or someone would just shoot me—since I was too weak and hurt to shoot myself."

She hesitated, or perhaps she was only tired.

But Briar asked, "Then what happened?"

"Then I got better. It took a long time, about a year and a half before I felt like myself again. And then, I could only think of one thing: I needed to go back and take care of Charlie. Even if that meant putting a bullet through his eye, he deserved better."

"But by then we had a wall."

"That's right. There's more than one way inside, though, as you learned yourself. I came up through the runoff tunnel, same as your boy did. And I wound up staying."

"But . . ." Briar shook her head. "What about the other hand? And what about the replacement?"

"The other hand? Oh." She shifted again in bed, and the feathers in the mattress rustled together with the blanket. A great yawn split her face, and she used the tail end of it to blow out the candle beside her bed. "The other hand I lost about two years later, down here. One of the newer furnaces exploded; it killed three of the Chinamen who worked it, and blinded another one. My hand got caught by a scrap of white-hot metal, and that was the end of *that*."

"God," Briar said. She leaned forward and blew out her own candle, too. "That's terrible, Lucy. I'm so sorry."

Lucy said into the dark, "Not your fault. Not anybody's fault, except my own for being down here after all that time. And by then we had our wicked old doctor, and he fixed me up."

Briar heard a settling swish of legs turning over underneath flannel.

Lucy sealed off another yawn with a high, satisfied note like the warning whistle of a teakettle. "It took him a while, figuring out how he was going to do it. He made up all these plans and drew all these pictures. It was a game to him, putting me back together. And when he had it all made, and all ready to wear, he showed it to me and I like to have died. It looked so heavy and weird, I thought I'd never be able to carry it, much less wear it.

"He didn't tell me, either, how he planned to make it work. He offered me a drink and I took it. I went out like a light, and I woke myself up screaming. The doctor and one of his fellows was holding me down tight—they'd strapped me onto a board like for surgery, and they were drilling a hole in my bone with a wood bore."

"Christ, Lucy . . ."

"It was worse than the other times, and worse than losing the arms in the first place. But now, well." She must have rolled, or tried to move the arm again. It jangled beneath the blanket, clattering against her chest. "Now I'm glad to have it. Even though it cost me."

Briar heard a hint of something bad in the last thing Lucy said before she finally went to sleep, but it was late and she was too exhausted to ask about it. She'd spent almost her entire time in the walls running, climbing, or hiding—and she hadn't yet found any sign of Zeke, who for all she knew might be dead already.

As Briar tried to calm her mind, her stomach grumbled and she realized that she hadn't eaten anything in longer than she could remember. Even thinking about the lowest of possibilities nearly sent her belly crawling out on its own in search of food. But she had no idea where she would go, so she clutched it hard, curled up into a ball, and resolved to ask about breakfast in the morning.

Briar Wilkes wasn't much of a praying woman, and she wasn't sure she believed too hard in the God she swore by on occasion. But as she closed her eyes and tuned her mind away from the intermittent squealing of the heating pipes, she begged the heavens for help, and for her son . . .

. . . who, for all she knew, might be dead already.

*And then she* was awake.

It happened so fast that she thought she must be crazy and she hadn't slept at all, but no—something was different. She listened hard and heard no sign of Lucy in the other bed, and there was a crack of dusty orange light leaking under the door.

"Lucy?" she whispered.

No answer bounced back from the other mattress, so she fumbled around with her hands until she settled on the candle and a stray scattering of matches.

Once lit, the candle revealed that yes, she was alone after all. A half-moon dent in the featherbed showed the shape where Lucy no longer lay, and the pipes were silent, though when Briar leaned the back of her hand against them they were warm to the touch. The room was comfortable but empty, and her lone candle didn't do enough to shove the darkness aside.

Beside the basin there was a lantern with a hurricane glass. She lit the lantern and added its light to the candle flame, which she abandoned to the table by the bed. There was water in the basin. The sight of it made her so spontaneously thirsty that she almost drank it, but she stopped herself and remembered that there were barrels of fresher stuff down the corridor.

She splashed a little on her face, pulled her shoes back on, and relaced her waist cinch. Down in the underground, she liked wearing it; it felt like armor, or a buttress that kept her upright when she was too tired or frightened to stand up straight.

The door was a lever latch, which answered her question about how Lucy might've left the room unaided. Briar leaned on it and it clicked open. Out in the hallway, small flames were mounted along the walls every few feet.

It was disorienting. Which way had she come from?

The left, she thought.

"All right, left," she said to herself.

She couldn't see the end of the tunnel, but after a few yards, she could hear it. The furnace wasn't howling and the bellows weren't pumping at full blast; they were cooling quietly, clicking and fizzing as the lava-hot fires inside mellowed during the cyclical downtime.

The barrels were beside the doors as promised, and a stack of wooden mugs were jumbled on a shelf above them.

God only knew when they'd last been washed, but Briar couldn't make herself care. She grabbed the first, least dirty-looking one and picked the barrel lid away with her fingertips. Inside, the water looked black, but it was only dark from the shadows. It tasted no worse than the runoff they cooked at the processing plant, so she drank it down.

Her empty stomach gobbled at the liquid, and a little farther down in her bowels another gurgling told her to find the privy. At the other end of the hall she located a door and tried it. She emerged a few minutes later, feeling better than she had when she'd gone to sleep.

She also felt as if she were being watched, and she wasn't sure why—until she realized she could hear voices nearby, and she'd misunderstood the sensation of barely being able to hear for that of being overheard. If she held very still she could recognize the voices. If she took a step to the right she could catch them more clearly.

"It's a bad idea." It was Lucy, sounding just short of openly confrontational.

"It might not be. We could ask her."

"I've been talking to her. I don't think she'll go along with it."

The other voice belonged to Swakhammer, without his mask. He repeated, "We could *ask* her. She's not a kid, and she can answer for herself. It could be helpful; she could tell us for sure."

"She thinks she already knows for sure, and she's got other problems right now—speaking of kids," Lucy said.

Briar slipped around the corner and pushed her back to the wall beside a door that had swung inward an inch.

"I think she talks like a woman who knows more than she's saying, and if she does, then it's no call of ours to drag it out of her," Lucy said.

Swakhammer paused. "We don't have to drag anything out of anybody. If she sees him, and he sees her, then everybody knows. He won't be able to hide underneath some other crook's mask; and the folks down here who are scared of him will have a reason to stand up.

"Or he could try and kill her, just for knowing the facts about him. And that means he'd kill me too, if I bring her to him."

"Your arm needs fixing, Lucy."

"I've been thinking about that, and I think I'm going to ask Huojin. He's good with mechanical things, too. He's the one who fixed up the furnaces after they went down last month, and he fixed Squiddy's pocket watch for him, too. He's a smart fellow. Maybe he can make it work all right."

"You and those Chinamen. You keep making friends with them like that, and tongues will wag."

"Tongues can wag all they want. We need those men, and you know it same as I do. We can't keep half this equipment running without them, and that's a fact."

"Fact or no, they worry me. They're just like those goddamned crows who hang out at the roofs—you can't understand them, they talk amongst themselves, and they might be for you or against you, but you'd never know it until it's too late."

"You're an idiot," Lucy said. "Just 'cause you don't understand them don't mean they're out to get you."

"What about Yaozu?"

She made a snort. "You can't call them all bastards just for one bad apple. If I did that, I'd never be civil to any man again. So get down off your high horse, Jeremiah. And leave Miss Wilkes alone about Minnericht. She don't want to talk about him; so she sure as hell don't want to talk *to* him."

"See, that's what I mean! She avoids the subject and she's not stupid. She must wonder. If we asked her, she might be willing—"

Briar leaned her foot on the door and pushed it open. Swakhammer and Lucy froze as if they'd been caught at something naughty; they were facing one another on either side of a table with a bowl of dried figs and a stack of dried corn.

"You can ask me anything you want," she said, though she made no promises about what she'd answer. "Maybe it's time we put all our cards on the table. I want to talk about this doctor of yours down here, and I want Lucy to get her hand fixed, and I want one of those figs worse than I ever wanted a piece of pie on Christmas—but most of all, I want to go find my son. He's been down here for . . . how long? A couple of days now, I suppose, and he's alone and I don't know—maybe dead already. But one way or another, I'm not leaving him down here. And I don't think I can work this place on my own. I think I need your help, and I'm willing to give you mine in return."

Swakhammer picked up a fat, soft fig from the top of the pile and tossed it to her. She caught it and chomped down on it, killing it off in a bite and a half, and sitting down beside Lucy, facing Swakhammer because she suspected he'd be easier to read.

Lucy was red, but not with anger. She was embarrassed to have been caught gossiping. "Darling, I didn't mean to go behind your back and talk out of turn. But Jeremiah here has a bad idea and I didn't want to show it to you."

Briar said flatly, "He wants me to go with you and see Minnericht, to ask about your hand."

"That's the long and short of it, yes."

Swakhammer leaned forward on his elbows, fiddling with an ear of corn and making the most earnest face he could manage. "You've got to understand: People will believe you if you set eyes on him, and if you say he's not Blue—or he *is*. If Minnericht is Blue, then we have a right to hold him accountable for this place, and throw him out of it—give him to the authorities and let them handle him."

"You can't be serious." Briar made it a statement.

"Of course I'm serious! Now, whether or not other people down here wouldn't drag him into the street and feed him to the rotters . . . I'm not in a position to say. But I didn't get the impression that you were real worried about anyone hurting him."

"Not remotely." She took another fig, and a swig out of the wooden mug she still toted. Swakhammer reached into a box behind his chair and pulled out a pouch of dried apples, which Briar pounced upon.

"Here's the thing," Swakhammer said while she chewed, again

with his earnest face firmly established. "Minnericht . . . he's . . . he's a genius. A real bona fide genius, not the kind you read about in dreadfuls, you know? But he's crazy, too. And he's been down here, treating this place like it's his own little kingdom, for the last ten or twelve years—ever since we figured out that we needed him."

He didn't like saying that part; Briar could see it in the way he balked around the word "needed." He added, "At first, it was all right. Nothing was very organized, and this place was a real madhouse, since we didn't have all the tricks nailed down yet."

Lucy interrupted and agreed. "It was all right. He kept to himself and didn't bother anybody, and he could be real helpful when he wanted to be. Some of the Chinamen treated him like he was some kind of magician. But," she was quick to point out, "they didn't treat him like that forever."

"What changed?" Briar asked around a mouthful of apple. "And is there anything else to eat around here? I don't mean to be rude, but I'm starving."

"Hang on," Swakhammer said, and he rose to a set of crates that must have functioned as cabinets. While he rummaged, Lucy continued.

"What changed was, people figured out that you could make good money off the Blight gas, if you turned it into lemon sap. And by 'people' I mean Doctor Minnericht himself. As I heard it, he was experimenting with it, trying to turn it into something that wasn't so bad. Or maybe he wasn't. Nobody knows but him."

Swakhammer turned around with a tied-up sack. He pitched it to Briar, and it landed on the table in front of her. "What's this?" she asked.

"Dried salmon," he said. "What Lucy is leaving off is that Minnericht used to test it on his Chinese friends. I think he wanted them to treat it like opium. But he killed a bunch of them that way, and finally the rest of them turned on him."

Lucy said, "Except for Yaozu. He's Minnericht's right-hand man, and he's the business arm of the operation. He's mean as a snake and—in his way—he's smarter than Minnericht, I'd wager. The pair of them make an amazing amount of money together, running their little empire based on that nasty yellow drug, but God knows what they spend it on."

"Down here?" Briar took a handful of salmon jerk and gnawed it. It made her even thirstier, and she was out of water, but she didn't stop.

"That's what I mean," she said. "Money isn't worth much down here. People only care about things you can trade for clean water and food. And there's still lots of houses with good stuff left for salvage. We haven't combed over every inch of the walled innards by a long shot. All I can figure is that he's using the money to bring in more metal, more cogs, more parts. More whatever. He can't manufacture the stuff out of thin air, and most of the metal that's been found up topside isn't any good anymore."

"Why not?"

Swakhammer answered. "Water and Blight rust it out crazy fast. You can slow it down if you oil up your metal parts good, and Minnericht has this glaze he uses—like a potter's glaze, I guess—that keeps steel from going too brittle."

Lucy said, "He stays out there, out on King Street—or that's what he calls it, because he's the king, or something. No one goes out there and looks too close, though some of the Chinamen keep homes out that way, on the edges of their old district."

Swakhammer added, "But most of them moved for higher ground, once they got tired of being treated like rats. The point is this, Miss Wilkes: Dr. Minnericht controls almost everything that happens down here. Those airmen—Cly, Brawley, Grinstead, Winlock, Hainey, and the rest of them—they're all subject to Minnericht. They pay him taxes, sort of, in order to take Blight out; and all the chemists who cook it in the Outskirts, they had to buy the knowledge off him.

"And the runners, and the dealers—they all owe him, too. He set them all up on consignment, saying they could pay him later out of their profits. But somehow, no one ever manages to pay him in full.

He adds on interest, and fees, and tricks, and eventually everyone understands that they belong to him."

Briar gazed down at Lucy's lone, broken arm and said, "Even you."

She fidgeted. "It's been, what did I say? Thirteen, fourteen years now. And somehow, he's never satisfied. Somehow, there's always something else I owe him. Money, information, something like that."

"What if you don't give it to him?"

Her lips twisted together, hugging each other and finally parting. "He'd come and take it back." She added fast, "And maybe you think that's not excuse enough to let myself be owned by the old rascal, but you've got two good arms and I don't have half of a good one without this machine."

"And Swakhammer?"

He hemmed and hawed, and said, "It's hard to live down here without certain supplies. I nearly died more times than I could count before I got this gear. And before that, I lost a brother and a nephew. Down here, things run different. Down here, we . . . we do things that . . . if people up in the Outskirts knew about them, we'd get hauled up in front of a judge. And Minnericht uses that, too. He threatens to get us all thrown out and left to the mercy of whatever law is left."

Lucy said pointedly, "And Maynard's dead. So there's no one in charge out there who we'd trust as far as we could throw a horse."

Swakhammer came back around to his original idea. "But if you could tell us for sure if he's Blue, then people would have a little leverage back against him. You understand?"

Briar tipped her mug upside down and let the last drops of water fall down into her mouth. She set it down hard. "Here's a crazy question," she said. "Has anyone tried asking him? I mean, couldn't someone just walk right up to him and say, 'Is Minnericht your real name, or might you be a certain Leviticus Blue?'"

"I'll get you some more," Swakhammer said. He reached for her mug and she handed it over.

He left the room and Lucy said, "Sure, people've tried it. He won't confirm or deny anything. He's happy to let the rumor grow and spread. He wants to keep us all under his thumb, and the less we know about him—and the more scared of him we are—the happier he stays."

"He sounds like a real peach," Briar said. "And I'm *still* sure he's not Levi, but it sounds like they're cut from the same cloth. I don't mind going down there with you, Lucy. Maybe he won't even know who I am. You said he didn't come here until after the walls went up, so maybe he's not local."

Swakhammer returned bearing a full mug of water, and behind him came an older Chinese man with his hands folded politely behind his back. Swakhammer said, "Here's your water, Miss Wilkes, and here's a message, Miss Lucy. You talk to him. I can't make heads or tails out of what he's saying."

Lucy rattled off an invitation to sit or talk, and the man spoke in a string of syllables that no one present but Lucy could follow. At the end of his spiel she thanked him and he left as quietly as he'd entered.

"Well?" Swakhammer said.

Lucy stood. "He said he just came back from the east tunnel and main blockade down at Maynard's. He says there's a mark left out there, a big black hand plain as day. And we all know what that means."

Briar looked at them questioningly.

So Swakhammer told her, "It means the doctor is taking credit for his handiwork. He wants us to know that the rotters were a special gift from *him*."

## *Nineteen*

Ears ringing, Zeke kicked against the hatch until it was wide enough for him to squeeze himself out into the city, which was exactly where he didn't want to be. But all things being equal, he'd rather be outside in the Blight than inside with the airmen, who were slowly unfastening themselves from their belted seats and moaning or fussing as they patted themselves down.

The silent and inscrutable Fang was nowhere to be seen, until Zeke located him standing beside the captain and looking back at Zeke with one eye.

The captain said, "Where do you think you're going?"

"It's been fun, but it's time for me to get going," Zeke said, trying to come across as droll and not shaken. He thought it'd make a great line to leave them with, but the hatch wasn't quite clear enough to permit him to pass. He shoved his feet against it, using his legs as levers.

The captain unfolded himself from his leaning seat and murmured something to Fang, who nodded. Then the captain asked, "What's your name, boy?"

Zeke didn't answer. He scaled the lip of the hatch, leaving bloody handprints on every spot he touched.

"Boy? Fang, grab him, he's hurt—boy?"

But Zeke was already out. He leaped to the ground and shoved his shoulders back against the door, jamming it shut only temporarily, but long enough for him to stumble into a run across the compound.

Behind him, from inside the belly of the crippled ship, Zeke could've sworn that he heard someone call his name.

But that was ridiculous. He'd never told them what it was.

It must've been something else they cried after him, some other word that his ears took to be his name in a fit of confusion.

He swiveled his head left and right, and his vision swam, though the sights told him almost nothing. There were walls—the city walls, he thought at first—but no, these were smaller and made of great, mushy logs with pointed tops; and the spots between them had been cemented with something else, so they presented a uniform front.

Someone on the ship had said something about a fort.

He racked his brains to recall his maps and remembered something about Decatur, where settlers used to hole up against the locals during times of trouble. Was this it?

The log walls that surrounded him looked like they could be punched down in a pinch. They'd been standing and rotting in the wet, poisonous air for a hundred years, or that's what Zeke guessed in his addled state. A hundred years and they were crumbling to spongy splinters but still standing—and there weren't any handholds anywhere he could see.

Around him the Blight-fog clumped and cluttered the air, and he could not see more than a few feet in any direction. He was panting again, losing control of his measured breathing inside the mask, and wheezing against the filters. The seals made his face itch, and every gasp he drew tasted like bile and whatever he'd last eaten.

Behind him, somewhere in the soupy air, someone was kicking at the door of the crashed ship. Soon, the crew would be out. Soon, they could come for him again.

All the "soons" were scaring him; and all the stretches of rumpled wood walls were bleak and blank under his hands as he felt his way along them. He thrust his palms and fingers out, even though they ached and he didn't know if they were bruised or broken or merely bent and exhausted. He flung his fingers and wiggled them at every crevice, trying to find a crack or a door or any other means of crawling under and out. He wasn't a big kid. He could fit through an astonishingly small gap if it came to it, but without a sound and without a warning . . .

. . . it didn't come to it.

A hand so strong that it didn't feel real clamped down across Zeke's mask-covered mouth, yanking him by the head and pulling him off his feet—into a recessed nook along the wall where the darkness was thick enough to hide almost anything.

It hid the pair of them, the boy and the hand that grabbed him; and the man who held him had arms that might be made of iron for all the softness in them.

Zeke didn't struggle for two reasons. First, he could already tell that it was more useless than not; whoever was holding him was stronger and a little taller, and breathing without sounding like he was going to vomit or pass out at any moment—so clearly, the advantage went to his opponent. And second, he wasn't entirely certain that he wasn't being helped. After all, he didn't want the men from the airship to find him, and they were scrambling out of their craft swearing and hollering as they surveyed the damage some fifty yards away.

Just when Zeke thought perhaps they were going to resume their search, find him, and drag him back to the wounded vessel, the hands that held him began to haul him backward and sideways.

Zeke did his best to cooperate, but his best involved a collection of trips and stumbles on the way to whatever black place he was being drawn. A tiny creak peeped in the dark, and he felt a gust of cooler air brush across his shoulders.

A few more steps, another twisting of his feet against each other . . . and a door shut behind him. He was closed into a small room with a set of stairs and a pair of candles burning feebly above a railing.

His captor or rescuer—he didn't know which—released him and allowed him to turn around.

Because Zeke wasn't sure of his standing or peril, he hoped for the best and tried, "Thanks, sir. I think those guys were going to kill me!"

A pair of narrow brown eyes blinked slowly back at him. They were dark eyes, and calmly intelligent—but utterly unreadable. Their owner didn't speak. He gazed down at the boy, for he was several inches taller than Zeke, with a long waist and long arms that folded across his chest. He was wearing what looked to Zeke like pajamas, but they were clean and unwrinkled, and whiter than anything that Zeke had yet seen inside the city walls.

And because the man had not yet said anything, Zeke mumbled, "They were going to kill me, weren't they? And you . . . you're not, are you?"

"What is your name?" the man asked, with only the faintest trace of a foreign accent.

"That's a popular question today," Zeke said, and then, because he was trapped in the semidark with this strange, strong man, he added, "It's Zeke. Zeke Wilkes. I'm not trying to make any trouble. I just wanted to get out of the city. My mask is clogging up, and I don't think I can last down here much longer. Can . . . can you help me?"

Again there was a protracted pause. Then the man said, "I can help you, yes. Come with me, Zeke Wilkes. I believe I know someone who would like to meet you."

"Me? Why me?"

"Because of your parents."

Zeke held still and tried to keep the pounding of his heart down to a dull roar. "What about them?" he asked. "I'm not here to make trouble or nothing. I was just looking for . . . I just wanted . . . Look. I know that my dad made problems and that he's not exactly a local hero or anything, but—"

"You might be surprised," the man said lightly. "This way, Zeke." He indicated the stairs and the corridor at the bottom.

Zeke followed him on legs that shook from exhaustion, injury, and fear. "What does that mean? I might be surprised? Who are you—and did you know my father?"

"I am Yaozu, and I did not know a man named Leviticus Blue. But I know a Dr. Minnericht who can, I am sure, tell you quite a lot." He checked over his shoulder, looking to meet Zeke's eyes.

"What makes you think I want to ask him anything?"

Yaozu said, "You are a young man of a certain age. In my experience, young men of a certain age begin to question the world, and what they've been told about it. I think that you will find our strange doctor to be a most . . . interesting resource in your search."

"I've heard about him," Zeke said carefully.

"How long have you been down here?" Yaozu asked, turning a corner and stopping at a large, misshapen door surrounded by flaps and seals. He lifted a latch and pulled it hard, and the door retreated from its frame with a whooshing gasp.

"I don't know. Not long. A day. Two days," he guessed, though it felt like a week.

Yaozu held the door open and gestured for Zeke to walk through it. There was light on the other side of it, so he left the candle in a cranny on the wall. "If you'd been here longer than an hour, I would assume that you've heard of our doctor."

Zeke stepped against a distinct and pulsing breeze, and once he was inside the next room, Yaozu followed him.

"So he's important, huh?"

"Very important, yes," the man said, but he sounded blandly unimpressed.

"And you work for him?"

The man didn't answer immediately. But when he did, he said, "You could say that. We are partners, in a way. He is a great man with electricity, and mechanisms, and steam."

"And what about you?" Zeke asked.

"Me?" He made a little noise that might've been a "hmm" or might've been an "oh." He said, "I'm a businessman, of a sort. It is my business to maintain peace and order so that the doctor can work on his projects." And immediately he changed the subject. "One more door, and then you may remove your mask. These are sealed, you understand. The clean air we catch, we must keep."

"Sure." Zeke watched as another door was dragged open against its flaps. On the other side was not another corridor, but a small room filled with lamps that lit all four corners. He said, "So you're a law-man down here? Something like that?"

"Something like that."

"My grandfather was a lawman."

Yaozu said, "I know." He shut the door behind them both and re-moved his mask, revealing a perfectly bald head and a smooth face that could have been twenty-five or fifty-five years old—Zeke found it impossible to guess. "You may remove yours as well. But be careful," he said, wiggling a finger at the boy's head. "You seem to have hurt yourself."

"Good thing you've got a doctor down here, huh?"

"A good thing indeed. Come with me. I'll take you to him now."

"Now?"

"Now," he said.

Zeke did not hear any request. He heard a command, and he didn't know how to refuse it. He was afraid, of course, because of what Angeline had told him with her spittle-flecked fury; and he was nervous, because something about this calm Chinese man unsettled him deeply, and he could not put his finger on what it might be. The man had been exceedingly polite, but the strength in his arms and the insistence in his voice were not the tools of a friendly negotiator.

This was a man accustomed to being obeyed, and Zeke was not a boy accustomed to obeying.

But his queasy-stomached nervousness did not want to know what would happen if he fought, or ran—and his chest was aching from the struggle of simply breathing. He could figure out the details later. He could plot and plan and escape later, but for now, he could remove his mask. And that was enough.

The itching, burning, rubbed-raw spots around the mask's straps burned like pepper on his skin, but then, with a buckle and a clip, the visor and filters came falling off his face. Zeke dropped the mask on the floor and tore at the red places with his fingernails.

Yaozu grabbed the boy's forearm firmly and pulled it away. "Do not scratch. It will only make it worse. The doctor will give you an ointment, and the sting will ebb in time. This was your first time in a mask?"

"For longer than a few minutes, yeah," he admitted, lowering his hands and struggling to keep them still.

"I see." He picked up Zeke's mask and examined it, turning it over and picking at the filter locks, and the visor. "This is an older model," he observed. "And it needs to be cleaned."

Zeke cringed. "Tell me about it." Then he asked, "Where are we going?"

"Down. Underneath the old station that never was." He gave Zeke an appraising sort of stare, taking in the boy's battered clothes and uncut hair. "I think you'll find the accommodations quite exceptional."

"Exceptional?"

"Indeed. We've created a home down here. Perhaps you'll be surprised."

Zeke said, "Most of what I've seen down here looked pretty rundown and crummy."

"Ah, but you haven't yet been to the station, have you?"

"No, sir."

"Well then. Let me be the first to welcome you." He went to the wall, where he pulled another lever.

Off in some place Zeke couldn't see, chains rattled and gears turned. And right in front of him, the wall slid along a track, revealing a glorious room on the other side, filled with light.

It was also filled with marble and brass, and polished wood seats with velveteen cushions. The floor was a mosaic of tiles and metal. It shined a reflection off every corner, every crystal and candle. But the longer Zeke looked at the lights the longer he thought that maybe they weren't flames at all; that maybe they were something else. After all, the lovely curved ceiling was not burned or smudged with soot.

Once he'd caught his breath, and once the wall had resumed its seamless position behind him, Zeke asked, "What are those lights up there? What powers them? I don't smell gas, and I don't see smoke."

"They are powered by the future." It was a cryptic answer, but it was not offered with any flair or tease. "This way. I'll arrange a room for you, and a bath. I'll ask the doctor if we can scare up any clothes, and perhaps some food and water. You've had a long set of days, and they haven't treated you kindly."

"Thanks," he said without meaning it. But he liked the idea of food, and he was thirstier than he'd ever been before in his life—though he hadn't noticed until the mention of water. "This place is beautiful," he added. "You're right. I'm surprised. I'm . . . impressed."

"It is easy for it to be beautiful. No one ever treated it like a train station. It was not finished when the Blight came. The doctor and I finished small parts of it, like this waiting area, with the materials that had already been brought for its construction. It was almost perfect, but it needed some *alterations*." He pointed at the ceiling, where three giant pipes with fans were installed in a row. They were not turning at that moment, but Zeke thought that the noise of them must have been amazing when they were active.

"Is that for air?"

"Very good, yes. It's for air. The fans only run a few hours a day, for that is all they're needed. We bring it in from above the Blight, above the city. We run pipes and hoses up over the wall's edge," he said. "That's why you can breathe in here. But we do not treat this as a living area. The rooms, kitchens, and wash areas are this way."

Zeke followed almost eagerly, wanting to see what was next. But he noticed before he was ushered out of the gleaming room with its high ceiling and padded chairs that there was a door at the room's far end. This door was sealed like the others, but it was also barricaded with iron crossbeams and heavy locks.

Yaozu led Zeke to a platform the size of an outhouse and pulled a low gate shut, then tugged at a handle on a chain. Again the sound of metal unfurling clanked and clicked in some echoing distance.

The platform dropped, not like the broken airship but like a gentle machine with a job to do.

Zeke grabbed the gate and held onto it.

When the platform stopped, Yaozu retracted the gate and put a hand on Zeke's shoulder, guiding him to the right down a hallway lined with four doors on alternating sides. All of the doors were painted red, and all had a lens as big as a penny built into them—for seeing out or seeing in.

The door on the end opened without being unlocked first, a fact that Zeke noted with some confusion. Was it comforting, the impression that they did not mean to lock him in? Or was it unsettling, for he would have no assurance of privacy?

But the room itself was nicer than any he'd ever visited before, plush with thick blankets on a bed with a fat mattress, and bright from lamps that hung from the ceiling and sat on the tables beside the bed. Curtains hung long and thick from a rod on the far end of the room, which struck Zeke as strange.

He stared at them until Yaozu said, "No, of course there's no window there. We're now two floors underground. The doctor just likes the look of curtains. Now. Make yourself comfortable. There's a washbasin in the corner. Make use of it. I'll tell the doctor you're here, and I'm sure he'll see to your wound himself."

Zeke washed his face in the basin, which nearly turned the water to sooty mud. When he was as clean as he was going to get, he wandered the room and touched all the pretty things he saw, which took a while. Yaozu was right; there was no window, not even a bricked-up place, on the other side of the curtains. It was merely a bare patch of wall covered in the same wallpaper as everything else.

He checked the doorknob.

It turned easily. The door opened, and Zeke poked his head out into the corridor, where he saw nothing and no one except for a few stray bits of furniture against the wall, and a carpeted runner that flowed the length of the corridor. The lifting and lowering platform was still parked, and its gate was open.

The message was clear: He was free to leave if he could figure out how, and if he wanted to. Or that's how they wanted it to look, anyway. For all Zeke knew, once he got to the lift an alarm might sound and poisoned arrows might fire from a dozen directions at once.

He doubted it, but he didn't doubt it enough to try anything.

And then he noticed that Yaozu had taken his mask, and he understood the situation a little bit better.

Zeke sat on the edge of the bed. It felt like something smoother and thicker than a feather mattress, and it bounced under his body when he moved. He was still very thirsty, but he'd dirtied the only water in the room. His head hurt, but he didn't know what to do about it. He was still hungry, but he didn't see any food handy, and when it came down to it, he was more exhausted than famished.

He pulled his feet up onto the bed without removing his shoes. He curled his knees up and hugged at the nearest pillow, and he closed his eyes.

# *Twenty*

Briar left to wash up, and when she returned, Lucy was sitting in a chair with her arm laid out on a table. The arm was surrounded by bolts, gears, and screws. A Chinese boy who couldn't have been a week older than Ezekiel was rooting around in Lucy's wrist joint with an oilcan and a long pair of tweezers.

He looked up at Briar through an elaborate pair of spectacles with adjustable, interlocking lenses attached at the corners.

"Briar!" Lucy said happily, though she was careful not to jostle the arm. "This here is Huojin, but I call him Huey and he doesn't seem to mind it."

He said, "No, ma'am."

"Hello . . . Huey," Briar said to him. "How's her arm coming along?"

He aimed his forehead back down at the splayed machinery so that the lenses would show the work space better. "Not bad. Not great. The arm is a fine machine, but I didn't invent it or build it. I have to feel my way around it," he said. His English came glazed with an accent, but it was not very thick and he was quite understandable. "If I had the copper tubes I need, I think I could make it work just right again. But I had to improvise."

" 'Improvise,' did you hear that?" Lucy laughed. "He reads English out of books. And when he was a little thing, he used to practice it on all of us folks down here. Now he talks a damn sight better than most of the men I know."

Briar wondered what Huey had been doing down in the underground as a small child. She nearly asked, but then she thought it might not be any business of hers, so she didn't. She said, "Well, I'm glad he's here working on you. Can you tell me more about that mark outside of Maynard's? What does it mean?"

Lucy shook her head. "It means that Minnericht likes to mark his territory like a dog, pissing all over it. I wonder what his gripe was with Maynard's? He's left us alone for a while; maybe he just figured it was time to stir things up to keep us paying attention. Or maybe Squiddy still owes him."

Briar said, "Mr. Swakhammer thought maybe one of Minnericht's men saw me. Maybe the doctor's mad that I went down to Maynard's without visiting him first."

Lucy didn't respond. She pretended to watch Huey as he closed up the panel on her arm and sealed it back into place. Finally she said, "That's possible. He's got eyes just about everyplace, damn him. And he couldn't just knock on the door or leave a note, God no. Instead he's got to send down the dead, soften us up, and maybe pick off a man or two in order to make a statement. I wonder how he'd like it if we went down to the station and popped his locks. Let *him* deal with the dead in his own home space. It'd be an act of war. And maybe we could use an act of war."

Huey wrapped up his work and tightened the last screw. He leaned back and pulled the heavy glass contraption off of his forehead. The straps stuck around his ears and then came loose with a snap. "All done, Mrs. O'Gunning. I wish I could fix it up better for you, but that's the best I can do."

"Sweetheart, it's just amazing, and I can't thank you enough. Anything you want, anything you need—you let me know. Next time the airmen come through town, I can put in a request."

"More books?" he asked.

"More books. As many books as they'll carry for you," she swore.

The boy thought for a moment and then said, "When will the *Naamah Darling* come back again? Do you know?"

"I'm sorry sweetheart, but I couldn't say. Why? You want to leave a message for Fang?"

"Yes ma'am," he said. "I would like some books in Chinese, and he would know where to get them. He'd know which books are good, I think."

"Consider it done. I'll stop by the tower on Tuesday, and ask around for you." She carefully ruffled her fingers in his hair, and although they were stiff, the gesture came across as friendly as she meant it. "You're a good one, Huey. A fine boy, and a smart one."

"Thank you, ma'am," he said, and with a bow, he excused himself back into the halls of the Vaults.

Briar said, "He sure does talk good."

"I wish I could take credit for it, but I can't. I just gave him what I had and let him learn it all himself." She twisted the arm left and right, and up and down. "You know," she said, "I think this'll be fine for a while. It's not perfect, but it works well enough."

"Does that mean you don't want to go to Minnericht after all?" Briar asked.

Lucy said, "Maybe, maybe not. Let me give this a few hours and see how it goes. What about you? Are you still interested in going all the way out to King Street to meet him?"

She said, "I think so, yes. Besides, if Mr. Swakhammer's right, you can't hide me forever. He knows I'm down here someplace, and he'll keep trying to flush me out if I don't go introduce myself. I don't want to make any trouble for you, Lucy."

"Trouble's fine, darling. We get trouble all the time, and if he wasn't giving us grief about you, it'd be something else. So how about this? Let me holler for Squiddy. We'll see if he'll take you down to the old bank blocks. He knows his way around that place better than anybody else, I'll tell you what. If there's any sign of your boy down there, he'll be the man to find it."

Briar's eyebrows pinched up into her forehead. "Really?" She tried to remember which patron of Maynard's they were discussing. "The thin man with the muttonchops and the goatee?"

"That's him. He's a mad old boy, but we all are, down here. Now, listen: Squiddy used to be a small-time crook, when he was Huey's age and younger. Back before the walls, he was making a big plan to break into the banks himself. He drew up all sorts of plans, and he learned all the nooks and crannies real good . . . and I think it made him madder than hell that the Boneshaker took the block first." She moved her arm again and winced. "But don't get me wrong; he's all right. He's sharp, in his own way, and he likes to look helpful. He won't screw you up or leave you stuck."

"How reassuring," Briar said.

"Oh, don't I know it. Here now—you'd better hurry up. It'll be getting dark before long. It hardly stays light at all up there, this time of the year, so go get Squiddy and take your look around while there's still time for you to do it. He knows to expect you. I already told him he was going to show you the sights, and he said he was all right with it."

Briar found Squiddy playing cards with Willard and Ed.

Squiddy folded his hand and tipped his hat at Briar, who wasn't sure if she should tip hers back or not. So she nodded and told him, "Hello. Lucy said you'd be kind enough to show me around the bank blocks for an hour or two real quick, before sundown."

"That's right, ma'am. I've got no trouble working on the Lord's day. Let me just get my gear."

Squiddy Farmer was a narrow man from chin to toes, dressed in skinny pants and a buttoned jersey that fit so close you could count his ribs. He threw a wool sweater over the whole ensemble; and although the sweater was large enough to hit his hips, its neck hole was small enough to squeeze his head. The salt-and-pepper puff of his balding scalp and fluffy sideburns popped through the opening.

He smiled, showing a mostly full set of teeth that didn't often see a brush. From a side table behind the spot where cards were being shuffled, he picked up a bubblelike helmet with a portal on the front.

When he saw her looking at it with frank confusion, he said, "It's one of Dr. Minnericht's models. He said I could have it, because no one liked it very well and it was just collecting dust."

"Why?" she asked. "Does it work?"

"It works. It works real good, but it's real heavy—and I have to cut my own filters for it. I don't mind it, though. I like being able to see almost all the way around, you know?" He showed her the way the curved glass wrapped from ear to ear, and she had to admit that it looked convenient.

"Maybe someday he'll make a lighter version."

Squiddy said, "I heard he was working on it, but if he ever made a new one, he didn't let me near it. Are you ready?"

She held up her mask and said, "Sure am."

He donned his globe-shaped mask and it gave him the look of a lollipop. "Let's go then."

Briar strapped her own mask onto her head as she followed him. It seemed like she'd only just pulled it off, but she understood the necessity and—against all expectations—she was almost growing accustomed to it.

Through a dark warren of corridors she hiked, down another stretch of poorly repaired staircases and deep into a grated level where the hum of machinery filled her ears.

Squiddy wasn't a man who was often asked to play tour guide, so he didn't give much in the way of highlights. But he did think to mention, "We're putting more filters down here." He gestured at the metal latticework under his feet. "It's an experiment."

"What kind of experiment?"

"Well, see, right now if we want to keep clean air in the safe spots, we have to pump it down from all the way up over the walls. But that China-boy said maybe we didn't need to do that. He says maybe we can clean the dirty air as easy as we can pull in clean air. I don't know if he's right or not, but some of our people think it's worth a try."

"Pumping down all that air must be a real chore."

"So it is, so it is," he agreed.

The grates beneath their feet clanged under their steps, and before long they gave way to a landing with three equally barricaded doors. Squiddy adjusted his massive headpiece and reached for one of three levers that were fixed in the floor.

He told her, "This is as close as we can get from inside, so here's the end of the line. We leave and come back through that one in the middle." He pointed at the door. "You can't see any of these doors from the outside. We were real careful with it. It all had to be sealed real tight, because the gas is worst over here."

"Of course," she said. "It *would* be worse, here at the center."

"Are your filters new?"

"I changed them out just before we left the Vaults."

He gripped the lever and leaned against it. "Good. Because that eight- or ten-hour rule? It's not so helpful over here. Those filters won't work longer than a couple of hours, maybe two or three. We're going down close to the crack."

"We are?"

"Sure we are." The lever bent all the way back, almost to the floor. With it, a chain was drawn somewhere out of sight, and a crack appeared around the center door. "It's right underneath the old First Bank. That's as deep as the Boneshaker ever got, and that's where the worst of the Blight seems to be. That's the *bad* news."

"You say that like there's good news," Briar observed as the door grinded back, out into the crushed old blocks where the banks used to be.

"There *is* good news!" he insisted. "The good news is that there aren't half so many rotters down here as there are farther out. The gas eats them right up, so they stay away—or the ones that don't, don't last too long. That reminds me. You might want to fasten up that coat. You've got gloves, don't you?"

"Yes," she said, wiggling her fingers to show them.

"Good. Pull your hat down tight, too. Over your ears if it'll fit. You don't want any skin showing if you can help it. It'll burn you," he said solemnly. "Just like knocking your hand on a stove. It'll turn your hair, too, and you've already got a bit of gold in it."

"It's orange," she said dully. "It used to be black, but it's getting those orange stripes from all the rain with Blight in it."

"Tuck it down into your collar if you haven't got a scarf. It'll protect your neck."

"Good plan," she said, and she did as he suggested.

"Are you ready?"

"I'm ready."

His sharply carved face wobbled behind the imperfect curve of his mask's glass front. He said, "Let's go then. Keep as quiet as you can, but don't worry yourself too bad. Like I said, we'll mostly be alone." He gave her Spencer a pointed stare. "Jeremiah says you're a real good shot."

"I *am* a real good shot."

He said, "Good. But just so you know, odds are good that if you've got to shoot out here, you won't be shooting at rotters. Minnericht's got friends; or he's got employees, anyway. Sometimes they patrol down here. This is the edge of the turf between the Chinamen's quarters and the old transportation depot. You know how they were building a new train station, when the walls went up?"

"Yes," she said, and then she headed him off. "I heard that Minnericht lives out there, under the half-built station."

"Right. That's how I heard it too." He leaned against the door to open it another foot or two, and it opened up almost as much as it opened out. It wasn't until it fell to the side that Briar realized she'd be climbing up from underground.

"Have you ever seen him?" she asked. "Dr. Minnericht, I mean?"

"No, ma'am," Squiddy told her, but he didn't look at her.

"Really? Is that so?"

He held the door for her, and she emerged up into a spot that was still underground, but with a perilous canopy of broken street looming over their heads. The afternoon drizzle of sun cut around its edges to illuminate the pit.

He said, "Yeah, that's so. Why wouldn't it be?"

"It's just that you said he gave you the helmet. And I heard you might owe him money sometimes, that's all. I thought maybe you'd seen him. I'm just curious. I wondered what he looked like." She figured he'd heard the rumors—it seemed everybody had—and since Squiddy didn't know of her chats with Swakhammer and Lucy, he wouldn't know that she'd already made up her mind about the mysterious doctor.

Her guide scrambled up behind her and let the door drop down. Once it had closed, it was all but impossible to spot; its exterior had been fixed with detritus, and when it swung out on those croaking hinges, it must've looked like the earth itself was opening to let them out.

Squiddy finally said, "I've owed him money once or twice, that's a fact. But really I just owe his men. I used to run with them, a little. Not much," he added fast. "I never worked for him proper-like. But I'd run an errand or two for some extra food or whiskey."

He stood beside the door and looked as if he'd like to scratch his head, if he could reach it. "When the walls first cut us off in here, we didn't have it all figured out right away. Times was hard for a few years. Aw, times is hard now, too. I know. But it used to be you could die for breathing. It used to be, you were fighting the rotters for spoiled fruit peels and rat meat."

"You did what you had to do. I understand."

"Good, good. I'm glad you're the understanding kind." He flashed that yellow-toothed smile. "I thought you might be. You come from a fair sort of stock."

At first she didn't catch his meaning, but then she remembered why they'd taken her in so quickly. "Well," she said, because she wasn't sure what else to say. She'd spent twenty years trying to prove she wasn't a thing like her father, and now she had his reputation to thank for her own safety in a very strange place. She wondered what he would've thought of it if he'd known. Privately, she suspected that he would've been appalled, but then, she'd been wrong about him once or twice before.

So she said, "I appreciate you saying so." And she didn't ask him any more questions. She'd rather listen to his silence than listen to his lies.

"Now tell me, Miss Wilkes. What are we looking for, precisely?"

"Some sign," she said. "Of my boy, I mean. Anything at all that shows he might've been here."

"Like what?"

She thought about it as she poked her way through the debris. Chunks of decaying wooden walkways hung over the edges of the shattered streets, and splinters rained down to settle on her hat. There was no wind and there was no sound. It was like standing underwater in a stagnant pond. All around them the dirty yellow air hung in place. At any moment, Briar thought, the world might freeze and she would stay there, stuck in amber.

She said, "Like anything different from last time you were here. Like footprints, or . . . or things like that. I don't know. Tell me about what I'm seeing, could you please? I don't understand. Where are we, exactly?"

"This is where the Boneshaker cut through under the street. The street fell in. We're standing on it now, but up there"—he pointed at the jagged ceiling above—"that's the rest of the street. And the walkways. And whatever else was up there sixteen years ago."

"Fantastic," she said. "It's dark down here. I can hardly see a thing."

"I'm real sorry. I didn't bring a lantern."

"Don't apologize," she told him. She picked her way around to a spot that seemed to be the back, or the edge, or some far corner of the pit. Directly in front of her, a black chasm opened up in the shape of a crushed circle, and disappeared deeper into the earth. Beyond a few feet, she could see nothing of where it might go or what it might hold.

She called into it. "Hello?" But she didn't use her loudest voice, and she would've been shocked to receive an answer.

None came.

"We can go up to street level, if you want. Over here," Squiddy said. He led her to a steeply cut ledge and pointed at the boards and bricks that had been jammed and stacked together. "It's a climb, but it's not bad. You can see better up there."

"All right. I'll follow you."

He scaled the slope with ease, scampering like a man half his age, until he crested the edge and stood, backlit against the lip of the gaping hole. Briar came up behind him and took his hand when he offered it. He pulled her over the edge and beamed inside his helmet mask. "Beautiful, isn't it?"

"Sure."

If she'd been asked to pick ten words to describe the scene before her, "beautiful" wouldn't have made the cut.

If she hadn't known better, she might've guessed that it had hosted a war in some other time; she might have assumed that some terrible scourge or blast had destroyed the whole landscape. Where once there had been stately structures that held money and the bustle of patrons, now there was only a long, open wound in the ground. The wound had gone rough around its massive edges, and it was beginning to fill with rubble.

In one place there seemed to be a stack of rounded river boulders. A closer look revealed them to be skulls, crusty and gray. They'd collected in a low gully, having rolled away from their forgotten bodies.

Briar fought to catch her breath. It was difficult, as she should've expected, given Squiddy's warning about the air. But it was a real and hard-fought struggle to bring a lungful at a time through her filters, which strained against the incoming impurities. It was like breathing through a feather mattress.

And how could she ever tell if her son had come by this place?

Gazing down into the pit she could see no sign of a trail—not even the one she'd so recently used. The terrain was unfit for keeping footprints. An elephant could've trod through the rubble and it wouldn't have left a mark.

A wave of hopelessness splashed against her and she cringed, tightening and hugging herself against the possibilities. She was out of ideas. She couldn't have discerned it if an army of Zekes had come this way. It was all she could do to swear to herself that no, he must not be back inside that tunnel with the edges as big as a house's roof. No, he couldn't be lying suffocated or squirming at the bottom of a hole Zeke's father had dug before he was born. No, it didn't matter that he couldn't have known about the air in this place. No, no, and no again.

"He's not here," she said, and the words bounded around inside her mask.

"That's good, isn't it?" Squiddy asked. His fluffy eyebrows twitched beneath his glass faceplate. "You wouldn't want to find him here, not really."

"I suppose not," she said.

"We could come back with a light, early tomorrow. We could look inside the tunnel. You wouldn't have to do a whole lot of crawling or anything. If he got up inside there, he didn't go far."

She squeaked, "Maybe. Yes. I don't know. Maybe. It's getting dark." She added the observation because she couldn't convince herself to choose an answer. "What time is it?"

"It's always getting dark down here," he agreed. "I don't know what time it is. Coming up on lunch, that's all I know. What do you want to do now?"

She didn't have an answer for that, either. So she tried, "Do you have any ideas? Any thoughts on where we might look? Are there any other safe places, or cleared-out breathing places nearby?"

Squiddy's oversized head swiveled back and forth as he surveyed the area for suggestions. "I'm forced to tell you no, Miss Wilkes. There's no place where the breathing's good until you get out to where the Chinamen keep themselves at night. They live near their old blocks, that way," he pointed.

"And Dr. Minnericht?"

"That way." He pointed ninety degrees away from his first gesture. "About the same distance. Where we just came from, that's the closest spot for getting away and getting some air, and I don't think anybody could find it if he didn't know it was there."

Back down in the pit Briar could barely see the place where they'd come out. "I'm sure you're right," she said. And she was glad that he couldn't see her face as well as she could see his.

As the white-gray sky above them lowered its lids and sank to a darker hue, Briar and Squiddy trudged back down the slope and reentered the tunnel beneath the ledge. The door sealed behind them with a grinding suck, securing them once more in the fire-dim brightness of machinery and filters.

"I'm real sorry," he said to her, still through the helmet because they hadn't yet passed enough seals to breathe freely. "I wish we'd found some sign of him. It's a shame we didn't."

"Thank you for taking me out here," she told him. "You didn't have to do it, and I appreciate it. I suppose now I'll go find Lucy and see how she's doing. Maybe, if she still wants to, we can go and catch this doctor of yours."

Squiddy didn't answer right away, as if he were chewing on a sentence before spitting it out. Then he said, "That might be a good idea. There's always a chance that Dr. Minnericht found your boy and brought him in. Or maybe one of his folks did. He's got folks just about everywhere."

Briar's throat seized as if it were being held in a fist. The thought had already occurred to her, and even though she was firmly, totally, thoroughly certain that the doctor was not her former husband . . . it still churned her stomach. If she'd ever had one thing to be thankful for, it was that Zeke had never met his father; and she had no intention of letting a pretender insert himself into that role.

But instead of screaming all this through the mask, as she desperately wanted to do, she cleared her throat and said, "He has people who work for him, does he? This doctor? I've heard them mentioned, but I haven't seen any sign of them yet."

"Well, they don't wear uniforms or nothing," Squiddy said. "But you can pretty much pick them out of a crowd. They're usually downed airmen, or dealers who come and go. Some of them are chemists who work with the doctor. He's always looking for new ways to make the sap, or make it easier to make. Sometimes they're big old thugs from outside the walls, and sometimes they're just sap-heads who hang around close and run errands, or do favors. He's got a little bit of an army down here, if you want the truth. But it's never the same army twice."

"Sounds like people come and go a lot. Sounds like he's not an easy man to work with."

"Ain't that the truth," he mumbled. Then he said, "Or that's how I've heard it. But you're new to the Inside, and you aren't making any trouble. You're just looking for your boy, that's all, and I don't think he'll make any problems for you. He's a businessman, you know? It'd be bad for business, I think, if he did you any harm. The kind of folks who work with him, they're real fond of your daddy's memory."

She stepped out in front of him and led the way along the path. Without turning around to meet his eyes, she said, "As I heard it, that's not always the case. I hear the doctor doesn't care much for the peace, and maybe he might not like me much."

"Maybe," he conceded. "But from what I've seen, you're a lady who can take care of herself. I wouldn't worry about it too bad."

"You wouldn't?" The Spencer beat a patient rhythm against her back.

"Naw. If he doesn't want anything from you, like as not, he'll leave you alone."

And that was the problem, wasn't it? He might very well want something from her. Heaven only knew what, but if he'd heard she was in town and if he had a reputation to protect, she might have a favorite new enemy. She glowered inside her mask until she passed the next seal and heard the whooshing, gushing, pounding thrust of the bellows driving air down through the tunnels. "I'm taking this off now," she said.

"Now that you mention it, I think I'll do away with my own."

Briar pried her hat away and popped the mask up off her hair.

"Not so fast, honey." Lucy parted the sealed flaps at the far end of the corridor and said, "I wouldn't get too comfortable yet, if I were you. Not if you want to meet the good doctor."

"Ma'am," Squiddy greeted her with a tip of his helmet. He pulled his own mask off and said, "I hope you're not talking to me. I think I'm done with the topside for now. It's harder to breathe every time I poke my head up there."

"No, Squiddy, I'm not talking to you. I'm glad I caught you two, though. I figured you might be headed back about now. If you don't mind my saying so, Miss Wilkes, you're looking grim but not grieving. You didn't find anything, did you?"

Briar shook her head, then stretched her neck so it could pop. "No, we didn't. We didn't look very long, but there wasn't much to see."

"Your lips to God's ears," she said. "It looks like an explosion out there, and it never does get any prettier, because, really—who would take the time to fix it? We've got better things to do down here, and we surely don't have the filters or the manpower for it. So all that debris, and all those toppled and sunken old buildings, they just sit there and crumble."

"Nothing to be done about it," Briar said. "But I'm a little surprised to see you out this way."

"My arm's acting up again. The temporary tubes Huey used to fix it are more temporary than I hoped. I've got a sling here for tying it up and holding it." It took her a moment of discomfort to bring herself around to saying the rest. "Fact is, I can't live real well without at least one good arm. And I don't mean to make you take me out there. I wouldn't do that, and if you don't want to go, I'd be the last one alive to insist on it. But since we'd talked this morning, I thought maybe—"

"Yes, that's fine. I don't mind, and now that you've all got me so curious about the man, I may as well catch him for myself." She punched the interior of her mask to fluff it out again. "If I seem surprised, it's only that it's getting dark up there, and I thought everyone tried to stay underground when the sun goes out."

Squiddy answered before Lucy could. He said, "Oh, getting over to King Street is easy as pie from here, and you wouldn't be heading out into the streets. Lucy, is that a pair of lanterns in your pack?"

He indicated the lumpy canvas sack she wore slung around her neck and arm.

"I brought two of them, yes, and extra oil for good measure."

Briar asked, "But aren't lights a bad idea? We'll draw rotters, won't we?"

Lucy said, "So what if we do? We'll be out of their reach. And anyway, you don't want to sneak up on the doctor. Best thing to do is walk up loud and bright, and don't let him think you're trying to hide. That's why I came up after you, hoping to catch you. The shortest, loudest, brightest way to Minnericht's is another tunnel south from here, and there was no sense in making you backtrack."

Even though Briar was technically willing, her motivation waned. "Isn't it getting late, though?"

"Late? No, it only looks late. It's just the time of year, and the shadow from the walls, and the thickness of the Blight. It makes you feel like the sun never comes up good, so it's hard to tell when it's actually going down." She shifted her shoulder, and the pack nestled against the curve of her waist. "Listen, honey, if you don't want to do this, it's all right. I'll go back and grab Jeremiah, and he can escort me in the morning. There's a rush, but not such a rush that I can't survive another night with a half-working hand. It'll be fine if you'd rather not expose yourself just yet."

Guilt won out over nervousness, and when Briar considered that perhaps Minnericht could point her toward Zeke, she had no choice but to say, "No, no. We'll go tonight, right now. Let me just change out these filters. They weren't quite new, but it didn't take them long to fill right up out there."

"Oh my, yes. I hope Squids gave you a warning about that."

While she unscrewed the filters and replaced them with clean ones from her satchel, Briar said, "He did indeed. He's been a most excellent guide, and I've appreciated his company."

"I'm sorry we didn't find anything about your boy," he said again.

"But that's not your fault, and it was worth trying, wasn't it? And now I've got no more leads to follow except this Minnericht." She popped the cap back over the filter, and it snapped into place. "Lucy, do you need any help carrying your supplies?"

"No, dear, I don't. Ask again in an hour, and see if you don't get a different answer, though." She was visibly relieved to be heading out, and Briar didn't wonder why. It must have been a hideously vulnerable feeling to be so crippled in such a dangerous place.

Squiddy said, "If you two ladies are all set up, I suppose I'll be on my way. There's a game running next door to the west-wall furnace room, and some of those Chinamen bring *gold* every once in a while. I may not win any, but I sure do want to set eyes on it," he beamed.

"Well then, you get a move on, and head back to the Vaults. We'll head out for the doctor's place, and if all goes without any trouble, we'll be back by bedtime," Lucy vowed.

Squiddy retreated back down the way Lucy had come, disappearing between the brown sealing flaps and darting back to the Vaults. Together, the women listened to the fading slap of his footsteps on the tunnel walkway.

*Twenty-one*

As soon as Squiddy was gone, Lucy turned to Briar and said, "Are you ready?"

"I'm ready," she promised. "Lead the way."

In front of her, Lucy was battling her arm to make her mask stay in place. Briar offered, "Can I help you with that?"

"Maybe that'd be a good idea."

Briar adjusted the other woman's mask until it settled firmly and buckled behind her ears. She noticed that Lucy had traded the one-hour model she'd sported before for a more substantial mask. "It's not sticking in your hair or anything, is it?"

"No, baby, it's fine. And thank you." She put on a brave smile, straightened her back, and said, "Now it's time to head up, and out. I might need you to open a door or two, and the path is wide enough that we can walk side by side most of the way, so it would be best if you could stay close to me."

"How far are we walking here?"

"Not more than a mile, I shouldn't think—but it's hard to say when we'll be climbing stairs and hunkering down hallways. It feels twice as long, I swear."

And Lucy wasn't joking. She couldn't hold a lantern with any steadiness, either, so Briar kept one lit and held up close for the both of them to see. Down a warren of tunnels, seals, and flaps, they came to a place with a crooked stairway and a sealed door. Briar unlatched the thing and climbed up with the light, and she kept an eye on Lucy behind her. The arm's integrity was failing, and it was becoming more useless by the moment.

Finally, at Lucy's request, Briar secured the arm as firmly as it could be caught. From that point on she walked in front when the going was tight. In this way, they hopscotched farther and farther south, until they'd come so close to the wall that its shape covered the sky when they emerged onto a new building's rooftop.

"What was this place?" Briar asked. It didn't look like the other rooftop vistas she'd seen so far; the floor was covered with plywood patches and the deeply rooted bases of metal poles. Overhead, a system of trapezes suspended walkways that moved at the pull of a handle.

"This place? Oh, I don't know. I think it was a hotel, once upon a time. Now it's . . . well, it's almost like a train station. I don't mean that there are any trains, because obviously there aren't, but—"

"But it's a junction," Briar surmised.

She stood back from a nailed-down piece of wood sheeting as big as a wagon and held her lantern aloft so she could better read the message written across it in red paint. It was a list of instructions and pointing arrows, almost like a stationary compass.

"See?" Lucy said, pointing down at it. "We want to go to King Street. That arrow there next to it, that tells you which walkway you need to pull."

"There, to the right?"

"Uh-huh. Beside it, see? There's a lever. Give it a good hard tug."

Briar pulled down hard on a lever that once was a broom handle; it had a green-painted end that matched the arrow pointing to it, which she thought was a nice touch. Somewhere up above, the clanging slide of a slipping chain was accompanied by the brittle protests of rusted metal. A sharp-edged shadow darted overhead and swayed, then settled, and lowered, and behind the shadow came a wood platform coated in pitch.

"It's not too sticky," Lucy said before Briar had a chance to ask.

"The tar keeps the wood from falling apart out here in the wet and the Blight; but it gets dusted with sawdust pretty often. Come on up. It's sturdier than it looks."

The platform was ringed on all four sides with a gated rail that opened front and back, and it now rested on a track that looked burly enough to support a herd of cattle.

"Go ahead," Lucy told her. "Get on the lift. It'll hold us both, and then some."

Briar took the suggestion and Lucy climbed up behind her, wavering with a lack of balance until Briar steadied her. "We follow along this?"

"That's right," she said.

The walkway disappeared into another tangle of platforms, lifts, and other contraptions meant to move people. Eventually it terminated at an interchange, and Lucy pointed out the green arrow aiming at a path that began with four green boards. Her eyes shifted back and forth in her mask and she said, much more quietly, "Don't look now, but we aren't alone. Up on the roof, to the right; and down in the window on the left."

Briar held her head still but followed the verbal directions. Lucy was right. Above them on the next roof over, a masked fellow with a long gun leaned into a corner and watched the women approach. Below them, one seamless glass window was blotched dark with the silhouette of a man with a covered face and a hat, also armed, and also hiding out in the open—not much caring if anyone saw him.

"Guards?" Briar asked.

"Don't get too nervous about them. We're coming up the right way, out in the open and plenty loud. They won't bother us."

"But they're watching for newcomers, aren't they?"

"Newcomers and rotters, and disgruntled clients," Lucy said.

Briar pointed out, "I'm a newcomer."

"Sure. But they know *me*."

"Maybe I should ask them—," she started to say.

Lucy interrupted. "Ask them what?"

"Ask them about Zeke. They're watchmen, aren't they? Maybe they saw my son while they were watching the streets."

The barkeep shook her head. "Not yet. Not these men. They won't talk to you, even if they can. They're only mercenaries, most of them. And they aren't friendly. Just leave 'em be." She lowered her voice again, and marched straight ahead behind Briar.

Briar picked out a third armed man on another nearby rooftop, and then a fourth. She asked, "Are there always this many of them?"

Lucy was looking another direction, for she'd spotted yet a fifth. "Sometimes," she said, but she sounded unconvinced by her own assessment. "This *does* seem like a lot for a welcome wagon. I wonder what's going on."

Briar didn't find this particularly reassuring, but she resolutely refused to hold her gun any tighter or walk any faster along the narrow, pipe-and-wood-frame corridors that held her up over the Blight-poisoned streets. "No one's aiming at us, at least," she said.

"True enough. Maybe they've had some problems. Maybe they're looking out for somebody else. Honey, could you do me a favor?"

"Name it."

"Stick a little closer by me. This part's uneven, and it's hard for me to straighten myself without my arm."

Briar shifted her shoulder, twitching her satchel and gun until they wouldn't clap Lucy in the face; then she put one arm around the other woman and helped her walk across the crooked beams. At the end of the way she pulled another lever, and another lift dropped down to meet them.

Lucy said, "This is the last of them. It'll take us down, into the basement. Can you see the station over there?"

Briar squinted and thought that she might be able to spy a dark point and a circle crossed by two lines through the shifting sheets of curdled air. "Over there?"

"That's right. That's the clock tower, there. They'd just got it up when the Blight hit us all. This place right here," she said as the gear-work mechanisms that held the platform aloft buckled and began to lower, "this was supposed to be a garage where the train cars were stored when no one needed them. It's been turned into a lobby of sorts."

"A lobby?"

"Sure. Think of it as a hotel. It's pretty nice inside," Lucy said. "Nicer than the Vaults, anyhow. Even down here, money has plenty to say—and Minnericht's rich as can be."

One level at a time, the rickety lift dropped the women. Through the skeleton of the huge, stillborn station their stomachs raced to beat them to the bottom; and at the bottom, the doors opened into more startling bareness—more blank reminders that there were no trains, and no tickets, and no customers. This was a place that had never been brand-new, and now it felt more ancient than the wings of flies trapped in dirty amber.

A puff of dust accompanied the settling of the lift.

Briar sneezed, and Lucy lifted her arm to wipe her nose on her sleeve, but the mask kept her from success. "Come on, dear," she said. "It's not much farther, and the deeper we go, the more comfortable the station becomes."

"How long has he lived here?" Briar asked as she followed Lucy off the lift.

"Oh, I don't know. Ten years, maybe? He's had quite a long time to spruce the place up to his liking, that's for sure."

They walked across flat stone without any shine or tiling, and their footsteps banged an announcement echo up to the room's edge. The vast, blank space terminated against a set of red double doors that were sealed with smooth black flaps at all the seams. Briar touched one of the flaps and stared at it more closely. It looked cleaner and more manufactured than the hastily improvised seals of the other quarters.

"How do we get inside? Do we have to knock a special way, or pull a bell?" Briar asked, noting that the door had no external knobs or latches.

Lucy said, "Help me pull the arm out of this sling, will you?"

Briar assisted with the detangling, and then Lucy swung the arm three times against the rightmost door. The sound was sharp and clanging. It was the sound of metal on metal.

"The doors . . ."

"Steel, I think. Someone told me he made them out of a train car's siding. But someone else told me he yanked them down from the entrance, so I don't know where he got them, really."

"And they're just going to let us inside?"

Lucy shrugged, and her mostly limp arm swung jauntily against her belly. "Rotters don't knock. Everybody else, they figure they can manage."

"Wonderful," Briar mumbled, and soon the jerk and squeal of interior braces revealed that they'd been heard.

The door took half a minute to open, as bars and locks were twisted, lifted, and set aside; and then came the squeal of unhappy hinges as the portal split open. Behind it, a thin man with an oversized mask glared suspiciously out into the area that Lucy had called "the lobby." An averagely tall fellow, he was dressed like a cowboy in canvas pants, a buttoned-shut shirt, and a pair of gun belts that overlapped one another around his hips. Across his chest another strap held another gun, a larger one like Briar's Spencer. He was younger than many of the other people she'd seen inside the city walls, but he was not as young as her son. He might've been as old as thirty, but it was hard to tell.

"Hello there, Richard," Lucy said.

If he had a frown or a smile to return the greeting, Briar couldn't see it through his mask. He said, "Miss Lucy. Something wrong with the arm?"

"That's right," she told him.

He gave Briar a frank sort of appraisal and said, "How'd your friend get inside the city?"

Lucy frowned. "What's that got to do with anything?"

"Maybe nothing. How'd she get inside?"

"You know, I'm standing right here. You *could* just ask me," Briar groused. "Fact is, I dropped down off the *Naamah Darling*. Captain Cly was kind enough to give me a ride."

Lucy held very still, like a prey animal afraid it's been spotted. Then she added slowly, "She's been here since yesterday. I was going to bring her sooner, but we had trouble with rotters. And anyway, she's here now."

Briar had assumed it had been longer, but when she thought about it, she realized she'd only been down in the city for one night and almost two full days. She said, before he could ask, "I'm looking for my son. He would've come inside here a couple of days ago. It's a long story."

He stared at her without blinking, for a moment too long. "I'll bet." After giving her another long look, he said, "I guess you'd better come inside." He turned his back to lead Briar and Lucy inside and they followed him.

The red double doors sipped a gust of air as they slapped back together.

"This way," said Richard. He drew them through a narrow room that was only just too wide to be called a hallway. The walls were pocked with gas lamps that looked like they came from ships. They reminded Briar of the lights on the *Naamah Darling*, and she thought that if she touched them, they might sway on their suspending arms.

They walked together in silence for so long that Briar jumped when Richard spoke again. "I think you're expected," he said.

Briar couldn't decide if this revelation gave her hope or made her feel sick. "I beg your pardon?" she asked, hoping for clarification.

He didn't offer any. "Miss Lucy, did you bang up your hand hitting on Willard again?"

She laughed, but it sounded more nervous than happy. "No, and that was only once. He's not very often a problem. Just that one time . . ." Her voice evaporated, and returned. "No, this was a clot of rotters. We had some trouble at Maynard's."

Briar wondered if Richard already knew about the trouble, or if he could have been involved in it. The man didn't respond, and Lucy didn't try any more conversation; and before long the stretched-out room ended in a set of curtains made of the same black rubber, but hung as if they were proper drapery.

Richard said, "You can take your masks off now, if you want to. The air's all right back here." He pried off his own and stuffed it up under his arm, displaying a broad nose marred with dimpled scars—and a set of hollow cheeks so deep they could've stored plums.

Briar helped Lucy first, stashing the barkeep's mask inside her sling. She pulled her mask off too, and stuck it into her satchel. "I'm ready whenever you are," she announced.

"Come on, then." He pushed the flap aside and nearly blinded Briar with the light behind the veil.

"I should've warned you," Lucy said with a squint. "Dr. Minnericht has a thing about light. He loves it, and he likes to make it. He's been working on making lamps that run on electricity or gas, and not just oil. And this is where he tests them."

Briar let her eyes adjust and she took a look around. Lamps of all shapes and sizes blazed around the room on pillars and poles. They were strapped to the walls and to each other, and bundled into groups. Some functioned with an obvious power source, and their lemony flames cast a traditional glow; but others broadcast beams made of stranger stuff. Here and there a lamp burned blue and white, or created a greenish halo.

"I'll go tell him you're here. Miss Lucy, you and your friend want to wait in the car?"

"Sure," she said.

"You know the way."

And he was gone, disappeared around a corner. The open and shut of a door said he was going quite a ways away, so Briar turned to Lucy and said, "What car?"

"He means the old train car. Or one of them in particular. Minnericht cleaned them out, and he puts furniture in them or uses them for storage, or work space. Some of them he turns into little hotel rooms, here under the street."

Briar asked, "How'd he get the railway cars down under the street? And what were they doing here, since the station wasn't finished when the walls went up?"

Lucy strolled past a row of candlesticks that were surely waiting to set the place ablaze. She said, "We had trains coming and going before the whole station was done. I think several of the cars dropped down here during the quake. But I couldn't say for sure. Hell, maybe he dragged them down himself, or paid somebody to do it. Baby, could you get that door for me?"

Briar leaned on a latch, and another set of double doors yawned themselves apart. Beyond them there was nothing but darkness, or so it seemed after the noontime brilliance of the lighting room. But glass-covered torches flickered insistently in the opaque blackness, and warmly glowing sheets of tarnished metal threw dim patches of light against the walls and ceiling.

When Briar lifted her head she saw too much above her, too close.

Lucy saw her looking. "Don't worry about that. I know it looks like a cave-in, and it *is*. But it happened ages ago, and it hasn't moved any farther since. He's braced it up, and he's reinforced the cars underneath it."

"So these cars are buried?"

"Some of them. Here. Look, darling. This is the one where he takes visitors. This is where he lets me meet him, at least. Maybe we do it here because this is where he stores his extra tools—I don't know. But this is where we're going."

She cocked her head toward a door that Briar almost missed, for it was obscured by rubble and dirt. A trestle of railroad ties framed it like an arch, and next to this door there were two others, one on each side.

"The middle one," Lucy said.

Briar took this as a cue to open the door. It felt like such a fragile thing, after all the heavily braced portals she'd passed through recently. The latch was only a tiny bar that fit in the palm of her hand. She held it softly, for fear of breaking it.

It clicked and the door swung out.

She held it open while Lucy let herself inside, where more shimmering lamps illuminated an intimidating array of trinkets, tools, and assorted devices whose function Briar could not begin to guess. The interior seats had been removed, though a handful had been repositioned to line the far wall instead of occupying space in rows. In the center, running lengthwise through the railroad car, a long table was almost totally buried by the bizarre items that were stacked upon it.

"What is all this?" she asked.

"They're . . . that's . . . it's tools, that's all. This is a workshop," she finished, as if that explained everything.

Briar picked at the edges of the heaps, running her fingers through tubes, pipes, and wrenches in sizes so odd she couldn't imagine what nuts they might twist. Stacked along the outer edges of the room more equipment had been abandoned or stored, and none of it looked like it could've possibly done anything more useful than beep or chime. But there were no clocks, only clock parts and hands; and she saw no weapons, only sharp instruments and bulbs with tiny wires running through them like veins.

The unmistakable slapping rhythm of incoming feet filtered inside, past the slim barrier of the old train's dented door.

"He's coming," Lucy breathed. A look of panic crossed her face, and her malfunctioning arm jerked in her lap. She said quickly, "I'm so sorry. I don't know if this was the right thing to do, but in case it wasn't, then I'm so sorry."

And then the door opened.

# Twenty-two

Briar held her breath while she stared.

Dr. Minnericht's mask was as elaborate as Jeremiah Swakhammer's; but it made him look less like a mechanical animal than a clockwork corpse, with a steel skull knitted together from tiny pipes and valves. The mask covered everything from the crown of his head to his collarbones. Its faceplate featured a flat pair of goggles that were tinted a deep shade of blue, but illuminated from within so it appeared that his pupils were alight.

No matter how hard she looked, she couldn't see his face. He was neither short nor tall, fat nor thin. The whole of his frame was covered by a coat shaped like a duster, but made from dark maroon velour.

Whoever he was, he was staring right back at her. The sound of his breathing exhaled through the filtering tubes was a small musical of whistles and gasps.

"Dr. Minnericht?" Lucy said. "I thank you for making the time to see me. And this is a new friend. She came down off the *Naamah Darling*, and she helped me find my way to you, since my arm's giving me hassle again."

He said, "I'm sorry to hear about your arm," but he didn't take his eyes off Briar. His voice was altered like Swakhammer's when he spoke. But the noise was less the sound of speaking through a tin can, and more the tune of a grandfather clock chiming underwater.

He came inside the warmly lit workshop, and Lucy chattered nervously as he shut the door behind himself. She said, "Her name's Briar, and she's looking for her boy. She was hoping maybe you'd seen him or heard about him, since you've got so many men out on the street."

"Does she speak for herself?" he asked almost innocently.

"When she feels like it," Briar answered, but offered nothing more.

The doctor did not quite relax, but he settled into a deliberately nonchalant posture within his oversized coat. He gestured at the table, inviting Lucy to come and sit on the bench beside it and set her arm down on the surface so he could see. He said, "Won't you have a seat, Mrs. O'Gunning?"

Behind the door was a box that Briar had not yet seen. The doctor retrieved it and approached the place where Lucy had come to sit. Briar backed away from the pair of them, feeling her way along the cluttered walls until she came to a clear spot beside a window.

It was a horrible game—wondering if he knew, and wondering if he'd say anything. She was still very certain, wasn't she? He wasn't Leviticus Blue—she could swear as much, and she had sworn as much before, and she would swear as much again; but she could not deny that he moved with a certain controlled swagger that seemed almost familiar. And when he spoke, there might be a cadence that she'd heard someplace before.

Minnericht unfastened the box a buckle at a time, then opened it and added a set of articulated lenses to the faceplate on his mask. "Let me take a look at that," he said, as if he intended to wholly ignore Briar. "What have you done to it this time?"

"Rotters," Lucy said, and her voice was shaky.

"Rotters? That's no surprise."

Briar bit her tongue so she would not say, "Not for you, I don't imagine—since you're the man who sent them."

Lucy mumbled, "We were leaving Maynard's and Hank got sick. His mask wasn't on him good, and he turned, and we ran into trouble. I had to bust my way to the Vaults with Miss Briar here."

Within his mask he made a clucking noise that sounded like a parent's gentle admonishment. "Lucy, Lucy. What about your crossbow? How many times do I have to remind you: This is a delicate piece of machinery, not a truncheon."

"The crossbow . . . I didn't have . . . there wasn't really time. In the chaos of it all, you know. Things get lost."

"You lost it?"

"Well, I'm sure it's still down there somewhere. But when I got up topside, it wasn't there anymore. I'll find it later. I'm sure it's still in one piece." She cringed when he opened the top panel of her arm and began to poke through its interior with a long, thin screwdriver.

"You've let someone else work on this joint," he said, and Briar could hear the frown she couldn't see.

Lucy looked as if she'd like to go crawling away from him, but she held still and almost simpered, "It was an emergency. It wasn't working at all, except to spasm and kick, and I didn't want to hurt anyone so I let Huey take a crack at it."

"Huey," he repeated the name. "You mean Huojin. I've heard about him. He's developing quite the reputation in your quarters, or so I hear."

"He's . . . talented."

Without looking up from his work, he said, "I'm always interested in talent. You should bring him here. I think I'd like to meet him. But, oh dear—just look what he's done. What is this tube made from, Lucy?"

"I . . . I don't know." Lucy clammed up, but Minnericht wasn't finished with the subject.

He said, "Oh, I see what he was trying to do. Of course, he couldn't have known what kind of heat the friction inside can generate, so he wouldn't have known that this couldn't work. Even so, I do want to meet him. I think that'd be a fair means of repayment, don't you, Lucy?"

"I don't know." She sounded like she might be choking. "I don't know if his grandfather will let him—"

"Then bring his grandfather too. The more the merrier, as they say." But it didn't sound merry at all to Briar, who wished that the compartment were bigger—if only so she could farther remove herself from the man's presence.

"Miss Briar," he said, suddenly directing his attention her way. "Could I impose upon you for a very small favor?"

She said, "Sure, ask." Her throat was too dry to carry the message with any coolness.

He used his screwdriver to indicate a place. "Behind you, over there. If you turn around, you'll see a box. Could you bring it to me, please?"

The box was heavier than it looked, and she would've preferred to hit him over the head with it than hand it to him; but she lifted it off the table and carried it to his side. Beside him, there was a cleared space on the bench. She placed it there and backed away again.

He still did not look at her. He said, "You know, Miss Briar, I can't bite you through this mask."

"I shouldn't think so," she said.

"I'm forced to wonder what dear Lucy here has told you of me, to send you so far out of my reach. Won't you have a seat?"

"Won't you tell me if you've seen my son?"

His hand froze and the screwdriver hung midair, suspended in his grip. He dipped it again, gave it a twist, and reached for a fresh tube from the box. "I'm sorry. Were we talking about your son?"

"I believe he was mentioned."

"Did I mention that I'd seen him?"

"No," Briar admitted. "But you didn't say you hadn't. So pardon me if I get a little more direct."

Minnericht closed the panel that exposed the insides of Lucy's arm; she tested it, and her face registered the deepest sort of relief as it worked in all the ways she required. She singled out her fingers and pointed them as if she were counting, then bent her wrist forward, backward, and left to right.

The doctor slid sideways, pivoting on his hip to face Briar while

remaining seated. "Did you ask the airmen? Captain Cly—he's the
fellow on the *Naamah Darling*, isn't that right?—he sees and hears
more than most men. Perhaps it's that unnatural height of his."

"Don't be ridiculous," Briar said, and she hated herself for being
childishly rude. It wouldn't serve her purposes, and it wouldn't move
him to help her, but there was an old pattern in play and she couldn't
find a different track. She was angry, and frightened on top of that,
and in those conditions she regressed into someone she didn't like. "I
asked him, and I asked every other airman who'd give me five minutes of his time. No one's seen hide nor hair of him, which isn't so
crazy given that he came in from the water runoff, not from the sky."

A flicker of the gleaming, flickering blue lights behind the mask almost implied a lifted eyebrow. He said, "Then why didn't you do likewise? Surely it would've made for a much less . . . traumatic entrance
into our fine and Blighted city."

"The earthquake the other night. It flattened the tunnel and I had
to come another way. Believe me, dropping a thousand feet through
a tube into a furnace wasn't my idea of a fun time, either."

"It's not nearly a thousand feet," he murmured. "It's only a couple
hundred. But that's useful to know, about the runoff tunnel. I'll need
to get it repaired, and the sooner the better. I'm surprised that you're
the first to say something about it. I would've thought . . ."

Whatever he'd been prepared to say, he abandoned it and said instead, "I'll make a point to have it fixed. But tell me, Miss Briar, how
did you intend to leave the city? If you knew the tunnel had collapsed, what sort of exit did you plan for him?"

"Where's my son?" she asked bluntly, again forcing that sharp
change of subject.

His answer oozed with something too theatrical to be meaningful.
"Whatever makes you think I know?"

"Because if you didn't know, you would've said so by now. And if
you know where he is, and you're giving me this runaround, then you
must want him for something—"

"Miss Briar," he interrupted, with more volume than was strictly necessary. The force of his voice, laden with strange weights and brass bells, brought her to silence in a way that chilled her. She didn't mean to obey him when he told her, "There's no need for abruptness. We can talk about your son if you like, but I won't be subject to your accusations or demands. You are now a guest in my home. So long as you act the part, you may expect to be treated accordingly."

Lucy's breaths were coming in quick, asthmatic squeezes that counted the time like a second hand on a pocket watch. She still hadn't risen from her seat on the bench, and now she looked positively unable to. The barkeep's skin was nearly green with fear, and Briar thought that she might vomit at any moment.

But she didn't, not then. She held herself upright and dry, and she said, "Please, I think—Briar, I think—let's all stay calm. There's nothing to be short about. We're guests; it's like he said."

"I heard him."

"Then I'd ask you, for my sake, to accept his hospitality. He says you can talk, and he'll let you talk. I'm only asking you—in a motherly way, if you don't mind it—to mind your manners."

It wasn't motherly at all, the way she was suggesting restraint. It was the trembling attempt of a child trying to appease two bickering parents.

Briar swallowed whatever else she was going to say. It took her a moment; she was forcing down a great knot of things she wanted to shout. And then she said, with words she'd measured as neatly as buttonholes, "I'd appreciate the chance to speak with you, yes. Whether it's here in your home, as a guest, or elsewhere, I have no preference. But I only came here for one thing—not to make friends, or to be a pleasant guest. I came here to find my boy, and until I do, you'll have to forgive me if my attention lies somewhere other than my manners."

The blue lights behind his mask—those flame-bright nubs that stood in place of his eyes—did not blink or waver. He said, "I understand, and my forgiveness surely follows." And immediately afterward, a gentle pinging noise sounded from his chest.

For one irrational, delirious moment Briar thought it must be his heart, a carved or assembled thing without a soul or a drop of blood; but he reached into a pocket to remove a round gold watch, checked its face, and made a small grunt.

"Ladies, I see that it's getting late. Please allow me to offer you quarters for the evening. It won't be the Vaults, but you might find it suitable, regardless."

"No!" Lucy said, too fast and too loud. "No, we couldn't impose on you like that. We'll just be heading on our way."

Briar argued, "Lucy, I'm staying until he tells me what he knows about Zeke. And I'll stay as a guest if that's how he wants it. You don't have to, if you don't want to," she added. She looked into Lucy's eyes with what she hoped was a meaningful gaze, and she said softly, "I won't take it personal if you want to see your own way home, now that you're all fixed up."

It wasn't just fear Briar saw on Lucy's face. Suspicion crept there too, and curiosity too strong to be extinguished even by terror. "I won't leave you here alone," she said. "And anyway, I don't want to go back by myself."

"But you could, if it came to that. I'm happy for your company," Briar said, "but I wouldn't ask you to stick around if you don't want to."

Minnericht rose from the stool and assumed his full height once again. Briar was closer to him now, and she couldn't decide, or couldn't remember, if his height was the same as Levi's—or if he was shaped the same way.

He said, "Actually, come to think of it, Lucy—I have a bit of an errand I'd like for you to run."

"You already said you wanted me to bring Huey out here, and that would pay you for fixing the arm." She did not sound even remotely charmed by the prospect.

"And I note you made me no such promise or agreement," he said with some displeasure. "But that's neither here nor there. You'll bring him here, or you'll wish you'd done so later. I thought you valued Maynard's, Miss Lucy. I thought it was worth something to you. Worth preserving, if nothing else."

"Don't be a bastard," she spit, her own manners forgotten in the face of his unveiled threats.

"I'll be a bastard and worse, if it pleases me." Briar thought she could see some curtain being drawn aside; she could see one mask sliding slowly away, even as the one he wore seemed bolted onto his very skeleton. He said, "Tomorrow or the next day, you'll bring me Huey so that we can discuss tinkering and other assorted things; and tonight, you will go out to my fort."

"Decatur?" Lucy asked, as if the prospect honestly surprised her. Briar did not like his claim to the place.

"Yes, I want you to go there and deliver a message for me," he declared. "We have more unexpected guests inside our walls than just your friend here, and I want to make sure they understand their place."

"And what place is that?" Lucy asked.

"*My* place." He reached a gloved hand into an interior pocket of his vest and withdrew a sealed letter. "Take this to whatever captain you find there. I understand that someone is using my old lot to make repairs."

Lucy was furious, but not stupid enough to put it on display. She said, "You could get anybody to carry a message for you. There's no sense in sending me out into the streets, late at night, through crowds of hungry rotters just to get me out of the way. I'll just leave, if that's what you want, and if Briar says it's all right with her."

"Lucy." He sighed as if she were truly tiring him with her protests. "You and I both know that you won't set foot on any street this evening. If you haven't figured out the fort block tunnels by now, then I've overestimated you for many years. Take the south fork at the third split, if you aren't so certain. It's marked in yellow. If you would rather not return all the way to your place in the Vaults, you may return here if you like—and we'll have Richard set you up in the bronze wing."

He presented the last sentence with a resounding vibe of dismissal. His hand was still holding the envelope with whatever instructions or requests for bribery it might contain.

Lucy glowered at his hand, and at his mask. She snatched the envelope and shot Briar a look that was too loaded to decipher.

Briar said, "Do it, if that's how this works. I don't mind, Lucy. I'll be all right, and I'll see you back at the Vaults in the morning."

Minnericht did not agree with this claim, but he did not contradict it either, even though Lucy gave him time to do so.

"Good. If anything happens to her"—she indicated Briar—"we won't be so easy to dismiss. You won't be able to pretend we're all friends here, not anymore."

He replied, "I don't care if we're friends. And what makes you think anything untoward will happen to her? You won't threaten me, not in my own home. Get out, if you're going to make a nuisance of yourself."

"Briar . . . ," Lucy said. It was a plea and a warning.

Briar understood that the conversation was crowded with things she didn't understand, and for which she had no context. She was missing something in the forced exchange, and whatever it was, it sounded dangerous. But she'd dug her own grave now, and she'd lie in it if she had to. She said, "It's all right. I'll see you in the morning."

Lucy took a deep breath. The mechanisms in her clockwork arm gave a rattling patter as if they were straining. "I won't leave you like this," she said.

"Yes, you will," Dr. Minnericht corrected her as he ushered her to the door and shoved her past its threshold.

She turned on her heel with rage in her eyes. "We're not done here," she said, but she left, letting the train door slam in her wake. From the other side, she shouted, "I'll be back tonight!"

Dr. Minnericht said, "I wouldn't recommend it," but Lucy couldn't hear him. Her retreating footsteps sounded like fury and humiliation.

Briar and Dr. Minnericht gave one another space, and the silence to think of a conversation safe enough to share. She said first, "About my son. I want you to tell me where he is, or how he is. I want to know if he's alive."

It was his turn to kick the subject ninety degrees without a transition. He said, "This isn't the main body of the station, you know."

"I realize that. We're in a buried car, is all. I don't know where you live down here, or what you do. I just want my boy." She balled her hands into fists and unclenched them, using her hands to smooth her pockets instead. She wrapped one row of fingers around the strap of her satchel, as if feeling its weight and knowing what it held might give her some strength to stand her ground.

"Let me show you," he said, but he didn't clarify what he intended to share. He opened the train car door and held it for her like an ordinary gentleman.

She stepped outside and immediately twisted to face him, because she could not stand the thought of him walking behind her. Her mind was churning with reassurances and logic, and with all her heart she knew that this was not her husband, who was dead. But that didn't change the way he walked, or the way he stood, or the way he watched her with polite scorn. She was dying to yank his helmet away and see his face, so that she could quiet the screamed warnings that distracted and harangued her. She was wishing with all her heart that he would say something—say anything—to either confirm or deny that he knew who she was and he intended to make use of that knowledge.

But no.

He led the way back into the corridor that ended in lights, and he guided her to another platform on pulleys. This platform was not like the rough-edged wood of the walkways outside; it was more carefully assembled, and designed with something like style.

Dr. Minnericht pulled a lever, and an ironwork gate slipped shut, closing them together inside a box as big as a closet. "Down one more level," he explained. He reached for a handle overhead and tugged it.

A chain unspooled, and the lift began to drop, settling on the floor below only seconds later.

On the other side of the ironwork gate, which slid aside with a thunderous rattle, Briar found a place like a ballroom—all gleaming and gold, with floors as bright as mirrors and chandeliers that hung from the ceiling like crystalline puppets.

She found her breath, and said, "Lucy told me this place was nicer than the Vaults. She wasn't kidding."

"Lucy wouldn't know about this level," he said. "I've never taken her here. And this is not our destination—it's only a place we're passing through."

Briar walked under the glittering lights and they seemed to turn as if to follow her—and they weren't crystals, they were glass bulbs and tubes, laced together with wires and gears. She tried not to stare, but failed. "Where did those come from? They're . . . they . . . they're amazing." She wanted badly to say that they reminded her of something else, but she couldn't confess it.

As the light tinkled down in shattered rays, sweeping the floor with white patterns that said strange things to the shadows, Briar remembered a mobile Levi had made when they'd talked about a baby.

She hadn't known about Zeke when the Boneshaker had ravaged the city. She hadn't yet suspected, but they'd planned.

And he'd made a lighted fixture—so clever and so sparkling that although she was no infant herself, she'd been fascinated with the trinket. She'd hung it in a corner of the parlor, intending to use it as a lamp until they had a nursery to put it in, though the nursery never happened.

But these lights were much larger, big enough to fill a bed. They would never fit in a corner or over a crib. Still, she couldn't deny that the design was similar enough to startle her.

Minnericht saw her looking and said, "The first one is there." He nodded up at the center light, the biggest of the assortment. "It had been shipped to the station for use in the main terminal. You can see, it's not like the rest. I found it on a car, boxed and covered in earth like everything else on the south quadrant of the city. The rest of them took some assembling."

"I bet," she said. It was too much, this familiarity. It was too strange, the way he rambled the same way about the things that pleased him.

"It's an experiment, I admit. Those two over there are powered by kerosene, but it's a bit of a mess and they smell more strongly than could be called pleasant. The two on the right are run by electricity, which I think might prove the better option. But it's tricky, and it can be just as dangerous as fire."

"Where are you taking me?" she asked, as much to break the spell of his mellow enthusiasm as from a desire to know.

"To a place where we can talk."

"We can talk right here."

He leaned his head in a mimed shrug and said, "True, but there's nowhere to sit, and I'd prefer to be comfortable. Wouldn't you prefer to be comfortable?"

"Yes," she said, though she knew it wasn't going to happen.

It did not matter that he'd shifted back into the civilized personality that had slipped when she'd confronted him. Briar knew what waited on the other side of his social warmth, and it was marked with a black hand. It smelled like death, and it moaned for the flesh of the living; and she was not swayed by any of it.

Finally they came to a carved wooden door that was too dark to be stained and too ornate to be merely a piece of salvage. Made from ebony that grew the color of coffee, the door was marked with scenes from a war, and with soldiers in costumes that might have been Greek or Roman.

It would have taken Briar time to decipher the decoration fully, and Minnericht did not give her any time.

He whisked her past the door and into a room with a carpet thicker than oatmeal, but about the same color. A desk made from some lighter wood than the door hulked in front of a fireplace that looked like nothing Briar had ever seen before. It was made of glass and brick, with clear pipes that bubbled with boiling water, burbling like a creek and warming the room without any smoke or ash.

A round, red settee with plush dimples sat in front of the desk, at an angle; and an overstuffed armchair lurked beside it. "Pick one," Minnericht invited.

She picked the armchair.

It swallowed her with squeaky, slick leather and brass rivets.

He took a seat behind the desk, assuming authority as if it were his birthright. He folded his hands together and rested them on the top of the table.

Briar felt herself getting hot, starting with the spots behind her ears. She knew without looking that she was flushing, and that the dark pink was blossoming down her neck and across her breasts. She was glad for her coat and her high-collared shirt. At least he could only see the color in her cheeks, and he might assume that she was merely warm.

Behind the doctor, the bright tube fireplace hummed and gurgled, occasionally spitting small burps of steam.

He looked her in the eye and said, "It's a ridiculous little game we're playing here, isn't it, Briar?"

The easiness with which he used her name made her teeth grind, but she refused to be drawn in. "It certainly is. I've asked you a simple question and you're disinterested in helping me, even though I think you can."

"That isn't what I mean, and you know it. You know who I am, and you're pretending you don't, and I can't imagine why." He templed his fingers and let the structure fall, patting his hands against the desk surface in an impatient sort of patter. "You recognize me," he insisted.

"I don't."

He tried a different approach. "Why would you hide him from me? Ezekiel must've been born . . . so shortly after the walls went up, or right around that time. I've not been much of a secret inside here. Even the child had heard that I survived; I find it difficult to believe that you did not."

Had she mentioned Zeke's name? She was almost certain she hadn't, and so far as she knew Zeke had never implied that he thought his father might have survived. "I don't know who you are." She stuck to her story and kept her words as flat as if she'd let all the air out of them. "And my son knows that his father is dead. You know, it's very improper for you to—"

"Improper? You're no one to speak to me of improper behavior, woman. You left, when you ought to have stayed with your family; you fled when your duty was to linger."

"You don't know what you're talking about," she said with more confidence. "If that's the worst you've got to accuse me of, then you may as well confess your deception now."

He feigned offense and leaned back in his chair. "My deception? You're the one who came here acting as if perhaps it had been so long I might not know you. Lucy knows what's going on too, I suppose. She must have, or else she would've used your full name to introduce you."

"She was being careful because she feared for my safety in your presence, and it seems she had good reason to."

"Have I threatened you? Shown you anything apart from courtesy?"

"You still haven't told me what you know of my son. I consider that the very height of rudeness, when you must be able to guess how much I've worried for him over these last few days. You're tormenting me, and taunting me with the things you keep to yourself."

He laughed at her, softly and with condescension. "Tormenting you? Good heavens, that's quite a claim. Here, then. Ezekiel is safe and well. Is that what you wanted to hear?"

Yes, but she had no way of knowing if it was true. It was almost too hard to hope through his screens, and lies, and deliberate misleading. "I want to see him," she said without answering his question. "I won't believe you until I do. And you might as well say it. Say what you're implying so strongly, unless you don't dare—and I think you shouldn't. Half your power over these people comes from the mask, and the confusion. They fear you because they aren't certain."

"And you are?"

"Quite."

He rose from his chair as if he couldn't stand to sit there another moment. He vacated it with such force that it rolled out from under him and knocked against the desk. With his back turned and his gleaming mask facing the faux fireplace he said, "You're a fool. The same fool you've always been."

Briar kept her seat, and kept her grim tone intact. "Maybe. But I've survived this long in such a state, and maybe it'll keep me a little longer. So say it, then. Tell me who you are, or who you're pretending to be."

His coat flourished when he whirled around to face her. Its hem scattered papers on the desk and caused the crystals on the desktop lamp to tinkle like wind chimes. "I am Leviticus Blue—your husband then and still, who you abandoned in this city sixteen years ago."

She gave him a moment to revel in his announcement before saying very quietly, "I didn't abandon Levi here. If you were really him, you'd know that."

Inside the doctor's mask something squeaked and whistled, though he gave no outer sign of feeling her rebuttal. "Perhaps you and I have different ideas of what abandonment means."

She laughed then, because she couldn't help herself. It wasn't a big laugh or a loud laugh, but a laugh of pure disbelief. "You're amazing. You're not Levi, but whoever you are, you're amazing. We both know who you're not, and you know what? I don't even care who you *are*. I don't give a good goddamn what your real name is or where you came from; I *just want my boy*."

"Too bad," he said, and he made a swift yank on the desk's top drawer. In far less time than it would've taken Briar to ready her Spencer, Dr. Minnericht was pointing a fat, shiny revolver at her forehead. He cocked it and held it steady. He said, "Because your boy is staying here with me, where he's made himself quite comfortable over the last day or so . . . and I'm afraid you'll be staying here too."

Briar forced herself to relax, letting her body settle more deeply into the chair. She had one card left to play, and she was going to play it without giving him the satisfaction of seeing her scared. She said, "No he's not, and no *I'm* not, and if you've got any sense, you're not going to shoot me."

"Is that what you think?"

"You've been building this up a long time, slowly feeding people clues that you might be Levi, and getting them so nervous about you that it's made you powerful. Well, they've been arguing out there in Maynard's, and in the Vaults, and in the furnace rooms—trying to get me to come out here and take a look at you because they want to know for sure, and they think I can tell them."

He came around the side of the desk, bringing the gun up closer but still not firing it, and not telling her to stop talking. So she didn't.

"You tried to convince me you were Levi, so that must be your goal—to make it official. It's one hell of an identity to steal, but if you want it, I say you can have it."

The gun jerked in his hand; he aimed it at the ceiling and angled his neck like a dog asking a question. "I beg your pardon?"

"I said, you can have it if you want it. You can be Levi—I don't care. I'll tell them that's a fact if that's what you want—and they'll believe me. There's no one else in the world who can confirm or deny your claim. If you kill me, they'll figure I knew you were a liar and you felt the need to shut me up. But if you let me and Zeke go, then you can be whatever legend you want. I won't muck it up for you."

It might have only been her imagination, but Briar thought that the bright blue flecks took on a crafty look. He said, "That's not a terrible idea."

"It's a damn fine idea. I'd only ask for one provision."

He didn't put the gun down. He didn't aim it at her face again, either. He said, "What's that?"

She sat forward in the chair, and it released her back and her satchel with a squeak. "Zeke has to know. I won't let him think you're his dad, but I'll sell him on the story, and he'll run with it. He's the only one who needs to know the truth."

Again the blue lights flashed. Minnericht didn't argue. He said, "Let me think about it."

And faster than Briar would've believed the man could move, he struck her across the head with the butt of the gun.

A searing bolt of pain sounded like a gong against her temple.

And everything everywhere went dark.

## *Twenty-three*

When Zeke awoke in the princely room beneath the train station, the lights had been somewhat dimmed and the cottony taste in his mouth suggested that he'd been asleep for longer than he'd meant to be. He smacked his lips together and tried to moisten his tongue.

"Ezekiel Wilkes," said a voice, before Zeke even realized that he was not alone. He rolled over on the bed and blinked.

Sitting in a chair beside the fake window, a man with folded arms and a monstrous air mask was tapping one gloved hand against his knee. He was wearing a red coat that looked like it was meant for a foreign king, and boots that were shiny and black.

"Sir?" Zeke said. He could scarcely force the question out.

"Sir. You call me 'sir.' I suppose it belies your appearance, that simple indication of manners. I'll take it as a good sign."

He blinked again, but the strange vision didn't change, and the man in the chair didn't move. "Of what?"

"Of how breeding might overcome raising. No," he said as Zeke began to sit up. "Stay down. Now that you're awake, I'd like to see that gash on your head, and the one on your hand. I did not want to examine them while you slept, lest you awaken to this." He motioned at his mask. "I'm aware of what it looks like."

"Then why don't you take it off? I can breathe in here."

"So could I, if I chose." He rose then, and came to sit on the edge of the bed. "Suffice it to say, I have my reasons."

"Are you all scarred up or something?"

"I *said*, I have my reasons. Hold still." He pressed one hand against Zeke's forehead and used the other to push the matted hair away. His gloves were warm but so snug that they might as well have been his naked fingers. "How did this happen?"

"Are you Dr. Minnericht?" he asked instead of answering the question.

"I am Dr. Minnericht, yes," he said without changing his tone in the slightest. He pressed a place here, and nudged a spot there. "At least that's what they call me these days, in this place. You ought to have stitches, but I think you'll survive without them. It's been too long since you sustained the injury; your hair has gummed up the wound; and for the time being, at least, it isn't bleeding and it doesn't appear inflamed. We should keep an eye on it, all the same. Now, let me see your hand."

If Zeke heard anything after the "yes," he didn't react to it. "Yaozu said you knew my father."

The prying hands withdrew, and the doctor sat up straighter. He said, "He told you that, did he? He phrased it exactly that way?"

Zeke scrunched his forehead, trying to remember more precisely. His furrowed eyebrows tugged at the torn skin farther back on his skull, and he winced. "I don't remember. He said something like that. He said you could tell me about him, anyhow."

"Oh, I certainly *could*," he agreed. "I wonder, though. What has your mother told you?"

"Not much." Zeke scrunched his body up to a seated position, and he almost gasped to see the doctor from this other angle. He could have sworn that the man did not have any eyes, but behind the visor of the elaborate mask, two blue lights burned sharply where his pupils ought to be.

The lights flared brighter for a moment, then dimmed. Zeke had no idea what it might mean. The doctor retrieved the boy's hand and began to wrap it in a thin, light cloth.

"Not much. I see. Should I guess instead that she's told you nothing at all? Should I furthermore assume that everything you've heard, you've heard from history—and from your schoolmates, or from the gossip of men and women in the Outskirts?"

"That's about right."

"Then you don't know the half of it. You don't know a fraction of it." The lights flickered as if he were blinking, and his words slowed down, and grew more calm. "They blamed him for the Boneshaker's failure, because they are ignorant, do you understand? They blamed him for the Blight because they knew nothing of geology or science, or the workings of the earth beneath the crust. They did not understand that he'd only meant to begin an industry here, one apart from the filthy, violent, bloody sport of logging. He was looking to begin a new age for this city and its inhabitants. But those inhabitants . . ." Minnericht paused to gather his breath, and Zeke surreptitiously burrowed more deeply against the pillows at his back. "They knew nothing of a researcher's process, and they did not understand that success is built on the bones of failures."

Zeke wished he had more room to retreat, but he didn't, so he made small talk instead. He said, "You knew him pretty good, then, did you?"

Minnericht stood, and strode slowly away from the bed, folding his arms and pacing a short path from the basin to the bed's foot. "Your *mother*," he said, like he meant to begin a new train of conversation.

But he stopped there, leaving Zeke to feel sick about the venom he heard. "She's probably pretty worried about me."

He did not turn around. "You'll forgive me if I don't give a damn. Let her worry, after what she's done—hiding you away and abandoning me to this place, these walls, as if I'd made for her a prison and not a palace."

Zeke froze. He was already holding still, and he didn't know what else to do except hold even stiller. His heart was banging a warning drum between his ribs, and his throat was closing up with every passing second.

The doctor, as he said they called him now, gave the boy time to absorb the implication before he turned around. Then he did, his red coat following with a flourish, and he said, "You must understand, I had to make choices. I had to make compromises. In the face of these people, and in the face of their catastrophe and loss—which was no fault of mine—I was forced to hide and recuperate in my own way.

"After what occurred," he continued, playing his voice like a symphony of sorrow and story, "I could not simply emerge and make my case for innocence. I could not rise from the rubble and announce that I'd done no wrong, and created no harm. Who would have heard me? Who would believe such a protest? I am forced to confess, young man, that I would likely not believe it either."

"Are you trying to tell me . . . you're . . ."

The smooth timbre of Minnericht's monologue cracked. He said flatly, "You're a smart boy. Or if you're not, you ought to be. Then again, I don't know. Your *mother*"—and again he poisoned the word as he spoke it—"I suppose I can't vouch for her contribution to your nature."

"Hey," Zeke objected, suddenly forgetting all of Angeline's advice. "Don't you talk about her, not like *that*. She works hard, and she's got it hard, because of . . . because of *you*, I guess. She told me, just a couple days ago, how the city, the Outskirts, how people out there would never forgive her for *you*."

"Well, if they can't forgive her, then there's no reason I should either, is there?" Dr. Minnericht asked. But seeing the reflexive defiance in his ward, he added, "Many things happened back then—many things that I don't expect you to understand. But let's not talk about those things—not yet. Not now. Not when I've freshly discovered a son. This should be an excuse for a celebration, shouldn't it?"

Zeke was having trouble soothing himself. He'd had too much fear and too much confusion since coming under the wall. He didn't know if he was safe, but he suspected he wasn't—and now his captor was insulting his mother? It was too much, really.

It was so much that it almost didn't matter that this Dr. Minnericht professed to be his father. He wasn't sure why he found it so hard to believe. Then he remembered some of the princess's parting words.

*Whatever he tells you, whatever he says, he's no native of this place and no man he ever claimed to be. He'll never tell you the truth, because it's worth his trouble to lie.*

But what if Minnericht wasn't lying?

What if *Angeline* was the liar? After all, she could say Minnericht was a monster and the whole world feared him, but she'd been on awfully good terms with those air pirates.

"I brought you some things," Minnericht added, proffering a bag, either to break the silence of Zeke's inner battle or as a parting missive. "We'll take supper in an hour. Yaozu will come for you, and bring you to me. We'll talk all you like, then. I'll answer your questions, for I know you must have some. I'll tell you anything you want to know, because I am not your mother, and I do not keep secrets like she does—not from you, and not from anyone."

As he stepped toward the door he added, "You might want to keep close to this room. If you'll notice, the door reinforces from the inside. We're having a little problem upstairs. It would seem that some rotters are wandering a bit close to our perimeter defenses."

"Is that bad?"

"Of course it's bad, but it's not terrible. The chances of them getting inside is quite low. But still—caution is always prudent," he said.

And with that, he left the room.

Again, Zeke heard no lock. He could see for himself that yes, the exit could be barred from within; but again, he remembered that he no longer had an air mask. How far could he expect to go without it? Bitterly, he concluded aloud, "Not far at all."

Then he wondered if he was being watched, or if anyone was listening. He clamped his mouth shut to play it safe and approached the bundle wrapped in a fabric bag. The doctor had left it beside the basin, along with a freshly refilled bowl of water.

Not caring that it looked terrible, or that it might be a ridiculous display of bad manners, Zeke thrust his face down into the bowl and drank until the porcelain was dry. It amazed him how thirsty he'd become; and then he was amazed by his hunger. The rest of it amazed him too—the airships, the crash, the station, the doctor—but he did not know how much of it to trust. His stomach, though. That could be trusted; and it said he hadn't fed it in days.

But how many? How long had it been? He'd slept twice, once beneath the rubble of the tower and once there, under the station.

He thought of his mother, and of his tightly made plans that had been guaranteed to get him in, out, and home safely in time to keep his mother from going mad with worry. He hoped she was all right. He hoped she hadn't done anything crazy, or that she wasn't sick with fear; but he had a feeling he'd blown it.

Inside the bag Minnericht had given him he found a clean pair of pants and a shirt, and socks that didn't have a single hole. He peeled off the filthy things he was wearing and replaced them with the cleaner clothes, which felt soft and brand-new against his skin. Even the wool socks were smooth and not scratchy. His feet felt funny while wearing them in his old boots. The boots knew where his old socks were worn through, and they'd come to hug the calluses on his toes. Now they had nothing to rub.

In a frame atop the basin, Zeke found a mirror. He used it to examine the bloody sore spot on his head, and to check the bruised places he could feel but not quite see.

He still looked like a dirty kid, but he looked less like a dirty kid than he had in years. He liked it. It looked good on him, even with the thickly bandaged hand to spoil the overall effect.

Yaozu arrived and opened the door without a sound. Zeke nearly dropped the mirror when he caught the Chinese man's tiny, distorted reflection in its corner. The boy turned around and said, "You could knock, you know."

"The doctor wishes for you to join him at supper. He thought you might be hungry."

"Damn right I'm hungry," Zeke said, but he felt silly about it. Something about the fine surroundings and the nicer clothes made him think he ought to behave better, or speak better, or look better—but there was only so much improvement he could muster on short notice. So he added, "What are we eating?"

"Roasted chicken, I believe. There might also be potatoes or noodles."

The boy's mouth went soggy. He hadn't even *seen* a roasted chicken in longer than he could remember. "I'm right behind you!" he announced with honest enthusiasm that overwhelmed and sank any fear he might've let linger in the back of his mind. Angeline's warning and his own discomfort vanished as he followed Yaozu into the corridor.

Through another unlocked door—this one with dragons carved into its corners—the pair of them passed into a room that looked like a windowless parlor; and on the other side of that, there was a dining room that could've come from a castle.

A long, narrow table covered in a crisp white cloth ran the length of the room, and tall-backed chairs were pushed under it at regular intervals. Only two places were set—not at opposite ends where the diners would not even see one another, but close together at the table's head.

Dr. Minnericht was already seated there. Over his shoulder he whispered to an oddly dressed black man with a blind left eye, but Zeke could not hear what they said. The conversation came to an end when Minnericht dismissed his conspirator and turned to Zeke.

"You must be starving. You look half-starved, at any rate."

"Yeah," he said, flinging himself into the chair by the place settings without wondering if Yaozu ate elsewhere. He didn't care. He didn't even care if Minnericht was a false name, or that this man was pretending to be his father. All he cared about was the golden brown and juicily dripping flesh of the carved bird on the plate before him.

A cloth napkin was folded into the shape of a swan beside the plate. Zeke ignored it and reached for the bird's drumstick.

Minnericht reached for a fork, but he did not critique the boy's dining style. Instead he said, "Your mother should have fed you better. I realize that times are difficult in the Outskirts, but really. A growing boy needs to eat."

"She feeds me," he said around a mouthful of meat. And then something about Minnericht's phrasing stuck in his teeth like a tiny bone from a bird's wing. He was about to ask for clarification when Minnericht did something remarkable.

He removed his mask.

It took a moment, and it looked like a complicated procedure— one that involved a small host of buckles and latches. But when the last loop was unfastened and the heavy steel contraption was set aside, the doctor had a human face after all.

It was not a handsome face, and it was not a whole face. Skin bubbled up in a gruesome scar as big as a handprint from the man's ear to his upper lip, sealing his right nostril shut and tugging at the muscles around his mouth. One of his eyes had difficulty opening and closing because the ruined skin verged on its lid.

Zeke tried not to stare, but he couldn't help himself. He couldn't stop eating, either. His stomach had taken over and now controlled his face and hands, and he couldn't imagine setting the chicken aside.

"You may as well look," Minnericht said. "And you may as well be flattered. I only feel safe going barefaced in two rooms, this dining room and my own private quarters. I could count on one hand the number of people who know what I look like beneath the mask."

"Thanks," Zeke said, and he almost ended the word with a question mark because he didn't know whether to be flattered or concerned. Then he lied, "It's not that bad. I've seen worse in the Outskirts, people who've been burned by the Blight."

"This isn't Blight-burn. It's merely a burn from a fire, which is bad enough." He stiffly opened his mouth and began to eat, taking smaller bites than the hungry boy, who would've stuffed the bird's whole leg in his mouth if no one were watching him. The doctor's face was partially paralyzed—Zeke could see that, when he watched the way the lips moved and the one working nostril failed to flare when it breathed.

And when the doctor talked without the mask to filter his words, Zeke detected the small struggle required for him to speak clearly.

"Son," he said, and Zeke cringed but did not argue. "I'm afraid I have a bit of . . . potentially distressing news."

Zeke chewed what he could and swallowed the rest before it could get away from him. "Like what?"

"It has come to my attention that your mother is looking for you, here in the city. A swarm of rotters overran the place where she was seeking information, and now there is no sign of her. Rotters are a perennial problem down here, inside the walls. I believe I mentioned that we're having a bit of an issue with them right now, ourselves, so she could hardly be called careless for encountering them."

The boy stopped eating. "Wait. What? What? Is she all right? She came inside here, looking for *me*?"

"I'm afraid so. I suppose we must give her points for persistence, if not for exceptional mothering skills. Have you never seen a napkin?"

"I'm not—*where is she?*"

The doctor seemed to reconsider his approach to the situation, and quickly reframed his explanation. "No one's told me that she's dead, and there's no sign that she's been bitten and turned. She's simply . . . missing . . . in the wake of that particular event. Perhaps she'll turn up yet."

There wasn't much left on his plate, but Zeke couldn't see himself finishing it. "Are you going to go look for her?" he asked, but he couldn't decide what he wanted the answer to be, so he did not press the matter when Minnericht took a few extra seconds to respond.

"I have men watching for her, yes," he said.

Zeke didn't like the forced caution he heard, and he didn't like the tone Minnericht used. "What's that supposed to mean?" His voice climbed higher and louder as he said the rest. "Hey, I know she's not a perfect mother, but I ain't no perfect kid, either, and we've done all right by each other so far. If she's down here, and she's in trouble, I've got to help her out! I've got to . . . I've got to get out of here, and go find her!"

"Absolutely not." Minnericht said it with authority, but his body language had frozen, as if he were not certain how he ought to proceed. "You'll do no such thing."

"Says who? Says you?"

"It is not safe beyond this station. Surely you've noticed that by now, Ezekiel."

"But she's my mother, and this is all my fault, and—"

Minnericht broke his stillness and stood, pushing his chair back and letting his napkin tumble to the floor. "All your fault though this may be, I am your father, and you will stay here until I say it's safe for you to leave!"

"You're not!"

"Not going to keep you here? Son, you are *mistaken.*"

"No, you're *not my father.* I think you're a liar. Though I don't know why you'd want anybody to think you're Leviticus Blue anyway, since everybody hates him." Zeke leaped up out of his chair and almost planted his hand in his plate in his hurry to back away. "You talk about my mother like you knew her, but you didn't. You don't even know her name, I bet."

Minnericht reached for his mask and began to wrestle it back onto his head. He donned it like armor, like it would bolster him against these verbal attacks. "Don't be ridiculous. Her name was Briar Wilkes when I married her, and Briar Blue afterwards."

"Everybody knows *that.* Tell me her *middle* name," Zeke demanded triumphantly. "I bet you don't know it!"

"What does that have to do with anything? Your mother and I— it was a long time ago. Longer almost than you've been alive!"

"Oh, great excuse there, *Doctor,*" Zeke said, and all the tears he was holding back were distilled into sarcasm. "What color are her eyes?"

"Stop it. Stop this, or *I'll* stop it."

"You don't know her. You never knew her, and you don't know *me,* either."

The helmet finally snapped into place again, even though the doctor had barely eaten. "I don't know her? Dear boy, I know her better than you do. I know secrets she's never shared with you—"

"I don't care," Zeke swore. It squeezed out more desperate-sounding than he wished. "I just need to go and find her."

"I told you, I have men looking for her. This is my city!" he added with a jolt of fervor. "It's mine, and if she's inside it—"

Zeke cut him off. "Then she's yours too?"

Somewhat to his surprise, Minnericht didn't contradict him. Instead he said coldly, "Yes. Just like you."

"I'm not staying."

"You don't have a choice. Or, rather, you do, but it's not a very good one. You can stay here and live comfortably while others seek your wayward mother, or you can go up topside without a mask and suffocate, or turn, or die in some other horrible manner. That's all. You'll find no other options available to you right now, so you may as well return to your room and make yourself comfortable."

"No way. I'm finding a way out of here."

"Don't be stupid," he spit. "I'm offering you everything she's denied you for your whole life. I'm offering you a legacy. Be my son and you'll find that it's a powerful position, regardless of old prejudices or rumors, or misunderstandings between me and this city."

Zeke was thinking fast, but he wasn't thinking much. He needed a mask; he knew that much. Without a mask he was screwed and doomed—Minnericht was right about that. "I don't want . . . ," he started to say, but didn't know where to finish the thought. He tried it again, with less passion and more of the blankness he saw in the doctor's mask. "I don't want to stay in my room."

Minnericht sensed a winning compromise, so he calmed. "You can't go topside."

"Yeah," he conceded. "I get that. But I want to know where my mother is."

"No less than I do, I assure you. If I make you a promise, will you behave like a civilized young man?"

"I might."

"Very well, I'll take my chances. I promise that if we find your mother, we'll bring her here unharmed and you'll be free to see her—and then you'll both be free to go, if you like. Does that sound fair?"

But that was the problem, really. It sounded too fair. "What's the catch?"

"There is no catch, son. Or if there is, it will come from your mother. If she cares for you as much as she claims, she'll encourage you to stay. You're a bright boy, and I think that together we could learn much from one another. I can keep you in a much finer lifestyle than she can provide, and for that matter—"

"Oh, I get it. You're going to pay her to go away."

"Don't be crass."

"That's the point of it, ain't it?" Zeke asked, not even angry anymore. He was surprised, and disappointed, and confused. But he'd gotten a promise, and whether or not it was kept or broken, it was a place to begin. "And I don't care. You two can work it out between yourselves. I don't care. All I want is to know she's all right."

"Then we *can* work together, see? I'll find her and bring her here. We can iron out the details later. But for now, I think that this first attempt at a family dinner . . . Let us conclude it," he said, looking past Zeke at a man who was standing in the doorway.

It was the same black man with the milky eye. He bucked his chin up as if he wanted Dr. Minnericht's attention.

"I want a mask," Zeke said before the moment fully passed and he lost the doctor's attention.

"You can't have a mask."

"You're asking me to trust you. How am I supposed to do that if you won't trust me back, just a little?" Zeke pleaded.

"You *are* smart. I'm glad to see evidence of it. But the only reason you'll need a mask is to leave the grounds, and I am not yet prepared to take your word that you'll remain here of your own volition. So I'm afraid I'll have to refuse your eminently reasonable request."

"What's that mean?" Zeke asked, thrown by the big words and getting mad about them.

. "It means no. You can't have a mask. But it also means you don't need to stay in your room. Roam wherever you like. I know where your boundaries are, and believe me when I say this: Within the confines of my kingdom, there's nowhere that I can't find you. Do you understand?"

"I understand," he said with a sulk and a slouch.

"Yaozu will . . . Damn it all to hell, Lester, where's Yaozu?"

"I couldn't say, sir," Lester replied, which did not mean that he did not know—only that he declined to say anything in front of Zeke.

"Fine. That's just wonderful. He's off doing . . . I don't care. You. Come with me," he said to Lester. "You," he said to Zeke. "Make yourself at home. Explore the grounds. Do as you like, but I'd recommend that you stay close to the core, here on this floor. When I find your mother, I'll bring her to you. No matter what you think of me or what you believe, you can rest assured that even should you somehow make it to the topside and mount your own search, I'll find her first. Unless you want to be left out and lost when I locate her, you'll stay close to home."

"Not 'home,'" Zeke echoed with displeasure. "I said I understood, all right?"

"Good," Minnericht said. It was less a positive declaration than a dismissal, but it was the doctor who flounced out of the room, almost dragging Lester behind him.

When they both were gone, and Zeke had the dining area to himself, he paced back and forth and then returned to his plate—though he did not sit down. He needed to think, and thinking was easier to do on a full stomach and in motion, so he carried the chicken with him. He gnawed it until there wasn't a scrap of flesh left on the small bones; then he turned to the food that Minnericht had left behind on his plate.

After cleaning that plate too, and wondering briefly where the kitchen might be, Zeke let out a mighty belch and thought some more about gas masks.

Dr. Minnericht—whom Zeke refused to think of as his father—

must keep some down there someplace. Clearly the doctor's own was a custom model, made for him and no one else, but Zeke had seen several people down below. There was Yaozu, for starters, and the one-eyed black man. And with all those other rooms, locked or unlocked, there must be other people who manned the facilities. Upstairs Zeke could hear footsteps—heavy ones, like men in boots. Sometimes they walked as if on a guard's dull circuit, and sometimes they ran in groups.

Whoever these men were, they weren't stuck down below. They came and went. They must have masks someplace, and if Zeke could find a big storage closet or a room where such devices were stashed, then he wasn't above stealing one.

*If* he could find one.

But after wandering around for a while, he could immediately locate neither a secret stash of gas masks to pilfer nor any other people. The underside of the train station was a ghost town except for the intermittent background noise of distant feet, conversations barely beyond earshot, and pipes in the walls that hissed and strained to accommodate water or warming steam.

Surely someone, somewhere tended the guest rooms; and certainly someone must have cooked, and must be coming back to clean up later—or so Zeke assured himself as he wandered the levels that had been deemed acceptable by his host.

In time, he successfully followed his nose to the galley; and from the cupboards he scavenged wax-paper packets of jerky, a pair of gleaming red apples, and some dried cherries that tasted as sweet as candy when he gnawed them. He couldn't find the source of the fresh food that had been served at dinner, but Zeke was pleased with his loot. He hauled it back to his room for a later meal, or a midnight snack.

He hadn't found what he'd meant to find, but his need to swipe and hoard something had been appeased for now. He went back to his room, sat on the edge of the overstuffed bed, and fretted idly about what would come next, the roasted chicken warm and heavy in

his stomach. The weight of the meal pinned him onto the blankets
and lured him into deeper and deeper comfort. It coaxed him back
under the sheets, and though he'd only meant to close his eyes for a
few moments, he did not awaken again until morning.

 *Twenty-four*

Zeke awoke the next morning determined to carry out the leftovers of last night's plan. He stuffed his pockets with the food he'd gathered (minus a few mouthfuls for breakfast) and wandered back out to the corridor with its lift. The gate was down, but it was easy to move; and once inside the boy had no idea what to do with it. Four levers hung from a wire-frame ceiling overhead, and for all he knew one of them was an alarm.

There must be stairs.

Somewhere.

There must be other people, too, or so he was thinking when a peculiarly tall Chinese man and a peculiarly short white man conspired their rushed and distracted way around the corner. They stopped their chattering and quit their brisk pace in order to gaze curiously at Zeke.

"Hey," he said to the men.

"Hey," the white man said back. He was a round little fellow, Zeke's height but three or four times his girth, with a belt that circled his waist like an equator and a military cap squashed down over his overgrown hair. "You the Blue boy?"

"I'm Zeke," he said, neither confirming nor denying. "Who are you?"

They didn't answer him any better than he'd answered them. "Where you heading off to? There's rotters upstairs, boy. If you've got any brains in your skull, you'll stick down here, where it's safe."

"I wasn't going nowhere. I was just looking around. The doctor said I could."

"Did he now?"

"Yeah, he did."

The thin, tall Chinaman leaned down to see Zeke better, and asked in a rough, hoarse voice, "Where's Yaozu? Looking after boys, that's not our job."

"Is it Yaozu's job?"

The smaller man said, "Maybe he likes it, being the doctor's right hand. Maybe he don't. I couldn't say, except that he puts up with it."

Zeke nodded, absorbing the information and filing it away in case it was important. "All right. Well, let me ask you this, then. How do I get upstairs? I've seen pretty much all there is to see down here."

"Didn't you hear me? Can't you hear the commotion? Them's *rotters*, boy. I can hear them all the way from here."

The tall man with the thin brown eyes said, "It's dangerous, next floor up. Doornails and rotters are a bad, bad mix."

"Come *on*, fellas," Zeke wheedled, sensing that he was losing their attention to whatever task they'd been chasing when he'd stopped them. "Help a kid out. I just want to take a look around my new homestead."

The men shrugged back and forth at one another until the taller of the two walked away, leaving the small man. He shook his head. "No, I don't think so. And don't go upstairs, if you know what's good for you. There's trouble up there. Rotters been coming inside from all over the place, like someone's deliberately letting 'em in. And there's other problems, too."

"Like what?"

"Like your pa don't have many friends outside the station, and sometimes they make a stink. You don't want to get stuck in the middle of that. And I don't want to be the one who gets blamed for putting you there."

Zeke said, "If I get up there and get killed, I won't tell a soul it was you who sent me. Deal?"

The fat man laughed, and squeezed his thumbs into the band of his belt. "You've got me there, don't you? That's real fine, sure enough. I won't tell you how to work the lift, because that ain't my job and I don't like pulling all them strings; but if you were to follow that hallway behind me, and take it all the way to the left, you'd find a set of stairs down at the end of it. But if anybody asks, I didn't tell you anything. And if you stick around, then you remember who done you a favor."

"Thanks!" Zeke said brightly. "And I'll remember, don't worry. You're a champ, man."

"You said it," he replied.

By then, Zeke was already headed down the hall at a pace halfway between a jog and a sprint. He found the stairs a moment later, and he crashed up them with a newfound sense of direction. There might be trouble upstairs, but there might also be people with gas masks. It didn't matter what kind, and it didn't matter whom he had to steal it from—Zeke was going to get his hands on one if it killed him.

There was no light in the stairwell, and he couldn't find any obvious way to illuminate it, but he only needed to scale one flight and he could follow the noise that was rising steadily from above.

It sounded like heavy men running back and forth. Shouts added to the chaos, and as he climbed higher in the dark, stumbling over every other step, an explosion shook the floor.

Zeke flailed and grasped for a rail or a support, but found none. He fell down to his hands and knees.

The last vibrations thudded away and he scrambled to his feet. He dusted off his hands on his pants and felt along the wall until a white line on the floor revealed the bottom of a door with some light behind it. But if there was a handle, he couldn't find it. As he pressed himself against the door and frantically fought to open it, the commotion outside escalated further, making him wonder if this was *really* the way he wanted to go.

The unmistakable percussion of gunfire joined the shouting and the running.

Zeke stopped searching for a way out and held still, jarred by the shots and on the verge of changing his mind. It sounded like open warfare up there, in contrast to the calm, rich, quiet surroundings just one floor below. Was this what Lester had been whispering about in Minnericht's ear?

He hadn't yet seen a rotter up close. Not a real one, not a hungry one—and certainly not a pack of them.

An irrational burst of curiosity sent him seeking the handle again.

His fingers wrapped around something that could've been a lever, set a little higher than an ordinary doorknob. He squeezed it and yanked, and nothing happened. He tugged again, using his weight to pry the thing downward, but the door didn't budge.

But then it was hit from the other side.

Something big and hard smashed against it, throwing it inward and violently sandwiching Zeke between the panels and the wall. The force of it knocked the wind out of him. He crumpled to the floor holding his injured head, although it was too late to protect it. He gasped, and drew in ragged breaths of air that stunk of gunpowder and Blight residue. The air was sticky against the back of his throat and he gagged—a tiny sound that no one should've heard above the clamor on the door's other side.

Except that someone heard it.

Someone pulled the door aside and looked behind it, discovering the battered, folded form of Zeke trying to keep his head and face covered. This someone cast a very wide shadow; even as Zeke was peering between his fingers, he could see the block of darkness clogging the doorway.

"*You there. What are you doing? Get up,*" a man said through a device that turned his voice into a mechanical hum. It was as if all his words came filtered through a metal sieve.

"I . . . um . . . shut the door, would you?" Zeke was flustered and frightened, and more gunshots were springing from wall to wall, fired from nearby at a terrible volume. He moved his hands and squinted up, peering at the backlit hulk and seeing nothing but a shape that was not human, exactly. It was the shape of a man wearing armor, or a suit made of steel with a mask shaped like an ox's head.

The man in the mask didn't speak for a few seconds while the bullets whizzed and clanged, ricocheting off his shoulders. Then he said, *"This place ain't safe for a boy. What are you doing here?"* He asked it slowly, like the answer might be very important.

Zeke said, "I'm trying to get out of here! They took my mask, downstairs. I thought—"

His thoughts were cut off by something louder and longer than the mere firing of a revolver sounding through the semibrightness on the other side of the armored man.

"What's that?" Zeke almost screamed.

The man quavered against the blast behind him; he braced himself against the doorframe, his wide, bulky arms spreading and stretching to hold himself upright. He said, *"That's Dr. Minnericht's Sonic Gusting Gun. It . . . it throws sound at people, like a cannon."* For a moment he seemed as if he had more to say about it, but he changed his mind and said, *"Out of here's a good idea. But not this way. You'd better not . . ."* And then he added, *"Ezekiel. That's you, ain't it?"*

"Who are you? And what do you care?"

*"I know someone's who's looking for you,"* he said, but the answer wasn't too comforting. The first face that sprang to Zeke's mind was the giant who'd piloted the ship that'd crash-landed in the fort.

This man who blocked the way purely with his size could be kin to the pilot, or worse. He could be crew or mercenary, and of all the things Zeke wanted to do, going back to that man with the hands as big as buckets was at the bottom of the queue. He was furthermore concerned that this masked man seemed to know his name, which only made the situation worse: Now the air pirate knew whom he was looking for, and was sending soldiers after him.

"No," Zeke said, as a general answer to everything that was being asked of him. "No, forget it. Let me go."

The man shook his head, and the seams on his mask creaked as the metal squeaked against his reinforced shoulders. *"You can go, but you can't come up here. You'll get yourself killed."*

"I need to get myself a mask!"

*"Tell you what,"* said the man. He looked back over his shoulder and spied something promising. He said, *"You stay here, and I'll go get you one."*

The masked man looked as impassable as a moat, even with all the confidence Zeke could muster. But if the other man was willing to wander off for a few seconds, it'd give the boy time to bolt.

"All right," he whispered, and nodded his head.

*"You'll stay here, and you won't move?"*

"No, sir, I won't move," Zeke assured him.

*"Good. I'll be back in a minute."*

But as soon as the clanking armored man pivoted on his heel, Zeke zipped out behind him and dived into the fringe of the fray.

Too frightened to freeze and too exposed to stand still, he crouched and ran for the closest cover he could find: a stack of crates that were splintering, dissolving by slow degrees as bullets chipped away at their corners. A hot streak of something fast and hard went burning across his back, searing a hole in his shirt.

He struggled to wrangle his arms behind himself so he could touch the stinging line between his shoulder blades, but it was hard to reach and he gave up once he concluded that he was not dead, and not dying. All things being equal, his head still hurt far worse than any other part of him, even his torn-up hand.

Zeke crouched, cornered and horrified by the scene.

Around him, the room had divided into factions. Just like it had sounded below, it was war up there. But contrary to everyone's explanation, he saw no rotters—no shambling, wheezing undead like the ones he'd heard described. He saw only men, armed and scowling and shooting back and forth across a shining expanse of chipped-up marble that had once been a beautiful floor. On one side were a group of three Chinamen, joined by a pair of men who were dressed like the airmen aboard the *Clementine*. On the other, Zeke saw Lester and a handful of fellows who looked like they'd come from underneath the station.

From the ceiling, a cascade of glimmering lights dripped like formations inside a cave, lending plenty of light to show the horrible events unfolding in all the dusty, cobwebbed corners.

Along the windowless walls there were padded seats and plants made of silk that would never need watering, though they'd need mending from bullet holes. Behind those plants, and crammed under seats, and behind the rows of chairs that were locked together and bolted to the floor in tidy, waiting-room lines, pockets of scowling, grimacing men were doing their best to force their opponents to surrender, or to kill them all outright.

Zeke wasn't sure where he was. The room looked a bit like the lobby of a train station. And he didn't know who any of these people except Lester were, or why they were fighting. Some were wearing masks and some weren't, and at least three of them were dead, sprawled across the shiny-hard surface—two facedown, one faceup. The faceup man was missing most of his throat and his eyes were open, glazed, and staring at nothing but heaven beyond the ceiling.

But one of the facedown men was wearing a mask.

And to Zeke's total astonishment, the burly, armored fellow who'd confronted him in the corridor was in the process of stripping that mask away. The dead man's neck wobbled like an empty sock, and with a slip of a final strap, the mask came loose.

The armored man turned around, seeking the corridor entrance and the door behind it. Seeing that the door was open and Zeke wasn't there anymore, he swore loudly and spun in a circle. A bullet pinged against his shoulder blade with the light chime of a cymbal, but it didn't seem to harm him any.

He spied Zeke jammed behind the crates.

For a moment, Zeke thought that the man was going to pull that enormous gun down off his back and fire it, and then Zeke would dissolve into a thousand pieces and not even his mother would recognize him.

Instead, the man palmed the mask, wadded it into ball, and chucked it into the boy's lap before turning around and pulling an oversized six-shooter out of his waistband and firing it again and again and again. He made a line of bullets from one side of the room to the other, creating cover for his own getaway or for Zeke's—suddenly, Zeke wasn't sure.

At the far edge of the room there was another door, and something big was beating against it from the outside. Or maybe it wasn't something big. Maybe it was something *many*.

It wasn't one beating bash, like a battering ram or a machine. It was a constant, pounding, pushing, thrusting pressure being forced against the door—which seemed to be strongly reinforced. Even from his own limited perspective, Zeke could see that the door was barricaded as if it expected an army to fling itself against it.

Was this that army?

The door was holding for now, but the armored man was shouting, "*Go on, go back downstairs! Find another way out. Ezekiel!*" he added, in case his audience wasn't clearly enough defined. "*Get out of here!*"

Zeke wrung the mask into a knot and stood to a crouch.

Off to his left, behind a curtain, a man shrieked and flopped to the ground, dragging the curtain down with him. It covered him like a shroud. Around its bottom fringe a puddle of red crept and sprawled across the gray-and-white swirls of the polished floor.

## *Twenty-five*

Zeke's eyes flicked back and forth, scanning the room from corner to corner in search of some other exit. Wasn't that what the armored man had said? Find another way out? But except for the door that strained against some shoving force on its other side, and the corridor through which the boy had initially come, he didn't see any other outlets.

The man in the steel suit was out of bullets.

No, only one of his guns was out of bullets. He jammed the empty piece into his belt, against his belly, which was guarded by a metal plate. There was another gun wedged between his belt and his hip; he pulled it out and began a firing retreat.

Zeke counted eight more quarreling, shooting men holed up behind the chairs and around the occasional crates. He assumed that at some point they'd all run out of ammunition and everyone would have to stop. But for the moment, lead crashed in piercing straight lines, splattering like hail driven sideways by the wind.

Zeke wanted out. And the big man's back was closing in on the corridor—he was trying to flush Zeke back downstairs, and maybe that wasn't the worst idea in the world, after all.

It was a straight shot across the floor, and he had a big man in a suit of armor drawing all the bad attention away from him. On the other hand, the big man in the suit of armor was no doubt going to follow him downstairs. But here, upstairs, there was nothing but death and confusion.

Zeke decided to take his chances.

He took a leap that became a very short, very low flight from the crates to the middle of the floor—and he finished up his course with a sprinting scramble that sent him headfirst down the stairs on his hands and knees. Fifteen seconds behind him the armored man came backward, more gracefully than Zeke would've expected.

He grabbed the door and closed it with the full force of his weight at exactly the moment someone else came slapping against it from the other side.

Zeke tumbled down, tripping and catching himself and falling around the corner until he couldn't see what was happening above him—he could only hear it. He was back downstairs. It was much quieter there; even the blasts of the guns upstairs were muffled by the ceiling and the stone walls around him.

Back where he'd started from, he felt a sense of failure, until he remembered the mask he clutched like a lifeline.

Minnericht had said Zeke couldn't have one, and he'd been wrong about that, hadn't he? Granted, it had come off a corpse, but the boy tried hard not to think about the face that the visor had most recently covered. He tried to take the philosophical view that the other man couldn't use it anymore, so there was nothing wrong with taking it, and that made sense. But it felt no less disgusting when he smudged his thumb along the inside of the glass and felt the dampness of someone else's dying breath.

Now that he had a mask, he didn't know where to go or what to do with it. He wondered if he ought to hide it—maybe stash it in his room and wait for things to settle down—but that didn't sound right.

At the top of the stairs the armored man was holding his ground, but Zeke had no way of knowing how long that would last.

At the bottom of the stairs, in the corridor with the row of doors and the lift at the end, there was nobody around but Zeke.

Whether this was a good or bad thing, he had no idea. He couldn't escape the impression that something had gone off the rails, and that the quiet supper he'd so recently escaped had terminated in a terrible situation. The chaos above was swiftly working its way down, held at bay by only one stairwell door that was under a steady assault.

Paralyzed by indecision, Zeke listened as the shots slowed above. The distant sound of beating, banging, and shoving was dim at the edge of his hearing, and it didn't mean anything pressing. The grunts of the armored man holding the door were stern and determined.

Down at the far end of the hall, the lift began to move with a clustering rattle of chains. Zeke was still holding the contraband mask. He balled it up into a wad and jammed it under his shirt. And lest he be accused of acting sneaky, he called out, "Hello? Is anybody there? Dr. Minnericht? Yaozu?"

"I'm here," said Yaozu before Zeke could see him.

The Chinaman swept off the lift before it had even settled properly. He was dressed in a long black coat that he hadn't been wearing the last time Zeke saw him. Aggravation was carved into his face, and when he saw the boy these unhappy lines deepened.

He snapped out one long arm with a billowing sleeve and settled his grip on Zeke's shoulder. "Go to your room and shut the door. It barricades from within, by a tall bolt. It would take a catapult to knock it down. You'll be safe there, for a while."

"What's going on?"

"Trouble. Secure yourself and wait. It will pass." He ushered Zeke hastily down the hall, away from the stairwell door and the armored man holding his ground at the top.

"But I don't want to . . . to . . . secure myself." Zeke looked over his shoulder, wondering about the stairs.

"Life is difficult, isn't it?" Yaozu said dryly. He stopped at the door to Zeke's quarters, jerked the boy to face him, and said the rest quickly. "The doctor has many enemies, but they tend to be a fractured lot, and they pose little danger to this small empire under the walls. I do not know why, but these fractured forces have suddenly joined. I suspect it has something to do with you, or with your mother. Either way, they are *coming*, and they are raising quite a lot of racket."

"Racket? What's the racket got to do with anything?"

Yaozu held a finger to his lips and pointed up at the ceiling. Then he murmured, "Do you hear that? Not the guns, and not the shouts. The throbbing. The groaning. Those are not men. Those are *rotters*. The commotion draws their attention. It suggests to the walking dead that food is nearby." He said again, "If you wish to survive the night, close your door and leave it closed. I'm not trying to threaten you—only preserve you, as a matter of professional courtesy."

And then he was gone, heading down the hall and around its sharp bend with his dark coat swirling behind him.

Zeke immediately abandoned his own doorway and trotted back to the stairwell, hoping to learn something new or find it open and the way above it cleared of havoc. For all he knew, the fight may have migrated elsewhere, leaving him alone to explore for a way out.

He could hear more tussling up there, and then a howl that was more of a lion's roar than a man's exclamation.

It almost sent him running, but a new noise snagged his attention—and this new noise was less threatening. One part moan and one part gasp, the faint cry was coming from somewhere close, from behind a door that was not quite closed and not quite an open invitation to investigate.

He investigated anyway.

He pushed at the door and discovered a small kitchen that looked nothing like a kitchen. But what other room might have such bowls, lights, stoves, and pans?

Inside, the room was too warm from the cooking fires. Zeke squinted against the heat and listened, and he heard the distressed panting once more, from underneath a table that was half covered with a burlap cloth that had once been a sack. He drew the cloth aside and said, "Hey. Hey, what are you doing here? Hey, are you all right?" Because Alistair Mayhem Osterude was cowering there, curled in a fetal shape with pupils so ghastly and large that they seemed to see nothing, or everything in the whole world.

He was drooling, and around his mouth he sported a series of fresh sores that looked something like a line of bubbling burns. With every exhalation, he wheezed. It was the sound of a violin string being scratched slowly lengthwise.

"Rudy?"

Rudy slapped at Zeke's outstretched hand, then retracted his arm and clawed at his face. He mumbled a word that might have been, "Don't," or "No," or another short syllable that expressed resistance.

"Rudy, I thought you were dead. When the tower got busted, I thought you'd done died at the bottom someplace." He did not add that Rudy looked half-dead now. He couldn't think of a good way to work it in.

The closer he looked, the more certain he was that Rudy *had* been hurt badly—not badly enough to kill him, maybe, but badly all the same. The back of his neck was scraped and bruised, and his right arm was hanging funny. His shoulder had bled itself so extensively that his whole sleeve was damp and crimson. His cane was fractured; a long crack had opened up along one side. It didn't look like it worked anymore, not as something to lean on and not as something to shoot with. Rudy had dropped it off to the side, and was ignoring it.

"Rudy," Zeke asked, tapping his knuckle against a bottle tucked against the man's chest. "What's that? Rudy?"

His breathing had gone from shallow and noisy to almost imperceptible. The wide black pupils that stared at nothing and everything all at once began to shrink until they had turned to pinpoints. A dull twitching made Rudy's stomach jiggle, then worked its way up his torso until his throat was rattling and his head was shaking. Spittle splattered against the underside of the table, and against Zeke's shirtsleeves.

The boy backed away. "Rudy, what's happening to you?"

Rudy didn't answer. Someone else did, from the doorway. "He's dying. Just like he wants."

Zeke whipped around and stood so fast that he clipped his

shoulder on the edge of the table. It smarted. He held it. He griped, "Dammit, Miss Angeline, couldn't you knock or something? I swear to God, nobody ever knocks around here."

"Why should I?" she asked, entering the room and lowering herself into a crouch that made her knees pop loudly. "You weren't going to get all surprised and shoot me, and he's too far gone to even know I'm here."

Zeke joined her, copying her position—hanging onto the table's edge and ducking his head to see underneath it. "We should do something," he said weakly.

"Like what? Like help him? Boy, he's so far beyond help that even if I wanted to, there's nothing to be done for him. Hell. The kindest thing we could do is shoot him in the head."

"Angeline!"

"Don't look at me like that. If he were a dog, you wouldn't let him suffer. Thing is, he ain't a dog, and I don't mind him suffering. You know what's in that bottle? The one he's holding there, like it's his own baby?"

"What is it?" He reached for it and dislodged it from Rudy's slipping grasp.

The liquid inside the scratched glass bottle was runny and not quite clear. It had a yellowish-green tint to it, and it smelled a little bit like the sour odor of Blight, and a little bit like salt, and maybe kerosene.

"Jesus only knows. This is a chemist's lab, where they tinker with the nasty stuff and try to make it drinkable, or smokable, or sniffable. The Blight's a bad, bad thing, and it's hard to turn it into something people can stand. Rudy here, this old deserter, he's been stuck on it for years. I tried to tell you, back at the underground tunnel. I tried to get it through your head that he was only taking you back here because he thought Minnericht might reward him for it. This miserable poison was bound to kill him one day, and I think today will be that day." She frowned at the bottle, and frowned at the man on the floor.

"We should help him," Zeke said, protesting the man's death as a matter of formality.

"You want to shoot him after all?"

"No!"

"Me either. I don't think he deserves it. He deserves to feel the pain, and die from it. He's done some mighty nasty things in his time to get that stinking drink, or paste, or powder. Leave him alone. Cover him up if you think that's polite. He's not coming back from this one."

She stood up, tapped the top of the table, and said, "I bet he didn't even know what that stuff was. He probably just wandered in here, looking to get all sloppy from his drug of choice, and started sucking down the first thing he found."

"Is that what you think?"

"Yeah, that's what I think. Alistair never had a drop of brains to spare, and what little he started out with got burned away by the sap."

Zeke stood up too, and he pulled the burlap cloth over the spot where the vibrations from Rudy's head were tapping a gruesome hum against the floorboards. He couldn't stand looking. He asked Angeline, "What are you doing here?" partly because he wanted to know, and partly because he felt the need to talk about something else.

"I told you I was going to kill him, didn't I?"

"I didn't think you were serious!"

She asked, with what appeared to be honest confusion, "Why not? He's not the first man I'd like to kill down here, but I was willing to work him onto the list."

Before Angeline could speak again, Zeke noticed that the crashing upstairs was gradually fading to a sporadic, angry rumble. He no longer heard the thrashing against the door back down the hall, not even faintly. He said in a gasp, "The stairs. There was a man on the stairs."

"Jeremiah, yes. That's right. Big fellow, wide as a brick wall. Wearing a bunch of gear."

"That's him. Is he . . . all right?" Zeke asked.

The princess understood what he meant. "He's got his faults, like all men, but he's here to help."

"Help who? Help me? Help *you?*" Zeke recoiled and jerked his head out the doorway, looking left and right. "Where'd he go?"

Angeline joined him at the doorway, then stepped past him into the hall. "I think he's here to help your mother," she said. "She's down here in the station someplace. Jeremiah!" she called out.

"Don't yell!" Zeke tried to hush her. "And he's here for my mom? I thought nobody knew where she was!"

"Why'd you think that? Is that what Minnericht told you? Don't you remember what I told you, you dumb boy? I told you he's a lying snake. Your mother's been down here a day or two, and Jeremiah's here now because he's afraid the doctor's done her some kind of mischief. Jeremiah!" she hollered again.

Zeke took Angeline's arm and shook her. "She's here? All this time she's been down here?"

"She's here somewhere. She was supposed to be back at the Vaults by morning, but she didn't come back, so now the Doornails have all come spilling into the station, looking for her. I don't think they mean to leave without her, either." And once more she shouted, "*Jeremiah!*"

Zeke told her, "Don't! Stop shouting like that! You've got to quit shouting!"

"How else am I going to find him? It's all right. There ain't nobody else down here anyhow, at least not that I could find."

"Yaozu was here, a few minutes ago," Zeke argued. "I saw him."

Angeline stared at him hard. "Don't you lie to me now, boy. I saw that evil Chinaman upstairs. He ran down here, did he? If he ran down here, then I need to know which way he went."

"That way." Zeke indicated the bend in the corridor hall. "And off to the right."

"How long ago?"

"A few minutes," he repeated, and before she could dash away, he clutched her arm and asked, "Where would he have put my mother?"

"I don't know, child, and I don't have time to figure it out. I've got to follow that murdering old bastard."

"Make the time!" Zeke did not quite shout, but the words carried some force to them, in a tone that he'd never heard himself use. Then, more quietly and with more control, he let go of her arm and said, "You told me everything Minnericht ever said was a lie. Well, he told me my mother came into the city, chasing after me. Is that true?"

She drew her arm back down to her side and gave him a look he couldn't read. She said, "That's true. She came here looking for you. Minnericht lured her here, with Lucy O'Gunning. Lucy got clear of the station yesterday and went back to the Vaults to round up help."

"Help. Lucy. Vaults," he repeated the words that sounded important, though they didn't mean much to him. "Who's—"

Angeline's patience was running out. She said, "Lucy's a one-armed woman. If you see her, tell her who you are and she'll do her best to get you out of here."

She took a step away from him and started to run, as if she was finished talking.

Zeke grabbed her arm again and pulled her back, hard.

Angeline didn't like it. She let him yank her into his personal space, but she brought a blade with her and she held it up against his stomach. It wasn't a threat, not yet. It was only an observation, and a warning. She said, "Get your hand off me."

He let her go, just like she told him to, and then he asked, "Where would he have put my mother?"

She gave the bend in the corridor a nervous glance and Zeke an aggravated one. "I don't know where your mother is. But I'm guessing he's just stashed her someplace. Maybe one of these rooms, maybe downstairs. I've been sneaking around in here before, once or twice, but I don't know this place like the back of my hand or nothing. If you find Jeremiah again, stay with him. He's a monster of a man, but he'll keep you in one piece if you let him."

Zeke figured that was all he was going to get, so he started to run;

behind him, he heard the swift patter of Angeline's feet dashing away in the other direction.

He ran to the first door across the hall and whipped it open.

There was only a bed and a basin, and a chest of drawers—much like the quarters he'd been given, though not quite as clean or posh. Something about the smell of dust and linen made him think no one had used it in a very long time. He exited the room, calling for Angeline before he remembered that she had taken off without him. Even her footsteps had left him, and he was alone in the corridor with all the doors.

But now he knew what to do.

He reached for the next door and it was locked.

Back in the chemist's room, Rudy wasn't breathing anymore—or maybe he was, but it was so light and frail that Zeke couldn't hear it when he tiptoed over to the table. Without looking under the burlap covering, the boy kicked his feet around and found the cracked cane.

It was heavy in his hands. Even with the long, gaping crack in the side it felt solid.

He ran back out to the locked door, and he beat the knob with the sharp, heavy cane until the hardware broke and the door smashed inward.

Zeke shoved his way past the broken door and charged wildly into a room that was packed with junk. None of it looked important; all of it looked old; some of it looked dangerous. One box was missing a lid. Inside were pieces of guns, cylinders, and spools of wire. The next-nearest open crate was crammed with sawdust and glass tubes.

He couldn't see any farther back than that. There wasn't enough light.

"Mother?" he tried, but he already knew she wasn't there. No one was there, and no one had been there in a while. "Mother?" he asked once more just in case. No one answered.

The next door was open, and behind it Zeke found another laboratory, crammed with tables shoved closely together and lights on hinges that could be adjusted for better illumination. He called out,

"Mother?" as a matter of general principle, received no answer, and moved on.

He whipped himself around and stopped with his nose half an inch from the metal-covered chest of the man whom Angeline had called Jeremiah. How Jeremiah had been able to move so quietly in so much armor Zeke had no idea, but there he was, and there was Zeke, breathless and driven by his first real direction in days. He blurted, "Get out of my way—I have to find my mother!"

"*I'm trying to help, you stupid kid. I knew it was you,*" he added as he took a step back, letting Zeke escape the laboratory and step back into the hall. "*I knew it had to be you.*"

"Congratulations. You were right," Zeke said.

There was only one unopened door left. He started toward it, but Jeremiah stopped him. "*It's a storage closet. He wouldn't be keeping her there. My guess is, he took her down one more level, where his living quarters are,*" he said.

"These aren't the living quarters?"

"*No. These are the guest quarters.*"

"You've been here before?"

"*Yeah, I've been here before. Where do you think I got this gear? Get on the lift.*"

"You know how to work it?"

Jeremiah didn't respond except to stomp up to the platform and jerk the gate aside. He held it open for Zeke, who had to run to keep up; the lift was dropping before the boy could land both feet inside it.

While the lift shook and descended, Zeke asked, "What's going on? No one will tell me what's going on."

"*What's going on*"—Jeremiah reached up to tug on a lever that must've been a brake—"*is that we've had it up to here with that goddamned deranged doctor.*"

"But why? Why now?"

Jeremiah shook his head crankily. "*Now's as good a time as any, ain't it? We've let him treat us like dogs for years, and we've taken it, and taken it, and taken it. But now he's taken Maynard's girl, and* there's not a Doornail or scrapper down here who'll stand for that kind of horseshit."

Zeke felt a surge of real relief, and real gratitude, on top of it. "You really *are* here to help my mom?"

"*She was only down here trying to find you. He could've left her out of it, and left you both alone. Obviously,*" he said, leaning his weight on the lever and drawing the lift to a stop, "*he didn't. Neither of you ought to be here, but you are. And that's not right.*"

He shoved the gate aside with such force that it broke and dangled.

Zeke kicked his way past it and into yet another hallway lined with carpets, lights, and doors. He could smell a fire burning somewhere. There was a warm and homey scent around its edges, like the burning of hickory logs in a fireplace.

"Where are we? What is this? Mother? Mother, are you down here? Can you hear me?"

Upstairs, something awful happened in one crashing, crushing blast that made Zeke think of the tower when it'd been smashed by the *Clementine*. He felt that same shuddering immediacy, and being down underneath the world only made the fear worse. The ceiling cracked above him, and the dust of crawlspaces and riggings rained down.

"What was that?" Zeke demanded.

"*How the hell would I know?*"

A growling roar hummed upstairs in the wake of the explosion, and even Zeke—who had been thinking it'd be a shame if he left the city without ever seeing a rotter—could guess what the sound was.

"Rotters." Jeremiah said. "*A lot of them. I thought the downstairs was better reinforced than this. I thought that was the point of all these levels. I guess Minnericht doesn't know everything after all, eh? I'd better get upstairs and hold them.*"

"You're going to hold them off? By yourself?"

"*Some of Minnericht's boys might join in; they don't want to wind up rotter shit any more than I do, and most of 'em are only here because they're paid to be. By the way, if you hear a big boom in a few minutes, don't get too worked up about it.*"

"What does that mean?" Zeke demanded.

Jeremiah was already back on the lift, thumbing through the levers in search of the right one. He said, "*Stay here and look for your mother. She might need help.*"

Zeke ran to the edge of the lift and asked, "And then what do I do? Where do we go, when I find her?"

"*Up,*" the armored man said. "*And out—however you can. Things are going to get worse down here before they get better. The rotters moved faster than our boys thought they would. Go back to the Vaults, maybe—or go to the tower and wait for the next ship.*"

And then the lift jerked, and lurched, and carried Jeremiah up into the ceiling until even the tips of his toes were gone. Zeke was alone again.

But there were more doors to open, and his mother was missing, so at least he had something to take his mind off the commotion upstairs. The door at the end of the room was open, and since that door represented the path of least resistance—or fastest access—the boy barreled towards it and shoved it inward.

Here was the source of the smoke smell: a brick fireplace with smoldering logs turning the room a golden orange. A blocky black desk squatted in the middle of the floor, atop an Oriental rug with dragons embroidered into the corners. Behind the desk was a fat leather chair with an overstuffed seat, and in front of the desk were two other chairs. Zeke had never been in anybody's office before and he didn't know what the point of it might be; but it was a beautiful room, and warm. If it had a bed, it would be a perfect place to live.

Because no one was looking, he walked around the far side of the desk and opened its top drawer. Inside he found papers written in a language he didn't understand. The second drawer—a deeper one, with a lock that wasn't fastened—held something more interesting.

At first he thought it was his imagination that the satchel looked familiar. He wanted to believe he'd seen it before, on his mother's shoulder, but he couldn't be certain at a glance, so he opened it and jammed his hands inside. His swift rummaging revealed ammunition, goggles, and a mask, none of which he'd ever seen before. And then he found the badge with its ragged MW initials and his mother's tobacco pouch, untouched for days, and he knew that nothing in the bag belonged to the doctor.

He reached down and scooped it up. When he bent to shove the drawer shut, he saw a rifle stashed under the desk, where it couldn't be seen except from behind the tall-backed chair where Zeke probably wasn't supposed to sit.

He snatched the rifle, too.

The room was empty and quiet, except for the flickering chatter of the fireplace. Zeke left it that way and charged back into the hall with his treasures.

There was a door across the way, but Zeke couldn't open it. He beat against it with Rudy's warped cane, but when the knob broke it simply fell off, and whatever braced the other side held firm. He flung his weight against it enough times to bruise his shoulder. Nothing budged. But there were other doors to be opened, and he could come back to that one if it came down to it.

The next one across the hall opened into an empty bedroom. And the one next door to it failed to open at all, until Zeke bashed the knob into fragments with the butt end of the cane. The lock tried to hold, but the boy could kick like a mule—and within half a minute the frame splintered, and the door opened violently.

## Twenty-six

Briar dreamed of earthquakes and machines so huge that they mowed down cities. Somewhere, at the edge of the things she could hear, she detected the sound of gunfire and something else—or maybe nothing else, because whatever it was, it didn't come again. Somewhere else it was soft and the lights were turned down low, and the bed was deep enough to cradle a family of four.

It smelled like dust and kerosene, and old flowers dried and left in a vase beside a basin.

Levi was there. He asked her, "You never did tell him, did you?"

From the bed, where her eyes were so heavy she could hardly hold them open, Briar said, "I never told him anything. But I will, as soon as I can."

"Really?" He did not look convinced; he looked amused.

He was wearing the thick linen apron he often wore in the laboratory workshop, and it was covered by a light coat that went down to his knees. His boots were unlaced, as usual, as if it never occurred to him to fix them. Around his forehead a set of conjoined monocles was strapped, wearing a groove into the skin that never fully went away.

She was too tired to object when he came to sit on the edge of the bed. He looked exactly how she last remembered him, and he was smiling, as if everything was all right and nothing had ever been wrong. She told him, "Really. I'm going to tell him, no matter what it costs me. I'm tired of keeping all these secrets. I can't keep them all anymore. And I won't."

"You won't?" He reached for her hand, but she didn't let him take it.

She rolled over onto her side, facing away from him and clutching at her stomach. "What do you want?" she asked him. "What are you even doing here?"

He said, "Dreaming, I think. Same as you. Look, my love. We meet here—if nowhere else."

"Then this *is* a dream," she said, and a sick feeling spread through her stomach like acid. "For a minute I thought it wasn't."

"It might be the only thing you ever did right," he said, moving neither toward nor away from her. His weight on the edge of the bed bowed the mattress and made her feel as if she were rolling or falling into his space.

"What? Not telling him?"

"If you had, you might've lost him before now."

"I haven't lost him," she said. "I just can't find him."

Levi shook his head. She could feel the motion of it, though she couldn't see him. "He's found what he wanted, and you'll never get him home again. He wanted facts. He wanted a father."

"You're dead," she told him, as if he did not know.

"You won't convince *him* of it."

She crushed her eyes closed and buried her head in the pillow, which almost wanted to smother her with its musty, warm odor. "I won't have to convince him, if I show him."

"You're a fool. The same fool you always were."

She said, "Better a live fool than a dead—"

"Mother," he said.

She opened her eyes. "What?"

"Mother."

She heard it again. She turned her neck to pull her face away from the pillow, and lifted her head. "What are you talking about?"

"Mother, it's me."

It felt like shooting through a tunnel, the speed and ragged jolt with which she awoke. She was being dragged from warm darkness and into something colder, fiercer, and infinitely less comfortable. But there was a voice at the end of it, and she crawled toward it, or slid toward it, or fell up as she tried to reach it.

"Mother? Oh shit, Mother. Mother? Come on, wake up. You've got to wake up, 'cause I sure can't carry you, and I want to get out of here."

She rolled over onto her back and tried to open her eyes, then realized that they were already open but she couldn't quite see. All the world was blurry, though light did flicker off to her right, and above her there loomed a distinctly dark shadow.

The shadow was saying, over and over again, "Mother?"

And the earthquake in her dreams was rumbling still, or maybe he was only shaking her. The shadow's hands gripped her shoulders and hurled them back and forth until her head snapped on her neck, and she declared, "Ow."

"Mother?"

"Ow," she said again. "Stop it. Stop what you're doing, that . . . Stop it."

The brighter her vision became, the more aggressively it was accompanied by a burning sting, and a dampness that drooled over her cheekbone. She touched the sore spot with her hand, and when she drew it back, it was wet.

"Am I bleeding?" she asked the shadow. Then she said, "Zeke, am I bleeding?"

"Not real bad," he said. "Not even as bad as I was. Mostly you're just bruised up. You got blood all over the pillowcase, but it ain't ours, so I don't care. Come on. Stand up. Get up. Come on."

He wedged his arm underneath her back and hauled her bodily off the bed, which was every bit as soft as her dream suggested. The room was the same too, so she must've been awake enough—in fragments— to gather her surroundings. But she was alone except for the boy, who dragged her to her feet and forced her to stand.

Her knees buckled, then locked. She stood, leaning on Zeke. "Hey," she said. "Hey, Zeke. Hey, it's you. It *is* you, isn't it? Because I was having the weirdest dream."

"It's me, you crazy old bird," he said with affection and a grunt. "What are you doing in here, anyway? What were you thinking, coming inside this place?"

"Me? Wait." As much as it made the sore spot on her head swim, she shook her head and tried to make it clear enough to object. "Wait, you're stealing all the things I was going to say." Slowly, then suddenly, the understanding landed. She said, "You. It's you, you dumb boy. You're what I'm doing here."

"I love you too, Momma," he said around a smile so big he could hardly shape the words.

"I found you, though, didn't I?"

"I might argue that I found *you*, but we can fight about it later."

"But I came *looking* for you."

"I know. We can fight about it later. First, we need to head on out of here. The princess is waiting for us. Somewhere. I think. We ought to go find her, and that Jeremiah guy."

"The what? Or the who?" The warbling throb around her ear kicked hard, and she wondered if maybe she hadn't been wrong about her state, and maybe she was dreaming again after all.

"The princess. Miss Angeline. She's real helpful. You'll like her. She's real smart." He released his grip on Briar and left her to stand by herself.

She wavered, but held steady. She said, "My gun. Where's my gun? I need it. I had a bag, too. I had . . . some things. Where are they? Did he take them?"

"Yeah, he took 'em. But I took 'em *back*." He held out the rifle and the satchel and all but shoved them into her hands. "You'll have to work that thing, because I can't shoot it."

"I never taught you how."

"You can teach me later. Let's go," he ordered, and Briar wanted to laugh but she didn't.

She liked the look of him, even frantic and controlling—even leading her like a child while she came all the way to her senses. Someone had given him nice clothes and maybe a bath. "You clean up nice," she said.

He said, "I know. How you feeling? Are you all right?"

"I'll survive," she told him.

"Good. You'd better. You're pretty much all I got, ain't you?"

"Where are we?" she asked, since he seemed to have a better handle on the situation than she did. "Are we . . . under the station? Where did that bastard put me while I was out?"

"We're under the station," Zeke said. "You're two levels down from the big room with all the lights on the ceiling."

"There's another level underneath?"

"At least one, maybe more. This place is a maze, Momma. You wouldn't believe it." He stopped her at the door and opened it fast, then looked left and right outside down the hall. He held out his hand and said, "Wait. Do you hear that?"

"What?" she asked. She came to his side and let him listen and squint while she checked the rifle. It was still loaded, and inside the satchel all her belongings seemed to be in place. "I don't hear anything."

He listened longer and then said, "Maybe you're right. I thought I heard something, but I've been wrong before. There's a lift at the end of the hall, over there. You see it?"

She leaned her head around the door and said, "Yes. That's it, right?"

"Right. We're going to run for it. We've got to; otherwise Yaozu is going to catch us, and we don't want that."

"We don't?" Briar didn't mean to make it sound like a question, but she was still pulling herself together, and for the moment, it was the easiest way to participate in the conversation. Besides, she was so happy to see him that all she wanted to do was touch him and talk to him.

Off in the distance, she heard gunfire. It was a large crack and loud, the sound of a rifle, not a revolver. More shots answered it, bullets from a smaller gun with a faster firing rate.

"What's happening?" she asked.

"Long story," he said.

"Where are we going?"

He took her hand and pulled her into the hallway. "To the Smith Tower—the big one where they dock the dirigibles."

A memory flickered as her footsteps followed his in a furious patter. "But it's not Tuesday yet, is it? It can't be. We can't get out that way—I don't think it's a good idea. We should head back down to the Vaults."

"But we *can* get out that way, at the tower," he swore. "Jeremiah said there's ships there."

She tore her arm away from his as they reached the lift. The iron grate covered the same lift as the one she'd taken from the top side; she pulled it over and pushed Zeke onto the platform. As she joined him and closed the gate, she said, "No. I've got to go see Lucy. I need to find out if she's all right. And—"

More shots exploded, somewhere closer.

"And something bad is happening up there." She pulled the Spencer around and held it in position as the lift rose to the next level. "We should get off here. Let's avoid as much of it as we can."

"It's probably just rotters," Zeke said, and tried to keep her on the lift as she stubbornly hauled the gate aside. "But we can't leave yet. The princess might be up there!"

"Well, she *isn't*."

Briar swung the Spencer around and pointed it at a smallish woman with skinny limbs and long gray hair that was braided into a rope. She looked native, though Briar couldn't have guessed which tribe; and she was wearing a man's blue suit with a tailored coat and pants that were too big for her.

The woman was holding her side. Blood squished out from between her fingers.

"Miss Angeline!" Zeke ran to her.

Briar lowered the Spencer, then changed her mind and held it out, ready for any trouble that might come from some other direction. After all, they were in the midst of a large room with several doors, all of them closed. There was nothing to mark this room as different from any other, or as having any particular purpose. It was mostly empty, except for a stack of tables against one wall and a clump of broken chairs that were piled on top of one another and left to collect dust.

"Ma'am," she asked over her shoulder. "Ma'am, do you need some help?"

The reply came without a drop of patience in it. "No. And don't touch me, boy."

"You've been stabbed!"

"I've been scratched, and it's ruined my new suit. Hey," she said to Briar, tapping her on the shoulder with a bony finger. "If you see a bald-headed Chinaman in a black coat, you shoot him between the eyes for me. That would make me happy," she fussed.

"I'll keep a lookout for him," Briar promised. "Are you the princess?"

"I'm *a* princess. And I'm mad as hell right now, but we've got to get out. If we stay here, they'll catch us."

"We're on our way back to the Vaults," Briar said.

"Or the tower!" Zeke insisted.

Angeline said, "Either one of those would work, but you might want to head to the fort instead. When the *Naamah Darling*'s fixed, you can get old Cly to take you out, if you're looking to leave."

Briar frowned. "Cly's here? At the fort?"

"He's making repairs."

More commotion upstairs told Briar that she'd have to ask about it later.

Zeke asked, "Wait. We're going back to that ship? With that big old captain? No; no way. I don't like him."

"Cly?" Briar asked. "He's good. He'll get us out of here, don't worry."

Zeke said, "How do *you* know?"

"He owes us a favor. Or he thinks he does, anyhow."

Around the bend something fell and broke, and on the other side of the walls, the trundling waves of heavy, rotting feet were beating a gruesome time. "This is bad," Briar observed.

"Worse than that, probably," said Angeline, though she didn't sound too upset. She pulled a big-barreled shotgun out of a quiver she wore on her back, and checked it to make sure it was loaded. The injury in her side oozed, but did not gush when she let go of it.

"You know your way around here?" Briar asked her.

"Better than you folks do," she said. "But not by much. I can find my way in and out, and that's about it."

"Can you take us out to the Vaults?"

"Yes, but I still think you should head for the fort," she groused, and pushed Zeke so he wouldn't help her walk. "Get off me, boy. I'm walking all right. It stings a little, but it won't be the end of me."

"Good," Briar said. "Because we've got problems."

From inside the lift, a mournful groan came echoing. Pounding hands beat at the roof above, or from some other spot around the lift's basket. Then there was a splintering, breaking smash . . . and they came tumbling inside. One or two blazed the trail, and then they poured in greater numbers through whatever passage they'd forced.

The first three rotters off the lift and into the corridor were once a soldier, a barber, and a Chinaman. Briar pumped the rifle and aimed it fast, catching the first two in the eyes and blowing off the third one's ear.

"Mother!" Zeke shouted.

"Behind me, both of you!" she commanded, but Angeline wasn't having any of it and she used her own shotgun to take down the third.

Scrambling hungrily over those three bodies came another round of rotters, half a dozen bodies wide and at least that deep.

"Back!" Angeline cried. "Back, this way!" she said, even as she continued shooting.

The noise in the corridor was deafening, and both Zeke and Briar had heads that were already throbbing. But it was either shoot and aim high or sit down and die; so the women kept firing as Zeke blazed a backward path around the bend, acting as scout and lookout while he tried to follow Angeline's directions.

"To your right! I mean, to your other right," she corrected herself. "There ought to be a door there, at the end of the way. Beside the office!"

"It's locked!" Zeke shouted. The second word was drowned out by the calamity of his mother's Spencer, but Angeline got the general idea.

She said, "Cover me, just a second."

Before Briar had time to do anything but comply, Angeline turned around and shoved Zeke out of her way. She unloaded her shotgun's second barrel into the lock and the door flapped inward, shattering on its hinges.

"It's a back exit," the princess explained. "He tells people it's a dead end, but it's his own personal escape hatch, the bastard."

Zeke kicked the door's fallen shards aside and wished they had something to close behind them, but it wasn't going to work out that way and he didn't have time to complain. He tried to let the women clamber up first, but he was unarmed and no one would let him.

His mother took him by the crook of his neck where it met his shoulder and half threw him into the corridor, then almost tripped over him backward with her next shot. Angeline told him, "Get a move on!" and reloaded as she retreated. The hallway was dark and crowded, but Zeke could see stairs going up one direction and down another.

"Which way?" Zeke asked, perching at the edge of the platform where the steps swapped angles.

"Up, for Christ's sake," Angeline swore loudly and cocked her shotgun again. "We're cutting past the main trouble, and if we go down they'll trap us there. We've got to try up and out, if we want to survive."

Briar breathed, "We can't keep this up," and fired her last shot from within the doorway.

She knocked down the foremost rotter with a bullet; its forehead

blistered and popped as it fell. That cleared perhaps ten yards between the surge of decomposing flesh and the narrow bottleneck of
the emergency escape hall.

"Up, all right. Up," Zeke wheezed as he started to climb.

"There's another door on the first floor up. It's dark. Feel around.
You'll find it. It should be unlocked; it usually is. I *hope* it is." Angeline gave instructions from some black-blanketed corner where Zeke
couldn't see her. As soon as they'd rounded the bottom bend and begun their ascent, the stairwell had become perfectly dark. Arms, elbows, and the burning-hot barrels of guns knocked against shoulders
and ribs as the three tried to beat a retreat back up into the mere ordinary chaos of the living.

"I found the door!" Zeke announced. He yanked on it, and almost
flopped past it when it opened. Briar and the princess squeezed out
behind him, then slammed the door. A brace as big around as Briar's
head was leaning helpfully against the wall, and together they shoved it
up under the latch to hold it.

When the horde of starving rotters crashed against it, the door
jolted, but held. The brace strained and scooted slightly against the
floor, but Angeline kicked it into place and stared at it, daring it to
move.

"How long will that hold?" Zeke asked. No one answered him.

Briar said, "Where are we, Princess? I don't recognize this place."

"Put your mask on," Angeline said in response. "You're going to
need it soon. Boy, that goes for you too. Put it on. We're going to make
a run for the topside, but it won't help us any if you can't breathe."

Briar's satchel wasn't settled on her shoulder the way she liked it;
she'd grabbed it in such a hurry that there hadn't been time to adjust
it. She did so then, lodging it into the familiar groove across her torso.
She retrieved her mask and wormed her head up into the straps,
watching while Zeke did the same. She said, "Where'd you get that?
That's not the mask you left home with."

He said, "Jeremiah gave it to me."

"Swakhammer?" Briar said. "What's he doing here?" she asked no one in particular, but Angeline answered.

"You took too long getting back to the Vaults. Lucy went down there and grabbed your friends, and then all hell broke loose." She took a deep breath that sounded like it hurt, like her lungs were snagged on something sharp. When Briar looked down at the woman's side, she could see that the bleeding there was fresh.

"They came after me? To rescue me?"

"Sure, to rescue you. Or to start the war they've wanted for years. I'm not saying they don't mean to help you, because they surely do— but I will say that they've needed an excuse to rise up like this, and you're the best one they ever got."

Above, a rickety string of rope was knotted around hanging lights powered by no source that Briar could see. But twisted together with the rope she could see metallic veins, wires woven together and transmitting whatever energy it took to illuminate them. They weren't bright, but they showed the way well enough to keep them from stubbing toes or shooting one another from surprise. Large tarps covered things shaped like monstrous machines that had been pushed into corners, and stacks of crates were piled along the edges of the room, which was low-ceilinged, damp, and chilly.

"What is this place?" she asked.

Angeline said, "Storage. Extra things. Things he stole, and things he'll use later, someday, if he gets the chance. If we had the time or wherewithal, I'd say we ought to set fire to this place behind us. There's nothing here but things designed to maim and kill."

"Like those chemist's labs, downstairs," Briar murmured.

"No, not like those. These are things he can sell to a different market, if he can work out how they operate. They're leftovers from the big contest the Russians held, looking for a mining machine that could dig through ice and lift out gold. He'll be a rich, rich man if the war goes on any longer."

Zeke said, "He's already a rich man, ain't he?"

"Not as rich as he'd like to be. They never are, are they, Miss Wilkes? Now he's turning these things into war machines, since they weren't much use as drilling machines. He wants to sell them back east, to the highest bidder."

Briar was only half listening. She'd picked up the corner of the nearest tarp and she was gazing up underneath it, like she was lifting a lady's skirt. After squinting into the murky brown darkness there, she said, "I've seen this before. I know what this is—what it was supposed to be . . . But these aren't all left over from the contest."

"What?" Zeke asked. "What do you mean?"

"He's been stealing Levi's inventions and retooling them for his own purposes." She said, "These are your father's things. This machine, under here . . ." She yanked the sheet away to reveal a long, ghastly, crane-shaped device with wheels and plating. "This was a device to help build big boats, or that's how he tried to sell it. It was supposed to do . . . I don't remember. Something about moving large parts to and fro on a dock, so men didn't have to carry them. I didn't believe it then, and I don't believe it now."

"Why not?" Zeke wanted to know.

· She told him, "Because how many boat-builders do you know that need artillery shells and gunpowder reservoirs? I'm not stupid. I guess I just didn't want to know."

"So Minnericht's not—," Zeke started to say.

Briar said, "Of course he isn't. He scared me for a minute there, I don't mind telling you. He's about the right size, and about the right . . . I don't know. The right *type* of man. But it's not him."

"I knew he wasn't. I knew it all along."

"You did, did you?"

Zeke turned to Angeline and said proudly, "You told me not to believe anything he'd tell me, and I didn't. I knew he was lying all along."

"Good," his mother said. "So what about you, Princess? What makes you so sure that the good doctor isn't my dead husband? I got my own reasons for knowing. What are yours?"

She poked at her injury and winced, and covered it up with her hand. She stuck her shotgun back in the quiver and said, "Because he's a son of a bitch. Always has been. And I'm . . ." Angeline started walking away from the battered door and down the corridor along the string of lights that lit the way overhead. "Well, I'm that bitch."

Zeke's jaw dropped. "He's your *son*?"

"I didn't mean it quite like *that*. A long time ago, he was married to my daughter Sarah. He drove her mad, and he killed her." She didn't swallow, and her eyes weren't warming with tears. This was something she'd known and held against her chest for years, and merely saying it didn't make the truth of it any worse. So she continued. "My girl hung herself in the kitchen, from the ceiling beam. So maybe he didn't shoot her, or cut her wrists, or feed her poison . . . but he killed her as sure as if he *had*."

Briar asked, "So what's his real name, then? It can't be Minnericht. He didn't sound like any Hessian I ever heard of."

"His name's Joe. Joe Foster. No man was ever baptized with a more boring name, and I guess he didn't like it any. If he could've gotten away with it, after the Blight and after the walls, I think he would've taken Blue's life over. He would've done it right away if he could. But he got hurt in the leaving. If you've seen his face, you know what I mean; he got burned up in a fire, back when people thought maybe the Blight could be burned away. So he did it slow, stealing another man's life a piece at a time as he took these things— these inventions, toys, and tools. It took him a while to learn how to use them."

Briar couldn't think of the sinister Dr. Minnericht with the name Joe Foster. It didn't fit. It didn't match that odd man with a big personality and a big controlling streak that reminded her so immediately of her long-gone husband. But she didn't have long to ponder it.

Listen," Angeline said, putting her bloody fingers to her lips. "Listen, you can still hear them, can't you?"

She meant the rotters, still knocking against the braced-up door to the corridor behind them. "I can still hear them," Briar admitted.

"That's good, that's good. As long as we can hear them, we know where they are. Now, do you hear anything up there?" She used the two fingers over her mouth to point at the ceiling.

Briar asked, "What's up there?"

"We're under the lobby, where all the shooting and trouble started."

Zeke said, "Oh, yeah. Jeremiah went back up that way, 'cause there were rotters."

Just then, an impossibly loud explosion shook the whole underground station, and in its wake the sound of falling masonry, brick, and rubble rained down from somewhere else, echoing the blast and dragging it out.

The trio stopped. Angeline frowned and said, "That didn't sound like the Daisy to me." She asked Briar, "Do you know what I'm talking about?"

"Yes, I do. And no, that didn't sound right."

Zeke said, "I heard that, once before. Jeremiah called it a Sonic Gusting Gun, I think."

"Ooh, that can't be good," the princess murmured. "Jesus, I hope he's all right. But he's such a big man, and he's got so much gear. I'm sure he must be," she said. "We'll stop, and be real quiet, and take a look."

"I can't leave him here," Briar said. "He's been real helpful to me. If he's hurt—"

"Don't start counting those chickens, Miss Wilkes. Not yet. I don't hear any more fighting up there, do you?"

"I don't," she said.

Zeke agreed. "I don't either. Maybe they moved on, or maybe everybody's dead."

"I'd rather you didn't put it like that," his mother complained. "I like those people. Those people from Maynard's and the Vaults, they've been good to me, and they didn't have to be. They helped me go looking for *you*. I don't know if I'd have lived this long without them."

Behind another door that was unmarked and unremarkable, Angeline pointed out another set of stairs. Briar thought that if she never saw another step in her life it would be too soon, but she led the way and let Zeke take up the rear. She was increasingly worried for the Indian woman with her bleeding belly; and she appreciated toughness, but Angeline wasn't fooling anybody anymore. She needed a doctor—a real one, and a good one, and that didn't bode well.

The only doctor Briar had ever heard anyone mention inside the walls was . . . well . . . it was Minnericht. And she had a feeling that if they caught up to him, he wouldn't be very helpful.

# Twenty-seven

Briar leaned against the door, pressing her ear to the crack and listening for all she was worth. On the other side she detected only silence, so she stopped and reloaded there in the dark, filling the rifle by feeling her way through her bag. It took an extra moment, but it was an extra moment she was willing to spare.

Finally she said, "I'm going first. Let me take a look."

"I can go first just fine," Angeline argued.

"But my gun will fire more than twice, if it needs to. Keep a watch on my son, will you, ma'am?" she said, and she pushed at the door's latch and let the wooden barrier creep back out of its frame.

Briar led with the barrel of her rifle, and followed with her masked face, swiveling back and forth to take in the whole scene despite the limitations of her visor. She could hear her own breath too loud in her ears, echoed and amplified in her mask, and it was still the same as when she'd first put it on and dropped down the tube. She didn't think she'd ever get used to it.

The room before her was very different from the last time she'd seen it. The glorious unfinished lobby was littered with the aftermath of a localized but very vicious battle. Bodies were sprawled and folded across the regimental rows of chairs; she counted eleven at a glance, and she spied a magnificent hole in the wall that looked like it could've been cut by the Boneshaker machine itself.

And directly inside the hole, where the wall was bitten off and dangling in heavy, scarcely lifted chunks, Briar saw a foot atop the rubble, as if its owner had bodily created the hole and now languished within it.

She didn't quite forget to scan the rest of the room, but her subsequent sweep of the area was perfunctory and fast. Without warning her son or the princess, still in their dark little cubbyhole, she ran to the foot and crawled up over the jagged blocks of broken masonry and marble until she could drop down beside it.

She let the Spencer fall off her shoulder, and set aside her satchel.

"Swakhammer," she said, patting at his mask. "Mr. Swakhammer."

He didn't respond.

The mask appeared intact, and mostly he did too—until she began to stick her fingers between the seams of his armor and feel for things that might be broken. She found blood, and quite a lot of it. She found that his leg was bending in an unlikely manner, broken somewhere below his knee and dangling inside a heavy boot with a steel-toed shell.

She was wrenching his mask away from his head when Zeke got tired of waiting in the stairwell. He came to the wall's edge and asked into the hole, "Is somebody in there?"

"It's Jeremiah."

Zeke asked, "Is he all right?"

"No," she grunted. The helmet came mostly off, but it was attached by a series of springs and tubes. It fell away, but didn't roll far. "Swakhammer? Jeremiah?"

Blood had pooled inside the mask; it was coming from his nose and—Briar noted with real alarm—it was dripping steadily from one of his ears.

"Is he dead?" Zeke wanted to know.

Briar said, "Dead folks don't bleed. He's done up brown, though. Jesus, Swakhammer. What happened to you? Can you hear me? Hey." She gently slapped his face, both cheeks. "Hey now. What happened to you?"

"*He got in the way.*"

Minnericht's filtered, masked voice came down like the hammer of God, echoing loudly through the chamber with its dead souls and split-open walls. Briar's chest seized up in a tight flash of fear, and she wanted to scream at Zeke for leaving the relative safety of the stairwell. He was standing there, out in the open at the foot of the stone-cluttered hole, vulnerable as could be.

Briar stared down at Swakhammer, whose pupils were darting back and forth behind closed lids that were caked with drying blood. He was still alive, yes, but not by much. She looked up and said, loud enough that she could be heard from outside the hole and across the room, "You're not Leviticus Blue. But you could've been his brother," she added with as much bland apathy as she could muster. "You've got his sense of timing, that's for sure."

Over the lip of the hole in the wall, she knew she had a bare ridge of shelter. The doctor, if in fact he was one, couldn't see what she was doing—not very well. She used the moment and the cover to lightly frisk her friend in case he was carrying anything helpful. She'd chucked the Spencer aside. Even if it was within easy reach, she'd never get it up, cocked, aimed, and fired before Minnericht had time to do something worse.

One big revolver was lying alongside Swakhammer's ribs, but it was empty.

"I never said I was Leviticus Blue."

Briar grunted as she tried to lift Swakhammer enough to feel around underneath him. "Yes you did."

Zeke piped up, "You told *me* that's who you were."

"Hush, Zeke," his mother warned him. There was more she wanted to say to her son, but she turned back to the masked bastard again before he could respond. "All God's children know it's what you wanted these folks to think. You wanted them to be afraid of you, but you couldn't make that happen with your name alone. You might be mean as a snake, but it turned out you're not as scary as one."

"Hush your mouth, woman. I've made this place what it is today," he said, defensive and angry, and possibly smarting from a slight wound to his pride.

Briar hoped he was smarting. She hoped he was as much like Levi as he acted. She said, "I won't hush; and you can't make me, Joe Foster, even if you try. And you might. You're the kind of man who likes to hurt women, and I hear I'm not the first."

He barked, "I don't care what you heard or where you heard it. Except that I *do* want to know, and I want you to tell me *this moment*, where you heard that name."

She stood up fast and straight. Instead of answering his demands, she said, "I want to know who the hell you think you are, dragging us into your little western front, you son of a bitch"—she borrowed Angeline's favorite label.

When she stood, she could see him as clearly as he saw her, and the triple-barreled shotgun in his hands was something of a terror. It wasn't aimed at her. It was aimed at Zeke, who, to his credit, had successfully hushed as his mother told him to—though whether it was due to her orders or Minnericht's amazing firearm, Briar didn't know and didn't care.

She'd expected him to threaten *her*, but Minnericht was smarter than that, and meaner. Well, that was fine. She could be smart and mean, too. She said, "You made this place what it is today? So you think you've got some kind of power down here? You sure act like you do, but it's horseshit, isn't it? It's all a big show so people will think you're the smartest man with the most money. But it ain't like that. If you were half as smart as you pretended to be, you wouldn't have to steal Levi's inventions, or scare up the leftovers from the mining contest. I saw them back there, in your storage room. You think I don't know where they came from?"

He roared, "Stop talking!"

But she was determined to keep his attention on her instead of on Zeke, and instead of on the slender, boyish old woman who was slinking out of the stairwell to creep up behind him. Briar continued, talking louder so she'd be heard over him, "If you were half the man you pretend to be, you wouldn't need me to prop up your story—and you wouldn't need to bring in the boys, like you do. Levi was crazy and he was bad, but he was too smart for you to just pick up his toys and run with them. You need Huey because he's smart; and you tried to talk my own boy into staying by telling him a pack of lies. But if you'd really made this place what it is, you wouldn't *need* to."

His aim shifted so that the fat-barreled triple gun pointed between her breasts. She'd never been happier. He said, "You say another goddamned word and I'll—"

"You'll what?" she shrieked. She spit out the next part in a frantic, desperate tirade—all in one breath, skipping from pause to pause and trying to keep him angry, because Angeline had almost reached him. "You don't even know how to work that gun, I bet. You probably didn't even make it. All the ideas you ever got you stole from Levi, who designed it all and built it all. You know just enough of it to make yourself look like a king, and all you can do is pray to God that no one figures out how useless and weak you really are!"

Beyond roaring, beyond howling, he simply shouted, "Why are you here? Why are *either of you* here! You never should have come! This wasn't about you," he swore. "You should've both stayed home, in that disgusting little hovel in the Outskirts. I offered you more—I offered you both much, much more than either of you deserves, and I didn't have to! I didn't owe you anything, either one of you!"

She shouted back. "Of course you didn't! Because you're not my husband, and you're not his father, and none of this was our fight, or our problem. But you didn't figure that out in time, Joe Foster."

"Stop using that name! I don't want that name; I hate that name, and I won't hear it! *Why do you know that name?*"

Angeline was there to answer.

Before Briar could blink, the old woman was on him, wrapped around him as tight as a vise, as mean as a mountain cat, and much, much more deadly. One of her knives was in her hand, and then it was under Minnericht's chin, in that narrow seam where his skin met his mask.

She used her weight to jerk his head back and stretch that seam, exposing his Adam's apple and a white stretch of flesh. As she did so, Briar gasped and Zeke leaped over the debris and into the near-shelter of the hole, beside his mother.

Angeline said, "Because of Sarah Joy Foster, whose life you ended twenty years ago."

And with one slash, swift and muscle-slicingly deep, she cut a line across that seam.

He fired two of the gun's three barrels, but his aim was lost to imbalance and shock. He spun and stumbled, and slipped and skidded across the scuffed marble floor that was soaked with his own blood. It gushed in a pair of amazing sprays that shot out from both sides of his neck, for Angeline had cut him hard from ear to ear. She rode him like an unbroken horse as he flailed, grasping for the woman, or his throat, or anything to steady himself. But he was bleeding too fast, and too much.

He didn't have long to struggle, and he wanted to make it count. He tried to turn the gun around in his hands—to aim it back, over his shoulder, but it was too heavy. He'd lost too much blood, and he was too weak. He fell to his hands and knees, and finally, Angeline let go of him.

She kicked the big gun out of his reach and stared down while he sputtered, and while his glorious red coat grew redder still.

Briar turned away. She didn't care about Minnericht's death; she cared about Swakhammer, who wasn't bleeding with quite so much spectacular gore, but whose life was ebbing all the same. It might well be too late already.

Zeke took a step or two back. Until he did so, Briar hadn't noticed that he'd been all but hiding behind her.

He opened his mouth to say something, then closed it again as a bustle of incoming activity prompted his mother to grab, hoist, cock, and aim the Spencer.

"Get down," she told him, and he *did*.

Angeline hobbled over to the hole, scaled its lip, and readied her shotgun just in time to point it at Lucy O'Gunning as she stomped around the corner and into the room where the battle had just ended.

Lucy had found or fixed her crossbow, and it was affixed to her arm, ready to fire. She aimed it back at Angeline before she realized who she was. Then she brought it down and said, "Miz Angeline, what are—?" Finally, she saw Briar, and she almost laughed when she spoke the rest. "Ain't this a pairing? I swear and be damned. We don't have too many women down here inside the walls, but I sure wouldn't mess with the ones we've got."

Briar said, "You can count yourself in that number, Lucy. But don't start smiling yet." She pointed down at Swakhammer, whom Lucy could not see over the edge of fallen wood and wall. "We got trouble, and it's big, and it's heavy."

"It's Jeremiah!" Lucy exclaimed as she poked her head over the rubble.

"Lucy, he's dying. We've got to get him moved out of here, and back someplace safe."

Angeline said, "And I don't know if that'll save him or not. He's hurt bad."

"I can see that," Lucy didn't quite snap. "We'll have to take him . . . We'll have to put him . . ." she said, as if—should she talk long enough—an idea would eventually occur to her. And then, one did. "The mine tracks."

"That's a good thought," Angeline said approvingly. "He'll be easier to take down than carry up, and if you can get him in a cart, you can roll him all the way back to the Vaults without a lot of trouble."

"If, if, and if. How are we going to—?" Briar said.

Lucy interrupted. "Give me one minute," she said. She added to Swakhammer in particular, "Don't you go anywhere, you big old bastard. You hang on. I'll be right back."

If he heard her, he didn't give any indication of it. His breathing was so shallow it could scarcely be detected, and the twitching of his pupils beneath his eyelids had slowed to a faint roll, corner to corner.

Half a minute later Lucy returned with Squiddy, Frank, and Allen, if Briar remembered the other men's names correctly. Frank didn't look so hot. He had a black eye so broad that it nearly made a black nose and a black forehead too; and Allen was nursing a hand that had been injured in some way. But between them, they crawled into the hole, lifted up the armored man, and began to half tow, half carry him out and down.

Lucy said, "We can take him to the lift. At the bottom level, we ought to find mining carts—this is where all the lines ended when Minnericht drew them up. Come on now, and hurry. He ain't got long."

"Where will we take him?" Squiddy asked. "He needs a doctor, but—"

And that's when they noticed the bloody puddle with a masked villain lying dead at its center.

"Jesus. He's dead, ain't he?" Frank asked with awe.

"He's dead, and thank Jesus for it," Angeline told him. She reached for one of Swakhammer's dangling feet—the one that did not appear broken. She picked it up and propped it over her shoulder. "I'll help you carry him. I could use a peek from a doctor myself," she confessed. "But this corner of ol' Jeremiah ain't so heavy. I can help."

"I know a man," Lucy said. "He's an old Chinaman who lives close to here. It's not medicine like the kind you're used to, but it's medicine all the same, and right now, you'll both have to take what you can get."

"The medicine I'm used to?" Allen grumbled. "I'd sooner die, if you want the truth."

"Swakhammer'd maybe rather die than get cleaned up by a Chinaman," Lucy said as she used her uncommonly strong mechanical arm to brace Jeremiah's back. "He's scared to death of them. But I'm willing to scare him if it keeps him in one piece."

"Momma?"

"What, Zeke?"

"What about *us*?"

Briar hesitated, though she dared not hesitate long. Jeremiah

Swakhammer was being toted away under the straining backs of his friends, and he was leaving a dripping blood trail like a ball of yarn unspooling behind them. Upstairs the sounds of rotters moaning and stomping continued. Their infuriated, starving demands grew louder and louder as their numbers climbed, and they struggled to find their way inside the pried-open crannies and left-open entrances.

"They're everywhere," Briar said, not really answering his question.

"Down's going to be as bad as up. I don't know how this room has stayed so clear," Lucy said with a grunt. "Where's the Daisy?"

"Here!" Briar said quickly, like she'd had the same thought at the very same moment. The massive shoulder cannon was half buried beneath a slab of ceiling, but she pried it out and held it up with no small degree of effort. "Christ," she said. "Zeke, this thing weighs almost as much as you do. Lucy, do you know how to work it?"

"Roughly. Turn that knob there, on the left. Turn it all the way up; we're going to need all the juice that thing can give us."

"Done. Now what?"

"Now it's got to warm up. Jeremiah says it has to collect its energy. It gathers up electricity in order to fire. Take it with us—come along, come over to the lift. Fire it inside the lift—that'll be the best place, don't you think?"

"You're right," Briar said. "The sound will carry from floor to floor, not just the one. That will work, if we can get to the lift." With that thought, she handed the Daisy to Zeke, who strained to hold it. "Take this," she told him. "I'm going to go ahead and clear the hallway. There were rotters there before; they might be there still."

She readied the Spencer and ran ahead of the clot who carried Swakhammer, and ahead of her own son, whose back was bent backward nearly double as he tried to balance his body's weight against the weight of the gun.

Briar kicked open the stairwell corridor and charged down unopposed.

"Stairway's clear!" she shouted to the group behind her. "Zeke, come ahead of them with that gun! Lucy—how long until it's warmed up properly? It ain't been fired lately. Please tell me it's not a quarter of an hour!"

"Not if he didn't fire it. Just give it a minute," the answer dribbled down through the stairwell.

Briar didn't hear the last part. The corridor on the guest floor was peppered lightly with rotters in varying states of gruesome decay. She counted five of them, shambling between the bodies of their comrades and gnawing on the limbs of more freshly fallen men. Thus distracted, they barely noticed Briar, who picked them off quickly, one after the other.

The floor was cluttered with limbs that ought to stink, but then she remembered that she was still wearing her mask and that's why she could only smell the charcoal and rubber seals. For the first time since arriving, she was glad for the singular odor of her own face.

Here and there an arm had fallen away from pure decomposition; and over there in a corner, the decapitated forms of other seminaked, putrefying corpses were collected as they'd toppled. It bothered her for a moment, wondering who'd decapitated them. But then she decided that she did not care and it did not matter. All the living—even those who fought amongst themselves—had a common enemy in the rotters, and whoever had separated those heads from those bodies had her gratitude.

She kicked at the limbs she could easily move, trying to clear a path and test the state of the prone and prostrate forms. One faker opened its lone remaining eyelid and bared its teeth, which Briar promptly shot out of its face.

Zeke popped out from the stairwell corridor with the Daisy shoved behind his neck, his arms draped over it so he could support it like a set of stocks. "Momma, what are we going to do?" he asked with real urgency, and Briar heard a question that she wasn't quite prepared to answer.

"I don't know," she said. "But we need to get out of here, that's plain enough. We'll start with that."

"Are we going with them? To Chinatown?"

"No, don't," Angeline said.

She was the one who emerged first from the stairwell, still bearing Swakhammer's leg over her shoulder. Behind her came Frank with the other leg, then Squiddy and Lucy with the rest of the unconscious man borne between them.

"I beg your pardon?"

"Get yourself to the fort. Go to that ship, the one they fixed there. It ought to be ready to fly," Angeline added, each word abbreviated and stressed with her own exhaustion. "It'll take you out."

"Out of the city?" Zeke asked.

"Out of this part of it, at the very least," Lucy said from underneath Jeremiah's neck. "Help us get him on the lift, and then send us down. And as soon as we're gone . . ." She shifted Jeremiah's weight, and he let out a tiny moan. "You get on the lift, Briar Wilkes, and take that goddamned gun and fire it. And then you get up, and you get out of here."

Still uncertain, Briar followed the first part of the order and helped maneuver the big man onto the lift. They rested him against Frank and Squiddy while Lucy poked through the levers up above. She said, "Once we hit bottom and get Jeremiah off to the tracks, I'll send it back up, you understand? You'll have to jump for it, 'cause it's not going to stop."

"I understand," Briar said. "But I'm not sure—"

"I'm not sure of anything, myself," Lucy told her. "But this much is for damned sure: You've got your boy, and this station is about to be overrun full tilt by those rotters, and anyone who stays in here is going to get eaten."

Zeke said, "Are you the one who let 'em inside?"

Lucy gave a hard toss of her head to Frank and Allen and said, "Turnabout's fair play, ain't it? I only wish I knew they'd make it this deep. I wasn't expecting that."

"We could go with you. We could help," he insisted.

Briar was thinking the same thing. She added, "We could see you safely back, at any rate."

"No, no you couldn't. We'll either make it or we won't. He'll either make it or he won't. We don't need no one else to carry him. But you two, well. *You*, Miss Wilkes. You need to go tell the captain you didn't die down here. He needs to know that he paid a debt, not that he incurred an even bigger one. He's down at Fort Decatur, where they've fixed his ship and he's waiting to take off, out of the city. He knows your boy's down here, now. He told me so, when I gave him Minnericht's message."

Swakhammer's shoulders stretched and he made a gurgling sound like something trying to breathe with a chest full of tar. The last part of it came out in a whimper, which tore Briar up. It wasn't a sound that Jeremiah Swakhammer ought to make, ever. "He's dying," she said. "Oh God, Lucy. Get him out of here. Get him to your Chinese doctor. I thank you, and I'll be seeing you again sometime, I swear it."

"On my way," she said. She didn't even bother to close the iron gate, just yanked a pulley overhead. The lift began to drop. As the crew was lowered and they disappeared a foot at a time, Lucy said again, "You've always got a place with us in the Vaults, if you want it. If not, it was an honor to fight beside you, Wilkes."

And then the precipitous slide of the lift down its cables and chains took them out of sight.

Briar was left alone with her boy.

The great gun was almost too much for him. He strained against its weight, but he did not complain, even though his knees were shaking and the back of his neck was burning from the warmth of the slowly heating metal.

At the bottom of the lift shaft, something stopped.

Briar and Zeke heard Lucy shouting orders, and she heard arrangements being made, and Swakhammer being toted and dragged off the lift and into the deepest depths of the underground levels. Hopefully there was a mine cart down there someplace; and hopefully, Lucy could take him somewhere to get him help.

With a rustling clank of cables and chains, the lift began to rise once more, climbing back to Briar and Zeke.

They held their breath and prepared to jump for it.

Briar and Zeke held the Daisy between them, and when the lift climbed into view they chucked it onto the deck and followed it. Once they were safely aboard, the lift rose slowly but steadily, a fraction of a floor at a time. Briar rolled the gun over and propped it up on its butt end.

A trigger as big as a large man's thumb jutted out from the undercarriage.

The whole machine was buzzing with pent-up energy, ready to fire.

Briar said, "Cover your ears, Zeke. And I'm very, very serious about that. Cover 'em good. This'll stun the rotters, but only for a couple of minutes. We'll have to move fast."

Leaning as far away from the gun as possible, Briar waited until the top floor came dawning into view, and then she squeezed the trigger.

The pop and the pulse pounded up, and down. Compressed by the shaft, it echoed and bounced and crashed, coursing from top to bottom and spilling out from floor to floor in a series of waves that might have amplified its power—or might have only dispersed it. The lift rang and rattled; it shook on its cable supports, and for a dazed, almost blinded moment Briar was afraid it was too much. She feared that the lift couldn't handle it and couldn't hold them, and at any moment it would drop them both to their deaths.

But the lift held, and it crawled upward into the darkness of yet another lightless place.

Zeke was stunned—every bit as stunned as Briar had been the first time she heard the Daisy. But his mother lifted him out more easily than she'd lifted the gun, and she pulled him off the platform, right into a door.

Without knowing what was behind it, she opened it swiftly, dragging the staggering boy in her wake and aiming her Spencer in a sweeping arc that covered the whole horizon.

The glowing orange bubbles of a dozen bonfires dotted the

streets, and around each bonfire there was an empty ring of space. No one had ever told Briar that rotters would keep their distance from a flame, but it stood to reason, so she didn't question it.

The fires were built up and fed by masked men who cared nothing for whatever fight still raged beneath the station. These men were reeling, but recovering. They'd heard the Daisy too, and they knew what it was when it sounded. They were far enough away, up here— and sheltered some by the crackling loudness of the fires—that only a few had actually fallen. Some of them shook their heads or boxed at their own ears, trying to shake away the dreadful power of Dr. Minnericht's Doozy Dazer.

Briar hadn't known they were up there. But if she had, likely as not she would've fired the Daisy anyway. After all, the living recovered faster than the dead.

Briar spied one ponytail, and then another two or three jutting out from the backs of gas masks. The Chinese quarter was out near the station at the wall's edge; and these were its residents, defending the streets in order to protect themselves.

All of them ignored her. They ignored Zeke, too.

She told him, "Drop the Daisy."

"But it's—"

"We won't get a chance to use it again. It'll take too long to charge, and it will just slow us down. Now," she said, because suddenly it occurred to her that she did not know. "We have to find this fort. Do you know where it is?"

She could barely see through the smoke and the Blight, and she wanted to ask someone for directions. But all the busy men, feeding their fires, did not look her way when she shouted for their attention. She doubted they spoke English.

Zeke tugged at her arm. "It's not far away from here. Follow me."

"Are you sure?" She dragged her feet, but he took her hand and started to pull her along.

He said, "I'm sure. Yeah, I'm sure. This is where Yaozu brought me, and I remember it from my maps. Come on. It's back down this street, around this way. The fires help," he added. "I can see where I'm going!"

"All right," she told him, and she let him tow her away from the fires, and away from the strong-armed Chinamen with their masks and shovels.

Zeke rounded the nearest corner and drew up short.

Briar slammed into the back of him, pushing him forward two short steps—over a small sea of rotters. All of them were lying down, but some of them were beginning the first tentative flops and jerks of awakening. There were dozens of them, with maybe hundreds more behind them, beyond where the dark and the Blight would let Briar and Zeke see.

"Don't stop," she told him, and she took the lead. "We've got less than a minute. For God's sake, boy. *Run!*"

He didn't argue and didn't pause; he only leaped after her—charging from body to body, seeking the street beneath them when he could find it. She led him in the direction he'd picked, setting an example by stomping on any heads or torsos that got in her way. She tripped once, sliding on a leg as if it were a log roll, but Zeke helped her recover and then they were off that street with its legion of irate, immobilized corpses.

"Go right," he told her.

She was still in front, so she was both leading and following his directions. The smell inside her mask was an elixir of fear and hope, and rubber and glass and coal. She breathed it deeply because she had no choice; she was panting, forgetting so fast how hard it was to run and breathe at the same time while her head was bound by the apparatus. Zeke wheezed too, but he was younger, and maybe, in his way, stronger.

Briar didn't know, but she hoped so.

The time they'd bought with the Daisy was all but up; and even if it wasn't, they were getting so far from the blast site that the rotters wouldn't have heard it, and it wouldn't have stopped them.

Two streets more, and another turn.

Zeke stopped, and sought his bearings.

"Please tell me we aren't lost," Briar begged. She threw her back against the nearest wall and pulled Zeke back, urging him to do the same.

He said, "Not lost. No. There's the tower, see? It's the tallest thing here. And the fort was over this way. We're right on top of it, just about."

He was right. They felt their way through the gas-filled, starless dark until they found the front gate, buckled and latched from within. Briar pounded on it, knowing that she might be drawing the wrong kind of attention, but knowing also that it *had* to be worth the risk. They had to get inside, because the rotters were coming: She could hear them rallying far too close, and there was only so much farther she could run.

The satchel that hung across her chest and beat against her hip was perilously light, and she couldn't bring herself to see how much ammunition was left. The answer was "not much," and any more knowledge than that would only make her sick to her stomach.

Zeke joined in beside her, knocking against the fort's door with his fists and his feet.

Then, from behind the blocked door came the sound of heavy things being set aside and shoved to the ground. The rows of logs that made up the fort's wall and doors began to move, and the crack between the wood opened enough to let inside one woman and one boy, just before the first huffing rotter scouts turned the corner and charged.

## Twenty-eight

Briar recognized the men by their shapes, because she could not see their faces.

Fang, a slight and perfectly motionless man.

Captain Cly, a giant who could be mistaken for no one else.

Light did not flood the walled compound, but it pooled enough to see by. Lanterns were strung the way the Chinese placed them, bound by ropes and lighting the pathways from above. Two men worked with a tool that spit fire and sparks, and a third pumped a steam generator that gasped and huffed hot clouds, sealing up the torn seams on the *Naamah Darling*.

It surprised Briar, how she almost hadn't seen it through the pudding-thick air, but there it was: nearly majestic, despite its multitude of patches.

She said to Cly, "I thought you weren't passing through again for a while?"

He said, "I didn't intend to." He cocked a thumb at another man, who had his back turned and was watching the ongoing repairs. "But old Crog got himself in a bind."

"Got myself in a bind?" The captain spun and glowered so hard that Briar could see it behind his mask's visor. "I got myself into no bind at all. Some miserable goddamned son of a bitch thief flew off with the *Free Crow*!"

"Hello, erm . . . Captain Hainey," she said. "I'm very sorry to hear about that."

"You're sorry; I'm sorry. All God's children are *sorry*," he said angrily. "The most powerful ship for miles, in any direction. The only warship ever successfully stolen from either side, and someone had the temerity to steal it from *me*! And you'd better count your lucky stars, ma'am," he said, pointing a finger at Briar.

"Oh, I do. Every day, as of late," she assured him. "For what?"

"With the *Free Crow* gone," Hainey replied, "I'd have no way to lift you out, and heaven knows who else you might've met. But this big bastard agreed to help me catch the bird, so here we are."

Cly added, "As you can see, it didn't work out for Crog, but I'm glad to see we caught *you*, at least. We took a little damage," he said, cocking his head to indicate the workmen, who had turned off their tools and were sliding down ropes that descended from the side of the ship. "You could ask your boy about that. What were you doing on board the *Free Crow*, anyway? I've been trying to figure that out ever since I realized who you were."

Zeke, who'd been keeping quiet in hopes of being ignored, said sheepishly, "They told me the ship was called the *Clementine*. And I was only trying to get outside, back to the Outskirts. Miss Angeline set it up for me. She said they'd take me out and set me down. I didn't know it was a stolen ship, or nothing," he fibbed.

"Well, it *is* a stolen ship, or something. I stole it first, fair and square as a stamp on a letter. *I* changed it up. *I* made it worth flying. *I* made her into the *Free Crow*, and she's mine as sure as I'm the one who built her from the rudder up!"

"I'm real sorry," Zeke said weakly.

"So Angeline's the one who put you up to it, is she? But she knows most of us who fly in and out of here," Cly said, scratching idly at a spot where his mask wasn't quite big enough to comfortably fit over his ear. "I don't think she'd set you up blind, with a captain she don't know."

Zeke said, "She *said* she knew him. But I didn't think she knew him real well."

"Where is she, then?" Croggon Hainey all but shouted his demand. "Where is that crazy old Indian?"

"She's on her way back to the Vaults," Briar said, trying to inject some finality into the statement. "And we need to see about taking off. Things are bad back there, over at the station, and the badness is going to spread."

Hainey said, "I ain't worried. This fort'll keep out almost anything. I'm gonna go find that woman and—"

And because he was trying to be helpful, Zeke said, "Mister, the captain's name was Brink. He was a red-haired guy, with a bunch of tattoos on his arms."

Hainey froze while he absorbed this information, and then his arms flew up again—and he began to punch at the air. "Brink! Brink! I know that old horse's ass!" He turned around, still kicking and striking at everything and nothing, and wandered back toward the ship, swearing and making threats that Brink couldn't hear.

Andan Cly watched his fellow captain storm across the fort's yard until he disappeared behind the *Naamah Darling*. Then he turned to Briar and started to say something. She beat him to the punch.

She said, "Captain Cly, I know you didn't plan to be back inside the city walls so soon, but I'm glad to see you all the same. And"—she paused, unsure of how best to phrase her request—"I hope I can impose on you for one more small favor. I can make it a profitable one, and it won't even take you anywhere out of your way."

"Profitable, eh?"

"Profitable, absolutely. When we lift up out of here, I want to stop by my old house. I want Zeke to see where I used to live. And as you must remember, my husband was a rich man. I know where some of his money is hidden away, and I don't think even the most industrious looters could have found it all. There are . . . hiding places. I'll be happy to share whatever I can scrape up and carry out."

As if he hadn't heard the rest, Zeke said, "Really? You'll take me there? You'll show me the old house?"

"Really," she said, though saying it made her sound tired beyond her years. "I'll take you there, and I'll show you around. I'll show you everything," she added. "That is, if the good captain would be so kind as to carry us over there."

Croggon Hainey came out from around the back side of the *Naamah Darling*, still swearing to turn the air blue. "I hope Brink has the time of his life flying my ship, because when I catch up to him, I'm going to kill him dead!"

Cly watched Hainey with a narrowing of his eyes that was more a grin than suspicion. He said, "For the prospect of profit, I can probably talk him into a little detour. Besides, it's my ship. We'll swing by your house if you want. Is there anyplace we can dock, or at least tie down an anchor?"

"There's a tree in the yard—a big old oak. It's dead now, I'm sure, but it should hold you steady for a few minutes."

"I'll take your word for it," he said. He looked her up and down, and looked Zeke over as well before saying, "We can take off as soon as you like."

"Whenever you're ready, Captain," Zeke said. He leaned back and put an arm around his mother, which startled and charmed her.

It pleased Briar even as it made her feel a little sad. She'd always known he'd grow up someday, but she hadn't quite expected it so soon, and she wasn't sure what to make of it now.

She was hopelessly tired, and her eyes ached in her skull from the days of too little sleep and too much worry, not to mention the odd blow to the head. She leaned into the boy, and if she hadn't been wearing her father's old hat, she might've put her head on his shoulder.

Cly checked over his shoulder, and seeing that the workmen had finished with the last of the tools, he asked Fang, "Did we get Rodimer back on board?"

Fang nodded.

"Oh, yes, Rodimer," Briar said. "I remember him. I'm a little surprised he's not been out here chatting."

Without any ceremony, Cly said, "He's dead. When we crashed down, he broke something—inside, you know what I mean. He was all right for a bit, and then he wasn't. And now, I don't know. Now I guess we'll take him home. Let his sister decide what to do with him."

"I'm so sorry," Briar said. "I rather liked him."

"So did I," he admitted. "But there's nothing to be done about it now. Come on, let's get out of this place. I'm sick of this mask. I'm sick of this air. I want to get out, and get moving. Come on," Cly said. "It's time to go home."

And in less than half an hour, the *Naamah Darling* was airborne.

It lifted with caution as the captain tested its thrusters, its tanks, and its steering. It rose up lightly for such an enormous craft, and soon it was high above the fort.

Croggon Hainey took Rodimer's seat and grumpily performed the services of a first mate. Fang strapped himself in and performed his navigational duties in silence, by hand signs and head movements. Briar and Zeke hunkered together by the farthest edge of the slightly cracked windshield corner and looked out over the city.

Cly said, "We're going to stay within the Blight for now. If we go up any higher, we'll meet crosswinds, and I want to baby this bird until I'm sure she's working right. Look down and to the left. You see the station?"

"I see it," Briar said.

She saw the crosswalks that interlaced like helpful fingers, giving pedestrians a way in, out, and around the quarter where the half-built station stood against the mudflats at the edge of Seattle's great wall. The fires below showed her plenty, and the men who tended them looked like mice.

The *Naamah Darling* drifted past the station's clock tower a little too close for comfort. The blank face of a clock as big as a bedroom stared dully back at them, no mechanisms to make it keep the time and no hands to display it. It was a ghost of something that had never happened.

Over the streets the airship flew, and the rotters were filling the roads beneath it. They moved in pockets and clusters, bumping mindlessly from wall to wall like marbles spilled from a bucket. Briar felt a great swell of pity for them, and she wished with all her heart that maybe someday someone would put them all down—every one of them. They had been people once, and they deserved better. Didn't they?

As the craft drifted higher, along the slope of the city's sharpest hill, Briar thought of Minnericht and she wasn't so sure. Maybe not all of them deserved better. But some of them.

And she looked at her son beside her. He stared out the same window, and down at the same shipwreck of a city. He smiled at it, not because it was beautiful, but because he'd beaten it after all—and now he would get the only reward he'd ever wanted. Briar watched him smile. She peeked at him, trying not to catch his attention by staring. She wanted him to smile, and she wondered how long that smile would survive.

"Miss Wilkes, I'm going to need some directions," Captain Cly announced. "I know you lived up this hill, but I don't know where precisely."

"That way," she pointed. "Along Denny. Straight up, to the left. The big house," she said.

It rose up out of the bleak, smeared stretch of low-lying gas like a tiny castle—gray and sharp edged, and clinging to the side of the very steep hill like a barnacle on a boat. She could just see its flat tower and widow's walk, and the gingerbread frosting that banded the gutters. What colors remained from the lovely old house were just light enough to show it in the darkness.

The exterior had once been painted a pale gray shade of lavender, because it was her favorite color. She'd even confessed, to Levi and no one else, that she'd always liked the name "Heather" and she wished her parents had thought of it. But Levi had said her home could be the color of heather; and maybe, should they ever have a daughter, Briar could name her whatever she wanted.

The conversation haunted her. It was sharp and hard, as if the memory had frozen and stuck in her throat.

She looked again at Zeke, from the corner of her eye. She hadn't known about him at the time. So much had happened before he'd ever been thought of—and by the time she'd figured out why she felt so ill, and why she was hungry for such strange things . . . she was in the Outskirts, having buried her father for the second time. She was living on the silverware she'd taken from Levi's house, selling it a piece at a time to survive while the walls went up around the city she'd called home.

"What?" Zeke caught her looking. "What is it?"

She made a nervous laugh so small that it might've been mistaken for a sob. "I was just thinking. If you'd been a girl, we were going to call you Heather." Then she said to Cly, "There's the tree. Do you see it?"

"I see it," he said. "Fang, get one of the rope hooks, will you?"

Fang disappeared into the cargo hold.

Beneath it, a panel retreated and a weighted grappling rope was pitched into the top of the long-dead tree. Briar could see it from the window, how just below her the branches snapped and fractured; but when the rope was yanked and wiggled it stayed. The *Naamah Darling* drifted, and caught, and hovered.

Beside the tree, a rope ladder unrolled and dropped to within a few feet of the ground.

Fang returned to the ship's bridge.

Cly said, "That won't hold us too terribly long, but for a few minutes it'll be all right."

Captain Hainey, now reluctantly serving as first mate, asked, "Do you need any help?"

Briar understood what he really wanted, and she said, "Could you let us have just a few minutes alone? Then come on inside, and I'll help you find the gold that's left. You too, Captain Cly. I owe you plenty, and anything you find is yours to carry home."

"How many minutes?" Hainey asked.

Briar said, "Maybe ten? I want to find a few personal items, that's all."

"Take fifteen," Cly told her. "I'll restrain him if I have to," he added.

Hainey said, "I'd like to see you try it."

And Cly replied, "I know you would. But for now, let's give the lady the time she's asking for, all right? Go on now, before the rotters get wise that all the action isn't down there at the station and make for the hills again."

Zeke didn't need to hear it twice. He dashed for the hold, and the rope ladder, and before Briar could catch up Cly was out of his seat. He caught her gently by the arm and said, "Are your filters all right?"

"They're fine, yes."

"Is there something . . . ? Is there anything . . . ?"

Whatever he wanted to ask, Briar didn't have time for it and she told him so. "Let me go after him, will you?"

"Sorry," he said, and let her go. "You'll need light, won't you?"

"Oh. Yes, we will. Thank you."

He handed her a pair of lanterns and some matches, and she thanked him for them. She jammed her wrist through their handles and held them by her forearm so she could freely climb the ladder.

Moments later she was standing in her old front yard.

The grass was as dead as the big old oak tree, and the yard was nothing but mud and the slickly rotten film of long-gone grass and flowers. The house itself had turned a yellowed shade of brownish gray like everything else that'd been smudged by the Blight for sixteen years. Around the porch where rosebushes had once grown there was only the skeletal aftermath of brittle, poisoned flora.

She set the lanterns down on her porch and struck the matches to light them.

The front door was open. Beside it, a window was broken. If Zeke had done it, she hadn't heard him, but it would've been easy for anyone to reach inside, unlock it, and enter. "Mother, are you in here yet?"

"Yes," she said, not very loud.

She couldn't breathe, and it wasn't the mask.

Inside, everything was not as she'd left it, but it was close enough. People had come through; that much was obvious. Things were broken, and the obvious objects had been looted. A white-and-blue Japanese vase lay in shards on the floor. The china cabinet had been smashed and everything within it was missing or shattered. Beneath her feet, an Oriental rug was curled around the edges where it had been kicked by trespassers; and several sets of dirty footprints streaked across the parlor, and into the kitchen, and into the living area where Ezekiel was standing, staring at everything, taking all of it in—all at once.

"Mother, look at this place!" he said, as if she'd never seen it before.

As she handed him a lantern she said, "Here, have some light so you can actually *see* it."

Look, there was the velvet couch, covered in dust so thick that its original color could not be told. Look, there was a piano with sheet music still clipped into place, ready to be played. And over there—above the doorway—a horseshoe that had never brought anybody any luck.

Briar stood in the middle of the room and tried to remember what it'd looked like sixteen years go. What color had that couch been? What about the rocking chair in the corner? Had it once had a shawl or a throw slung across its back?

"Ezekiel," she whispered.

"Momma?"

She said, "There's something I need to show you."

"What's that?"

"Downstairs. I need to show you where it happened, and how it happened. I need to show you the Boneshaker."

He beamed from ear to ear. She could see it in the scrunch of his eyes behind the mask. "Yes! Show me!"

"This way," she said. "Stay close. I don't know how well the floor's held up."

As she said it, she saw one of her old oil lamps hanging on the wall as if she'd never left. Its blown glass reservoir was untouched—it wasn't cracked, or even crooked. As she walked past it, the light of her cheap industrial lamp flickered against it and made it look briefly alive.

"The stairs are over here," Briar said, and her legs ached at the thought of climbing yet more of them in one day; but she pushed the door open with her fingertips and the hinges creaked a familiar squeal. They'd rusted, but they held—and when the door was opened they sang with exactly the same old notes.

Zeke was too excited to talk. Briar could sense it in his quivery fumbling behind her, and in his permanent grin inside the mask, and in the quick, happy breaths that whistled through the filters as fast as a rabbit's.

She felt the need to explain.

"There was a contest, years ago. The Russians wanted a way to mine gold out of ice in the Klondike. Your father won the contest, so they paid him to build a machine that could drill through a hundred feet of ice." With every step down, she added a new piece of exposition, trying to slow their descent even as she forced herself to make it. "It hardly ever thaws up there, I guess, and mining is a tricky thing. Anyway, Levi had six months to build it and show it to the ambassador when he came to town for a visit, but then he said he'd run the drill engine early, because he'd gotten a letter asking him to."

She'd reached the basement.

She lifted her lantern and let it light the room. Ezekiel came to stand beside her.

"Where is it?" he asked.

The rays of her lantern illuminated a mostly empty room scattered with stray sheets that once covered machinery or other equipment. "Not here. This isn't the laboratory. This is only the basement. This used to be where he stored all the things he was working on while he waited for someone to buy them, or while he waited to figure out what he was going to do with them."

"What happened to it?"

"I'm guessing Minnericht made off with everything he could carry. Most of what I saw there in the station—well, a lot of it, anyway—came from here. Those beautiful lights—did you see them? Powered by electricity, generated from I-don't-know-what. Did you see the gun he had? That triple-barreled thing? I never saw one down here, but I saw some drawings for it. They were on that desk."

A squat, long piece of furniture was pushed against the wall. It was naked, without a single piece of paper or the smallest scrap of pencil left upon it.

"Minnericht, or Joe Foster, or whoever he was . . . I reckon he took everything that wasn't nailed down. At least, he took everything he saw. Everything he could move. But he couldn't move that goddamned Boneshaker, even if he knew how to find it."

She opened the top right desk drawer and slipped her fingers underneath a hidden panel, where she pushed a button.

With a pop and a crunch, a shape like a door appeared in the wall. Zeke squealed and ran to it.

"Watch out," his mother warned. "Let me show you." She went to the rectangular shape and ran her hands along the depression where the door had been revealed. She pushed the panel at a certain spot and it withdrew, sliding back with a squeak to reveal another set of stairs.

"Well," she said. She lifted the lantern up high and held it out into the room. "It looks like the ceiling's held."

But not much else had.

Part of one wall and all of the floor was totally lost, ground up like meat. Wires as fat as fingers dangled broken from the ceiling and lay scattered across heaping stacks of rubble that had been pushed up and back, shoveled aside as easily as snow by the giant machine that jutted out from the subterranean depths of the hill, and into the old laboratory.

The Boneshaker was intact, covered by the debris it had so efficiently generated. It was planted in the very middle of the room as if it had grown roots there.

The lanterns weren't enough to push back all the darkness, but Briar could see the machine's scratched steel panels between the slabs of fallen masonry, and the enormous drilling grinders still jabbed into the air like the claws of a terrible crab. Only two of the machine's four grinders were visible.

The drill engine had not so much broken as crushed to dust three long tables that glittered with shards of glass. It had knocked down and demolished rows of shelving and cabinets; everything it had brushed against even lightly was shattered to splinters.

"It's a wonder it didn't bring the whole house down," Briar whispered. "I tell you, at the time I thought it was *going* to." Even through her mask, the air was stuffy and cool, and clogged with the mold, dust, and Blight of sixteen years.

"Yeah," Zeke said, agreeing with anything she felt like saying.

At a glance, it appeared that the machine was on its side, but this impression was only a trick of the room's proportions. It was nose-up, a third of the way out of the cellar's floor. Its grinding drills—each one the size of a pony—had twirled and twisted around everything near them; Briar remembered thinking of giant forks twirling at a bowl of spaghetti. And although rust had taken the biting edges off the grooved, bladed drills, they still looked nastier than a devil's dream.

Briar swallowed hard. Zeke crouched like he was going to jump, but she put out an arm to stop him. She said, "Do you see, on the top of it—there's a thick glass dome, shaped like a bullet?"

"I see it."

"That's where he sat to drive the thing."

"I want to go sit in it. Can I? Does it still open? Do you think it still works?"

He jumped before she could stop him, leaping across the gap and landing lightly on the stairs at the edge of the litter-clogged room.

Briar said, "Wait!" and she came after him. "Wait, don't touch anything! There's glass everywhere," she admonished. The lantern in her hand was still swaying from her jump, so it looked like the dusty, half-collapsed room was filled with stars.

"I've got my gloves on," Zeke said, and began a scramble that would move him across the floor, past the drills, and up to the driver's bubble.

"Wait." She said it with urgency, and with command.

He stopped.

"Let me explain, before you demand that I explain."

She slid down the stairs and crawled up beside him, onto the stacks of rubble and rocks and what was left of the cellar walls that coated the Boneshaker like a lobster's shell.

She said, "He swore it was an accident. He said there was a problem with the steering and the propulsion, that the whole thing was out of his control. But you can see with your own two eyes how he put it right back in the basement when he was finished with it."

Zeke nodded. He got down on his knees and brushed away what dust his hands could move, revealing more of the steel plating with its fist-sized dents.

"He swore that he didn't know what became of the money because he didn't take it, and he swore that he hadn't ever meant to hurt a soul. And believe it or not, for a few days he was able to hide here. No one knew exactly where the machine had gone off to. At first, no one knew he'd driven it right back home, easy as turning a cart.

"But then your grandfather came around looking for him. I mean, everyone was looking for him, but if anyone knew where Levi'd gone off to, it'd be me, so this is where he came.

"I hadn't talked to him since I'd run off to get married. My daddy never liked Levi. He thought Levi was too old for me, and I guess he was right. But more than that, he thought Levi wasn't any good, and I guess he was right about that, too. So the last time I ever spoke to your grandfather, I called him a liar for saying my husband was a crook; and I lied through my teeth and said I didn't know where my husband was. But he was right down here, in this laboratory."

Zeke said, "I wish I'd got to meet him. Your pa, I mean."

She didn't know how respond to that, and a reply choked her until she could say, "I wish you had, too. He wasn't always a real warm man, but I think he would've liked you. I think he would've been proud of you."

Then she cleared her throat and said, "But I was awful to him, the last time I saw him. I threw him out, and I never saw him alive again." She added, more to herself than to him, "And to think it was Cly who brought him back home. It's a smaller world than you know."

"Captain Cly?"

"Oh, yes. It was Captain Cly, though he was a younger man at the time, and nobody's captain, I don't suppose. Maybe he'll tell you about it when we get back on the ship. He'll tell you how the jailbreak really happened, since you've always wanted to know so badly. If anyone can set the facts straight, it's *him*, since he was there.

"But later that same night, when my daddy came here looking for Levi, I went down into the laboratory like I knew I wasn't supposed to. Your father'd made a big stink about it, how I shouldn't go there without his permission. But I came on down and let myself inside while he wasn't looking. He was under that dome, working with some wrenches or some bolts, with his backside hanging out and his head buried down deep in the Boneshaker's workings. So he didn't see me."

Zeke was creeping up toward the driver's panel, up toward that glass bubble that was thicker than his own palm. He hoisted his lantern as high over his head as he could hold it and peered through the scraped-up surface. "There's something inside it."

Briar spoke more quickly. "I opened the laboratory door, and right over there was a stack of bags marked FIRST SCANDINAVIAN BANK. Over there, where that table's all broke up now, there were several sacks, lined up in a row and stuffed to busting with money.

"I froze, but he saw me anyway. He jerked up in that seat and gave me a glare like nothing I'd ever seen before. He started yelling. He told me to get out, but then he saw that I'd already seen the money and he tried a different approach: He admitted he'd stolen it, but told me he didn't know anything about the gas. He swore it was an accident."

Zeke asked, "What happened to the money? Is any of it still here?" His eyes scanned what was left of the room and, seeing nothing, he began to scale the Boneshaker's resting place.

Briar continued. "He'd already stashed most of it. What I saw was only a little bit that he hadn't got around to hiding yet. I took some of that with me when I left; and I stretched out every penny. That's how we ate when you were little, before I went off to work at the water plant."

"But what about the rest of it?"

She took a deep breath. "I hid it upstairs."

And she said, faster than before, trying to spill the whole thing out before Zeke got a chance to see it himself. "Levi tried to sell me some snake oil about running away together and starting over someplace else, but I didn't want to go anyplace else. And, anyway, it was plain as day he'd been planning to run off without me. He started shouting, and I was angry, and I was scared. And on that table, the one that used to be over here, I saw one of the revolvers he was trying to turn into something bigger and stranger."

"Mother!"

She didn't let his exclamation slow her down. She said, "I picked it up and I held it out at him, and he laughed at me. He told me to go upstairs and get whatever I planned to take with me, because we were leaving town in the Boneshaker, and we were leaving within an hour. Otherwise I could stay there and die like everybody else. And he turned his back on me; he went right back up into the machine and started working again, just like I wasn't there. He never did think I was worth a damn," she said, as if it had only just occurred to her. "He thought I was dumb and young, and pretty enough to look nice in his parlor. He thought I was helpless. Well, I *wasn't*."

Zeke was close enough to the battered glass that when he held his lantern up to it, he could see a sprawled shape beneath it. He said, "*Mother*."

"And I'm not saying he threatened me, or he tried to hit me. It didn't happen like that at all. How it happened was, he got back into the Boneshaker, and I came up behind him, and I shot him."

Zeke's hand found a latch down by his knee. He reached down to pull it, and hesitated.

She told him, "Go on. Look, or spend the rest of your life wondering if Minnericht was telling you the truth."

Zeke took one more glance back at the doorway, where Briar stood motionless with her lantern, then pressed the latch and pulled back the door. The glass dome lid hissed on a pair of hinges and began to rise.

A mummy of a man was seated inside, slumped forward and facedown.

The back of his head was missing, though pieces of it could be seen here and there in chunks—stuck to the inside of the glass, and to the control panel. The stray bits had gone black and gray, glued to wherever they'd splattered and fallen. The dried-out corpse was dressed in a light-colored smock and was wearing leather gloves that came up to its elbows.

Briar said, quieter, and slower, "I can't even pretend I was protecting you. I didn't figure out I was going to have you for another few weeks, so I don't have that excuse. But there you have it. I killed him," she said. "If it weren't for you, I don't suppose it would've ever mattered. But you're here, and you're mine—and you were his, too, whether he deserved you or not. And whether I like it or not, it matters."

She waited, watching to see what her son would do next.

Upstairs, they both heard the sound of heavy feet stomping through the parlor. Captain Cly called out, "Miss Wilkes, you in here?"

She yelled back, "We're down here. Give us a second; we'll be right up!"

Then Briar said, "Say something, Zeke. I'm begging you, boy. Say *something.*"

"What should I say?" he asked, and it sounded like he honestly didn't know.

She tried, "Say you don't hate me. Say you understand, or if you don't understand, tell me that it's all right. Say I've told you what you've always wondered, and now you can't accuse me of holding anything back anymore. Or if you can't forgive me, then for Christ's sake tell me so! Tell me I've wronged you, same as I wronged him years ago. Tell me you can't understand, and you wish you'd stayed with Minnericht in his train station. Tell me you never want to see me again, if that's what you mean. *Say anything.* But don't leave me standing here, wondering."

Zeke turned his back on her and stared again into the bubble of buttons, levers, and lights. He took a hard look at the shriveled body whose face he'd never see. Then he reached for the glass dome lid and drew it down until the latch caught with a click that held it closed.

He slid down the side of the big machine and stopped a few feet away from his mother, who was too terrified to cry, for all that she wanted to get it out of the way.

He asked, "What do we do now?"

"Now?"

"Yeah. What do we do now?"

She gulped, and released her death grip on her satchel's strap. She wanted to know, "What do you mean?"

"I mean, do we go through the house, take what we can salvage, and go back to the Outskirts?"

She said, "You think maybe we should stay here. Is that it?"

"It's what I'm asking you. Can we even go back to the Outskirts now? Would you have a job? You've been gone for days; I guess we both have. Maybe we should take whatever money's left and see if the captain would take us back east. The war can't go on forever, can it? Maybe if we go far enough north, or far enough south . . ." The idea faded, and so did his list of suggestions. "I don't know," he concluded.

"I don't either," she said.

He added, "But I don't hate you. I *can't*. You came into the city to find me. Ain't nobody else in the world except you would give a damn enough to try it."

Her nose went stuffy and her eyes filled up. She tried to wipe them both and forgot she was wearing a mask. She said, "All right. And good. Good, I'm glad to hear you say that."

Zeke said, "Let's get out of here. Let's go upstairs and see what we can find. And then . . . and then . . . what do you want to do?"

She put her arm around his waist and hugged him fiercely as they climbed the stairs together.

On the floors above, they could hear the air pirates rifling through drawers, poking their hands through shelves and cabinets.

Briar said, "Let's go give them a hand. There's a safe in the floor of the bedroom, under the bed. I always thought I'd come back for it someday, I just didn't know how long it'd take me." She sniffled, and was almost happy. She asked, "One way or another, we'll be all right, won't we?"

"I think we might be."

"And as for what we do next . . ." She took the lead and brought him back up into the hallway, where the combined light of their lanterns made the narrow space light up with warmth. "There's a little time left to decide. I mean, we can't stay *here*. The underground is no place for a boy."

"Or a woman either, as I heard it."

"Or a woman either, maybe." She gave him that much. "But maybe that don't apply to us. Maybe I'm a killer, and you're a runaway. Maybe we deserve this city, and these people, and maybe we can make something good of it. It can't be much worse than the life we've got outside the wall."

Captain Cly's hulking shadow met them in the parlor, and Croggon Hainey came in through the front door, adjusting his mask and still swearing softly about his missing ship. He paused long enough to say, "This is a strange thing, Miss Wilkes. I don't think I've ever been invited to steal from anyone's home before."

She looked around at the coiled strips of damp wallpaper, the mushy rugs, and the squares of strange colors where paintings had once hung. Shells of furnishings languished along the walls and beside the fireplace, and the crisp, sharp edges of broken window glass made funny lines of burned shadows across the dirty walls. Through the windows, she could see that the sun was coming up outside—barely enough to lighten the gloom within, and not bright enough yet to make the place look truly tragic.

Zeke's grin hadn't stayed, but he raised it again like a flag and said, "Hard to believe there's anything worth having in this old wreck. But Momma says there's money stashed upstairs."

She left her arm around him and kept him as warm and close as he'd let her. To the two air captains she declared, "This is *my* house. If there's anything left that's worth taking away, then let's go get it. Otherwise, I'm finished here. I've salvaged what I can, and it's enough to lean on."

Zeke held still while she ruffled his hair; then he turned to Captain Cly and asked, "Is it true you were there, at the jailbreak? Momma says you were one of the fellows who took my grandfather back home."

Cly nodded and said, "That's a fact. Me and my brother. Let's clean this place out, get back on board, and then I'll tell you about it, if you want. I'll tell you the whole story."

# Epilogue

At the 'works, a supervisor with a peevish face and very thick gloves told Hale Quarter that no, Mrs. Blue hadn't been to work that day. For that matter, she hadn't worked a shift in nearly a week, and as far as the supervisor was concerned, she was no longer employed at the plant. Furthermore, he did not know what had become of her. And no, he had no idea where she might've gone, or what she might be doing now.

But if Hale was truly interested, or desperate, or bored, he was welcome to rummage through whatever personal effects of hers remained. As far as the supervisor knew, no one had cleaned off her shelf or emptied her cubby.

Briar didn't have anything that anyone wanted.

The young biographer nodded and wormed his finger between his shirt collar and his neck, for the room was astonishingly warm. Steam oozed, billowed, and sometimes sprayed out from between the cracks on the big machines; and boiling water for processing was dumped from crucible to crucible in sizzling, foaming waterfalls of heat and heaviness. The other workers eyed him with suspicion and open contempt even though no one had told them who Hale had come seeking. It was enough that he was dressed in clothes that fit him, and that he carried a notebook under his arm. It was enough that he wore glasses that fogged with every fresh pour from a hanging vat above and beyond his head. He was not their kind, and they were not prepared to be kind to him. They wanted him out from underfoot, and off their working floor.

Hale accommodated them. He scuttled out of the main processing area, slipping a little on the steam-slicked grates that served as
floors between the stations. Before he was clear altogether, he asked
in a coughing yell, over his shoulder, "How will I know which things
are hers?"

The supervisor didn't even look up from the valves he was moni-
toring. A fat red needle was quivering between a blue zone and a
yellow one. He simply said back, "You'll know."

Hale wandered back to the rear entrance and to the room where
the employees kept their personal belongings, and within a few moments he understood what the supervisor meant. He found a shelf
with Briar's last name written on it—or presumably, that was the original idea. Graffiti had scrawled, scribbled, and argued its way across
the shelf's little ledge until there was no way to know for certain.

Atop the shelf lay a pair of gloves, but when Hale tried to lift and
examine them, they clung to the wood.

He stood on the tips of his toes and peered over the edge to see
the puddle of blue paint that had congealed into something as firm as
glue. He left the gloves where they were, and since the paint was dry
enough to work around, he fished past them, hoping to find some
trace of Briar's life. From the back corners of the cubby he withdrew
a single lens from a pair of cheap goggles, a broken strap from a bag,
and an envelope with Briar's name on the outside—but nothing
within it.

He found nothing else, so he rocked back down onto his heels until he stood flat on the floor again. He tapped one knuckle against the
edge of his belt, because it helped him think; but nothing new came
to him. This meant that he was fully out of ideas. Wherever Briar
Wilkes Blue had gone, she'd gone suddenly. She'd never said good-
bye, formally quit her job, packed her things, or breathed a word of
her plans to anyone, anywhere.

There was no sign of her son, either.

One last time, Hale decided to check her house. Even if no one
was home, he might be able to tell if anyone had *been* home, or if any-

one had visited. If nothing else, perhaps one of Ezekiel's friends might be lingering around the property. If nothing else, Hale might peek inside a window or two and confirm the obvious even further: Wherever Briar Wilkes Blue had gone, she wasn't coming back.

Hale Quarter tucked his notebook up under his arm and began the long hike up the mudflats, through the soggy Outskirts streets, and into the neighborhood where Maynard Wilkes was buried in his own backyard. It was still early, and the drizzling, noncommittal rain wasn't so bad. The sun strained weakly through veiny breaks in the clouds, casting inverse shadows on the horse and wagon tracks that cut through the soft roads. The wind shoved at his back and it was cold, but it didn't have the bite of some days, and it drove only a little water up against his papers.

By the time he reached the Wilkes house, the afternoon was turning dark a little too early, like it always did at that time of year. Down the street, young boys were lighting the street lanterns for a penny apiece, and what was left of the light sufficed to let Hale see the house in all its absent glory.

It was a squat place, and gray like everything else around it. The walls were tainted with streaks of Blight-tinged rainwater, and the windows were likewise etched, as if with acid.

The front door was closed, but it was not locked. Hale knew that much already. He put out a hand to turn the knob and stopped himself.

Instead, he took a moment to peer into the nearest window. Seeing nothing, he returned again to the door. His palm was damp around the chilled metal knob. He gave it half a turn, changed his mind for the hundredth time, and released it.

The rain picked up, jerking into a gust that flung cold needles of water into his ears. The porch would not shelter him much, or for long. He clutched at his notebook with its leather flaps holding the paper out of the weather; and he considered the unfastened door once more.

He sat down against it, as far out of the rain as he could get, and he pulled his notebook into his lap. The wind combed through the trees around the dilapidated little house, and the rain came and went like the drawing and undrawing of theater curtains.

Hale Quarter jabbed a pen against his tongue to moisten it, and he began to write.

As I believe *Boneshaker*'s premise makes clear, this is a work of fiction—but I've always enjoyed including local landmarks in my novels, and this one is no exception. However, let me take a moment to assure you that I'm *fully aware* of this book's particularly grievous and shameless warping of history, geography, and technology.

My motives were simple and selfish: I needed a Seattle that was much more heavily populated in my version of 1863 than real life's version of 1863. And so, as the first chapter explains, I've accelerated the Klondike gold rush by a few decades, and thus swelled the city's ranks exponentially. Therefore, when I speak of thousands of rotters and a large urban area having been evacuated and sealed, I speak of a population of some 40,000 souls, not the mere 5,000 or so that history was unkind enough to give me.

As some of you local buffs are aware, I've also ignored a couple of major turning points in Seattle's development: the 1889 fire that destroyed most of the city and the 1897 Denny Hill regrade. Since both of these events took place well after the events of this book (which transpired in 1880), I had a fair bit of leeway when making up my version of Pioneer Square and its surrounding blocks.

For reference's sake, I used a Sanborn survey map from 1884 to make sure that I loosely, generally followed the likely lay of the land, but heaven knows I went off the rails a bit here and there.

Ergo.

Assuming a much earlier, much bigger population base, it is not altogether outside the realm of reason that some of Seattle's landmark buildings might've been under way in the 1860s, before the wall went up.

That's my logic and I'm sticking to it.

So there's no need to send me helpful e-mails explaining that King Street Station wasn't started until 1904, that the Smith Tower wasn't begun until 1909, or that Commercial Street is really First Avenue. I know the facts, and every digression from them was deliberate.

At any rate, thank you for reading, and thank you for suspending your disbelief for a few hundred pages. I realize that the story is a bit of a twisted stretch, but honestly—isn't that what steampunk is for?